War of the Gestalt

Book 3 of The Behemoth Gestalt

A Novel In Behemoth's Shadow

Chad W. Knox

ALSO BY CHAD W. KNOX

In Behemoth's Shadow Universe

INTERESTED IN MORE OF THIS UNIVERSE'S INSANITY? CHECK US OUT ON FACEBOOK AT
"MUGZ INK BOOKS"

For more information, follow "Mugz Ink Books" on Facebook.

Paperback: ISBN 979-8-9891794-9-7
Hardback: ISBN 978-1-967333-99-8
E-Book: ISBN 978-1-967333-98-1

Edited by: Not gonna do it...

DEDICATION

For Sarah, who continues to be that girl who went when a stranger showed up at her door asking, "Sarah Connor?"
(I'll figure out something.)

For Pat M-S, I hope you're happy with what I did. There's still more to come.

CONTENTS

ACKNOWLEDGMENTS

For those who stuck around.

Thanks for turning the pages.

Author's Note

The first 2.5 books were, more or less, finished a long time ago. It wasn't until I hit the halfway point and the wall of this book that I stopped and started publishing the others.

Now I'm caught up and having to push through. The characters aren't talking to me very much with this one. They don't like where we're going.

But who knows what'll happen? I had zero intent to make James a vampire originally; that just happened as I wrote and shocked the crap out of me when I realized what was happening.

Now, characters from other stories are trying to pull my strings to be involved here. Since our crew isn't chiming in, those other voices are getting through and making more changes I didn't come up with.

So, yeah, things are happening.

[Still not happy. --Rhi]

Prologue

RHI

{OK, so, the author's told me to do these little intro segments for each character. Apparently, he's thinking about putting these chapters up on some writing website to stir interest, and he's starting with Book 3 for some reason. But, you know, he's a hack. So, he'll probably be lazy and leave them in for the main book as well.

Oh, the first three books (0-2) are already published and the big A owns the sole online rights, but that will be ending shortly. OK, whatever.

ME? It's not my turn yet, but I'm Rhi; I'm pretty much the only one of us who knows who you are, so he's given this job to me. Goodie.

SHAE: Hmmm...lots I could say, but let's start with Shae was born 300 years ago in Ireland and grew up with a checkered past until she was captured, enslaved, freed, and turned into a vampire where she served until she lost a bet with her friend in modern times and found James. After a few years of slap and tickle, she's once again enslaved and, this time, had her memory messed with. Then, 14 years later, she reunites with James, who helps free her and get her memory back right smack in the middle of a zombie apocalypse. Gotta love true love and all that crap.

She eventually makes James a vamp, talk about taking responsibility. They meet Moi and saved their family by taking over a not-so-secure vampire compound.

Oh, and the person who took and eventually gave back her memories? That's a bloodworker named Natalie who says she's blending Shae, James and my minds together into something called a gestalt. It's a good thing I came to love Shae cause we're always in each other's heads now.

Book 2 sees her...what? Book 0? Oh, that was her meeting James while he was still in high school and the slap and tickle part. Moving on.

Book 2 sees her going to Houston with James, meeting a lot of people, including some of her old, surviving "family." It ends with her and the rest of the gang being "captured" once again, this time by Beth, who I'll introduce shortly.

What she looks like? Uh, I dunno. She looks like she's not quite old enough to drink(she'd definitely get carded.) A pretty, slightly shorter than average girl, nice bod with a pixie cut that's naturally white and crazy blue eyes? That good enough?

I guess that sums it up...hey, you get what you pay for, and I ain't getting paid shit. --Rhi}

∞∞∞∞Ω∞∞∞∞

SHAE

I wasn't going to make it.

The scorching wind deafened and half-blinded me as it relentlessly buffeted my broken body. I fought to stay on my feet, to keep running, but the pain was making me nauseous. I could barely see James and Rhi in the distance now.

I'd ordered James to leave me. I knew he wouldn't, but I'd commanded him, and he'd had no choice. Those two had to make it; somebody did. Our list of fallen was growing too long. I never imagined this was how I'd join it.

My only comfort was knowing James and Rhi would make it. They'd get somewhere safe and I knew she'd take care of him. She'd keep him going as we'd kept her going after Tara.

The pair were scrambling over the rubble of the Alamo to get to our...their possible salvation.

I tumbled, out of control, down the last embankment as another wave of fire-laced air pushed me. When I finally came to rest in the field far below, I was too stunned to move.

Vampires were hard to kill, but it could be done if you had the tenacity. I couldn't keep track of the damage to my body anymore; everything hurt. First, the crash, then the explosion, then the run and constantly being tossed about like a rag doll.

Blinking the blood out of my eyes, I tried to start crawling. My legs were useless and only one arm would move as I dug my fingers into the dried dirt in an attempt to follow. The pain was a constant I could no longer ignore as my body threatened to black out on me again.

A noise made me look up just in time to see Rhi hit James in the back of the head with enough force that he collapsed into the hole.

Good, they found it, I mentally sighed in relief. Rhi was taking care of him...just as I'd hoped.

I saw the reflection in Rhi's face before I felt the sudden surge behind me. We were out of time. It was here.

I watched as Rhi climbed into the hole and grabbed the door to close it behind her. She paused, looking at me from across the field. Her expression held the hatred I expected...the hatred I deserved.

It's OK, I tried to send to her, to help her in that final moment.

I thought I saw the flicker of something else on her face just as she closed the door.

Then, it was on me, and the pain ended.

Awakenings

RHI

{Oh Tara...the things I could tell you about my wife. Whew, but big A won't let those parts be printed...I think he's finding a way around that, though. So, if you like smut, check his social media page. There may be links...eventually...maybe.

ANYWAY, Tara is a Daemon. This means she's humanoid, two arms, two very nice legs, one head, a lovely torso and a really fun tail. Her skin's also crimson, not that that should matter right? She's got claws on her hands and feet that can be fun and her eyes are red. As in, the eyeball is all red, and only the iris is black. Oh, and she has tasty fangs. And yes, she's shorter than Shae is. Shut up.

Biased? Why would I be biased in any way when describing my wife? Idiot.

Tara has a slightly mysterious background. She was discovered on her world (yeah, it's that kind of story) in the mountains and taken in by a tribe of giants. She was adopted by them and raised as part of the tribe for the 100+ years she spent with them.

She was on a misguided adventure in some caves when she met yours truly. She'd been living a...restricted lifestyle up until this point. You see, once she hit puberty, it turns out her scent could drive people to the point of insanity. So, she'd been covering up that scent by way of a full bodysuit of infused leathers.

When Tara met me, it seemed my scent drove her a little nutty. She sort of attacked me, and we ended up married. It's a weird story; you'd have to read it. Instead of rings, we got matching magical arm tattoos that change as we grow and move on. It was compulsory.

During our shenanigans on her world, we're attacked by a mysterious pair of flying powered armor who were dead set on killing Tara. After a fashion, we survived the attack and A post-mortem of one of the pilots revealed they're some version of a Daemon, just like Tara. Only bigger. Like twice the size, bigger! No one's ever seen these guys before and the technology is way beyond that of Tara's world.

Tara ended up following me when I went home to my own world; I mean, we were married, after all. As an added bonus, her scent doesn't drive anyone here crazy. So, she ditched the leather suit and has tried to wear as little as possible ever since.

She helped out in Houston as she could move metal with her mind. Why bother shooting zombies when she could just use her nugget to make her daggers fly around and take them out, right?

Two more of those flying powered armors showed up but one of James's really big guns made short work of one and scared off the other.

Tara had her own ability to touch my mind. By the end of Book 2, she was somehow talking in James and Shae's minds as well, as if she were part of our little gestalt.

Did I mention she was hot? I mean, like smoking hot. And she had this thing she did with her eyes that...sorry...got sidetracked there for a moment. --Rhi}

<u>TARA</u>

A steady beeping slowly drew me from the depths of sleep. I struggled to ignore the annoyance. I was warm and comfortable; I didn't want to be awake yet.

I tried to roll over and go back to sleep but my body met resistance. My limbs moved sluggishly and I couldn't find the comfort my body needed to return to my slumber.

Rhi, I needed Rhi. I reached for my mate, seeking her cool body to comfort me in this restlessness. My hand struck something hard, causing pain to radiate from my knuckles. Had I struck the nightstand or the headboard, perhaps?

With annoyed resignation, I slowly opened my eyes.

The first thing my sleep-addled brain took in was that the room was wrong. It took a moment before I realized it was vertical instead of horizontal. Had I fallen asleep standing up? No, I never did that.

My hand ran up against that firm surface again. I looked down and found my hand resting against the inside of a curved tube. Light from somewhere below reflected off my side of the tube and made the room beyond dim. My other hand found the opposite side of the tube, causing my brain to finally come fully awake.

I was inside a tube. There was just enough room for me to barely touch either side if I stretched my arms out. I looked up and saw the top was a good meter above me. When I looked down, I appeared to be floating a meter above the floor.

Floating? To be floating, you either had to be flying or in water. I didn't see any clouds, so...I pulled my hand to my face and realized the resistance I'd felt earlier was from the fluid filling the tube. A fluid I was in and it was in me.

As a young girl, I loved the water. I used to play with the other children of my adopted village. We had a few lakes around us that were warm and we'd splash and play often.

Then, when I got older and my body changed, I came to hate the water. I'd have to sneak off by myself to bathe, something I came to loathe. Had I been able to take my clothes off without

3

driving those around me insane, perhaps I'd still have my love for the water.

Panic set in. I was trapped underwater. I had to get out! I shot to the top of the tube, bashing my head on the metal ceiling. There wasn't a surface to escape to! I started banging on the tube walls, clawing, kicking anything to try and get out. I had to get out!

A cool current passed through the water and into my body. Each of my muscles relaxed in turn as the current washed over me. A relaxing calm cascaded through my mind, letting me know I was OK. I was safe. Nothing was wrong. I...I just needed to...go back to sleep...when I woke...everything...would be...just—

You're Doing What?

RHI

{Beth...OK...so Beth was a pop star both on her world and mine. Two separate people, though...again, long story.

Beth was on tour when the zombie apocalypse hit her world. She lost her husband and daughter trying to get home and went a little nuts. Can you blame her? Really?

She was picked up by the remnants of the military and ended up joining them. She proceeded to serve, helping rescue and save people over the next two years.

She'd met Rachel by this point, and they'd started a fragile relationship when they suddenly found themselves alone, trapped in Houston on my world.

Beth and Rachel are rescued by my crew (James, Shae, Tara and me) and temporarily join forces with us when they learn they couldn't go home until the portal they came through at Drakes (a weird bar, even by my standards) could be fixed in roughly two weeks.

They helped us rescue the folks who were still at NASA's Johnson Space Center before heading home to their world.

We thought that was it, but when we finally got back to Austin, the one flying powered armor that James hadn't killed showed up and started wreaking havoc on our home.

Out of nowhere, a new, bigger, flying-powered armor showed up and wasted the other one. After it landed, Beth popped out of the cockpit, looking battle-worn and ten years older. She then demands we come with her because "Behemoth" says so. She can be so demanding.

Oh, and she looks like, late 40s now, she's buzzed her spiky hair off and is pretty much all attitude now. But if you can get past the tired eyes, she's pretty, in her own way. --Rhi}

∞∞∞∞∞Ω∞∞∞∞∞

BETH

I stood rigidly at attention, not believing the words I'd just heard. It took every ounce of my self-discipline not to burst out laughing at the absurdity of the situation.

"You're pulling me from combat duty?" I said through clenched teeth, attempting to keep it together.

Herwn, my squadron commander, looked down on me from her nearly three-meter height. I'd gotten used to those red and black eyes examining me like a bug under a microscope. The eyes, the red skin, the tail...none of that scared me as much as her words did.

Relax, the soothing voice in my head said with the maddening calm it always carried. *Listen,* it practically hissed.

"You are needed to train the incoming Chosen Army candidates," Herwn said with finality.

"But I'm not a teacher," I attempted to say without the exasperation I felt contaminating my voice.

I'd spent 10 years of blood, sweat, and tears getting to where I was now. I'd bested everyone in the Chosen Army and the third wing to earn my place in the Daemon Corps. I wasn't about to lose all that now just to babysit a group of whelps.

"You will learn," Herwn said without emotion. "Just as you learned from the ones who taught you."

"But why now? Have I not maintained my proficiency? Have I done something to offend?"

"Your skill and combat record are still...exceptional."

Her comment didn't make me feel exceptional. It was well-known how Daemons felt about us, "Leirs," the term given to anyone who wasn't a Daemon. While the translation was something innocent enough, "Light Eyes" was still used as a derogatory term.

My high standing amongst the Daemons was a point of contention that made my life harder at times. But I didn't care how they felt about me; I didn't do it for them.

"Behemoth is especially interested in the candidates you retrieved. Your previous contact with them and your personal input will aid in Behemoth's evaluation."

"Behemoth requested me specifically?" I asked, my anger momentarily forgotten.

"Yes," Herwn's voice took on honest admiration instead of her customary disdain for a change. "You know how great an honor it is to be selected for the Chosen Army to begin with. Now Behemoth calls on you again for aid. Will you decline this opportunity?"

I stood a little straighter.

"Of course not; I will serve," I snapped out. A human being singled out by Behemoth was unheard of. Refusing Behemoth was...impossible.

"I thought as much," Herwn didn't smile but nodded slightly. "Now go, your things have already been transferred to your new resting area."

At the dismissal, I automatically pivoted and departed.

One thought repeated in my head all the way to the gate room: *Behemoth had wanted me.* I still couldn't believe it.

See? I told you that you were important, The voice again whispered in my mind.

I let the minder's sentiment seep into my thoughts for once, but only for a moment. I had a job to do.

You've Got To Be Kidding Me

RHI

{Then we have James. I think he was originally supposed to be the main character (hey, I was a friggin afterthought by the author) until this story turned into an ensemble.

James was a dorky high school kid that a 300-year-old vampire took an interest in (I did say she lost a bet, right?) James spent the next three years falling in love with Shae and eventually popping the question. Of course, he's shattered when she disappears the day after he proposes.

He eventually seeks escape in the military, who have their own plans for James. You see, the military knows about vampires and has a program(The Phobos Project) that takes previous tap boys(vampire chew toys) and turns them into super soldiers by way of a serum.

14 years later, James is home on leave for his mom's funeral. He's just in time to reunite with Shae, run out of super soldier serum, and for the zombie apocalypse to kick off.

Over the next several months, James manages to secure his friends and family, get the lost memories of his girlfriend back, and get himself turned into a full vampire.

He then goes to Houston to fulfill a promise. While there, he checks on more friends and family, apprehends a renegade Colonel, murders a gang of kidnapping rapists, CAPT Kirk's an alien(my wife, btw...it's OK, we traded,) and has a PTSD flashback so bad I pop him one.

It's a good thing I love this guy.

Oh, uh, him...yet another average heighter, has brown hair cut short, military style. He's what, mid-30s now? He's handsome, has a solid military bod, and has his moments when he's not being a mopey little bitch. --Rhi}

JAMES

The bed was soft and warm. I snuggled deeper into my pillow and pulled the blanket closer. It was nice waking up quietly, gently, for a change. It reminded me of those lazy Sundays as a kid. I could sleep in as late as I wanted, and the house was always quiet, as no one else wanted to get up either, unlike Saturdays, where I got up early for cartoons. You always got up early for cartoons.

Shae, my fiancée, lay in bed beside me. She seemed to sense my movement and cuddled closer. Her head rested on my shoulder, and her hand was on my chest. I gently curled my arm around her as she made a protesting noise at the disturbance.

Shae was warm against me, something I didn't use to appreciate, at least until I became a vampire. Shae's body temperature constantly fluctuated when I was a teenage human and she was a vampire. Sometimes chilly, sometimes blazing hot. It just depended on how much she'd had to "eat" recently. But, once she turned me, saving my life from my own stupidity, my tolerance changed. Now I enjoyed her at all temperatures.

I took a deep breath and blew it out, allowing my mind and body to settle into the warm, soothing comfort of the bed. Looking up, I realized I was beneath yet another alien ceiling. This one was a strange textured gray I'd never seen before. It almost looked as if the ceiling was lined with small scales. It took another minute for my eyes to seek out the walls around me. They were the same scale gray as the ceiling, and they were also without fixtures. Light seems to spill into the room from the top of all four walls.

The room was small, containing only the bed we both slept in. There was only a meter or so of clearance around the bed from each wall and I didn't see a door anywhere.

I shook Shae gently. She mumbled something unintelligible before slowly opening her eyes.

"Hmmmm?" Shae asked.

"Shae, wake up luv." I glance down in time to see her eyes blink a few times.

"Morning," she croaked, a sleepy grin crossing her face.

"Morning to you too," I said as I leaned down and kissed her on the forehead.

"What time is it?" she asked.

I looked down at my wrist but found my watch was gone. This concerned me because I never took off my watch, not even in the shower. As I continued to stare at my wrist, I noticed the pale white silhouette of where my watchband usually lay was also gone.

"Dunno," I said, looking around for a clock but failing to find one. "You got any idea where we are?"

This statement caused her to freeze, mid-yawn. She closed her mouth and slowly looked around at our sparse surroundings. Finally, she cautiously said, "No."

"Me neither," I said, frowning. "What's the last thing you remember?" I wondered if her memory was as foggy as mine.

"Last thing I remember was—" Shae started but was interrupted.

"Well, it's about time you two finally woke up!" a new voice said from the foot of the bed. Rhi stood in a doorway that hadn't been there a moment before. Her arms were folded, and her face was stern.

Rhi is the third vampire in our foursome. With ivory skin and long raven hair, her beauty was only matched by her insanity.

As we lay there with our mouths open, Rhi moved around to the side of the bed and touched the wall. A panel disappeared, revealing a small rack of clothing.

It was only then I realized Shae and I were currently without apparel.

"Hurry up and get dressed. We're scheduled for our newcomer's briefing soon. You're going to love this!" Rhi said before stepping out of the room.

We cautiously moved over to inspect the hanging clothes. They appeared to be some one-piece uniform made from a soft, lightweight material. Mostly black in appearance, they had dark gray trim. There were no symbols or patches adorning the plain uniforms. They covered everything from our toes to our fingers to the tops of our necks, clasping shut with what appeared to be a soundless Velcro material.

As soon as the clasps were fully closed, the clothes shifted and fit themselves to our bodies. While they weren't skin tight, they were mighty close.

Two pairs of boots were below the uniforms in the closet. A seam on top of the boots, running from the toe all the way up, split open and allowed me to slip my foot inside easily. When I pulled the top of the boot together, it sealed itself snugly all the way up to just below my knee. A moment later, the boot conformed to me and vanished as it blended into the uniform seamlessly. When I reached down, I could still feel the boot; I just couldn't see where the boot ended and the uniform began.

"What the?" I said as a quick glance told me Shae was feeling the same way.

We struggled into jackets that were hanging beside the uniforms but didn't seal them for fear of being strangled by the high collars. The jackets were as soft and flexible as the uniforms, only the material seemed more robust. They also sported a reversed color scheme from the rest of the uniform.

I absent-mindedly pulled at the crotch of my uniform as we exited the room.

Outside was a long hallway filled with doors identical to ours. A quick glance revealed the hallway appeared to extend to either side of us out to infinity. I swear I could see the hallway curve as if with the curvature of the land. When I touched the wall, it was smooth, plastic-like, and gave just a bit when pressed.

Rhi watched us from the opposite wall, where she was impatiently tapping her foot. She wore the same uniform as us but with a different-style jacket. Her jacket appeared to be a full-length copy of the leather coat she'd picked up in Tara's world. The only difference was that the coat was the same color and cut as our new uniform coats.

"Where's Tara?" Shae asked before I could open my mouth.

Rhi's face momentarily faltered. "She's...uh...in a meeting." Then she brightened. "But never mind that," she said and took us both by the hand, "you gotta come see this!"

Dragging us down the hall, she turned sharply when an opening to a hidden side hallway appeared. A few more turns, and we were standing in front of a huge eight-meter by eight-meter window overlooking a city.

"What the?" I looked out onto a massive metropolitan city made of shimmering steel. Skyscraper after skyscraper locked together like an enormous jigsaw puzzle in some artist's gallery. The sky above was a brilliant blue with crimson-colored clouds in the setting sun.

"What the?" Shae echoed as she watched cars move through the street, stop, and then suddenly begin to lift into the air before gliding into the clouds above.

People were piloting giant, multi-armed, and legged machines as they lifted construction materials on a building site. There were parks here and there with bright-colored playgrounds where children frolicked.

I watched as a small child climbed an unusually tall slide. When the child reached the top, the slide shifted from plane metal to a snake's back to a snowy field before settling on a river flowing rapidly down into darkness. The child squealed as it slid down.

When we looked over at Rhi, she was smiling at our expressions.

"No," Rhi said, holding up a finger, "Not yet. This way," she beckoned us down a nearby hallway.

Reluctantly, we followed.

Rhi stopped at the corner of yet another identical hallway and told us to close our eyes. After we reluctantly complied, I felt Rhi's hands slide over my already closed eyes.

"What gives?" I asked.

"I don't trust you, you cheater," Rhi whispered in my ear.

"Smart girl," Shae chuckled.

"Shut up," I mumbled.

Rhi moved us forward and around the corner. When we stopped, I heard Shae gasp and tried to open my eyes. Rhi giggled as she held my eyes shut for another moment before relenting and releasing me.

In front of us is another window, this one ten times the size of the previous one. But this one didn't look down on a city. It looked out into the star-filled vastness of space.

I immediately felt like I was falling and started to flail. Rhi caught my hand and steadied me.

Moving around in front of us, Rhi grinned at the childlike wonder on our faces.

A sudden flash blinded me. When the spots cleared from my eyes, Rhi was standing there with a small tablet pointed at us.

"Sorry, I had to save that Kodak moment," Rhi grinned evilly.

After a minute, Shae shook herself free of the hypnotic blackness and turned to Rhi.

"What's going on?"

Before Rhi could answer, something flew past the window in a burst of light that left even more spots in my eyes. I could just make out one of those huge flying armor suits as it passed by the window, this one as black as the space it flew in. Only a series of lights on the armor separated it from the darkness of the void beyond. I watched it make a slow, lazy turn before returning the way it came.

I realized my mouth was hanging open and closed it with a snap.

"I thought you might say that," Rhi smiled at my shocked silence. "Now y'all will be able to trust what I'm about to tell you and not think I'm out of my mind. Well, any more than normal, that is. Come on." Rhi turned and started walking down the hall, leaving Shae and me to continue to stare out the window in wonder.

Rhi stopped in front of a red door and looked back at us. We hadn't moved.

"AHEM!" Rhi cleared her throat loudly.

Shae was the first to tear herself away from the view and began pulling me away from the window.

I resisted for a moment before relenting and allowing myself to be pulled from the astonishing view. Even though it was only a simple starfield, something constantly depicted on TV shows and movies, I couldn't help but be drawn in by its depth.

The room beyond the red door appeared to be a tiered classroom. We entered from the back and descended row after row of individual chairs with small tablets attached to them. When we reached the front, Rhi directed us to sit as she stood behind a large table.

"What's going on, Rhi?" Shea asked again.

"Yeah," I added, "what happened? Where are we?"

Rhi held up a hand. "OK, bear with me as it took me nearly two weeks to accept it myself."

"Two weeks?" Shae and I said simultaneously.

"Well, that made things worse, didn't it?" Rhi chuckled nervously and paused momentarily before continuing, "OK, we're in space. Specifically, on a...sorta...space station."

"Figured that much out," I scowled.

"James," Shae's chiding silenced me.

"Sorry," I held up my hands.

"OK, what's the last thing you remember?" Rhi asked.

"The flying armor suits fighting," Shae said.

"And Beth popping out of one of them," I added.

"OK, immediately after that fight at the Alamo, the four of us were brought here. Don't ask me how; I still don't understand it. There was no magic door or anything, just *BAM* and here we were."

"You said two weeks?" Shae asked.

"Yeah," Rhi looked at the tablet she was carrying. "OK, so Tara woke me up in a room like the one you guys woke up in..." Rhi said as she started her tale.

∞∞∞∞Ω∞∞∞∞

<u>RHI</u>

{Hey, look, it's me, Mari-NO! Huh, OK...how to talk about one's self and my story...you know, the most important story. Wow.

So, I went to school with James and had a crush on him that never worked out, mainly because he didn't know I existed. So, I moved on with my life.

While my psychology degree (and the mountain of student loan debt that accompanied it) got me into the military, an IED got me out of it. As an added bonus, I'd become an insane, violence-addicted, MMA champion vampire that heard voices...well, no, just the one voice—

"Hello," my inner voice said, sounding like a limo driver from a good sitcom.

—in my head. This led me to be indentured to the very vamp whose compound Shae and James wanted to take over.

Of course, my running into James reignited those old, pesky feelings I had for him...which led us to end up in bed together. Something I didn't think Shae would appreciate, but it turned out I was wrong.

Shae's so weird, good thing I love her too.

After I helped them take over my boss's compound, they ran off to Houston. Shortly afterward, I got myself sucked into another world where I met up with Tara...and ended up in her bed.

You know, this is really making me sound like a slut, but I'm not. Despite everything you've heard, I'm really particular about who I sleep with.

Anyway, I ended up married to Tara, yeah...that's about as fast as it happened with me as well. But I love her. I'd say it was love at first *sight, but there was more...a lot more...like the tail...*

AHEM

While I was stuck on that backwards, reject renaissance fair world for a year, Tara was with me. As long as she was with me, I found I could bear anything.

When we got back to my world, while over a year had passed for me, almost no time had passed back home. Houston was our destination where we helped out James and Shae.

We stuck with them through all the broomstick-worthy shenanigans they went through and survived right up until Beth caught up to us in Austin and kidnapped us.

Fine...me...I'm not part of the average height crowd, I'm actually quite a bit taller than most girls...and some guys. I mentioned I was a vamp fighter and I've the body for it. It takes me several hours a day to keep it, but I take pride in what I got. Especially my girls, they're bangin'. I try to keep my hair nice and long as it's straight, black, and gorgeous, but events have made that a pain lately. Am I pretty? Fuck no, I'm hot!

That should pretty much catch you up on the main characters and what's happened so far. You'll only hear more from me if I decide to butt in...not that that would ever happen. --Rhi}

∞∞∞∞Ω∞∞∞∞

RHI

There was a buzzing in my head. That was the first thing I—

[Like hardly ever. I only make comments that are worth interrupting your time...or something really needs to be said...or I get bored. --Rhi]

There was a buzzing in my head. That was the first thing I

became aware of. It wasn't a hangover or the after-effects of any drug I'd experienced. I held still, trying to figure out what was going on. Out of instinct, I listened, smelled and felt, trying not to give away the fact I was awake.

"You can open your eyes, silly," a familiar voice said from off to my left.

I opened my eyes and saw my wife, Tara, sitting at the foot of the bed. She was wearing a strange red uniform that matched her skin and eyes. Her smile was gentle and warm, tinged with the slight mischief she always carried when looking at me.

"How are you feeling?" Tara cocked her head at me.

"Like I got hit by a truck. My head hurts." I sat up, rubbing the back of my head.

"It will pass. Come on, get dressed. We need to get a move on, or we're going to be late." Tara tossed a uniform similar to her own, only black, at me from a hidden wall locker.

"Late for what?" I asked, groaning as I started pulling on clothes.

"Beth's going to fill us in on what's what," Tara said.

"Beth?" I asked, starting to fumble with the closures. "Where's James and Shae?"

"Still sleeping. Apparently, the transport affects each of us differently. They need more time to recover," Tara said.

"Transport?" I continued to fumble with the closures until Tara took pity on me and helped me get dressed. Strangely, Tara wasn't offering any of her usual flirtatious commentary for such an occasion. I pondered this as I tried to figure out why my hands weren't working properly.

"Beth will explain it all if we ever get there," Tara smiled and touched the uniform, causing it to fit itself to my body.

"Oh!" I exclaimed as my clothes seemed to hug me.

"You want a coat?" Tara held one out.

I looked at the coat Tara was holding and wrinkled my nose at it. "Not one that looks like that. The unitard is bad enough." I tugged at the shirt, trying to stretch it out a bit so the girls could breathe, but the uniform went right back to practically being a sports bra.

Tara smiled and tossed the coat back into the locker. "I'll see what I can do. Come on."

We went out into the hall and passed windows like the ones I eventually showed James and Shae, with similar results. When we finally entered the same briefing room, Beth was waiting for us.

"Welcome to Behemoth," Beth started as we sat.

"What's..." I started, but Tara's hand on mine caused me to hesitate.

"Life and your world don't really exist as you know them. Your world exists within Behemoth in what is known as a 'Biological Habitat' or 'Bio-Hab.'" Beth touched a series of keys, and a 3D image of our planet appeared above the table, rendered in perfect detail. At the touch of a key, the image slowly began to zoom out to show the entire planet inside a massive spherical room.

"Wait," this time, I didn't stop at Tara's touch, "you're saying our planet is inside some huge metal sphere?"

"Correct," Beth said.

"What about the moon? The stars? Or the sun, for that matter?" I asked.

"All projections. Bio-Habs can be manipulated by Behemoth in any way, form or function," Beth nodded.

"Wait, that means that the government really did fake the moon landing!" I smiled at the random thought. "But why the manipulation?"

"You're not cleared for that information yet," Beth said with a finality I wasn't used to hearing from her. "What you need to know is that you were chosen by Behemoth. It is a great honor to be chosen. Only a handful from any Bio-Hab are ever chosen."

"Chosen for what?" I asked.

The image of the planet was replaced by a schematic of one of the white battle suits that had chased after us twice now...well, I guess three times now? Next to it was a technical print of one of its pilots.

"They call themselves the Angel Guard (AG). They were originally created to serve and protect Behemoth. But over time, they rebelled and now seek to overthrow Behemoth," Beth said.

"If this Behemoth created them, why doesn't it stop them? Shut down their suits or something?" I asked.

"At the time of the rebellion, Behemoth had been infiltrated, and they somehow managed to pull themselves out of the primary net. As a stop-gap, Behemoth created the Daemon Corps (DC) to combat the AG and take up their original duties," Beth said.

A second pair of images appeared on the display. This time, it was a black, flying-powered armor similar to the blue one Beth had been piloting, with a much larger version of Tara's race beside it.

"The DC were given better tech and broader powers as time passed," Beth continued. "The DC eventually beat the AG into hiding. The AG could no longer strike openly and began a long guerrilla war that's still ongoing. The AG changed tactics and began hunting down DC wherever they could find them. This is where Colonel Tara came in."

"Apparently, I was part of a colony of Daemons who, tired of fighting, broke away and tried to settle somewhere peacefully to live out their lives. It apparently didn't last long as they were discovered and wiped out. I was somehow overlooked by the AG and here I am today," Tara said.

"Colonel?" I asked.

"All true Daemons have the rank of Colonel unless they warrant something higher," Beth said. "Support personnel are enlisted and a handful of the chosen hold various other ranks. I, myself, have earned the rank of Colonel through ten years of hard work."

"Beth is the only chosen who's ever reached that high of a rank. Apparently, her ability to mesh with Behemoth's mobile weapon platforms is unheard of, rivaling that of a true Daemon. But don't mention it to anyone; it's a sore subject. My kind seems to have a superiority complex," Tara said.

Beth broke her serious face long enough to crack a grin. It was gone a moment later and her stern expression returned.

"As the latest recruit of the Chosen Army, you will begin a training regimen that will determine your optimum weapon platform and bring you up to speed with the latest technology before being placed into the field—"

"Wait," I interrupted. "Have I been drafted into this army, or do I have a choice?"

"You have been honored, and there's always a choice," Beth said flatly, meeting my eyes.

"Uh-huh. But I probably won't like my other choice, will I?" I asked.

"Rhi, it's all right," Tara said.

"No, it's not all right. I barely survived one war and I wasn't doing so hot in the zombie war. I don't like my chances a third time around."

"Tell her the rest of it," Tara said to Beth.

Beth seemed to hesitate before continuing. "The AG is targeting Bio-Habs in addition to any DC they can find. Once they visit a Bio-Hab, they continue to visit it until they find a way to destroy it."

"Destroy it?" My mouth hung open. "How do you destroy a whole planet? They got a death star or something?"

Fucking James and his references, I thought to myself. The longer we were all together, the more I found James, Shae, and Tara's thoughts in my head. James's sci-fi references seemed most prevalent, though.

"That's just it. Each Bio-Hab is set up differently. There are..." Beth searched for the words. "Fail-safe control points built into each Bio-Hab."

"Fail-safes?" I barked. "Why the hell would you put a self-destruct button on a planet?"

"Just in case," Beth said flatly.

"In case of what? I can't imagine any reason to have one," I shook my head.

"Exactly. The reason is for the events you can't imagine," Tara said.

"That only makes sense to a madman," I smirked.

"Regardless, these Bio-Habs each have their own control points that must be protected," Beth said.

"Why doesn't Behemoth just shut them down?" I asked.

"They can't be disabled; they're hard-wired into each Bio-Hab's core systems. The only way to shut them down is to take

21

the Bio-Hab offline," Beth said.

Shaking my head, "OK then, just plant a hundred troops in front of each control point," I said.

"They can't," Tara said.

"Why not?" I asked.

"Because we don't know where they are," Beth continued before I could say anything. "When Behemoth was compromised by the AG all those years ago, part of its contingency plan was to purge certain information from its core memory to keep it from falling into enemy hands."

"Well, that's just great! Whose bright idea was that?" I frowned. "So, what, we wait around until the AG finds it, and then we try to stop them?"

"Sometimes," Beth said. "Once we learn the AG has visited a Bio-Hab, we focus all our research on it to try to determine the control points' location. The idea is to get there first and protect it."

"Wait. Just how many Bio-Habs are there?" I asked.

The table's holographic display changed, and suddenly, a large sphere floated in front of us. Small rectangles with different landscapes were on the sphere. There were more images than I could count, but one of them caught my eye.

"Wait, there," I pointed at an image.

The sphere stopped its slow rotation and the selected image expanded till it almost covered the display. It was the image of a city perched on the edge of a waterfall within a massive cavern.

"Tara, is that?" I asked.

"An underground city from my world? Yes, yes it is," Tara nodded.

We were interrupted as Beth and Tara were called away, leaving me alone to stare at the slowly turning worlds.

∞∞∞∞∞Ω∞∞∞∞∞

JAMES

The same sphere of images now floated in front of Shae and

me.

"All of these worlds...these Bio-Habs are at risk from the AG." Rhi looked up and selected one. "This one is apparently next on the list."

We watched as the new image expanded to an aerial view of our home, what we called the Alamo. Our compound wasn't the real Alamo, but the main building looked similar enough. Once we'd taken it from its previous owner, a power-hungry vampire named Pagoda, I'd given the place its nickname.

The image seemed to be in real-time, as there was movement within the compound, but the view was too high for me to make out any details.

"Why would they be after our world...er...Bio-Hab?" I asked.

"Tara," Shae said.

Rhi nodded, "Yes. It's my fault. If I hadn't brought Tara home with me, our Bio-Hab would still be safe," Rhi's voice uncharacteristically faltered.

Shae was beside her before I even realized what was going on.

"You said yourself that these AG are eliminating these Bio-Habs systematically anyway. It was only a matter of time until they found us." Shae put an arm around Rhi. "But we're here now. We can help do something about it."

"True," I said, rising to my feet and joining them. "And if Tara hadn't come to our world, we might not have been picked to help out in this 'Chosen Army.' Now, what can we do about it?"

Rhi seemed to pull herself together.

"And why didn't Beth give us this brief like she gave it to you?" Shae asked.

"Oh," Rhi cleared her throat, "uh, two reasons really. One, she's in the field right now."

"And the other?" Shae asked.

Rhi looked at me, "And two, she doesn't like you, James, like a lot! I don't know what you did, but stay away from her."

I rubbed my eyes, trying to absorb and sort everything I'd been shown so far. "Rhi?" I finally asked.

"Yeah?" Rhi said.

"What the hell's going on?" I said, pulling my hands from his eyes and trying to blink the spots away. "You know I trust you; otherwise, I wouldn't have gone along this far. But just what happened? How'd we get here, and just what the hell is Behemoth?"

"Behemoth? Didn't Beth mention that once before in Houston?" Shae looked at me.

"Well, in a nutshell, we've been drafted," Rhi said, then chewed her cheek for a minute. "I don't know how we actually ended up here," she indicated the room around us. "From what I understand, Beth knocked us out somehow and she brought us here. I don't know if she flew us straight up, teleported us, or wished us here with pixie dust and naughty thoughts. There's a lot that she's not willing to or not able to talk about, saying we're not cleared for it yet. I'm guessing once we start our training, we'll get filled in."

I barked a laugh. "Yeah, I've heard that one before."

"Well, Beth did say there's a formal in-processing briefing they're going to give us before we get started." Rhi glanced at the tablet again. "Hopefully, it will have some more answers," Rhi said.

"Why does Beth look so much older?" Shae asked. "It's not just the haircut."

"Yeah, she's in contention with Sinead for the shortest haircut, ain't she?" Rhi said. "I'll be honest, guys, Beth won't talk about anything outside of what's going on right here, right now. I only figured out she's got a problem with James by the way she acts whenever I mention you. I've pretty much been locked up in this area since Beth's briefing. Apparently, I couldn't leave until y'all were up. I've been going nuts here by myself."

"How long was Tara here before you woke up?" I asked.

Rhi stopped and seemed to think about that for a minute. "You know, I don't know. I didn't think to ask."

"You said this is sorta a space station. What did you mean by that?" Shae asked.

"From what I've been able to figure out, this place is insanely large," Rhi said.

"Well, if they keep multiple planets as pets, I'd say so," Shae said.

"No, that's not big enough," Rhi's brows crinkled in thought. "Think about what kind of machinery that would be required to house a planet. I'm not talking about just the space needed to hold it, but all the support mechanisms. I'd guess it would easily be at least twice the size of each planet. With the number of planets on this screen," Rhi nodded to the still glowing display. "This place has got to be the size of our solar system or some such."

"That can't be right, it's not possible. Think about what it would take to make something that big, not to mention what something that large would do to the surrounding space," I couldn't wrap my head around it.

"Oh really, Mr. Wizard? And when did you become an astrophysicist, James?" Rhi smirked at me.

"Why would they have multiple planets in here?" Shae wondered aloud, ignoring us. "I mean, all these planets in here, why? For what purpose?" She asked, pointing at the display.

Rhi held her hands up, "Guys, I'm just as in the dark as you are. Beth got called away in the middle of the briefing she was giving me and took Tara with her. She never came back and finished up."

I suddenly had a thought, "Have you been able to contact home? They're probably wondering what happened to us."

Rhi just shook her head.

"What happens if we don't join this army?" Shea asked quietly.

"Apparently, we'll be sent home," Rhi said after a moment, "with our memories blanked."

"They can do that?" I gasped.

"If they can make whole planets, I'm pretty sure they can do a little mind vacuuming," Shea said. "I've had just about enough of people playing with my memories, thank you."

"Who are they? You keep saying they, but who are THEY?" I asked.

Rhi shrugged, "The only other person I've met is Beth. There's a room that dispenses food, but it's all machines."

"But I saw hundreds of doors out there," Shae said.

"I don't know what to tell you, but this place is dead. I haven't even heard anyone else. All the doors to this section are locked, and there's no way to get around them. Believe me, I've tried," Rhi sighed. "I was just glad Tara pointed out where you guys were before she left. Otherwise, I probably wouldn't have ever found you."

The conversation stalled at this point and silence reigned. I had so many questions that I didn't know where to start.

"So," Shae said after a minute of quiet. "Are we really going to do this? Join some sort of space army?"

"Doesn't seem like we have much choice," I said. "I mean, getting sent home and not knowing about this threat looming over us. Having zero control over preventing it? I don't think I'd trust anyone else to do this, to protect my family and friends."

"Nope," Rhi agreed with me.

"Besides, look at this place. It's a geek's wet dream. I mean...we're in space...after a fashion, but it's still space! Who knows what all tech they have here in this...future...place."

"Well put," Shae grinned.

"Hey, I was never going to leave my planet, no matter how many times I'd dreamed about doing it," I said.

"You wanted to be an astronaut?" Shae asked.

"What kid doesn't at some point?" I shrugged.

Rhi nodded, "Yeah, I thought about it as a kid, but that was all it was a thought."

"We didn't have astronauts in my childhood. The closest thing to explorers we had were sea captains," Shae added.

"Hey, they still had ships," Rhi said.

"Pinch me," I said to Shae.

Shae looked at me and then pinched me.

"No, harder. Ouch!" I said, rubbing my arm where Rhi had pinched me while I was looking at Shae. "So, I guess this is real? Us, here, space station, Behemoth, all that? It's all real, right? I'm not dreaming this? I'm not in some zombie infection fever dream or something? Cause, while this is terrifying, it's also pretty awesome!" I grinned.

I stood up, inadvertently pulling at my uniform. "Alright, what do we have to do...and why are these uniforms so tight?" I interrupted myself.

Shea slid to her feet, "Tight?"

"Yeah," Rhi agreed, "I don't know what you're talking about, James. Mine fits just fine."

"Same here," Shae said as they both turned and looked at me, slow smiles curling across their lips.

"Seems like someone's not been sticking to his workout routine," Rhi turned to Shae.

"Well, to be fair, Houston did keep us a bit preoccupied," Shae said in mock seriousness.

"No excuse," Rhi countered. "Physical fitness is at the forefront of any successful army."

"I hate you," I mumbled to no one in particular.

A chime made Rhi look at her tablet again.

"OK, it's time for the official in brief," Rhi said. "Let's go."

Newcomer's Brief

SHAE

"Hello, my name is Cr'eon, and I'll be your transition assistance officer during your tour," the bored voice of the Daemon said. She seemed to be a carbon copy of Tara, save for the darker red skin and the fact that she was three meters tall! She wore a disheveled uniform similar to ours, only a deep red bordering on black. It had red trim as well, but it was only a slightly lighter shade of red. Apparently, Daemons liked the color red.

"What's with her?" Rhi whispered. "She get up on the wrong side of the space station or something?"

Cr'eon leaned against a podium and looked out at the lecture hall full of mostly humanoid-looking people. Stifling a yawn, she pointed at the large table in the middle of the room and it lit up with a massive three-dimensional display like the one Rhi had used.

"She looks hungover," James said.

I shushed both of them.

"This briefing is intended to give you basic background information concerning Behemoth and the Chosen Army," Cr'eon paused before saying, "You all are members of the Chosen Army, by the way. At this briefing's conclusion, you should have a basic grasp of the operating concepts of your purpose here. Please hold all questions until the end of the presentation," she droned on.

Several images and small animations flashed on the screen. Some were in English, and some were in various other alien languages I didn't recognize.

"Oh my God," James whispered beside me.

"What?" I whispered back.

One of the first things we discovered after waking up here was that our telepathic link had been severed. If we did a bloodtouch, we could still speak in each other's minds. But without it, we were back to whispering for privacy. I hadn't realized how much I'd come to depend on being able to speak without words.

"Even in space, they have death by PowerPoint," James groaned.

I chuckled softly and looked around at the audience. There were easily 100 of us in a larger version of the classroom Rhi had briefed James and me in. The lights had been low when we'd entered so I hadn't gotten a good look around, but what I did see was like an encyclopedia of bad science fiction aliens.

They were all basically humanoid but with varied skin types, facial features, number of limbs, etc. It was like the early sci-fi shows where they just added makeup or prosthetics to an ordinary person to make them "alien." If I didn't know better, I'd say we were on one of those shows right now.

"Various parts of this briefing will automatically translate into your home tongue. Most of what I say should be converted and translated into the equivalent for your mode of communication. Concepts should translate as well, but if you are confused, please note it on the Personal Data Device (PDD) each of you was issued when you came in. Everything you see and hear will also be displayed on your PDD for your convenience. Again, questions will be addressed at the end," Cr'eon addressed a blue-skinned man with three arms who'd raised one of them.

Slowly, the alien lowered its arm.

I glanced down at the PDD, and sure enough, a live broadcast of everything in front of me was displayed. There were even closed captions at the bottom. I touched the screen and it moved, rotated and zoomed in 3D as if I were a drone flying about the room. It was like nothing I'd ever seen before.

When I pushed a random button on the PDD, the audio suddenly came into my ears, as if I were wearing earbuds while all other sounds were dampened. I saw James try this, and he immediately checked his ears for earbuds but found nothing.

When I glanced at one of my "alien" neighbors, I found I couldn't see what was on their PDD. Even when the person next to me moved, giving me a dead-on look at the screen, it was blank, as if it wasn't even on. When I checked James and Rhi's later, none of us could see the other's PDD. Talk about good privacy security.

"You're on Behemoth, what most of you would call a megastructure. Your worlds, which are called Biological Habitats or Bio-Habs for short, are contained within Behemoth. They were not captured or taken but created by Behemoth," Cr'eon paused here and looked around the room. "For any of you who are having a crisis of faith or whatever at this information, there are councilors available after this briefing to help you cope with your new life status.

"Behemoth was originally created to be a processing center for personnel in support of an intergalactic war," Cr'eon said. "Training in various environments was accomplished here, overseen by the Behemoth administrator. When continued support was no longer needed, Behemoth continued to maintain the various Bio-Habs it had created. The various species that developed on these Bio-Habs were left to grow and flourish independently.

"Behemoth originally had a specialized security force known as the 'Angel Guard,'" as Cr'eon said this, images of the AG and their flying armor appeared on the screen.

"This force eventually rebelled and was replaced by the current 'Daemon Corps.'" Cr'eon continued, "The AG, while diminished in numbers, is now a terrorist organization and seems to enjoy sowing chaos. The DC is dedicated to neutralizing the AG by any means necessary until they no longer threaten Behemoth."

"Are the AG and DC all women?" James whispered. "All the pics I've seen look female."

"Yes and no," Rhi whispered back. "Yes, they all have what we'd consider female bodies. But they're a single-sexed race and can't reproduce."

James and I stared at Rhi.

"What?" she said. "I take an interest in my wife's people." Rhi shrugged.

"As part of the Chosen Army, you will be assigned various duties dedicated to protecting the Bio-Habs and Behemoth as a whole," Cr'eon said. "If you are lucky enough to be selected to serve with the DC, you will be under the command of the most capable combat veterans you'll ever meet. Each DC officer has more combat experience than even the longest-lived race here. They've earned the respect you'll pay them for they're the ones who've kept your Bio-Habs safe so far."

"If they're so good, why have we seen two incursions on as many worlds...er Bio-Habs?" Rhi whispered.

I nodded at her and motioned for her to just hear Cr'eon out.

"If you're thinking there's been some kind of mistake and that you don't belong here, you're wrong. Behemoth chose you based on your abilities and Behemoth is never wrong."

I looked at Rhi, silencing her with a look. Before she had a chance to change her mind and get her barb in, Cr'eon continued.

"You will be entered into a training system designed to find your optimal occupation. At the end of this cycle, you will be placed with your permanent unit and given additional on-the-job training. Don't worry, we're not just going to throw you to the wolves," Cr'eon looked up at the audience with a forced smile. After a few awkward heartbeats, she returned to her brief.

"Pretty sure that part of the script said to smile at the audience and pause for laughter," James mumbled.

It was strange how I kept finding James and my mind having the same thoughts sometimes. Once again, I wondered if this was due to this "gestalt mind link" Natalie had established between James, Rhi and me.

Then I remembered Tara had spoken in our minds just before we were taken. Had Natalie added her to the gestalt, or had Tara's marriage to Rhi added her to our group? I didn't think I'd be getting a chance to ask Natalie about it anytime soon.

I patted James on the arm, which always served to soothe his nerves.

Cr'eon's briefing went on for some time on various subjects before finally coming to a close.

"Your PDD has in-depth records concerning everything I've touched on today so you can refer to it for more information. Additional in-depth information not in today's briefing will be passed along to you during your training," Cr'eon put her elbow on the podium and rested her chin in her hand before asking, "Are there any questions?"

"I'm starting to like this Daemon," Rhi chuckled. "She could be my spirit animal."

"Yeah, she could," James agreed, earning him a look from Rhi.

While I didn't quite share Rhi's sentiment, Cr'eon's communication skills left everything to be desired. It was almost as if she were suffering through a punishment. Had she been a courier like me, she'd have lost her head on day one.

Suddenly, a sentence appeared on the display:

"Who created Behemoth?"

Apparently, the questions from the audience were being sent via the PDDs. I looked down at mine and saw there was a large question mark on the screen now. I touched it and a blinking cursor appeared. Before I could look for a keyboard, words began to appear behind the cursor. They were the words I was thinking at the time.

"What the shit? This thing can read my mind?" Rhi also seemed to have discovered the question feature.

"The founders of Behemoth are called the—" The sounds Cr'eon made hurt my head. "This name is not translatable to most of you, so they will be referred to as simply 'The Creators' as this seems universally translatable."

Immediately, another question appeared:

"Are they still around?"

"They are, but unless there is a need for Behemoth, they will not contact us directly," Cr'eon droned.

"Who was the war with?"

"A coalition of species determined to sow chaos and disorder amongst the universe," Cr'eon said.

"How long ago was this?"

"That information is on your PDD now in your own time measurements," Cr'eon said.

"Uh, how many gazillion years ago?" James asked.

I glanced down at the number and didn't even know the name for one so large.

"This place has been around that long? How the hell is it still operational?" James asked.

"It's probably not made by Ford," Rhi whispered.

"Are we allowed to leave Behemoth?"

"No," Cr'eon said simply.

"Why?"

"Security reasons aside, because the location of Behemoth doesn't make travel feasible," Cr'eon yawned.

"Where is Behemoth located?"

"In order to maintain the utmost security, Behemoth was created in the depths of space between galaxies," Cr'eon held up her finger to pause the questions. "Travel to and from Behemoth and the civilized galaxies requires specialized ships, which Behemoth does not have nor can manufacture. Again, this is by design for security purposes." As Cr'eon dropped her finger, the next question appeared.

"Who is the Behemoth administrator?"

"Behemoth is its own administrator," Cr'eon said.

"You mean like an artificial intelligence?"

"No, there is nothing artificial about Behemoth," Cr'eon said.

"How long do we have to serve?"

Cr'eon shrugged her shoulders, "You don't have to serve at all. You can go home anytime you'd like." She then pointed to the left side of the room. "At the end of this briefing, you will make a choice. If you choose to serve in the Chosen Army, you will exit through that door and be sent to your training evaluation."

Cr'eon then pointed at the right side of the room. "If you do not wish to be a part of the Chosen Army, you will exit through that door and be returned to your Bio-Hab. But, you will not be allowed to take the knowledge of Behemoth with you when you do. All memory of your time away from your Bio-Hab will be erased."

"Lost time," James said. "All those people who claimed to have lost time or been abducted by aliens? Maybe this is what they experienced?"

I patted James's arm again.

The questions had paused after Cr'eon's words, but not for long.

"Can we visit home, like on leave?"

"No, you're not allowed to have any unauthorized contact with the inhabitants of the Bio-Habs. We do have several facilities both on and off Bio-Habs where you will be allowed to recreate," Cr'eon said.

"Can we bring family here?"

"No," Cr'eon said.

"What if they're in trouble?"

"You are more than welcome to resign and go home to help them," Cr'eon stretched her neck. "But again, your knowledge of Behemoth will be removed and you will not be allowed to return."

"How big is Behemoth?"

"Big," said Cr'eon simply.

"How can you build something this big? How do you get the resources?"

"Behemoth's original birthing location was a rouge system. Its core binary stars were captured, and its orbitals were dismantled for raw materials. Other materials were brought in as needed," Cr'eon said.

I saw Rhi entering something on her PDD and giggling to herself.

Oh no, I thought as a moment later, her question appeared on the screen. I knew it was hers as she snickered.

"How do I get out of this chicken shit outfit?"

Cr'eon didn't bat an eye as she deadpanned her response.

"The Chosen Army does not include any poultry excrement in its policies or procedures. Again, you are free to resign and return to your Bio-Hab at any time." She pointed at the door.

I saw Rhi frown at Cr'eon's lack of a rise. Before she could fire off what I was sure would be an even more vulgar question, I touched her thigh. She glanced at me, and I gave her my best "Seriously?" expression.

"You're such a spoilsport, Mom," Rhi grumbled but put her PDD down, crossed her arms and sat back to pout.

I typed in my question and waited for it to appear.

"If Behemoth created the DC for protection, why does it need us?"

35

"Yes, the DC were created to protect Behemoth. You are a bolstering force designed to aid the DC in all things. Your perspective could provide new insight into a critical situation. And while your skills may never be up to DC standards, you can still aid Behemoth in other ways to help protect your Bio-Habs," Cr'eon droned.

No matter the question thrown at her, Cr'eon never sounded surprised. It was as if she'd done this briefing a thousand times and heard every question that could possibly be asked.

We waited, listening to every question asked. Several people had already gotten up and made their choice, going through whichever door they chose.

When the questions finally ended, Cr'eon said she'd remain in case any additional questions arose. But as for the briefing, it was concluded and everyone needed to make their choice.

The three of us sat in silence for a long time, not saying anything.

"What did Tara have to say on this?" I asked finally.

"She voted for staying. From the way she talked, she already knew what decision the rest of us would make," Rhi shrugged. "As for me, she followed me, so now I'll follow her."

I turned and looked at James.

"I just don't trust anyone else to do it," he said.

"OK then," I said as it seemed our little gestalt had decided to go to war.

Training

SHAE

I was out of breath and questioning my choice to stay. That, in itself, was a testament to how hard I was working. I mean, I didn't even need to breathe most of the time. Sweat stung my eyes for the first time in a long time and my muscles were burning.

All morning had been grueling calisthenics on a beach. An area was set aside strictly for beach training on this "space station." Technically, there were entire worlds set aside for training here, but when you are standing in six inches of water and looking up through windows out onto the vastness of space, it's a little unnerving.

As part of our training regime, James, Rhi and I had calisthenics every morning along with a couple dozen other "chosen" from various Bio-Habs. There was even one other vampire in our class, but he kept to himself.

Tara was never present at these sessions as Daemons trained with their own kind. As a matter of fact, I hadn't seen Tara since we'd arrived here. Every time I brought it up with Rhi she tried to blow it off, saying Tara was in a meeting, or training or the DC were "reintegrating" her, whatever that meant. If I pressed, Rhi would clam up. I figured she'd tell us more when she wanted to and left it at that.

Each physical exercise was "adjusted" for an individual based on what their body could do. While I thought our strength as vampires was quite impressive, there was another race that blew us away. They were much shorter and stockier than anyone else and could lift what I thought only Superman could. I came to find out that their Bio-Hab had a higher gravity than ours. They had to wear specialized suits to counter the comparatively light gravity we were training in.

When I asked, Behemoth's "normal" gravity was slightly more than it was back home.

Our introductory training had consisted of a lot of orientation on how basic life on Behemoth worked, such as toilets-which were much different than back home. I guess when you had to worry about losing gravity, you made "adjustments."

James and Rhi called our first few weeks "basic training," but I called it babysitting. Having to tell someone when to get up, when to eat, how to dress, etc. That's babysitting! Thankfully we were out of that phase and were into our specialized training now.

The four of us were all chosen for training on Behemoth's mobile weapon platforms. Meaning: we were going to be taught how to pilot the flying armor that had chased us before. This job was apparently the cream of the crop as no one else had been selected for it from our class.

The flying armor had an official name that none of us could understand, let alone pronounce, but it translated to Behemoth's mobile weapon platform. Somewhere in the official name was a word that sounded like "augment." James latched onto this and started calling them AUGs. I think he just missed his rifle. Regardless, we all adopted it since "Behemoth's mobile weapon platform" was ridiculous.

During the weeks that followed, we'd been taught more about Behemoth, including a repeat of most of the questions that had been asked during our "newcomer's briefing." We'd been taught how to use basic military equipment that, to hear James and Rhi speak of it, was God-like in comparison to back home. Hand weapons and basic fighting styles were thrown in as well. It was pretty much all the staples of military training I'd come to expect from movies and TV shows. All of it was relatively simple. What was hard was piloting the AUGs.

The AUGs were supposed to be designed as an extension of the wearer. They were made so someone with the most basic of training could climb into one and operate it with the minimum of instruction. Unfortunately, whoever designed them had a specific definition of "operate."

Things I was told were supposed to be instinctive, weren't. The neural interface helmet allowed me to see out of the windowless giants in any direction. Wherever I looked, I had a window to the outside, as if my AUG were invisible. There were also two screens in either corner of my display that constantly showed what was behind me. Even with these "rearview mirrors," I still caught myself turning to look behind me.

I soon discovered why the AUGs weren't intuitive to us. They were designed for Daemons. Our Daemon instructors didn't want to hear any excuses from us for our "appalling" piloting skills either. This created quite a hostile learning environment. The only thing that made it bearable was the fact everyone was having a hard time adapting. This, at least, made me feel a little better and helped to form some sense of camaraderie. Misery truly loved company.

We finally caught a break during the second week of AUG training when one of our fellow chosen "hacked" our suits and did a rough recalibration specifically for each of us. The girl who managed it was a quiet, mousey type with spiked hair and an apparently never-ending supply of bubblegum. When I thanked her, she just shrugged and went back to chewing.

Our group's sudden skill increase took our instructors by surprise, but they didn't complain. They didn't praise either. If anything, they expressed relief that the group had finally "caught up" to where we should be. Regardless, the AUGs became much easier to handle, and soon, we found ourselves in advanced training.

I had never been in the military. The closest thing I'd been to that sort of structure was my loyalty to my mistress. But I found blindly following orders given to me by someone I didn't know and who didn't seem to care about me hard to swallow. I wondered, briefly, if this was how other vampires felt who had masters who didn't care about them.

Thanks to help from Rhi and James, I managed to bite my lip

and play along. They shrugged at the command structure, already used to it. But, by the end of the first month, even they were expressing doubts about the training structure and motives.

∞∞∞∞Ω∞∞∞∞

SHAE

I didn't like the cadet bar. Aside from the fact it wasn't really a bar, just a glorified robot café, it was the only "bar" cadets were allowed to go to for a drink. It was a sterile place, void of decoration. I was used to a warm, rich atmosphere from a drinking establishment. This place reminded me of a hospital. Brushed steel tables and chairs filled the sparse bar while robotic vending machines lined the walls like some big alcoholic arcade.

The entire class sat in the otherwise empty bar and silently sipped our beverage of choice.

"This sucks," Rhi said, leaning forward against the bar.

"It's not that bad," I said.

"I don't mean this artificial blood...well, yeah, that too. But I mean this," Rhi indicated the room. "Why is this the only place we can go?"

The three of us had been given an unlimited supply of artificial blood. We'd been instructed to remain "topped off" at all times. Anytime we needed some, the little metal pouches full of "not blood," as Rhi liked to call them, were always at hand. They pretty much tasted like nothing, which made eating them anything but pleasant.

Any time something was labeled as "unflavored," it had a flavor. Even if it didn't, your imagination would always give it a flavor. One that never tasted good.

Here, at least, we could get "alcoholic" artificial blood. It still didn't taste like anything, but it provided a small morale boost.

"It's all about control." James took another pull from his drink. "Here, they can control everything. What we eat, what we drink, they can listen to our conversations and watch what we're doing." James nodded towards a camera suite in the far corner of the room.

Rhi gave it the finger.

"Rhi," I chided. "Don't be childish."

"Just wanted to make sure they knew how I was feeling," Rhi said.

Sophia chuckled from a few seats down. She faced the room, leaning back against the bar and gulped from one of many cups she'd already destroyed. "Maybe if we could stop sucking so bad, they might let us drink at the good bar." She swallowed another mouthful.

"Doubt it," I grimaced.

"What? That we can stop sucking or that they'd let us drink somewhere else?" Sophia asked.

I smiled at the intoxicated pilot. Out of all of us, she'd been the only one able to get her AUG off the ground consistently. Granted, not far off, but still better than all the rest of us. From what I knew, she'd been some sort of spaceship pilot back in her Bio-Hab.

The girl was what was called a "fierce" in her Bio-Hab. Her race was a cross between an animal and a humanoid. I didn't know the details. The girl had light tan fur across her entire body, and a large white patch covered the front of her torso, which she enjoyed showing off by leaving her uniform "unzipped." She had small pointed ears on the top of her head, an elongated muzzle and a semi-fluffy tail that stuck out of her uniform.

I'd had fun giving James a load of grief as he'd immediately taken an interest. I had to admit the girl had a certain exotic allure, but I wasn't sure how it might work out.

"Anyone else feel this game is rigged?" that was Tech. I didn't know his real name as he refused to give it. Someone had given him the nickname as his entire body was made of smooth, curved metal, complete with electronically projected eyes. I glanced at what he was drinking as I'd never seen him eat anything. There was a small metal box with what appeared to be a couple of small electrodes sticking out of it in front of him.

"I mean," Tech continued, "we were supposedly chosen to

come here and help protect our homelands, but how are we supposed to do that if all we're doing is being berated at every turn by these Daemons?"

I couldn't help but agree. So far there hadn't been any sort of instruction, just trial by fire. Everything we'd learned was hands-on without anything but the barest of classroom guidance. It was almost like they were trying to make the class fail.

"It's obvious the Daemons we've encountered are not impressed with us," I said.

"They're not impressed with anything but themselves," An extremely drunk old man slurred from his table. His name was Gus and as far as I could tell, his only talent was the amount of alcohol he could consume and still stay upright.

"Rhi, where is Tara?" James asked. We had been in training for well over a month now and we still hadn't seen Tara. "And don't say in a briefing."

Rhi's drunken smile faltered, and she covered it by draining another drink.

Rhi— I growled, wishing I could touch her mind. We still couldn't touch each other's minds and so far, we hadn't found a reason why.

When Rhi finally looked up from the bar, she had tears in her eyes. "They won't let me see her!" she wailed and collapsed on the bar.

James and I looked at one another, alarmed by the ferocity of Rhi's anguish.

"What?" James asked as he and I moved around her. Even Sophia moved closer at the uncharacteristic sob that escaped Rhi.

"Daemons and humans aren't supposed to mix," Rhi managed, not looking up. "The idea of our marriage is repugnant to them. They've moved her to the Daemon quarter and ordered no contact between the two of us."

"Can they do that?" Sophia asked.

"Not if we don't let them," I was surprised by the steel in my own voice as it caused Rhi to look up.

"Shae?" James asked as he turned to me as well.

42

"You know where she is?" When Rhi nodded, I continued, "Good, let's go get her." I span and pointed at our resident hacker, "Mouse."

The girl looked up, "Yes?" she said timidly. Of all of us, she was the only one not drinking something alcoholic.

"You're with us," I said.

"I am?" Her eyes widened.

"Waz going on?" Gus shambled to his feet.

"A good deed," I said. "A stupid and dangerous good deed," I affirmed.

"Stupid and dangerous? That's got me written all over it," Gus slurred.

"Count me in, too," Sophia said.

"Our two resident drunkards are in? There's no way I'm missing this shit show," Tommlet, our resident cynic, said, picking up his floppy hat and stuffing it on his head. No matter how many times he'd been told to get rid of his hat or how many times it had been confiscated, Tommlet somehow always ended up with it on his head.

"What exactly is going on?" Barrett tried to speak over the sudden noise of the intoxicated group getting excited to do something.

"Don't worry about it, Barrett," James said. "We wouldn't want to defile your delicate sensibilities."

Barrett shot to his feet, "I don't..." he started, his voice an octave higher than normal. He cleared his throat and tried again. "We," he indicated his three companions from his Bio-Hab, "aren't about to get the cadre any more upset with us than they already are. You can count us out."

"Like I said, Barrett, don't hurt yourself," James chuckled at the young man. The two of them had been at odds since day one. "What's the plan Stan?" James said as he turned back to me.

"Who is Stan?" Tech asked as he approached our group. Everyone but Barrett's group was now crowded around, looking at me expectantly.

Suddenly, I wasn't so sure. I wasn't used to being the one people turned to in moments like this, even though I started the whole thing. I'd always managed to avoid leading groups of people. It wasn't for me...not since my breathing days. Then, an idea hit me and I grinned.

"Montage time."

∞∞∞∞Ω∞∞∞∞

SHAE

"Last chance Barrett," James taunted the boy from his AUG.

Thanks to Mouse's hacking abilities, getting past security and into the hanger bay had been a breeze. The whole squad was suited up now and started to move out on their assigned tasks. We still weren't great with the AUGs, but we could at least get them to walk in a straight line...except for Gus, whose AUG always seemed to stagger.

Barrett's group had followed us and watched from a safe distance. When Barrett refused to say anything, James shrugged and buttoned up his AUG before joining the rest of the group.

I hung back and waited for everyone else to leave the hangar before turning to Barrett. I had been watching him the entire time. I'd always been a good judge when it came to people, well, mostly. Sitting back and watching people, judging what they were thinking and feeling, was all part of my previous job as a courier. I was good enough at it to be comfortable taking this gamble.

"Barrett?" I asked.

He didn't answer.

"I am your acting wing leader, am I not?" I was made acting wing leader in charge of the class last week after the previous wing leader froze up during an exercise, and I covered for them.

When he didn't answer, I pressed. "Answer me, cadet!"

"Ye...yes." My uncharacteristic firmness startled him, and he added, as an afterthought, "Ma'am."

"Good. Now get in those suits and follow up," I ordered.

"But—" he started.

"No buts cadet. I gave you an order. And if I give you an

44

order, you must follow it, right?" I asked, already knowing the answer.

"Uh, yes? Ma'am."

"And if anything were to happen, it would fall on me for having given you the order, right?" I asked.

It took a while, but eventually, a slow smile curled across his face. "I guess that would be correct...ma'am." He said, seeming to gain a little confidence.

"Good. Now saddle up." I turned and rejoined the rest of the group, grateful for once, that the DC didn't acknowledge "unlawful orders." Apparently, whatever a DC ordered was law and acted as your CYA.

"Saddle up?" James asked.

"Heard it in a movie once," I shrugged, causing the AUG to do its version of a shrug.

The group lumbered across the training complex as Mouse locked the traffic system to reroute cars away from us on the fly. She kept the streets clear as our slow-moving parade advanced on the Daemon compound.

The training compound was roughly the size of a small city inside a massive metal room within Behemoth, not a Bio-Hab. The Chosen Army cadets were based on one side and the DC on the other. Between the two were various support agency buildings. Along each wall were tunnels to various training areas.

Barrett's group tapped into the various comm nets of the city and monitored for alerts on us. When they encountered one, they would either squelch the alert or redirect the responding party well away from us. This is how I learned we were in trouble.

"Daemon patrol en route," Barrett sounded off.

"How far?" I asked.

"Two minutes, approaching from two o'clock," Barrett said. Well, that's not really what he said. What he said was in his home language with his home time equivalents. What I heard was an automatic translation that replaced his voice with one speaking English and using my time equivalents. There were implants you could get that would do this automatically, but for now, we relied on small translation studs, similar to earrings.

"Can you divert?" James asked.

"Not a Daemon system," Barrett said.

"OK. Good work Barrett." I tapped my chin and then smiled at the idea that popped into my head.

When James, Rhi and I had been mentally linked, I'd found I came up with crazy ideas sometimes. When I asked Nat about them, she said our minds had "blended." When I asked what that meant, she said it meant exactly what she'd said. The three of us were sharing each other's minds. Not only could we think to one another, but, for example, we all shared some of Rhi's "crazy," some of James's "adaptive military style," and my "cunning thought process."

"Cunning?" I had asked Nat.

"Just take the compliment," Nat had replied.

As a result, I wasn't sure whose idea this was.

"Gus!" I barked.

"What?" the man replied, startled.

"Take Simone and break right. I want you to move as quick as you can and when I tell you, pop your baby bumpers," I ordered.

"What?" Gus slurred.

"Trust me," I said.

A belch came in reply.

"Are you drinking in your AUG?" I asked.

"I wasn't done yet," Gus replied, his AUG breaking off from the group as ordered.

I shook my head and stifled a grin.

Baby bumpers were what the cadre nicknamed the AUG's emergency system. If you ever got into serious trouble and were in danger, you were supposed to pop your baby bumpers. This would fire off a series of flares and an emergency tone that would bring the cadre running.

"Sophia," I said into the tactical communication network.

"Yup?" she said.

"You think you can repeat your DFA performance?" I asked.

I could hear the girl's grin through the radio.

"It would be a pleasure," she said as her AUG broke off,

following Simone and Jacobs. Her lateral boosters fired as she took flight.

"OK, folks, big push time," I said. "Barrett, give me a countdown on intercept."

Barrett began a slow countdown.

"You're doing well," James's voice came to me through a private channel.

"Well, this is normally your sort of thing. I'm just doing what you would do," I said cautiously.

"And then some. Love you," and James was off the channel.

When the count reached 30 seconds, I sent word to Gus. A moment later a red light and siren began to blare in each of our suits as the baby bumper alarm went off. Almost in unison, we cut the internal alarm.

As soon as I saw the two Daemon suits break away on the tactical map and head toward Gus, I spurred the rest into action.

"OK folks, there's the compound. Barracks are on the West side of the perimeter. If you can't hop the fence, you go through it. Mouse, how are you doing?" I asked.

"Almost there," Mouse grunted in frustration as she frantically maneuvered subsystem after subsystem until she found what she was looking for. "There's my bitch."

I was pleasantly startled. I'd never heard Mouse curse. The girl barely said anything. To hear her cut loose a bit was a pleasant surprise.

"Flare filters, now!" Mouse yelled into the comm system.

The compound lights burst to full power and then continued to build, putting spots in the eyes of those who didn't have their filters set to automatic. A second later, the entire illumination system crashed, plunging the Daemon outpost into darkness just as we hit the perimeter.

The darkness was negated for us by the technology of the AUG's optics system.

Rhi knew which building Tara was assigned to and which room. The plan was to pull her out through her balcony window. That was as far as I'd gotten in my plan. I hadn't thought of what we were going to do after that. I just knew I had to get Rhi and Tara back together, no matter what.

What was left of my plan changed as soon as we came into view of the building itself.

Each room of the multistoried building exited onto an exterior walkway that went all the way around the building.

When our group rounded the corner, we saw Tara standing on the balcony walkway, watching us approach with an apprehensive look on her face.

What changed our plans was the fact Beth was standing next to her with a master controller in her hand.

Beth had been a part of our advanced training from the start. While she wasn't in overall charge, the leadership had pushed most of the grunt work off on her to get done. I wasn't sure if this was the reason she always appeared angry or if it was something else. Either way, I'd learned from experience not to get on her bad side.

At Beth's command, the master controller made all the AUGs simultaneously shut down, freezing us in place. In unison, our canopies opened, but our restraints didn't release. We were trapped as the external lighting for each AUG came on.

Beth took her time, eyeing each one of us in turn before finally settling on me. The silent stare was broken as the two Daemon AUGs from earlier delivered our missing members. Beth gave the newcomers a quick once-over before turning back to the group.

"Theft of Behemoth property," Beth barked at the group. Destruction of Behemoth property," she punctuated each of the charges with a glare. "Transmitting false distress calls. Hacking Behemoth networks. Sabotaging said networks. Any of these would land someone back in their Bio-Hab with their memory erased at best. Death, at worst."

Beth took a long moment to let that sink in before continuing. "But as a group, these things show the beginning of an actual team." Beth looked at me. "A sloppy team we had to wait on to get off their butts and pull their collective shit together, but a team nonetheless. Something you have failed to show even the slightest semblance of since the beginning of your training."

Beth took a moment to rub her eyes. "I honestly thought we were going to have to recycle every last one of you. It literally took kidnapping a member of your team in order for you to pull it together!"

Beth leveled her gaze at me. "Cadet Commander Shae."

"Ma'am?" I asked cautiously, surprised by Beth declaring I was now the official class leader, not the acting leader.

"The slightest sign of backsliding, and I will recycle the lot of you," Beth warned.

"Yes, ma'am," I said.

"Do the rest of you understand me?" Beth didn't take her eyes off me as she said it.

"Yes, ma'am!" Came the answer from the group in unison.

"0500, Commander. Have your wing report to supply for repair detail on the mess you made."

"Yes, ma'am," I noted that was about four hours from now.

"Dismissed," at Beth's command, all our AUGs powered back on.

As each of us began to close our hatches, I spoke up, "Ma'am?"

"What is it, Cadet Commander?" Beth stressed the Cadet portion.

"You said you'd kidnapped a member of our team," I said.

"I did," Beth said.

"Are we getting her back, ma'am?" I looked at Tara. While Tara had never trained with us, Beth had said she was part of our team.

"Daemons and humans do not mix, Cadet Commander."

"I understand that, ma'am," I countered, looking back to Beth. "But we haven't been human in a long time, ma'am."

We stared at each other in silence for a long time.

"Return to your barracks, Cadet Commander," Beth said as she touched something on her controller.

What.The.Fuck? Rhi said in my head.

Shut up Rhi, I said quickly.

Since when— James started, also in my head.

I said shut up! The finality of my command caused them to be quiet. Somehow, the DC had been blocking our mind links and Beth had just given them back. I wasn't about to let that fact out in public in case our link might be revoked again.

Our group made our way back to the hangar in sober silence. Once there, we stored our gear and made our way back to the barracks. I ordered everyone to take sobriety chits, also known as sobes, to eliminate whatever intoxicants they had in their systems before sleeping.

What just happened? Rhi said as we were walking back to our barracks.

Some sort of test? James asked.

All I know is that we can talk to each other again. Somehow, they can control that part of us as well. Rhi, can you talk to—

No, Rhi said miserably, interrupting me.

I put my arm around Rhi's shoulders. *Hang in there.*

That night, the three of us stayed together. With our mental reunification, Rhi's mood caused us to band together to fight the loneliness.

Rhi's reaction to Tara's loss surprised me. I hadn't realized just how deeply Rhi had come to care for Tara. To James and I, they'd only been together a few weeks before we came to Behemoth. Not the actual year plus that Rhi and Tara had enjoyed on Tara's world.

The training was different after that. The morning after our "raid," Tara began training with us, which thrilled Rhi to no end. Rhi and Tara still weren't allowed to be together any other time than training, but at least they were getting to see each other again.

Implanted training was introduced at this point. Each of us was taken individually to a medical room with a massive chair in it. We sat down for a minute and when we stood up, we knew how to fully pilot the AUGs. When asked why we weren't given this before, we were simply told "because" and told to move along.

Daemons weren't known for being forthcoming with information to non-Daemons. We were getting used to it.

With the newfound knowledge, there was actual practical training now. All our newly implanted virtual knowledge was put into practice as we were paired off with Daemons who instructed us on all the intricacies of our AUGs.

Beth paired off with me and ran me through more controls than I could keep track of as I had been given the Cadet Commander's control suite. This allowed me to tap into other AUGs to the point of being able to take them over, slave them all together, or shut them down as Beth had done to us.

Anytime there was a break, Beth would disappear with the other Daemons, leaving us to ourselves. When asked, Tara told us it was true: Daemons and Humans didn't mingle. Daemons were looked at as a superior species as they were created directly by Behemoth for the protection of Behemoth. Those Daemons who chose to mingle were looked down upon. If one ever chose to have a relationship with a non-Daemon, they were ostracized almost to the point of being banished.

There were rumors of Daemons who'd quit the Corps to live with non-Daemons, but there was nothing to back it up, only rumor and speculation. The idea of a Daemon quitting the Corps was unheard of. The fact that Tara's family had been massacred was used as an example of what happened when one separated from the Corps.

Tara had been living in the barracks alone, and word had gotten around about her relationship with Rhi. She was already the outsider, both because of her size and her coming from an outcast colony. When you added her relationship with Rhi, it made for a lonely existence.

When asked about Beth, Tara said she was the exception. From day one, Beth seemed to have some sort of bond with AUGs. She was a natural. She'd bloodied herself in combat before she even left training. After a year, she was a proper Wing Commander, and within five, she'd earned her place with the Daemons, something unheard of. While she was respected, there were still those amongst the Daemons who shied away from her as unnatural.

I took to command surprisingly well. I still had trouble with terminology and frequently got tongue-tied, but I would revert to common terms and get the job done. The position made me nervous, more than I would admit. It was so far from the job I'd previously done, where all I had to do was look out for my mistresses' interests. Now, I had to look out for the mission as well as each person under me. It could be daunting, but it didn't stop me from getting the job done.

Our graduation day wasn't some huge celebration with parades and such. It was the simple acknowledgment we'd learned enough and orders came down for each of us to report to our various units.

Nearly every one of us was sent to a different unit. James, Rhi, Tara and I were all sent to the same unit, which caused me to wonder. There had been others from the same Bio-Hab who'd been split up even though they came as a group. Why were we being kept together? Not that I was complaining.

Even after graduation, Beth still wouldn't talk to James. Every time he tried to corner her, she flat-out ignored him and left. She'd not taken it easy on him during training, either. It seemed she rode him hard every chance she got, but he never had the chance to ask why. On the rare occasion he managed to catch her eye, she glared at him and moved on.

Wish I could figure that out, James thought aloud to us.

Never did huh? Rhi asked.

Could never pin her down. I'd almost say that's not the same Beth. She hates me so much. I just wish I knew what I'd done, James said in confusion.

Well, I think you'll get your chance, I chimed in. *We're assigned to her home unit.*

James groaned.

"Let me guess, James just saw his orders," Tara said as she walked up.

"Hey you," Rhi said and moved closer.

Tara glanced around to see if anyone was watching before touching Rhi's hand.

Tara hadn't spoken in our minds since the day we were taken. Every time I'd tried to ask her about it, something had pulled us from the topic. Tara was amazingly good at redirection.

"They still got you spooked? Even after training's over?" I asked.

"They're serious about the whole mingling thing. I don't get it myself, but you should see some of the looks I get. I sometimes wish I had my old leathers," Tara said.

"Why are we still here?" Rhi frowned.

"Trying to protect our home?" James offered.

"I'm starting to wonder if it's worth it," Rhi said.

"Rhi!" I scolded her.

"I'm joking," Rhi sighed. "It's just hard playing all prim and proper."

"You're so cute when you pout," Tara said. She started to reach out to touch Rhi's face but caught herself and stopped.

"We need to go find a place," Rhi said.

"Yes, we do," Tara agreed.

"Now that we're out of training, we're free to roam. I'm sure we can find someplace out of the way," I said.

"Let's go," Rhi said, practically pushing us towards the door.

New Digs For Old Dogs

SHAE

We didn't have to worry about our meager belongings as they were being transferred to our new quarters at our unit's ready bay.

We made our way via trans-mover to our new sector. While the mover was only in transit for a few minutes, we knew we were being taken a lot further than we could account for. We didn't know how the technology worked and frankly didn't want to know for fear of a headache.

Our sector was vastly different than the training sector we came from. Where we'd been accustomed to sparse and sterile corridors, the walls here were richly decorated with warm colors, plants, and various art pieces. I touched one of the plants and it moved, shuddering at my touch.

"Can't get much more real than that," I said, wiping off my fingers.

A quick look at a map directed us to the "eateries" area.

"Seriously?" James said. "Eateries? Who talks like that?"

We rounded the corner and stopped in our tracks. In front of us was a forest path. As the hallway continued, the floor became covered with a green moss-like substance and the smooth metal walls gave way to the round humps of tree trunks. The ceiling was a crisscross of tree limbs complete with leaves. What appeared to be blue sky and sunlight streamed in from above.

We entered the hallway cautiously and the warm smell of the forest affronted our senses.

"This is amazing," Rhi said, running her hand down the trunk of a tree.

"Are they real?" Tara asked.

"I can't tell," I said, feeling the cool, mossy ground that gave slightly as I stepped on it.

We continued forward and found that all the hallways in this section were forested. It continued as far as we saw at every intersection. The design was never repeated. As we walked, each tree was different from the last and sometimes the trees would spread their branches to allow the sunlight directly onto the mossy floor. Occasionally, a slight breeze would make the leaves shimmer, casting eye-popping designs on the floor and walls.

"I keep expecting a monkey to come swinging through here," James said, eyeing the tree limbs above us.

"With your luck, it would poop on you," Rhi said.

"Did you just say poop?" I asked.

"Yeah, sorry. I'm off my game." Rhi smiled.

After a few minutes, we managed to stop ogling everything and focus on reaching our destination.

We stepped out of the forest and into a large open area where several storefronts were. The forest motif ended at the hall and the warm and bright colors were back.

I looked down at my shoes, afraid I'd tracked moss into the open area. There wasn't a trace of our passage through the hallway.

"That was just...wow," James said.

"Yeah," I agreed.

The new open area reminded me of an upscale shopping mall. There were fountains and seating in comfortable chairs all over the place. Numerous humans and the occasional not-so-human filled nearly every chair. After the two months of training, I'd finally started growing accustomed to seeing non-humans here on Behemoth.

"I swear it's like we're on an episode of Star Trek," James said, glancing at a pair of non-humans talking animatedly with their hands.

"Where do you think they got their inspiration from?" I asked.

I glanced at a dark nighttime sky with stars and various nebulae. I knew it was an artificial projection of some kind, but

I couldn't help but marvel at the beauty of it.

There was every type of restaurant and every type of food we could imagine. Some we didn't recognize and some buildings were marked with a red stripe, meaning only Daemons could enter.

"Where do you want to eat?" I asked as we came to a halt at a large open intersection a few minutes later. Our training had kept us well supplied with synthetic blood, what we affectionately called "not-blood," and we had reverted to eating actual food in the presence of our fellow cadets. I rather enjoyed the nostalgia, even if it meant I had to start taking care of bodily functions again.

A fountain sat in the middle of the intersection, billowing fire instead of water. The flames flowed in strange shapes and designs. As we watched the fire took the shape of a large galleon that seemed to float in the air a moment before being blown into the shape of a large bird in flight. A moment later it was a woman ice skating and doing a spin in mid-air.

We watched in fascination for several minutes, open-mouthed. Waves of heat washed over us each time the image changed. A chuckle interrupted our gawking and impromptu sauna session.

"New into the district, I take it?" The man, who was sitting on one of the nearby benches, stood as he spoke.

"How could you tell?" I asked.

"You're not the first to be captivated by the flame dance fountain. I come here all the time and have lost hours to this alter," he said.

"Alter?" Rhi said.

"Yes. All the fountains in this district are dedicated to one religion or another. There's not enough intersections to go around, so some are combined," The man said.

"What's this one?" James asked.

"Let's see, today is Tuesday, so that would make this The Lamenting Crafter. At midnight, it becomes The Burning One until Friday." He smiled. "With all the different alters, it can get pretty confusing. That's why I only hang out here, it's the one I know. I'm Joseph, by the way." He held out his hand, shaking it side-to-side as if to show it was empty. It was a common enough greeting that didn't involve touching each other, like a handshake.

Introductions went around until it came to Tara, and he bowed stiffly without offering his little hand wave.

"You look like new members of the Chosen Army. Is there anything I can help you with?" Joseph asked, noting the style of our uniforms.

"We were looking for a place for dinner," I said.

"You're in the right place. Pretty much anything and everything is here. What are you in the mood for?" Joseph said.

"Can you tell us where a Drakes is?" Rhi asked.

"Drakes?" Joseph started. "Never heard of it. What do they specialize in?"

"A bit of this and that." I waved away the idea. Drakes was a pretty exclusive place, after all. "Just a cozy place with a little privacy. We're not too picky."

"Oh, well, down about three blocks on the right is a place called The Stuffy Grill. It's relatively quiet; I think you'll like it," Joseph said.

"Great. Thanks, Joseph. We'll give it a try," I said as I turned in the indicated direction.

"Have a nice night," Joseph said as we departed.

"They don't have a Drakes here? Seriously?" Rhi hissed as soon as we were out of earshot.

"Maybe he just doesn't know it," James said. "They weren't exactly public places back home."

"True. Regardless, let's find some food," I said.

We found the place a few minutes later, and true to Joseph's word, it was a quiet little place with the lights turned low. We found a large booth towards the back that kept us mostly hidden from the rest of the restaurant.

Was it me, or was the greeter just a little too happy to put us somewhere where no one could see us? James asked me.

Doesn't matter; it's what they want, I said, indicating Rhi and Tara, who were currently in a passionate embrace.

"Sorry," Rhi said uncharacteristically shy as they came up for air. "Been wanting to do that for way too long now."

"Oh, don't mind us," James smiled. "I was about to order some popcorn."

"Now, don't be crude." I patted James on the thigh. *Rhi is feeling really awkward. Don't make it any worse.*

Yes ma'am, James relented.

I leaned over and pecked James on the cheek.

Rhi was too occupied with Tara to pay any attention to the rest of us. She jumped when the waiter arrived to take our order.

After placing orders, we looked at one another a bit awkwardly.

"OK, we really need to figure out where we fit here," James said.

"True," I said. "We were shadow fringe back home. Here...I haven't the slightest."

We were wearing what passed as a dress uniform that everyone in The Chosen Army seemed to wear. The black and gray had been replaced with a deep midnight blue edged with gold trim. We had been given a dark red rope to wear on our right shoulder and a beret in the same color. We hadn't seen any other chosen with a rope, and all the other berets were gold.

We never saw the Daemons wear anything but their warskins. They were a red so dark they were practically black with trim that was only a hair lighter shade of red. We had similar warskins, only the pattern was reversed. This was the rookie warskin we were required to wear until we were blooded in combat and finally allowed to wear veteran warskins. The veteran warskins were identical to the Daemon version, only a shade lighter.

It seemed that not all the public was in the military. For every military member we saw, there were a hundred civilians who wore a wide mix of clothes. Some were as simple as jeans and a T-shirt, others so elaborate that I couldn't decide where skin ended and clothing began.

While our purpose was as a standing military force, there was more to Behemoth than that. There had to be. There were so many people that they had to do more than just support a military complex.

"Has anyone noticed," I started as we were waiting for food.

"That this feels like the first time we've been able to sit down and catch our breath?"

"What do you mean?" Rhi asked, giving me a puzzled look.

"It just seems like we've been running non-stop since we woke up here," I said, looking at each of them. "I mean, can any of you remember just hanging out like this without being pushed into doing something? It's like they want us constantly moving so we don't have any downtime."

"That's how the military works," James and Rhi said together, then looked at each other and chuckled.

I frowned. I was trying to make a point about...something... but the more I thought about it, the harder it became to remember what I was talking about.

"I'm just glad they fixed my tinnitus," James said.

"What's that?" I asked, coming out of my daze.

"When we started training, they told me they'd fixed my tinnitus. I had become so used to it I hadn't realized it was gone," James said.

"Wait, didn't becoming a vampire fix your illnesses?" Tara asked. "I thought that was how it worked."

"Me too," James said. "But I still had that nice high-pitched whine in my ears even after I turned."

"That's weird," Rhi frowned.

"James is just weird," I corrected.

Rhi nodded.

"Speaking of weird," James said, turning to Tara. "Now that we finally have two minutes to ourselves. How did you jump into our group mind chat back at the Alamo?"

Tara grinned and had the decency to look a bit abashed.

"Yeah. Rhi and I had been practicing our mind link for quite a while. When it first started out, we only got flashes of one another, but by the time I met the rest of you, we'd become pretty good at it. Not anywhere near the level the three of you all share, but we were getting there. That day at Drakes when I met the two of you, I found I seemed to have the same level of ability with you. Since then, it's only grown stronger."

"Why didn't you say something?" I asked.

"I wasn't exactly the most open person before I met Rhi. I

still tend to keep to myself, even after I get to know someone enough to trust them," Tara said.

"Even after—" James started.

"Yes, James, even after that night," then Tara smiled. "Although, I did find it much easier to connect to all of you after that."

"I bet," Rhi shook her head.

"Then we got here and it all got turned off until you 'rescued' me from the barracks," Tara said.

"Yeah, I still haven't been able to find out how they turn it on and off," I mumbled. "There wasn't anything on the command controller I was given that addressed that."

When dinner was over, we once again braved the forest corridors to find our new rooms. The rooms were right next to each other and pretty much the same as the small rooms we first woke up in. Each of us had our own room assigned, but the beds were large enough that we could double up, which both our couples did.

The other side of our rooms had a door that led into an open living space connected to all four rooms. The far wall of the common space was a floor to ceiling window easily three stories tall and at least 40 meters wide. It tilted at the top, making the "glass" almost seem curved. The view was of our planet from close orbit.

There were several chairs and couches around the common room that we ignored as we were drawn to the giant window.

I reached forward and touched the clear wall as the planet slowly rotated beneath us. It was smooth to the point of seamlessness, showed no distortion for its size, and was warm.

"Is that our planet?" James asked quietly.

"That's what I'm guessing," I whispered.

We sat in silence, watching the planet slowly turn below us. Looking away from the planet, we saw other windows like ours embedded here and there in the walls of the massive sphere that encased the Bio-Hab. While we could see the windows to other rooms, we couldn't see into them.

The giant apparatus that surrounded the planet was dotted with lights and windows of all shapes and sizes. The walls curved off in every direction, eventually being consumed by the appearance of space. I guessed whatever the projection system Behemoth used to make the illusion of deep space kicked in after a certain distance, even from up here.

We were so enthralled we didn't hear when someone entered the room.

"We have pre-flight at 0530 tomorrow," Beth's voice caused all of us to jump.

When I turned around, Beth was standing at the top of a set of stairs leading to a second level I hadn't noticed. She was in her warskin and looking stern as always.

"Get some sleep," Beth said before turning and walking through one of two doors I could see upstairs.

As the door slid shut, Rhi chimed in. "I don't know what you did, James..." she let her voice trail off as she grabbed Tara's arm and dragged her off to their room.

"I—" James started but stopped himself with a sigh.

I patted him on the shoulder and drew him away to our room for the night.

$$\infty\infty\infty\Omega\infty\infty\infty$$

SHAE

The flight bay was chaotic. I watched techs work furiously to get James and me buttoned up in our new AUGs. Things weren't going well. The only good thing was that Tara and Rhi were already out the door.

Our wakeup call hadn't come at 0530 hours for a pre-flight check, as Beth had said. Instead, it came at 0300 hours as a combat scramble. We stumbled towards the flight bay after discovering a side door off the living area that led to a people-mover that took us to the flight bay.

As soon as we entered the bay, Beth ordered a launch to get us out into space as quickly as possible. Since we'd never been fitted to our new AUGs, it was taking much longer than it should.

The AUGs we were assigned were not the basic models we'd used during our training. They were top-of-the-line and specialized models for each of us. They were also much larger than we were used to. Later, I'd learn these were the same models the Daemons used, so they were built to a Daemon's size. It was like going from driving a go-cart to a Formula One racecar.

The adaptive control system was the only thing that allowed us to use the suits. There was no seat, no joystick, no controls, and no helmet. The cockpit consisted of countless black threads that reached out and pulled us inside the beast. The threads surrounded us and, in some cases, entered us, merging the AUG with our body. This system allowed for a creature up to the size of a Daemon to pilot the massive machine.

Now, when I wanted to move the AUG, I didn't twist a joystick or throw a lever as I had in training. All I had to do was imagine moving the AUG as if it were my own body. The commands my brain sent to my muscles to move were redirected to the AUG. So, if I raised my right arm, my body's arm wouldn't move, but the AUG would. I tried not to think about it because it made my head hurt.

This was part of a system called a neural cockpit. It was an advanced version of the neural interface helmets we'd used in training, only it was all in our head. The helmets had helped us coordinate the movements of our suits, but we'd still had to physically manipulate controls. Doing this eventually made the body tired. With the new system, all I did was think about moving and it moved the AUG, my body never physically tiring.

[I'm sorry, but I have to cut in. I know it's not my turn and all, but Shae's too goody-two-shoes to ever tell you this. I just have to say that whoever designed this control system had seen too many tentacle hentai videos, if you know what I mean. Nuff said. --Rhi]

I watched my instruments as James's AUG turned green on my status board and bolted from its cradle. I looked down at my own AUG, still in the not-ready status depicted by yellow on my status board. Yet another tech came over to try and speed up the process. Unfortunately, the techs seemed to get in each other's way more than helping each other.

A long time later, I was finally cleared and flew from the bay. I met the others who were floating just outside the bay, above the planet.

"That," Beth's voice called, "was pathetic."

I turned to find her perched above the bay, the feet of her AUG gripping the side of the metal wall. The stylized black dragon art that twisted itself around the AUG seemed to watch us with malevolent eyes.

Before anyone could reply Beth ordered us into a series of basic combat maneuvers. She repeated the maneuvers again and again for hours. Her relentless drilling wore tempers thin, but eventually, the movements became second nature to us.

As soon as we thought we knew which maneuver was coming next, though, she switched it up, throwing something new into the mix. If we faltered, the whole process was repeated. We soon learned to hang on to her words, trying to anticipate what was coming next but never committing. This went on for the rest of the day.

When we were finally dismissed, we felt like we should have been soaked head to toe in sweat. Our muscles should have burned like nothing we'd ever experienced in training. But, somehow, the AUG's control system regulated our physical bodies as if we'd been asleep. We were mentally exhausted, but physically, it was like we'd just woken up from a nap.

That evening was short, as all anyone wanted to do was shower and sleep. Food didn't even factor into the equation.

The following morning was another scramble. This time, with our AUGs having been fitted, we were out in good time. Unfortunately, it wasn't good enough for Beth, as she sent us through yet another grueling day of maneuvers.

This routine went on for nearly two weeks, grinding each of us down more and more. Tempers flared as patience ran short. Even my patience finally ran out one evening as I waited until everyone else passed out before going to Beth's door. I touched the door chime panel and waited. I knew Beth was in there, I'd watched her go in. Even still, it took over a minute for the door to open.

"Come in, Lieutenant," Beth's voice called from the darkness. All new graduates from the Chosen Army started with the rank of Lieutenant.

I reluctantly entered the room. The door slid shut behind me as I joined the darkness. I saw a dull glow coming from a small room off to my right. I smelled the soap and synth-water in the air and guessed Beth had just finished a shower.

Synth-water was something I tried not to think about. Behemoth was so large that there wasn't enough fresh water to serve all the needs: showers, toilets, sinks, fountains, etc. Recycling helped, but it still only went so far. As a result, Behemoth used a similar substance and manipulated it into emulating water. The less I thought about it, the better.

"What is it, Lieutenant?" Beth's muffled voice came from the small room.

"Ma'am, I would like-" I began.

"Either come here or speak up, Lieutenant," Beth said.

I hesitated, then moved forward. This wasn't like me. I was never this reluctant. Something in our training had taken root and caused me to hesitate when dealing with a superior officer.

I made my way to the door and stopped just short of it without looking in. I took a deep breath, then turned and faced into the room.

The room was small. Beth sat, eyes closed, on a small mat in the middle of the floor. She sat lotus style, facing a small, lit candle on a stool. The shadows flickering across her didn't completely hide the fact that she was nude. Some sort of scented oil filled the air with a musky scent.

What appeared to be two golden eyes stared at me from Beth's left shoulder. They looked like the same eyes as the stylized dragon adorning Beth's uniform and AUG. When I blinked, they were gone.

"Still waiting, Lieutenant," Beth said, her eyes remaining closed.

"Yes, ma'am." I cleared my throat, and the image of the woman I had rescued in Houston months earlier flashed before my eyes. The flashback was so strong that I almost forgot what I was going to say.

"I was wondering about our training," I managed.

"What about it?" Beth asked without looking up.

"It just seems a bit...extreme." I added quickly, "I'm not complaining, ma'am. It's just...it seems much more strenuous than even our initial training program."

"Strenuous?" Beth seemed to contemplate the word. "Do you know what outfit you've been attached to?" Beth continued without waiting for an answer. "You're assigned to Reaper Flight, one of the premier units. Do you know those 'best of the best' units? You're on the elite version of that. You weren't assigned to it based on any talent; your performance levels show that, no question. But Behemoth put you here for a reason and it didn't feel the need to share that reason with me.

"You should be in a standard unit where you can be broken in properly, over time. But since I'm in charge of you, it's my responsibility to bring you not only up to speed, but up to the standards expected of long-time veterans. So, you'll have to excuse your 'strenuous' training as I need you sharp before we actually go into combat. I don't want to have to explain your deaths to Behemoth!"

Beth took a long, slow breath and exhaled loudly. "Is there anything else, Lieutenant?"

"Uh," I paused. There was a lot I wanted to ask, but I was pretty sure I wouldn't get answers from Beth tonight.

"No, ma'am. Thank you for your time." I frowned.

Beth nodded, but before I could turn, she added,

"Lieutenant?"

"Ma'am?" I said.

"Have you read your core manual?" Beth asked.

"Yes, of course, ma'am." I had read it. It was issued to every recruit in the Chosen Army and was mandatory reading. It covered all the essential customs, courtesies, and regulations.

"I suggest you read the associated reading list," Beth said.

I wasn't sure what Beth meant, but I felt I had gotten as much from her as I would for one night.

"Yes, ma'am," I said and smartly left.

Back in my quarters, I glanced at James, who was snoring softly with just the slightest amount of drool falling from his lips. It cracked me up that he still breathed when he slept. Some habits seemed to die hard. I smiled and shook my head before turning to my small PDD.

I pulled up the core manual and scrolled through it, not finding anything about another reading list. The second time through I found the small print in the back. After the index was a list of all the other publications the manual referenced or were pulled from. There were at least two dozen of them. I sighed and pulled up the first one on the list.

Stireen

SHAE

While the training didn't get any easier, it did change. We moved on from basic maneuvers to live fire and swarm techniques. By the end of the third week, we were feeling more confident and not nearly as exhausted as we had been.

I still wasn't sure if we, as vampires, could train and get stronger, but I do know we could increase our stamina. The past few weeks proved that.

It had taken me staying up late each night and nearly every free moment to read all the associated reading Beth had suggested. I now saw the pages and pages of text behind my eyelids when I slept. But it had been worth it. I'd found what I believed Beth wanted me to find.

That night, when the others headed out to get something for dinner, I told them to go ahead without me. We'd taken to sampling the various types of cuisine in the "eateries" section. Since we were always topped off, we could try all that Behemoth had to offer.

Once the others were gone, I pulled the bag from the closet and made my way up to Beth's room. Since all the doors were soundproof, I wasn't sure if Beth was in or not until she answered the door.

Beth was still in her warskin and was holding a PDD in her hand.

"Lieutenant?"

The look on Beth's face almost caused me to lose my nerve. I took a deep breath and started. "I read the additional reading, just as you suggested, ma'am."

Beth's stern visage faltered for a moment.

"You did? That's good. What did you take away from it?" she asked.

I swore I heard desperation in Beth's voice.

"Quite a bit, actually. Could I interest you in Stireen, ma'am?" my voice was filled with the nervousness I was feeling. It almost reminded me of how I first spoke with my master.

As I watched, Beth physically sagged as if a huge weight had been lifted off her shoulders. She recovered herself and stepped back.

"You'd best come in for Stireen," she said.

I walked in and closed the door. When I turned around Beth had tossed the PDD onto the bed and was pulling off her warskin as she walked into another room.

I got just the briefest glance of a series of scars across her body before she disappeared. They reminded me of the ones on James's back. It had to have been a trick of the light, but I swear I saw the shadow of something slithering across her back amongst those scars as well.

A moment later, I heard the shower start. Showering was just one option for getting clean on Behemoth. There was everything from synth-water to sonic to light, and then some I hadn't tried yet to get you clean. They were all available at the touch of a button.

Beth's room was easily four times the size of mine. I walked over and unloaded the contents of my bag onto a small table before taking a seat in one of the surprisingly comfortable chairs next to it.

Glancing at Beth's PDD, I was surprised I could see what was on the screen. I wasn't surprised that it was just more regs and battle doctrine, though.

A few minutes passed before the shower shut off, and Beth reappeared, toweling her head off. She draped the towel around her neck and padded over to the table without anything else on. She didn't appear bashful of her skin at all.

Beth picked up one of the bottles on the table, looked at it and then put it back down. She picked up one of the small canisters next to it and looked at the label.

"That's—" I started to say but shut my mouth as Beth looked at me and held the canister out to me. I cracked open the canister of alcoholic synthetic blood without a word before handing it back to Beth. I watched as Beth started draining it and walked back towards the bathroom.

I sat in stunned silence, my mind running a mile a minute, until Beth reappeared wearing a light-weight robe.

Beth walked over and sat in the opposite chair, dropping the empty canister on the table. She reached over and opened another, pushing it towards me before looking at me expectantly.

I recovered enough to remember my part of the ritual and opened another canister for Beth.

Beth reached over and took the canister before sitting back and taking a long pull from it.

I was still rattled but managed to find my voice. "How?"

"No," Beth ordered. "Do it properly, Lieutenant."

I stammered my way through the speech I had prepared about defeating the Angel Guard and protecting the Bio-Habs.

Stireen was something similar to the Japanese tradition of getting your boss and/or coworkers drunk so you could clear the air without fear of retribution. Here, it was a formal ceremony, regardless of the content, and had strict rules on how it was to be performed. I'd learned about it from one of the manuals in the associated reading list.

Beth nodded and simplified my speech, "Sometimes death is preferable."

Beth and I looked at one another and simultaneously said, "Adsel." We drained our canisters before opening another one for each other.

Beth waited until I drank half of my canister before speaking.

"OK," Beth slurred slightly. "I think I'm enough in. Ask."

"What happened?" I started, still in shock.

"Specificity, Lieuten...Shae." Beth corrected herself. Now that we were into it, formalities like rank had to be dropped.

"What happened when you got back to your world after leaving Drakes?" I asked.

"Oh, that's easy. Nothing. Nothing happened. The building

was still the empty hulk we'd first taken shelter in. The door we came through had closed after we came through. When we opened it, just to check, there was only a brick wall behind it.

Then, we wandered around until our team found us.

Come to find out, no time had passed—at least no time for our team. By my clock, we'd been gone a couple of weeks. But by my team's clock...no time had passed." Beth drank.

"Things went back to normal for us. Hunting, clearing...the usual. After a while, we started to think we'd somehow imagined all of you.

"Then came Corpus. We were down on the coast eight months later, scouting out what we'd heard was some sort of safe colony that had sprouted up. We'd been in the area before and never saw any colony. But we had to check out any possibility of survivors, safe harbors, etc." Beth drank.

"We found the colony alright...at least what was left of it. We never figured out what had gone wrong. They had safe walls, fresh water, and even a bit of power and food. But there wasn't a living soul left inside. Of course, we didn't realize that at first. Nope, walked right on in."

Beth finished her drink, and I gave her another. I was amazed by the amount Beth was putting away.

"We never saw them coming. Some fool had dug underground passages...in Texas...on the coast! We didn't know. We'd never heard of someone being that stupid. The ground was too soft, and the water table was WAY too high. We went into that small room underground...and then poor Henry opened that door." Beth paused, her eyes going distant, unfocused. "It was over in seconds; everything but the screaming, that is."

Beth's empty stare deepened. I saw her leg unconsciously moving up and down rapidly beneath the table as Beth recalled the memories. It reminded me of how Rhi had acted the first night she'd come to the Hacienda. I wished James was here; he knew how to read these things better than I did. But I couldn't call on him even if I wanted to now. Stireen wouldn't allow it.

"It was tight quarters. There was no room to move and only a small stairway out. In seconds, the room was full of them. Our team was trying to get out, but there were just too many. We couldn't get out fast enough."

Beth was quiet then. I was trying to figure out what to say when Beth finally continued.

"We were done by then, Rachel and I." Beth smiled sadly. "She'd finally given in and let herself fall for our stupid Sergeant, even though he was more than old enough to be her father. I dunno, maybe that was what she was trying to get back. I certainly couldn't fill that role." Beth drank.

"Did you know she was only 22? Barely old enough to drink." Beth shook her head and drank.

"What happened?" I asked softly.

"I pushed her towards the stairs. I told her to go, that I'd hold them off, buy her and the rest time. I guess I was ready by then. The monotony of constant loss had worn me down. Behemoth knows I'd been looking for a way out. I just didn't care about me anymore. The only reason I was still breathing was to take care of her.

"When our Sergeant reciprocated Rachel's feelings, I knew he could take care of her. But I just couldn't bring myself to let go of her. I needed to make sure she was OK. You don't know everything that kid went through before Z-Day. Rachel was damaged long before the rotters showed up."

Beth showed no signs of slowing down as I handed her another canister.

"I held my own for about a minute. Then, there were simply too many of them. I knew what was coming and I'd reached down for the grenade I'd told myself I'd never use." Beth hesitated a moment and looked at me for the first time since she'd started the story.

Beth reached over and touched the wall. A small compartment hidden in the wall silently slid open. She pulled out a small box and broke the seal on it, unceremoniously tossing the lid behind her.

Inside were three small tubes and several clear squares of plastic about the size of a small Band-Aid. The tubes resembled cigarettes.

Beth pulled out one of the tubes and tapped one end on the table. A brief spark of light and the end began to glow a soft blue. Putting the tube to her lips, she drew in a large lungful of something and held it.

I couldn't identify the odd odor as Beth exhaled. It was a gentle sweetness that made me think of a hard candy. But the smell was gone a moment later and there was no visible smoke like a regular cigarette.

"Then the dumbasses came back. Instead of using my sacrifice to get the hell out of dodge, they came back. But it was too late. Their gunfire surprised me, causing me to drop my 'just in case' grenade, unprimed. I couldn't get my gun up before they were on me. Three of them dragged me down, two biting me before I even hit the ground." Beth inhaled again, her pupils dilating as her empty stare returned.

"I don't know how many bit me. I just knew there was pain. Pain and pain and more pain. It wouldn't stop and I couldn't get away. Thankfully, time and Behemoth's treatments have dulled the memory...softened it so that I don't know how much of its true and how much I just imagined anymore."

Beth's eyes focused on me again.

"But I remember when I died. One second, I was staring up at the things chewing on me, unable to move. Then blackness, followed by a flash of blue, and then I was back. My body was on fire. It was an exquisite pain that coursed through me. My vision went red. There was a sense of moving, but I couldn't see. Time was gone as well. It was so loud, so hot, so bright. It was like all my senses were mixed up in my head."

I nodded absently, knowing what she was talking about and suddenly very aware of where this tale was going.

"Then there was a new fire in me. Something burning my throat, my stomach. Whatever it was, it made the rest of the chaos seem like a picnic. All I cared about was getting more of whatever it was. And I did. As I'd run out, I'd find another source and then another. Until, at last, my head cleared and I saw the carnage around me."

I didn't dare speak; I was pretty sure I knew what happened at this point, but I waited for Beth to continue. It was a long wait as Beth put down the first tube and grabbed a second. She sparked it on the table and put it in her mouth.

Whatever was in the tubes was potent as Beth was starting to sway slightly, a numb expression on her face.

"I'd killed them all. All the rotters and all my team. I didn't understand what had happened until I saw what was left of my team, how I'd killed them. How I'd drained them." Beth's hands were trembling by this point. She tried to cover it by taking another drink. When she'd drained the canister, she continued.

"I ate the first bullet I could find. When I woke up several minutes later, I tried it again, thinking I'd somehow screwed it up, grazed my brain or something."

"But it didn't work that time either," I said gently.

"No." Beth took another long pull from her tube. "So, I went back and found my grenade. I made sure I got as much of it in my mouth as I could before I pulled the pin."

Beth dropped the second tube and started to reach for the third but stopped, her hand hovering over it.

"Once I start the third one," Beth said, looking up at me. "I won't be able to stop until it's finished. When it's finished, I'll be unconscious and I would very much like to be out right now. But you requested this Stireen, so you let me know when I can have my release."

"I—" I didn't know what to say. So, I kept my mouth shut and thought. Finally, I just said, "How...who?"

Beth chuckled.

"Oh, the who is easy, the how as well. You see, I have only ever had direct contact with one vampire, one time," Beth slurred.

"But...he only...you two only had a bloodtouch. That's not how it works. You can't convert someone with a bloodtouch!" I insisted.

"When I woke up here, on Behemoth, after my failed grenade suicide, that's what Behemoth said as well. But Behemoth thinks there's something special about James. Apparently, he's something new," Beth slurred.

"Behemoth? You actually spoke to Behemoth?" I asked. Of everyone I'd talked to since arriving, no one had ever done that. There was always a friend of a friend who spoke to Behemoth once, but never any proof.

"There was nobody else with me when I woke, well, no one I could see at least. I couldn't move and they had some sort of blue screen covering my eyes. Behemoth talked until the screen went away, then the Daemons came in," Beth teetered in her chair dangerously.

"Something...new?" I repeated the words absent-mindedly, trying to remember where I'd heard them before...Drake. Drake had said that to James and me the night we met Natalie. The same night I got my stolen memories back.[1]

"So," Beth reached for another drink, missed, and picked it up on the second try. "I'm supposed to be dead. My team is supposed to be alive. But since I let that man touch me, everything is backward.

"And I've been here these last ten years drinking this stupid synthetic blood crap and praying I finally earn my release from this living hell. But it seems Behemoth has other plans and until those plans are complete, Behemoth is going to keep me around regardless of how I feel about the matter."

"Beth. There's no way he could have known—" I started.

"You think I don't know that?" she yelled, spilling part of her drink. "Do you think that matters to me one bit? The one person I gave any shit about in this crappy existence I murdered thanks to the little 'gift' he gave me. And do you think it makes me feel any better knowing that I was the one who asked for it?!? Do you?"

I remembered it had been Beth who'd asked James to bloodtouch her so she could see his memories of her alternative-universe self. But I was the one—

"And yes, in case you think I forgot, I remember it was you who suggested it to me," Beth spat.

I had no idea what to say.

"You see that PDD?" Beth pointed at the bed. "You know what's on there? What's always on there? War, that's what's on there. Nothing but war. I would kill to just read a dumb romance novel. Or Behemoth forbid, actually do some songwriting. But no, Behemoth wants me to be at war, so that's

---

[1] See all the way back in Book 1.

what I study. Day and night, I study. It's the only way I can keep up with the Daemons. I trained every day for ten years to keep my skills high enough to earn my place in their ranks.

"Then, here the four of you come again. And what does Behemoth do? It puts you in my unit, giving my superiors the perfect excuse to expel me from the position I earned. Now, I'm on babysitting duty for the four of you!" Beth started to reach for the third tube again but growled and jerked her hand away from the case.

"Do you have any idea how much I wish the two of you hadn't saved us that day in Drakes? Do you know how much simpler my life would be? No worries about saving billions of innocent lives from some intergalactic war between two species that have nothing to do with me! Not having to prove my worth every day to my supposed comrades. No matter how much I do or how well I do it, it's never enough!"

"Why don't you have them send you home? Erase your memory?" I asked.

Beth barked a laugh. "Wouldn't that be nice? Go back to simply trying to kill myself. But I can't even do that now."

I was afraid to ask, "Why?"

"Because my Bio-Hab is gone," The anger in Beth's voice fled, leaving nothing but exhaustion. "There's nothing left," she sighed.

"The AG?" I asked.

"No. The last human on my planet died years ago. Since all that was left was the zombie infection, Behemoth killed the planet," Beth said flatly.

"What?" I gasped.

"Yeah, instead of the living fire, Behemoth simply bled the atmosphere off and let it freeze. I guess they can thaw it out later and use it for materials or something, I dunno." Beth seemed to run out of energy.

"I can't keep doing this..." she mumbled.

I watched as Beth sagged in her chair, completely spent. There was more I wanted to know, so much more. But Beth was too far gone now and I wasn't cruel.

I reached over and picked up the third tube delicately.

Striking it on the table as I'd seen her do, I held it out to Beth, who just stared at it.

"Thank you, Beth," I said. "For being honest with me. For that, I'll return the favor. There's more I want to know, but not tonight. I can't..." I ran out of words. "I just can't." I placed the tube against Beth's lips before rising and leaving the room without looking back.

James was asleep already when I got downstairs. Stripping without a word, I crawled into bed. I wiggled my way into his arms and silently replayed everything Beth had told me in my head until I was holding my sobs in.

"What's wrong?" James mumbled groggily.

"Just hold me," I whispered.

James complied, wrapping his arms more tightly around me as I let go and sobbed openly.

"You OK?" he asked sometime later after I'd calmed down.

"I think so," I said, wiping my eyes.

"Anything I can do?" he asked.

"Just hold me, James, don't let me go," I whispered.

"Never."

The Morning After

SHAE

The following day, nothing was said about Beth and my conversation. As per the rules of Stireen, anything can be said, but nothing can be repeated. I hadn't said anything to James or the others about what I'd learned.

To be honest, I was afraid for James to learn of the results of his "hard kiss" with Beth. Knowing him, he'd get all angsty.

I was already surprised at how quickly James had managed to recover from Liam's death. I think Behemoth did something to him that dulled the memory or something to keep him going.

But then again, the non-stop training since we'd woken up here hadn't left us with much time to do anything other than study.

Beth had likewise shown no indication anything had happened the previous night. She was the same hardnosed, cranky commander she'd been before.

Today, we were sitting in a briefing room waiting for our AUGs to be readied. Beth was teaching us about the Point Transference System (PTS) that allowed our AUGs to get around so quickly. I was just getting interested in how it worked when Rhi chimed in.

"Ma'am, we're here for Bio-Hab protection, correct?"

"Yes," Beth said in her usual annoyed-for-being-interrupted-by-Rhi-again tone.

"Then why haven't we been training in our Bio-Hab? I mean, don't get me wrong. We've trained in all sorts of environments to include space but we haven't actually gone down to the planet itself. Ma'am," Rhi added the last as an afterthought.

"Behemoth can simulate any environment. There's no need to risk unnecessary exposure to train," Beth said.

"But how can a simulation be the same as the real thing?" Rhi asked.

Beth looked at her before Rhi added, "Ma'am."

"Behemoth can make very detailed simulations of anything," Beth said.

I caught Beth glancing at me briefly and wondered what she was really trying to say. The more I studied Beth, the more I was sure there was something very wrong going on here and Beth knew what it was but couldn't say.

"I have another question, ma'am," Rhi said.

"Of course you do," Beth said testily. "What is it?"

"The chosen are all pulled from different Bio-Habs right? Then they're trained and put back to guard those Bio-Habs, right, ma'am?" Rhi said.

"For the most part. Sometimes there are holes in units where there are no chosen, so the assets are split," Beth said.

"Assets?" I asked. "They're still people...or...sort of people, sometimes." I started off the sentence thinking one thing but had lost my train of thought by the end.

"Not when you're in a war, they're not," Beth said. "We're all assets in war."

"Why aren't you guarding your Bio-Hab, ma'am?" James asked.

Beth's eyes went cold as she looked at James. "Because lieutenant. My Bio-Hab was destroyed by the Angel Guard."

"Destroyed? But—" I started but caught myself before I could continue.

"How?" Rhi finished my thought in a surprisingly gentle voice.

"Because the chosen at the time weren't good enough," Beth stood up. "That's enough chatter. Suit up!"

That ended any further conversations with Beth for the day. Later that evening, when the four of us were at dinner, the conversation continued without Beth.

"I still don't understand how they can destroy a Bio-Hab," Rhi said. "I mean, how can you pull the plug on a planet?"

"I've been researching that, and from what I understand," I started. "Somehow, the atmosphere of Beth's world was shut down." I'd used my commander clearance to research Beth's Bio-Hab and found the information. So, me telling them wasn't in violation of Stireen since I could find it on my own. I just didn't mention it was Behemoth, not the AG that did it.

"Shut down the atmosphere?" Rhi said.

"Yes. Whatever Behemoth used to create and maintain the atmosphere was shut down. I don't know if it was the planet's gravity field or what. All I know is that the atmosphere bled off into space. Most everything still alive was dead shortly after," I said.

"Wasn't Beth's world overrun with zombies?" Tara asked.

"Yeah, without an atmosphere, wouldn't the planet freeze? That would mean the zombies may still be there, just frozen," James said.

Rhi shuddered. "That's just...wrong."

"No, what's wrong is the Living Fire," I said. It had been another phrase Beth had used last night that I'd learned about while researching Beth's planet.

"What's that?" James asked.

"The Living Fire is what is normally unleashed on a world when the self-destruct button is pressed at a control point. It's a ring of fire-like substance that expands out from the control point, engulfing anything it touches. It has the ability to destroy any and all life down through the mantle. From what I've read, it will sterilize a planet in just over 7 hours, depending on the planet's size." I paused, looking at their stunned faces.

"If Beth's world froze instead of burning, then something probably went wrong in the sterilization process," I said.

No one had anything to say and sat there in stunned silence until Rhi spoke up.

"Ever figure out why Beth's pissed at you?" Rhi asked James.

James shook his head, nearly getting whiplash with the sudden change of subject.

"She won't talk to me. To be honest, I was surprised she answered my question today," James said.

I just kept my mouth shut.

∞∞∞∞Ω∞∞∞∞

SHAE

I didn't trust my footing on the rocks that made up the bed of the railroad tracks. I'd already stumbled once and was trying to keep from faceplanting as I watched the man approach. The man who perfectly matched the description of the suspect down to the ripped Slayers jacket.

Moving my hand to my thigh, the built-in sidearm in my warskin "assembled" itself where I could now grab it if needed.

Warskins were the primary, most essential part of a fighter's kit here on Behemoth. The thin, lightweight body suit covered every inch of you, including a "hood" that could be pulled completely over your head to form a helmet in an emergency. It was capable of protecting you from any environment and was energy resistant.

It also had many built-in emergency features, such as the sidearm. When not needed, it resembled several small plates scattered about an area that would quickly assemble itself into a firearm when needed.

James liked to call them Swiss army suits.

"Halt!" I yelled at the man, who ignored me and continued to grow closer.

Like I'd been taught, I shifted my body to bring my sidearm away from the man, but at the same time, I was assuming a firing position.

Holding my hand out, palm facing the man, I tried again, "Stop right there!"

Again, the man ignored me...and was he speeding up?

I established my grip on the pistol and drew it, bringing it up to a "low ready" position. I wasn't pointing it at the man, just at the ground in front of me.

"I said stop!" I called again.

When the man was within 10 meters of me, he reached behind his back and I brought my pistol up, level with his chest.

"Halt! Put your hands up!" I tried again as my finger now rested on the firing stud.

The man began to pull something from behind his back.

I couldn't make out what it was, he was too quick.

As he brought it forward and started to point it at me, I pressed the stud.

The bolt that lanced out from my pistol offered no recoil. It raced across the distance faster than I could track and struck him in the lower right of his chest, knocking him to the ground, where he lay motionless.

The room froze.

"OK, why'd you shoot him?" Beth asked as she stepped out from behind me.

The simulator room was amazing. It would reproduce any environment, any scenario, anything. We usually used it for physical training, but right now, Beth was running me through a series of "shoot-don't-shoot" scenarios. It was supposed to help me understand situations I might get myself into and what would happen based on my decisions.

I had to say and act how I would in an actual shooting scenario. I wasn't allowed to run up and grab the person, it defeated the purpose of the training.

Beth had started working with us one-on-one to assess and train our skills, even James. While everyone else was out working on neural cockpit training, it was my turn in the simulator with Beth.

"Uh, he was the bad guy and he was going to shoot me?" I said.

"OK. You perceived him as a threat," Beth said, nodding.

"Well, the gun he was pulling from behind his back was the threat," I said.

"Sure, that's understandable," Beth said and pointed at the man on the ground. "Let's run it back and see what would have happened had you not shot."

The scene rewound to the point the man was reaching behind his back and then played forward.

I still found myself flinching as he pulled whatever it was from his back and pointed it at me. He held it up for me to see.

81

It was a large black wallet with the words "I am deaf" stitched on it. I just stared at the big white letters, my brain trying to wrap itself around what I'd done.

"Now, was this a legitimate shoot? Yes. The subject matched the description of the felon you were searching for. He failed to heed your directions, both verbal and visual. Nice putting your hand out there to try and make him stop, by the way.

"He entered into your danger range and pulled something from his person you thought was threatening. Show me the setting on your pistol."

My pistol was still in my hand, forgotten. I held the sidearm out to Beth to look at the setting I had it on.

"Perfect, non-lethal. But, just so you know, it would be grounds for lethal force in this scenario, at least legally," Beth said.

Legality was something that applied to the Chosen Army. We were given rules and regulations we were required to follow. From everything I read, that didn't apply to Daemons. They pretty much had free reign to do whatever they thought was right without repercussion. Now I understood why so many feared Daemons.

"Yeah, but I thought he had a gun and he didn't." I frowned. "And I still shot him."

"That's the whole point of this room. Putting you in a real situation and seeing how you would react under pressure. Then, look at what led you to the decisions you made. Here's where you need to make all the mistakes. Out there, you don't get to rewind and try again."

"Still..." I said.

"If it helps, every single person who runs through this scenario shoots and the man never has a weapon," Beth said.

"Everybody?" I asked.

"Yes. Untrained civilians have been placed in this scenario just to help them understand the types of choices a law enforcement officer has to make. They're always shocked that the man was unarmed AFTER they shot him. It opens quite a few eyes."

"I would have gone for a physical takedown. All the

information said the guy was just a normal human," I said.

"Sure, but this is shot decision training. And besides, the intel could have been wrong. In our old world, it was a harder choice because it was always lethal. Here, you get to choose," Beth said.

"It's still hard to pull the trigger, even non-lethal," I said.

I'd shot a lot of paper while practicing firearms under Pagoda. After Z-Day, I'd shot a lot of dead people. I hadn't pulled the trigger on that many live people before.

"It's supposed to be Shae. If it wasn't, you shouldn't be doing this job," Beth said. "Now, let's reset," Beth said as the room changed.

"Can I ask you a question?" I asked.

"You just did," Beth cracked part of a smile. It disappeared when I asked my question.

"How did you turn off our mindspeech?"

"What do you mean?" Beth asked.

"When we first arrived, our ability to speak to each other mentally was gone. Whatever you did with that controller when we 'rescued' Tara turned it back on again," I said.

"Oh. Behemoth dampens certain abilities it deems are detrimental to team building during your initial phase. When I flipped that switch, it promoted all of you to the next phase of your training. Behemoth must have restored your telepathy then."

"How can Behemoth do stuff like that?" I asked.

"Behemoth has a lot of power. There's not a lot it can't do," Beth said.

Minding the Store

BETH

When I caught myself rereading the same sentence for the third time, I threw the manual across the room. It wasn't that R'mmoth's third disciple principle was all that hard; I just couldn't get my brain to focus on the words.

I rubbed my eyes and stood up, padding my way over to the small sink. The cool synth-water on my face helped clear my clouded thoughts.

I looked down at the PDD I'd thrown and went to pick it up. I grunted slightly as I bent down to grab it. It seemed as if the deck was getting further away from me every day. Maybe it was time to get a body augment after all. I'd shied away from refreshing my physical body due to stubborn pride, but maybe it was time to take a serious look at it.

As expected, my throw hadn't damaged the PDD at all; Behemoth made them tough. I placed the PDD on the table and looked around my sparse room.

Once upon a time, I didn't mind the simple, cramped living spaces. Now, after having been around THEM for so long, I suddenly found my surroundings a bit duller than before. The DC had no need for frivolous items or bright living quarters. Our duty was all that drove us; most of our free time was spent training or studying. But watching their antics seemed to be slowly reminding me of the shadows of my humanity.

They were out on their "day off," exploring all Behemoth had to offer. I didn't go with them even though Shae had asked me. I didn't have time for anything other than my duty. I had to stay sharp. I couldn't afford to lose even one step; otherwise, they'd take my command from me permanently. Still, I found I enjoyed being asked. I tried to remember the last time I did anything that wasn't duty-related.

Shaking my head, trying to clear it of the chaos running loose, I departed my quarters and headed into the restricted area. Several corridors later, a large red door loomed before me. As I approached, the door read my bio-signature and automatically opened for me. Once through, I had to wait for the door to close before another opened, allowing me entry into areas reserved only for true DC. Not even the chosen army were allowed back here.

I nodded at the virtual guard as I passed. I don't know why I bothered; it never made any indication that I was even there.

The central gravity well was nowhere near as busy as I was used to. The large open area stretched as far as I could see in either direction up or down, allowing access to a variety of levels.

I stood on the transport ledge and waited as a transport sub-mind of Behemoth analyzed me, where I wanted to go and the traffic patterns. A moment later, I was gently lifted into the air and swiftly taken up the well.

Several AUGs, as James liked to call them, passed me. I don't know why the nickname stuck, but it did. The AUGs were heading down and were followed by a transport shuttle. Behemoth easily moved all of us without fear of collision. The levels swam past me until I slowed and was gently deposited on another transport ledge.

Leaving the well, I made my way to an operations node and entered quietly. The room was silent except for the gentle hum of the automated machinery within. The interface was empty and I stepped inside of it.

A warmth in the base of my skull marked me entering rapport with Behemoth's training interface. A moment later, my vision changed to that of a vivid cyberscape. With practiced ease my thoughts swiftly navigated the menu grid and brought me the files I needed.

I took a moment to settle my mind before continuing.

The training interface could teach a variety of skills, but it could also reinforce them in your mind. I'd been told that once was enough to learn any skill, but I'd found that by repeating the process, things seemed to come easier to me when I needed them. As a result, I'd probably done more coursework than anyone else here.

I can practically quote the 18 program levels of AUG piloting in my sleep. This didn't stop me from repeating the training once again.

Hand-to-hand combat training had added an additional level based on some new organism Behemoth had developed. It wasn't often, but occasionally, there would be an update to various forms of training due to things like this happening. Some got annoyed with it because it meant they had to repeat the training with the new material. I treated it like buried treasure and relished anything new that I discovered.

The new organism was some sort of symbiont that allowed the host to create crystalline substances from within their own body. The symbiont could merge with any lifeform that produced enough bio-energy to sustain it.

I assimilated this new information with the rest.

Six hours passed quickly for me as I renewed most of my primary training. In that time, I was never bothered. My mind focused on the training, not the chaos that had constantly clattered at the back of my mind since their arrival.

It wasn't that I was suppressing my humanity, however annoying it may be. It was more that I was realigning my priorities, and the training programs helped me focus.

When I left, my mind felt sharp, my body alert and eager. I stopped long enough to fuel myself with the bland synthetic blood I'd come to despise and made my way to the AUG hanger.

My wing's bay was empty, this being our down cycle. I'd already signed off on maintenance's AUG tweaks this morning. There was always a software update, weapon system alignment, or something that needed doing. Maintenance only had so long to get their work done while we were off duty.

As I approached, my thoughts brought my hulking AUG to life and began the powering sequence.

What? The mind workout wasn't enough? Now you need to stretch your mechanical muscles as well? my minder's voice hissed in my head.

I gotta keep myself on my toes, I thought back to my minder. *And since when do you sound like Phil Hartman?*

Behemoth had gifted me a personalized AI, known as a "minder," to me when I first arrived on Behemoth. Ever since it'd kept an eye on every aspect of my life. It kept me in check both on and off the battlefield. It was a weird blending of shrink and friend.

When it was first assigned and physically attached to me in some weird tattoo-like setup, it freaked me out. I didn't despise it as it was one of the few "people" who wasn't condescending to me. It wasn't exactly a friend, but it wasn't an enemy either. The fact that it was designed as a snake did freak me out a little at first. I was never fond of snakes.

You do know that not only am I not a snake, but I don't have to look like one either? the minder said. *And what's wrong with Phil Hartman? A review of your mind found that you found comfort in this voice."

I do. I just didn't expect it is all. Why'd you change now?

I adapt to you. I become what you need. Apparently, you needed this right now.

What a cop-out, I frowned.

By the time I reached my AUG, the main hatch was open and it was ready to deploy. At my thought, the tentacles within reached out and pulled me inside. I was long used to the tentacles and barely flinched as they pierced my body.

Why didn't you go with the others? my minder asked as I finished my final flight prep.

Mind your own business, I growled.

You are my business. Regardless of what you may think, nowhere in your manual does it say you're not allowed morale time, the minder said.

*The DC don't take morale time," I countered.

The DC are a race genetically designed to be that way, and you're not one of them, no matter how hard you try to be, the minder said.

I didn't answer. Instead, I piloted the AUG out of the hangar and towards the transfer point for the training grounds.

The silent treatment, eh? Fine, but it's not like you have people banging down your door with party invitations. Maybe you shouldn't pass up on rare opportunities. That's it, I won't say anything else about it.

As always, the minder's words planted unbidden suggestions in my mind as I couldn't block the minder out. I tried to push the suggestions away, but they lodged somewhere in my brain as if to bide their time.

We'd been told that minders were only loyal to the host. Yes, they were created by Behemoth, but for a trusting bond to be formed, the host had to believe the minder had its best interests at heart, not those of Behemoth.

It was a nice thought, but I just couldn't bring myself to believe Behemoth would have created something that could be used against it so freely. Because of this, I always took anything my minder said with a grain of salt.

I tried to shake these thoughts from my head as I began my training practice. As usual, when it came to my minder, the thoughts tended to linger.

PTS Crossroad Demons

SHAE

"OK, today will be your first test with a Point Transfer System (PTS) Gate. Remember everything I taught you in your training and this will go nice and smooth," Beth yelled over the sound of the generators in the background.

The room was massive. Our normal hanger bay was down for maintenance so we were using a backup PTS bay. It was easily ten times the size of our bay and equally as loud.

One entire wall at the far end of the room was the actual PTS Gate. Massive cables ran from its edges into the machinery around it. It was this machinery that was making all the noise.

"Is it supposed to be this loud?" James asked.

Beth looked momentarily out of sorts, almost as if she was listening to something else before she regained her composure.

"This is normal. The backup is an older model, not as quiet as our current ones, but still just as safe. This is good practice; you need to know how to use this system in case the primary ever goes down.

"Now, I'll go through the gate first. Our destination is training room 331a. Each of you will wait until the deck boss, the tech over there with the purple suit, gives you the go-ahead."

"We know," Rhi said. "Once they give us the thumbs up, we proceed through the gate at a walking pace and immediately step off to the side once we're through. Ma'am."

"And then run your diagnostic to ensure your systems are all 100%," Beth reminded her.

"Uh, yes, ma'am." Rhi had forgotten that part.

Beth looked over at the gate and frowned. "Stay here and

check the prep on your suits one more time."

We were already in our AUGs and ready to go. We'd just had our cockpits open while Beth was talking to us.

At my thought, a slight tingling sensation swept across my body, indicating the system was running through a diagnostic. A moment later, it stopped, and I knew everything was running perfectly. It was the fourth time we'd done it today.

I already knew the others were good; the information was simply sitting in my brain when I asked for it, thanks to my neural cockpit.

The neural cockpit was exactly what it sounded like. Instead of having a physical cockpit full of hundreds of switches and displays, my cockpit was in my mind. All I had to do was think of something, and the information was delivered to me however I wanted it. Plus, it allowed me to access various Behemoth systems when I wasn't in an AUG.

Thanks to the advanced training Beth had put us through, if I wanted to envision myself sitting in a physical cockpit with all those switches, I could. They'd interact with me exactly as I thought they would. But the only cockpit I'd ever seen was in movies and they'd looked way too complicated.

So, instead, I kept it simple and had nothing present but what I would see if I weren't inside the AUG. If a problem arose or I needed some info, it would appear in my vision, but otherwise, my view was uncluttered. Beth told me if I kept up my training, I'd eventually get to the point where I wouldn't need a visual representation of data. Instead, I'd have the knowledge in my head without having to take the time to read a display. But that was a ways off yet.

I had several presets where if someone in my wing took damage or was having a problem, I'd automatically be fed the information, but that was it. I'm sure as I learned and gained experience, things would change, but for now, this method helped make piloting the AUG easier for me.

"Anyone else got a bad feeling about this drop?" James smiled.

I knew James was smiling—not from our mental link but from the AUG's systems. With a thought, I could see someone in my wing in real time. I didn't know how it worked and, frankly, didn't want to know. The details that went into this system were amazing.

"Shut up, Frost," I said as another of James's movie references popped into my head. Beth was talking to the deck boss, and I was trying to pay attention.

"Hey," Rhi said, "do we get paid?"

Without moving my AUG, I looked back at her. An image of Rhi talking in real time appeared, superimposed atop a live image of her AUG. While it was intuitive, it took some getting used to. Random thoughts could generate results, so I had to be careful.

"I mean, we have ranks and such. We have these bio-credit chip things we use when we eat. But do we actually get a salary?" Rhi asked.

"Why, you want to buy some shoes?" I asked.

"Well, yeah. It would be nice to wear something other than these stupid warskins all the time. Besides, James still owes me a lot of replacement clothes from all his shenanigans back in Austin," Rhi said.

"Hey!" James cut in. "I got you all those clothes at The Galleria in Houston!"

"Doesn't count," Rhi said simply.

"The warskins are all we're allowed to wear," I said. It was true. As soon as we'd reported to the Reapers, we were told to get rid of all our other uniforms, as rookie warskins were the only authorized uniform.

We were expected to be on constant alert, and if something were to happen, we wouldn't have the time to change clothes.

Ever since we started wearing our warskins out in public, we'd been treated much differently. People seemed to be genuinely afraid of us and averted their eyes when we walked past. I had even seen one lady move to the other side of a walkway to avoid us. I had yet to find out why this was.

"Besides, it shows off your curves," Tara added.

"Well, yeah," Rhi agreed. "But it would still be nice to have something else just to switch it up a bit, you know?"

"You still have your coat," James added.

Rhi had thrown everything out as ordered except the coat Tara had given her.

"You're missing the point, James," Rhi said testily.

"Knock off the chatter," I said. "She's coming back."

Beth returned a moment later and checked each of our systems herself to ensure they were ready.

"Alright, move up to the ready line and button up," Beth said as her AUG moved forward, picked her up, and sealed her inside. Even before the cockpit was fully sealed, she was leading the way to a green line on the floor about 25 meters from the gate.

Beth had given us our literal marching order, starting with me, then Rhi, then Tara, and finally James. We lined up in order.

"Wait for the deck boss," Beth repeated.

"Yes, ma'am," We replied over the comm system.

As soon as the deck boss gave Beth the go-ahead, she walked towards the gate.

When we first saw the PTS gate, we expected a big silver whirlpool or a black void or something else equally impressive. Instead, the gate was invisible to the naked eye. It could only be seen through our neural cockpits as a pulsing green square. Anyone without an authorized access key would simply pass through the gate as if it wasn't there. You had to have a key in order to interact with it.

As Beth reached the threshold of the gate, she didn't hesitate. We watched as her AUG disappeared, appearing as if she'd walked right through the wall.

"Wow," James muttered.

Twenty seconds later, I was given the thumbs up, and with only a slight hesitation, I walked through.

PTS Genesis

RHI

I watched as the two boss ladies disappeared into the wall and breathed a short sigh of relief. While I didn't begrudge Shae for the role she'd been forced into, I still didn't like following orders. I liked to give them, not take them.

So, as I was waiting for the deck boss to give me the signal, I reached out and touched the point transfer wall. I watched as part of my AUG's arm disappeared.

I didn't feel anything as I hadn't turned on the touch sensors of my AUG. There were sensors everywhere on your AUG that could be turned on to give you tactile sensation, but I left them off. I didn't want to feel it if someone shot my AUG.

So, when I wiggled my fingers inside the wall, I didn't feel anything other than the sensation I was wiggling my fingers. I slowly pulled my arm back and it seemed fine.

I hadn't been paying attention to the deck boss, who'd been yelling at me for messing with the wall the whole time.

I was still grinning when the deck boss finally cleared me to move out. I moved through the wall and was instantly somewhere else. The massive room I walked into was very much not training room 331a.

"Oh, what the fuck?" I said to no one as I appeared to be alone. Did my messing with the wall screw it up? I had a feeling I'd be getting an ass-chewing from Beth shortly.

The oversized room wasn't bare. Everywhere I looked were metal cabinets and computer banks lining the walls and filling the room.

My AUG was helpful and labeled everything as I looked at

it. But this didn't help me as there was barely enough room to cram my AUG in where I'd emerged from the gate.

As I looked around, I bumped into one of the towering computers, and it teetered. I turned quickly, trying to steady the computer and inadvertently bumped another, sending it teetering. This comical domino effect continued until I got myself under control.

Finally, I had to abandon the AUG. It couldn't move in these tight quarters without destroying everything it touched.

I started to exit the AUG, then paused and leaned back in. I ran my diagnostic just like Beth had instructed, grumbling the entire time. Everything appeared fine. I was right where I was "supposed" to be, according to the computer.

"So much for diagnostics," I mumbled.

Our onboard PTS engines had been disabled for this training to ensure we didn't accidentally gate ourselves somewhere we weren't supposed to be. There were so many stories of gate accidents and I wasn't interested in becoming a statistic, so I'd left them alone.

Even if I could get the PTS engines back online, it wouldn't help. I wasn't authorized to make a personal gate. Only Daemons (and Beth) could do that. The rest of us had to have Behemoth make the gate for us.

Unfortunately, Behemoth couldn't find me at the moment. According to the computer, I wasn't even on Behemoth anymore. Every instrument my AUG had was contrary to the rest. I wasn't a computer tech, but I was pretty sure my computer was busted. For all I knew, I was in the room next door to where I was supposed to be.

I jammed my finger as I reached into the emergency storage area. I shook my hand before pulling out what looked to be a small brick, cursing to myself the entire time. I ran my finger over the surface of the brick and it unfolded itself into what looked like a submachine gun. I quickly checked to make sure it was working before slinging it over my shoulder by its nano-strap.

I touched a small, inconspicuous, hard patch on the thigh of my warskin. The patch unfolded itself into the standard pistol we'd been trained on. I checked to make sure it wasn't damaged before touching it to my outer thigh, where my warskin held onto it and acted like a holster.

I didn't know what was going on. But being heavily armed made me feel better. Yeah, I know what you're thinking, "How can two little plastic guns be considered 'heavily armed?'" Well, these guns packed a variable punch from a light slap to something equivalent to the "noisy cricket." I'd found that last part out the hard way when I hadn't respected my pistol the first time I fired it at max setting.

My finger still hurt from jamming it earlier. I shook my hand and flexed my fingers, trying to get some blood back into it. I wanted to kick my AUG in frustration but knew it wouldn't help.

I did it anyway.

I'd been assigned a Tempest class AUG. Its primary weapon system consisted of these tiny missiles no bigger than my fist. They didn't look like much as they were designed for close-quarters fighting. But each of those Budweiser-sized missiles packed a serious punch. It only took one well-placed hit to cripple a full-sized AUG.

As long as my AUG's power plant was at full capability, it could manufacture replacements almost as quickly as I used them. This effectively gave me unlimited ammunition. Granted, it could only build one replacement at a time, but still. If I missed my target the first time, I had plenty more opportunities.

On a side note, this was the same weapon system Beth had used to destroy the AG AUG over the Alamo. She didn't pilot a tempest, but she had the same weapon system built into that Frankenstein AUG she drove.

Limping slightly, I began to explore the room. It was bitterly cold. If I'd been a normal human, I would have gone into hypothermia by now. Even though vampires had a higher tolerance for temperature, I still activated my warskin and was instantly warm. Why be cold if you don't have to?

The warskin had the capability of protecting the body, even in the depths of space. But it had a limited power supply and we were told only to use it in emergencies. When I'd asked how long the power would last, I was told it would last for several days before needing replenishing. I figured simply running the heater wouldn't drain it that much.

As I explored the near-frozen environment, I soon regretted not grabbing the coat from my emergency storage despite the warmth from my warskin. I considered going back for it, but a blue light from the next room caught my attention.

A large faceted sphere dominated the middle of the next room. The sphere was what emitted the blue light that had drawn me in like a moth to a flame.

A handrail made a barricade around the sphere, and more computer banks lined this circular room. On the other side of the room was what looked like a room identical to the one I'd just left.

I took my time exploring the computers, looking for any help in figuring out where I was. Unfortunately, none of the computers had screens, or keyboards or mice or anything! They were just big cabinets full of computer stuff.

[Yeah, I know, "computer stuff." I'm big on technical terms, huh? Oh, shut up. You know I'm not a nerd. --Rhi]

Guys? Can anyone hear me? I mentally kicked myself for not trying it earlier. The whole being without mental comms when we first got here had made me start thinking like a normal human again.

I can hear you, my inner voice said in a tiny voice.

Nice of you to join me. Where have you been? I asked testily.

Oh, I'm always around. But lately, you've had too much noise going on in your head to hear me, the voice in my head said.

Oh, shut up. I shook my head. When there was no answer from anyone else, I returned to the computers.

A few minutes later, I found myself wanting to kick the computer as it wasn't helping either.

So, I kicked it.

I limped on my other foot to the center of the room and

peered into the glowing sphere.

Shadows seemed to be moving inside the sphere. I squinted and shielded my eyes to try and see past the glare.

Just as I was about to kick the sphere, it cleared. The light died down to a soft hue and I could now see images flickering within. They were all a pixilated jumble, making it so I couldn't figure out what they were. I frowned and the images disappeared.

"Well, that wasn't helpful," I sighed, half expecting a computer voice to ask what I needed help with.

WHAT DO YOU NEED?

The voice was loud in my head but disjointed as well. I grabbed my head out of reflex.

What do you need? the voice said in a quieter tone.

Recovering from the blast of mindspeech, I straightened and looked around. *Who are you?* I thought to the new voice in my head.

I am assistance, the voice said.

Assistance in what? I asked.

I am assistance.

Well, that's helpful, I thought sarcastically.

You are welcome, the voice replied.

Are you trying to be funny?

No, the voice said.

I stopped myself before the conversation turned into an Abbot and Costello routine.

Where am I? I asked.

Sector— a screech of noise followed. That was followed by, *Corridor WQjdu, Terminal 6641b320092aQ.*

It cut me off before I could say anything.

Primary Archive Residence.

That caused me to pause. In all the time we had been on Behemoth, we had never found any history on the place outside simple variations of the story we'd been told during the transition briefing. It was as if Behemoth had always existed, but no one had kept records.

Am I still on the Behemoth? I asked.

Affirmative.

Can you show me the history of this place?

Affirmative, the voice said.

I waited. When it was obvious the thing was not going to continue, I added, *Show me the history of this place.*

Specificity error.

Speci...oh, for Pete's sake. Show me the beginning of this place.

Complying.

The large sphere of light shifted, and a bizarre mash of colors and shapes appeared. They shifted and folded in on themselves repeatedly as I watched. When they didn't resolve into something I could understand after a minute, I said, *What is this?*

File record 1.

Why does it look like this? I rubbed my eyes as the collage of colors was starting to give me a headache.

Clarification: "Look like this?"

It's all scrambled, I said.

Negative. There is no security scramble engaged.

Is it damaged? I asked.

Negative, the voice said.

Show me the next file. Chronologically, I added.

The image blinked out. What took its place was just as distorted.

I growled with frustration. This was worse than scrambled Cinemax.

Show me something I can see! I said.

The image winked out again. What replaced it was a starfield, one I didn't recognize. Something in the distance moved.

What is that? I asked.

That is the first unknown vessel encountered on 93938847. This file features enhancement capability. Do you wish to engage it now? the voice asked.

Still squinting at the tiny image, I said, *Sure.*

As I watched, it seemed as if I was getting closer to the ship, not it getting closer to me. Details began to resolve of the ship as the stars seemed to envelop me, almost as if I was falling into the glowing sphere.

Then, I was outside, floating in the depths of space. My stomach churned with the sensation of sudden weightlessness and I couldn't breathe. Before me was a massive ship painted with blues, reds and silvers in a pattern that seemed to shift before my eyes. I struggled a moment before the scene shifted again, and I found myself sprawled unceremoniously on a warm, soft floor.

When I managed to regain my wits and look around, I was in some sort of control center. People were sitting at various stations around me. None of them seemed to notice I was there.

"Where are we?" The captain pondered aloud. His ship, his beautiful ship, was in pieces.

She had been top of the line once, many years ago. But now, she was yet another ship in the financially tapped fleet that desperately needed an overhaul. But she was still his. All the captain had to do was make it through two more months, and then he could retire and put his feet back down on solid ground for a while. Why he'd let his now ex-mate talk him into this job was beyond him.

Wha... I stammered. I had no idea how I knew the man was the captain or how I knew anything about the aging ship. None of these details were spoken in my head like traditional mindspeak; they were just there. It was almost like I could hear his own inner monolog.

"I'm not sure, sir. NAVComs are down," Tess answered automatically.

Frantically, Tess tried to remember every shortcut and trick she'd picked up while part of the merchant fleet to repair the damaged console. Practically everything was non-operational. She knew this was Rosi's job, but until her pilot controls came back online, she had nothing better to do. That plus, she was faster than Rosi.

The console blinked off, causing Tess to slam her fists down on it in frustration. The panel blinked back on. Her previous Captain had called that maneuver the "Old tried and true."

Uh, hello? I tried, but again, no one paid me any attention.

I pay attention to you, my inner voice said.

The ship drifted in a slow tumble as the residual gray space energy crackled along the hull, slowly dissipating into the void.

Even that, I somehow saw in my mind. *What is this?* I asked myself.

Enhanced file recording 88989930, the sphere's voice came again to my mind.

I'll say it's enhanced, I said as I looked at the rug burns on my palms.

"Still venting atmosphere on deck three," the damage control (DC) officer called out.

"What else, DC?" the captain asked.

"Engines are offline, maneuvering jets are...also offline. Main power is spotty at best, but the auxiliary is still holding. The other two hull breaches are stable."

"No sign of pursuit. They appear to have broken off, sir." Tess said, managing to bring the long-range sensors online long enough to look behind them. They immediately failed again as another jury-rigged relay shorted out.

"Well, that's one piece of good news. Hopefully, they overshot us and won't be able to turn about before we can affect repairs." The captain sighed, turning to the damage control station, "DC, any idea what knocked us out of G-space?"

"Not at the moment, Captain, but I'll add it to the list." DC was clearly focusing on his board, trying to triage the never-ending damage reports and dispatch repair teams in order of priority.

The DC had specialized in mechanical engineering while at the academy, and he was good at it. Graduated top of his class, assigned engineering on the last three flagships that went out on shake-down cruises. But one little close encounter with an Admiral's son and daughter had landed him on the Atlas, hauling supplies around between systems.

Seriously? How do I know that he banged some Admiral's kids? What the actual hell? I rubbed my temples.

"Whatever it was, it didn't come from the other ship," Tess said. "She was running just as clean as we were right up until we transitioned."

The Atlas had been on a routine run from one supply base to

another. Its mission had been the reconstituting of distant outposts with necessities when they'd run into unwelcome company. The raider ship had been waiting at one of the standard, clear zone jump points and had attacked as soon as they'd dropped out of G-space.

"Good job, Tess. Had you been a few seconds slower, we wouldn't be having this conversation," the captain lauded.

"Tango, sir," Tess said, her eyes never leaving her panels.

"Captain..." Rosi started.

The captain looked over to his navigator, who looked at his display quizzically.

"What is it?" the captain asked.

"I'm not sure," Rosi said, fiddling with several instruments, attempting to reroute sensor data through various interpreting software.

Rosi hadn't gone through the academy like most of the others here. He'd been picked up freelance and brought in as a contractor. This caused no end to the ribbing he received. But, his ability to make the computers do things they weren't supposed to had made even Tess, the worst of his tormentors, shut up. "There's something out there," he said at last.

"Is it our not-so-nice friends?" the captain asked.

"Negative. It's way too big," Rosi said, frowning down at his console. He reran the results and then ran them again.

"What is it, Rosi?" the captain asked, impatient with his navigator's obvious reluctance to continue. Rosi was a good navigator. But, his need to be 100% right all the time caused him to second-guess himself constantly.

"The...instruments say...and this could be false readings from the damage—"

"Just spit it out!" the captain growled.

"Whatever it is, it's almost 190,000 AUs in diameter," Rosi said finally.

This caused the entire command staff to glance up at the blank view screen.

What the hell's an AU? I asked and was ignored by the crew.

*An AU stands for an Astronomical Unit. In this case, it's

the distance from their home system's star to their home planet. In this case: 23,342,422,686,345,974,233 rells,* the voice provided.

Yeah, that helps, I frowned.

You are welcome, the voice said.

I rolled my eyes.

"It also appears to be man-made," Rosi said.

"Man-made? We don't have anything this far out," Tess said.

"You figured out where we are?" the captain asked. Tess had always been quick on the uptake. While not the best in the books, she more than made up for it in sheer flying talent. The captain had watched her make the Altas do things that would have given her design engineers a heart attack.

"Rough estimate, sir. By piecing together the star clusters I can make out...and taking into account our..."

"Just tell me where we are, Tess."

"We're roughly...1,200 lites from our last known location. Approximating, of course," Tess said.

"1,200 lites? Are you sure?" at her nod, he continued, "No one has been this far out."

"It doesn't really matter at the moment as we're drifting into this behemoth's gravity well." Tess scrambled for her controls. "I could really use some juice here, DC."

"Trying to get you some jets now. They're working the relays as we speak," DC said.

"Don't bother with the jets," Rosi said. "If I'm reading this right, jets won't break us from orbit around this thing. It's too big. Its gravity well is what probably yanked us out of G-space."

"If it's strong enough to pull us out, it could have pulled that raider out as well," the captain said. "Any readings from it? Communication, power, anything?"

"Negative sir. There's nothing coming back from it. I wouldn't have even noticed it if it wasn't for the dead space it takes up," Rosi said.

"Are we going to collide?" the captain asked.

"Can't tell yet," Rosi said. "I'm trying to calculate the gravity well but something is interfering with what little instruments I have."

"Are we in visual range?" the captain asked.

"Yes, but it's not very clear. Our sensors are still trying to recalibrate from the system crash," Rosi said.

"Show me what you got," the captain said.

"Yes, sir," Rossi said.

The dark screen flickered and slowly came to life. The star-speckled blackness of space filled the screen. The view swam, causing momentary vertigo to those who looked upon it. The entire screen was now filled with blackness.

"Did we lose the feed?" the captain asked.

"No sir," Rosi said. "That is our current view. It's taking up the entire sensor field currently."

"What the..." the captain began, squinting at the screen.

"Estimating impact in roughly two hours at our current drift," Tess chimed in.

"Are we still dead stick?" the captain asked.

"Unfortunately, sir," DC said.

"Even if I had full thrusters, I could only keep us up another...20 minutes...maybe," Tess said.

"OK, DC," The captain said. "Primary engines first, then life pods."

"Already on it, sir," DC said.

"Good man."

To me, the entire world seemed to shutter, and suddenly, it was 90 minutes later. Don't ask me how I knew that; I just did.

"Course change!" Tess said, staring at her instruments in disbelief. They still had another thirty minutes before impact. "DC, are you reading any misfiring jets? I still have nothing on my board."

"Negative, they're still dead as far as I know," DC said.

"We're definitely changing course," Rosi confirmed.

"Where we heading Tess?" the captain asked.

"Whatever this thing is, it's pulling us out of the drift we were in and towards its surface," Tess said.

"Still no readings from the object itself," Rosi said.

"Dammit," The captain muttered. "OK, people, listen up. We're going to..."

That's when the universe turned itself off.

My entire field of view was blue, a strangely familiar blue. A string of characters scrolled across the ceiling, as if subtitles but at the top of a TV screen. Then, the universe returned.

Their own painful groaning was the only sound the crew woke up to. Each of them came to, still strapped into their console seats. None seemed the worse for wear.

"Everybody all right?" the captain asked, shaking his head. A round of groggy affirmatives slowly made its way through the command deck. "Status?"

"We're...in G-space, sir," Rosi said.

"Not only that, we're back on our original course before we were pulled out of G-space," Tess said, looking at her instruments incredulously.

"All systems show green, Captain," DC said.

"What?" the captain asked.

"All systems answer fully operational," DC repeated.

"How?"

"It appears," Rosi began, then stopped and did a double take at his screen. "The tactical clock indicates that over 48 hours have passed since we were last in contact with the 'Behemoth,' as Ms. Tess so eloquently called it."

"48 hours? I want a full system diagnostic and crew accountability now!" The captain didn't know what was going on, but he wanted to make sure all of his people were still here. "Are we still 1,200 lites out?"

"No sir, we're back where we were during the pursuit." Tess glanced up from her console at the rapidly shifting screen.

"Any sign of pursuit?" The captain asked.

"No, sir, the raiders are gone," Tess said.

Silence filled the room only broken by the quiet chime of instruments.

I looked around. Everything was shiny and clean like one of those "neat and tidy" sci-fi universe shows. There wasn't even a hint of smoke in the air anymore.

After a long moment, the captain seemed to come to a decision.

"Rosi, plot a course to the nearest Imperial-class station. Whatever happened to us, they'll be able to figure it out," the captain said.

"Rerouting now, sir," Rosi acknowledged.

I felt the sensation of falling backward and stumbled. When I righted myself, I was standing in front of the glowing sphere back in the—

Primary Archive Residence, The voice helped finish my thought.

Thanks. I frowned, fighting down a wave of nausea as my body righted itself. I chewed on my lip a moment. *What was that blue...whatever it was?*

A command screen, the voice provided.

And that is...? I asked.

A command screen.

Seriously, so helpful, I said sarcastically.

You are welcome.

Before the blue— I started.

Command screen, the voice corrected.

Knock it off, I growled.

Specificity error.

What was at the top of the command screen? I asked.

Continuity reference, the voice said.

Reference? Reference to what? I asked.

In this instance, referencing what occurred to the Atlas during the crew's "lost time."

What happened? I asked.

Analysis and processing, the voice said.

You're analyzing it? I asked.

No. The analysis and processing of the Atlas and its crew.

I stopped, unsure if I wanted to know. Finally, I gritted my teeth and said, *Show me.*

PTS CW

JAMES

The moment I passed through the portal, my AUG died. I stared in astonishment at nothing, seeing as it was pitch dark. I shook myself free from my shock and fumbled for the emergency power switches.

Unlike Shae, I preferred to have actual switches, dials, and controls for my AUG, so that's what my neural cockpit was. Unfortunately, there were no switches, dials, or controls for me to use as my AUG seemed good and truly dead, including my neural cockpit.

When we first arrived on Behemoth, I'd had the nerve to ask where all the "cool sci-fi shit" was. Meaning the insane technology that comes from a civilization that was so far beyond my own that I couldn't even fathom it.

It took me a while to realize that the "cool sci-fi shit" was all around me. It was so advanced that it had incorporated itself into daily life, so you didn't notice it. It didn't stand out in bright neon colors and burning chrome; that was kinda the point. This is where our motto of "don't know how it works, just happy it does" came from.

A moment later, words appeared in front of me.

"Platform connection interrupted...please wait for communication restoration." The words sat there in the middle of the darkness, blinking at me.

I pushed down the rising panic and forced myself to take some deep breaths to try and calm myself. Over the sound of my own breathing, I realized there were no other sounds or vibrations in the AUG. I also realized there was no gravity so I was pretty sure I wasn't in a room on the station. I wasn't even sure I was on Behemoth anymore.

Shae? Rhi? Anyone there? When no one responded, real fear began to creep in, along with a small sense of claustrophobia I didn't know I had.

Carefully, I retracted the system tentacles that connected my head to my AUG. I needed to use my old analog eyes to check my surroundings since my digital ones had failed. I kept the other tentacles in place as they were keeping me secure within my AUG.

I racked my brain for any of the emergency training I'd been taught. What I could remember, I tried. First, I touched my warskin's illumination toggle. To my relief, stripes along my warskin began to glow.

The feature was supposed to allow for rescue to find us in the dark, whether that be on land or in space. I could adjust the brightness to near blinding in an emergency and even have it strobe if needed.

Now, I adjusted the brightness to allow me to see my instruments, forgetting there weren't any instruments to see as they were all in my head! So, I used the emergency lights as a sort of nightlight to push back the darkness.

There wasn't much to see, but it was better than staring at the warning message in the dark. Unfortunately, I had a good view of the tentacles that were still attached to the rest of my body.

I'd been having reoccurring nightmares about the tentacles ever since we started using the new AUGs. I knew they were essential for the AUG's operation, and they were designed to protect me. But that still didn't stop my mind from going to some dark places with the possibilities.

Even with the light, there wasn't much to see, especially as I was trying not to look at the tentacles. AN AUG's cockpit was just an armored void within the AUG. As much as they unnerved me, thankfully, the tentacles were still active. They ran on a different emergency system as they had to protect me and hold me in place. They doubled as the link to my AUG and my restraints.

Several hours passed, with me mostly twiddling my thumbs. I'd occasionally reach out mentally, but I still hadn't heard a reply from anyone. I'd considered blowing the emergency seals to get out of my AUG but knew I had a lot more air in it than in my warskin's emergency tank.

My AUG was a Typhon class multi-weapon platform. It was big and designed to carry a variety of weapons. It reminded me of an A-10 in the versatility of its ordinance. I'd nicknamed it "Jack," as in jack-of-all-trades. It was the same style as the one Beth had piloted before she'd modified it to its current form.

I started to wonder what would happen once I ran out of air. I mean, I didn't need to breathe, but with the amount of blood in me, I was as close to being a "normal" human as I could be. Did the blood need oxygen to survive? Could I survive in space even without air? These thoughts kept me occupied for quite a while.

A loud clang woke me from the doze I hadn't realized I'd entered.

I tried to take a breath and realized there wasn't anything to breathe. Panic set in as the need to breathe became overpowering.

I was still a "new" vampire, only a few months old now. I still retained much of my humanity, or at least my human instincts, like breathing.

I thrashed without rational thought and clawed to activate my emergency warskin reserve. I was so preoccupied with getting my air back on I didn't notice the return of gravity.

Suddenly, the entire AUG shuddered as it tipped onto its side and crashed to the "ground." A moment later, there was a loud banging on the outside of the AUG. Someone was out there and I briefly debated whether to come out or not.

Deciding I didn't have anything left to lose, I made a certain series of motions, and the emergency hatch on my metal coffin blew, spilling me out with a loud hiss of air.

The floor and walls were a dark purple color but not made of metal. It seemed to be some sort of crystalline substance and it seemed to throb slightly underneath me.

I lay there for a moment, just trying to get my heart back under control. I'd managed to get my warskin's oxygen supply going and was taking deep, calming breaths.

The warskin was designed so you could either pull the hood over your head, forming a full helmet, or you could have the warskin create a simple mask to cover your mouth and nose so you could breathe. I'd chosen the latter option.

Suddenly, something leaned down into my visage.

It was a helmet made of some sort of faceted crystal similar to the walls and floor. Instead of being purple, this crystal was a deep red with something similar to a white frost suspended within it. It would have reminded me of a snow globe, but the frost didn't move. Two darker red spots marked where eyes would normally be, at least on a human.

A strange series of noises came from the general vicinity of the "face" and reverberated into my ears, almost as if a guitar string had been plucked. When I didn't respond, the noises came again, only to be followed by "Are you all right?" in a strange version of English.

I blinked several times and tried to sit up, but I'd been strapped into my AUG for so long that my muscles were slow to respond. A crystalline hand helped me into a sitting position but as I made to lean back against my AUG, the hands yanked me away from it and across the room as if I weighed nothing.

Only then did I realize the surface of my AUG was unimaginably cold. Had I leaned against it, I probably would have stuck like some bad holiday movie.

A new voice came from across the room. It was the same strange noises from before, only in a deeper chord.

I looked towards the sound and found another humanoid-shaped "crystal man" entering the room from a door that slid shut behind him. The newcomer's armor was an amethyst color but not as dark as the surrounding room.

"Not sure yet." The "crystal woman" said, not taking her eyes off me. I guessed it was a she, as her armor appeared to have small breasts. "Do you understand me?" This question was directed to me.

I tried to speak, but my mouth was dry, so I just nodded and hoped nodding was an affirmative to them and not something else.

"Can he breathe our air?" The red one asked.

I glanced down at my wrist and saw the steady green line. The instruments built into my warskin said I could breathe their air, but I wasn't quite sure I wanted to try it yet.

And again, did I need to breathe it? I'd have to put in some research time on vampires in space when I got back if I got back.

Vampires in Space sounds like a Mel Brooks movie, I thought.

"From what I can tell, we're within tolerances," the purple one said. "The bay has pressurized as well."

"All right then." The red one said as the crystal around her body seemed to shrink, disappearing until a human-looking woman with shoulder-length white hair in a blue jumpsuit remained. She was attractive in a stoic sort of way. I'd guess late 30s with an athletic build.

"Shashka!" the purple one hissed, but she waived him off.

The scene from Galaxy Quest popped into my head. The one where the engineer just pops open the door to a shuttle on an alien planet. Everyone else is yelling at him for not checking the air; he takes a sniff and says, "Smells all right to me."

"It's all right," she said to me. "You're safe here."

I glanced at the purple one again and then down to the slowly depleting air bar on my warskin. I touched the hollow of my throat and the seal on my warskin broke. The thin membrane that had been around my mouth and nose retreated into the neck of my warskin.

The first time I'd gone into space with only my warskin to protect me, I'd freaked out a little bit. The thought that this thin fabric could not only protect me from the dangers of space but also provide necessities like air was so alien I couldn't believe it. But it worked.

The fact the warskin was actually a living organism that partially fed off my body to survive was a whole other nightmare I tried not to think about.

I hadn't realized I'd been sweating until the cool, fresh air of the ship struck my face. I gulped huge lungfuls of air, more out of habit than anything else.

"My name is Shashka. Are you hurt?" the woman asked with

just the slightest hint of yet another accent I couldn't identify.

"No," I croaked out, my throat dry. "I'm OK," I said after swallowing several times. "Where am I?"

"You're on our ship. We found your..." She glanced at my AUG and then back to me. "We found you floating in space. We weren't sure if there was anyone alive inside or not, so we brought you aboard."

"I appreciate the rescue," I said. "My name is James Sable."

"Well, I'm glad we could help you out, James Sable. The overly cautious one back there is my husband, Krys." She pointed a thumb over her shoulder.

The man crossed his arms and stood mute.

"Hi," I said cautiously.

"How did you get all the way out here?" Shashka asked.

"Good question, I don't really know. One minute, I'm stepping through a transport wall heading towards a training area; the next, I'm floating in a dead AUG in the depths of space."

"Huh," she said simply. "Well, let's get out of this compartment and somewhere a bit more hospitable. Then you can tell us all about it," she said, offering me a hand up. Her hand was soft and warm, almost hot to the touch.

We walked through a pair of doors and down a short hallway to another room. This room looked like a lounge. There was a table and chairs in the middle of the room and several couches along the outer rim of the room which seemed to be a large hexagon. Everything seemed to be made from some form of crystal.

"Please, make yourself comfortable," Shashka said, pointing to one of the couches.

I eyed the couch suspiciously and wondered how a rock-hard crystal couch could be comfortable.

She saw my expression and laughed. "It's more comfortable than it looks."

The crystal surface of the couch gently gave at my touch.

She went over to one of the walls and touched it. A panel slid open, revealing multiple containers within. She pulled two small containers and closed the panel. After handing one to her husband, she turned to me.

"I'm sorry, I'd offer you something but I have no idea if you can eat it. For all I know, what we eat might kill you," she twisted the top off the container and quickly downed its green-colored contents. She made a face and returned the now empty container to the wall.

"Did it change the formula again?" Shashka said to Krys. "I swear it's getting worse every time. It's practically sludge now." She made another face and shuddered slightly as she sat down in a chair.

I sat on the strangely comfortable couch. The surface was warm and seemed to adjust, cradling me no matter how I moved. I couldn't help but bounce a little to see what it would do. It simply continued to cradle me.

Glancing over at Krys, I saw he was still watching me, his posture guarded. Instead of drinking from the container, he held it up against his crystal suit, clothes, armor? Whatever it was, as he touched the container to it, the crystal seemed to grow out and grab hold of the container, leaving Krys's hands free again. He didn't drink.

Shashka followed my gaze. "Krys quit showing off and relax. I don't think our friend James here means us any harm, do you?"

"Not that I'm aware of," I said honestly. "You guys rescued me." I turned towards Krys, "And my AUG's not exactly a wooden horse."

I guessed he understood the reference as I was rewarded with a chuckle from the man but he kept his armor in place.

"Where am I?" I asked.

Shashka rested an elbow on the table. "Truth be told, we're lost. We were hoping you might be able to tell us where we are."

"Lost?" I swallowed hard.

"Yeah," she sighed, "our ship has a tendency to wander."

"Your ship...wanders?" I said slowly.

"Yeah, she gets absent-minded sometimes when it comes to our destination," Shashka grinned.

"Sounds like you need to fire your navigator," I said.

"Can't really do that. The ship is the navigator."

"Uh...what?" I asked.

"It's a living ship," Krys said, finally breaking his silence. His voice also had a strange accent to it I'd never heard before. It was also way different from Shashka's.

"Huh," I said intelligently.

"We don't recognize any of the star references here...at all," Shashka said.

"We appear to be between galaxies," Krys said. "There is absolutely nothing out here."

"Behemoth is out here somewhere," I said. "It's where I'm from."

"A ship?" Krys asked.

"Not exactly. Behemoth is...a space station...sorta," I said helpfully.

"Sorta?" Shashka asked.

"It's also a living organism. But instead of a ship like you have, it's a massive space station," I said.

"How massive?" Krys asked cautiously.

"Big enough to house planets," I said.

"Planets...plural?" Shashka asked, her eyes widening.

"At least a hundred or so, I think," I said.

"A hundred...planets," if Shashka was trying to hide the shock in her voice, she was failing.

"I've never heard of anything that big before," Krys said. His crystal helmet seemed to fade away much as Shashka's had, revealing his visage.

He shared the same white hair as his wife, as well as the same length. He looked to be in his late 40s and, I had to be honest, one of the most handsome men I'd ever seen.

Krys caught me staring as he removed the container from his suit, opened it, and took a long drink, all while never taking his eyes off me. His eyes matched the color of the armor he'd been wearing.

The more I looked at his eyes...the more...I seemed...to be...drawn...into...I shook my head, trying to clear it. I wasn't sure if he had some sort of mental power or what, but I had to remember not to look into his eyes anymore.

When I glanced back, Krys was still watching me with an

expression I didn't recognize.

"Are you OK?" Shashka leaned down and peered into my eyes. She had perfectly normal brown eyes. Lovely yes, but not crazy hypnotic like her husbands.

She glanced at Krys, then back to me.

"Yeah, sorry. I was in that AUG for a really long time. I guess my head's still a bit woozy," I said.

"You feel like coming up to the cockpit and seeing if you might recognize something that might help us figure out where we are?" she asked.

"I would, but...I wouldn't be much help to you," I sighed.

"Why?" Krys drew out the word. He'd finished drinking, without the repulsive shudder Shashka gave, and placed the now empty container back into the wall. The place where the armor had held the container reshaped itself back into its smooth surface, leaving no evidence it had ever changed.

"Because I've never been outside of Behemoth before," I admitted. Before they could ask, I explained how I was part of a defense force that protected a Bio-Hab. We had no reason to leave Behemoth as our mission was inside. Not to mention, we'd been told there was nothing outside to worry about.

"Well, that's just great," Krys frowned.

"What about your...AUG?" Shashka said the word like it tasted bad in her mouth.

"What about it?" I asked.

"Could it find your home?" she asked.

"I have no idea. But even if it could, it's dead," I said.

"You don't know how to repair your own equipment?" Krys asked distastefully.

"Hey man, I'm just a pilot, not a mechanic," I said defensively.

"You're obviously a soldier. You should know how to maintain your equipment," Krys accused.

I was about to say something rude when Shashka intervened.

"Let's just go take a look at it and see what we can do, shall we?" She glared at Krys.

I recognized the look she gave him. It was the same one Shae gave me when I was being a pain in the ass. It also seemed to last a bit longer than necessary, making me think they might be able to mindtouch as well. I considered trying to make contact but thought better of it.

We went and checked on my AUG. In the time we'd been gone, it had warmed back up to room temperature, making it safe to touch. It was lying on its side and didn't appear to have any external damage.

Contrary to what I'd said, I did know how to perform basic inspections and safety checks on the AUG. It had been part of our training. It's just...since I'd been assigned to the Reapers, I'd always had techs that took care of that for me. All I'd had to worry about was the neural cockpit, which also took care of the inspections for me.

Needless to say, I was rusty. As a result, it took me a couple of tries to get the maintenance hatch open. I could feel Krys's eyes on me the entire time, which didn't make it any easier. I made a mental note to quit slacking off and start doing this sort of thing myself from now on.

"Yebena mat! Krys, look at this powerplant." Shashka said as she looked inside my AUG. "It's the size of my fist. I thought the one on my old fighter was small, but this is ridiculous."

"Yeah, if that is the powerplant," Krys frowned, looking at me.

"It is," I said tersely.

A few hours later, I stifled a yawn.

"Well," Shashka started, "this looks like the primary power junction." Shoving her arm into the machine up to her elbow, she pulled a small cable out and examined it. "This should be the auxiliary power supply if I'm right."

She turned to Krys. "You think you could come up with an adapter so we could feed it some juice?"

Krys looked at the cable and then at the port. "It would probably take a few hours, but yes, I believe so. The real question is if our systems are compatible."

"Well, it's not like you can make it any worse. The thing's dead," I said.

Krys turned those amazing amethyst eyes on me.

I really gotta stop it with his eyes, I thought. *I don't know how, but they read like a bad romance novel and I REALLY don't know how I feel about that.*

"If we screw this up, we could overload your powerplant. We do that and—"

"BOOM!" Shashka finished for her husband with a strangely evil smile.

"Yes, as my wife is so fond of saying, boom," Krys said. "Even a small explosion of that nature could cripple our ship, stranding all of us."

"So don't screw up?" I said in an attempt at playful.

Krys just eyed me, and not in a good way.

"James, you look exhausted. This is going to take some time; why don't you try and get some rest?" Shashka said.

I stifled another yawn at the mention of rest. "I'm OK," I lied. "I don't have to sleep that much anyway."

I don't know how long I had snoozed while floating in space, but I still felt tired. I don't know if it was from all the stress or what, but at the same time, I didn't want to look weak in front of Krys...who seemed—

"Go away," Krys said flatly, thankfully interrupting where my train of thought was heading. He turned back to my AUG, "You're distracting. My wife's just too nice to say it."

I started to say something, but, like before, Shashka saved me from myself.

"Come on. When he gets like this, I don't even want to be around him," Shashka rolled her eyes and motioned to the door.

I rose and followed her out, but not before glancing back at Krys and my AUG. As I watched, Krys's armor faded away completely, revealing a blue jumpsuit like Shashka's. He peeled the top part down, revealing his back. Not only was it ripped with solid muscle, but ugly scars crisscrossed it in an uncomfortably familiar way. I closed my still-open mouth and quickly caught up with Shashka.

"You have to forgive Krys," Shashka started as we returned to the lounge area and took a different hallway out of it. He's a very old soul."

"A crotchety one if you ask me," I mumbled.

She chuckled, "Yes, he does have his moments."

She touched a space on the wall and a doorway appeared. It hadn't been there a moment before. Inside was a small room with a bed and a couch.

"I hope this is all right. It's not much, but we don't have many frivolities on this ship," she smiled.

"Oh, this is just fine," I said. "I've slept in much, much worse conditions. Thank you." I stepped into the room and touched the bed. "Is everything on this ship made from crystal?"

Shashka's smile broadened, "Yes. Crystal is a large part of our being." She paused, "That sounded kinda cryptic, didn't it? Sorry. Maybe I should explain."

I sat on the crystal bed. It was soft and warm. If I closed my eyes, I didn't think I could tell the difference between this and a normal bed from my world.

As I watched, Shashka tugged at her forearm and the jumpsuit split, revealing long, elbow-length gloves. As she pulled the gloves off, she revealed three rows of small crystal chips running from the back of her hand to her elbow. Each was the same shade of red as her armor.

"We live with a symbiont that allows us to create a bio-crystalline structure at will. The armor we create allows us to survive and operate in almost any environment, including space," she said.

"Your armor provides life support in space?" I asked. I don't know why it surprised me so much. My warskin basically did the same. "And you can just...make it appear and disappear at will?"

"Yes, for the most part. The symbiont was designed to combat a space-faring plague that lays waste to any planet it touches. It allows us to create armor, weapons, and even ships, although that takes quite a while." She smiled and sat on the couch opposite me.

"So, you're not human?" I asked and realized how stupid the question was.

"Oh, I'm very human. Born and bred in Russia, on Earth, a long-long-long time ago," she chuckled to herself at some private joke, her eyes bulging slightly. "Krys, on the other hand...not so much." She sighed. "I've been to his planet...once.

It's just a big ball of sand. I wouldn't recommend a vacation there.

"The symbiont's also alien. Apparently, it was designed to be versatile, but at the same time, it is also very selective on who can be a host. What about you? I take it you are...human?" she asked.

I nodded. "Yeah, I'm from a place called Texas, actually. But, not that long ago." I smiled, then cocked my head at her. "If you don't mind me asking, how did y'all meet? You don't strike me as...well..."

"Compatible?" Shashka smiled. "Would you believe this isn't the first wandering ship Krys has been on?"

"Sounds like he needs to make better ships," I said.

Shashka laughed, "Yeah. But the previous one wasn't his; I have to give him that. I was hurrying to work when this guy literally fell out of the ceiling and landed on top of me. The next time I saw him, he was in the brig."

"Sounds like love at first sight," I smiled.

"Oh, I hated the guy," she said. "He was a constant thorn in my side after that. Constantly getting into trouble one way or another. At first, I thought he was just a scumbag. Then I thought he was a stalker as he just kept showing up in the weirdest places. Eventually, I realized he was just an idiot with terrible luck,"

"Been there," I sighed.

"You run into someone enough times, and it's only a matter of time before something happens, one way or the other. Then we went the rest of the way together. It's been a long road, and we've seen some stuff, that's for sure. But I wouldn't trade him for the world." She practically glowed when talking about Krys.

"You keep talking like y'all are an old married couple. But you're my age," I said.

She laughed explosively. "You're what, 30? 35? I was that age when I got infected by the symbiont; a long-long-long-long, long time ago. Don't ask me how many; that's just rude."

"That's what Shae says," I laughed.

"Oh? Who's Shae?"

"She's...my other half...no...my other quarter?

It's...complicated," I said.

"Sounds like you have many complications in your life," Shashka said.

"A few, but I wouldn't trade them for the world either," I said.

"Oh, now you must tell me," she said.

"I was way back in high school when I met Shae..." I started to tell the story of Shae and me. Then I added Rhi and, eventually, Tara. Then Behemoth.

"Vampires, military superheroes, zombies, parallel worlds, aliens, giant space stations," Shashka finally said when I was done with a not-so-brief summary of the last twenty years of my life. Are you sure you're not just describing your favorite holo-novel series?" she grinned.

"I couldn't make this shit up," I said, shaking my head.

"You're a vampire?" Shashka asked flatly.

I nodded, "Yup."

"And you drink...blood?" she cringed.

"Yeah, but don't worry. Like you said, I don't know if the food you have would kill me or not." I tried to smile but had a feeling it came off creepy. "Did that come off creepy? It felt creepy."

"A bit," she said, nodding.

"I was trying for funny," I said.

"Not so much," she said, shaking her head.

"Sorry," I held my hands up.

"And you have three full-time women in your life?" She eyed me suspiciously. "Did you use your vampire seduction powers on them?"

"What? No! Two of them are vampires themselves," I said in defense.

"So, you all used your vampire seduction powers on each other?" she asked.

I almost kept going but pulled up short. "You're fucking with me, aren't you?"

Shashka laughed. "Seriously, though. Your story reminds me of what my kind does when we are defending a world. We band together in small groups we call gestalts," she said.

"Gestalts?" I asked, sitting up straighter.

"Yeah. A handful of us come together and basically become one. We're better together than we are apart...like a...strudel," Shashka said.

"A strudel?" I asked.

"Yes. It's made up of several things that might taste OK by themselves, but when joined together, make something amazing!" Shaska smiled. "I know, that sounded pretty sappy, but it's true. When we're together it's like we balance each other. We work, fight and sometimes...love better as a group. It's hard to explain, let alone understand if you've never experienced it."

"Yeah, I think I understand. When my group is together, things are better, problems are easier, hell, I can think better...if that makes any sense. But this is because this woman Natalie linked our minds together, so it's almost like we're one...no, that's not it. Sometimes, I don't know who I am in the group anymore; it's like we all blend together."

"A gestalt." Shashka nodded. "Sounds like your group is still figuring it out. Give it time. You'll get there."

"Shashka...what is that? What does your name mean?" I asked.

"It's Russian. Does it have to mean anything? What does James mean?" she asked.

"Uh, supplanter, I think," I laughed.

She shook her head. "Shashka is a kind of Russian cavalry saber."

"Did your parents hate you or something?" I laughed.

"OK, substitute." She smirked. "No, when we get our symbiont, it's treated as a rebirth. As such, we choose a new name."

"And you chose a sword?" I asked.

"All of our names are based on bladed weapons," She explained.

"Oh," I said slowly.

She shook her head and held her arm out to the side. Slowly, crystal appeared to grow from her arm, elongating until it was a long blade the size of a sword.

"Wow!" I exclaimed.

She nodded and the blade slowly retracted until her arm was back to normal. She began to pull her glove back on.

"So...Krys?" I said.

"The kris knife. You know, the one with the squiggly blade?" Shashka said.

I nodded.

"You have no idea what I'm talking about, do you? No matter." She sighed and stood up. "I'm going to go check on Krys. Try and get some rest. I'll come get you if anything changes."

"OK," I said. "Thanks again for saving me out there."

"You're not rescued yet," She cautioned.

I looked around the room, "Compared to my cockpit, yes, I am." I smiled.

∞∞∞∞Ω∞∞∞∞

JAMES

Eventually Krys managed to work whatever crystalline magic he did and set up a trickle of power to my AUG. It wasn't enough to get it moving, but sticking my head into the AUG allowed me to access my neural cockpit. It couldn't tell me where I was, but it did manage to set up a sort of homing beacon we could follow back to Behemoth. The problem was, it didn't say how far away it was, just a direction.

We started following the beacon at whatever speed the ship did. Not having a clue as to when we would arrive made me slightly nervous as I wasn't sure how long I'd survive without "nourishment." I had a ration in the emergency pack, but it was only good for a day or two. I didn't think our AUGs were designed to ever leave Behemoth. Hopefully, it wouldn't take that long to get home.

Along the way, Krys loosened up a little, at least enough that he didn't constantly wear his armor around me. He was still pretty tightlipped, leaving the conversation to Shashka. I got the feeling he didn't say much, even when not around strangers.

Luckily, Shashka was a pretty good conversationalist. We compared notes about the mundane differences and similarities between our worlds. But the biggest information came unintentionally, two weeks after my arrival.

Having used my emergency ration last week, my condition had steadily been deteriorating with the lack of blood.

When the tremors appeared, Shashka put her foot down. She told me the ship was complaining that my shaking was disturbing it, whatever that meant. As a result, I had to sample their blood.

Krys was unusually vocal about it having to be his blood I took, not Shashka's. I wasn't sure if this was a protective thing or what, but she didn't seem to mind. He didn't seem shaken by the fact I drank blood, unlike Shashka, who feared a "creature of the night," as she called me.

At first, I took a small amount. The memory of what happened to Shae back at the Hacienda caused me to be gun-shy. We agreed that if there hadn't been any negative reactions in 24 hours, then I could take an amount that would sustain me.

Shashka assured me I could take a lot more blood from them than a normal human. Apparently, it had something to do with how the symbiont maintained them.

It was during the 24 hours that it happened. I was lying down and trying to rest in my room. I was entirely focused on my body and trying to monitor it for any changes from the new blood when I heard it.

I still don't know! It was Krys's voice in my head. He sounded frustrated and angry.

Relax. If it happens, it happens, Shashka's voice came into my head as well, but it seemed to be routed through Krys.

They seemed to be talking to each other telepathically and I was somehow eavesdropping. The only thing I could figure was that it was a residual from me taking blood from him.

Is it still as bad as it was?

Yes, Krys growled.

Well, when you did it to me, did it go away afterward? she asked.

I don't know, Krys said.

*How can you not know? That was a pretty intense feeling from what you told me," Shashka said.

*Yes, it was. But Symitar also told me it wasn't normal. She said the symbiont's need was never as strong as I described it. She joked that it was my personal desire for you that was driving me mad. The symbiont was just tagging along for the ride," Krys said.

Well, now, isn't that what every girl wants to hear? No wonder there's no Valentine's Day on your world, Shashka said flatly. *Are you saying you want him as much as you wanted me then?*

I don't know! I could feel Krys's frustration as if it were my own.

Krys, for as long as we've been together, you've never felt this way about someone else. At least, not that I've ever felt from you, and we both know how bad a liar you are. I would say you should sit down and talk to him about it, but we both know how much you enjoy talking about your feelings. I could feel Shashka's smirk through the link.

No. I'll just ignore this. We'll get to this Behemoth station, and he'll return to his people, and I won't have to feel this anymore, Krys said with some determination.

Riiiiiight. Shashka continued to smirk. *And when you give him more blood tomorrow?*

I'll control it like I did today, Krys said.

Shashka laughed. *You nearly jumped him as soon as his mouth touched your skin! Just ask him. I've seen some of the glances he's given you, it's probably mutual. Stop this high school pining and just ask!*

No. Besides, the exchange will probably satisfy Itam and all this will go away.

God, for being over 3000 years old, you can be such a baby sometimes! Shashka sighed.

Oh, really? And why are you suddenly so keen on me doing this? Krys asked.

Shashka was quiet for a moment. *Because I know a lot about missed opportunities. It took me a long time to accept who I am and be OK with that. Besides, I don't want to see you pass something up just because you're being stubborn.*

Now you sound like Cateia, Krys huffed.

Well, she's bright for her age. Just look at what she did with Tachi, and you know how stubborn he was. Maybe when we find her, I can have her start to work on you.

Whatever link I'd tapped into faded, leaving me with a lot of questions.

The next day, I still hadn't had a negative reaction to Krys's blood. So, I took more from Krys, a lot more. He didn't stop me as I topped off. In fact, the entire time I drank, we shared some uncomfortable eye contact.

I knew Krys had some sort of thing for me. But while he was pretty hot...for a guy, I wasn't exactly looking for something like that just now. I already had enough partners in my life as it was. Then a part of me started to imagine what the others would do if I brought Krys home and I had to derail that train of thought real quick.

Another part of me was worried Krys might take Shashka's advice and proposition me for whatever he had in mind. Yet another part of me was interested in finding out more about what the alien's proposition might be.

I had too many parts.

Luckily, my AUG pushed all of that to the side when it lit up at full power, all on its own. When I checked on it everything worked like nothing had ever happened. I also had all the information I needed about Behemoth's location, distance, and everything.

It was as if Behemoth was feeding power to the AUG directly or controlling its powerplant from a distance. We'd simply been out of the range of Behemoth's control. I didn't know how it worked; I was just glad it did.

"You know, I'm in range now. I can always leave the ship and make it back to Behemoth on my own, guys," I said as we stood around the ship's "bridge."

The "bridge" consisted of two pilot couches and no windows. There were also no controls that I could see. Apparently, they controlled the ship through direct mental contact, their version of a neural cockpit. This allowed them to see outside of the ship without the need for windows. They could technically tap into the ship anywhere onboard just by touching it, but they used the pilot couches for major events.

Krys was currently encased in one of the pilot couches as Behemoth was in extreme sensor range now.

"We'll bring you the rest of the way in," Shashka said. "We were traveling with friends when all this started. Since this Behemoth is the only thing out here, it's a good bet they may have ended up there."

The presence of my AUG made entry into Behemoth relatively easy. Whoever was in charge of docking on Behemoth was talking to my AUG, which was relayed to me through a comm node in my warskin. I didn't know it could do that until a voice had started talking in my ear.

I had no idea of Behemoth's immensity until we got close to an entry hangar. It made the Death Star look like a house garage in comparison. Actually, it looked like you could dock the Death Star in this hangar. My brain just couldn't accept that something so massive existed. Behemoth truly earned its name.

There were support personnel I'd never seen before running the hangar. They were mostly human, but I didn't recognize their uniforms. They said they could help Shashka find their friends if they were on Behemoth. They just had a few questions first.

In the meantime, I'd been directed to return to my AUG and prepare for gating. Apparently, whoever was in control had reactivated my PTS engines and was sending me home by remote. All I had to do was get inside and they'd do the rest.

I said my goodbyes to Krys and Shashka and thanked them again for rescuing me. They both hugged me, Krys's lasting a bit longer than Shashka's. I told them how to contact me and said we needed to have a drink together sometime under better circumstances. I wished them luck in finding their friends before I suited up.

As my cockpit was closing, I took one last look at Krys and couldn't help but wonder, "What if?"

PTS Aftermath

SHAE

"OK, Tara, tell him what happened to you," I said.

The four of us were sitting around the table in our dayroom, catching James up on the malfunctioning PTS incident now that he was back. The rest of us had returned within a day or so from when we'd left. James was the only one who'd been gone longer.

James's absence had been felt by the group. We had all been out of sorts the entire two weeks and it wasn't just because of worry. It was almost like phantom leg syndrome. We knew he was gone, but every time we needed something from him, the loss hit us all over again. Beth had stood us down after we had multiple near-miss collisions.

The malfunctioning transport had sent the four of us in opposite directions. Oddly enough, Beth had ended up right where she was supposed to. So far, James and Rhi had both told their stories.

"Oh, I'm easy. My AUG ended up embedded in a wall," Tara said.

"WHAT?!?" James sputtered.

"Yes. When I reappeared, the bottom half of my AUG's legs were dangling out in the level below me while the upper half was stuck in the floor. My power systems had been interrupted and the ejection system was fused. A couple of Felon's Rangers found me not too long after," Tara said.

Felon was the commander of a nearby wing of DC. Rumor had it they were the premier unit in the entire corps.

"You're too damned lucky, girl," Rhi said as she hugged her. "OK, Shae, tell him your story."

"Uh..." I started, looking around the table. The tone of my voice caused James to straighten up and pay attention. With that one word, he sensed something had happened.

"I appeared in darkness," I cleared my throat. "But, at least my AUG was functional. When I hit my external lights, it was a mess. There was so much debris floating around me, bumping into me." I swallowed.

"Then I realized what the debris was." I looked about the table but didn't see them. "There was metal, concrete, cars, bodies, trees, houses, you name it. I didn't understand it at first.

"I fired up my spaceborne sensors and discovered I was in orbit around a Bio-Hab. There was no light coming from the planet or the debris. There were no stars and even the wall-sphere's camouflage screen was off. I tried my radio, but there was no answer. The rest of my AUG seemed fine, so I made my way through the field and towards the planet. As I approached, I deployed atmosphere entry shielding, but I didn't need it. There wasn't an atmosphere," I said.

The rest of the group looked at one another.

"I was on the ground before I knew it. The entire planet was a frozen ball. Anything not physically attached to the planet was in orbit around it," I said.

"Wait," Rhi said. "If there wasn't any gravity, how was there stuff in orbit?"

I managed to focus on Rhi.

"They were bouncing off the walls that surrounded the Bio-Hab and again off the planet itself. It was like a horrific game of table tennis." I didn't laugh, neither did anyone else.

"Could that be one of the planets the AG destroyed?" James asked to the air in general.

"Has to be," Rhi said.

"I can't imagine something so horrific," Tara said.

I looked at her, "Be glad you can't." I focused on a spot on the far wall.

"At first, I thought it was some sort of test. But after an hour, I gave up and went up to the wall-sphere. My radio still wasn't working so it took me a while of searching before I found an entrance bay. Once I manually opened the doors and was inside, all my systems came back online and I called for retrieval.

"Was it our Bio-Hab?" James asked.

"Not according to my sensors. The land masses were off," I replied.

"Uh, James?" Rhi said, pointing a thumb at the planet outside our common room.

"I don't trust anything anymore," James said.

"Why would Behemoth just leave all that in there?" Rhi asked, rolling her eyes at James.

"What do you mean?" Tara asked.

"Behemoth is big on using all available resources. If our AUGs are damaged, the damaged pieces are fed into a recycling unit to be melted down and used again. The same is true for just about everything we use," I said.

"I don't want to think about the bathrooms," James said, trying a little levity, but it fell flat.

"So, with all those resources just floating around there, why not use them?" Rhi said.

"You mean recycle the planet?" Tara asked. "Can Behemoth do that?"

"I don't see why not," Rhi said.

The idea brought a quiet moment to the group in contemplation.

"Why did we all end up so spread out?" James asked. "I mean, I wasn't even on Behemoth anymore. If Krys and Shashka hadn't found me and brought me back, I'd still be out there, sealed away in that tin can." James shuddered at the thought.

"Where are they?" I asked.

"Shaska and Krys? I don't know. I haven't heard from them since I reported back in," James said. "Hopefully, they found their friends."

"What was the name again?" I asked.

"Cateia something, I think," James said.

"Huh," I said.

"What?" James asked.

"Wasn't there a Cateia in our basic training class?" I asked.

"I don't remember. Things were kinda crazy at the time,"

James said.

"Yeah...I think there was, but she got pulled—" My train of thought sort of trailed off as it became harder and harder to remember where I was going.

"I don't think I want to walk through another of those transport walls again," Rhi said.

"Same here," Tara agreed.

"I think we all share that sentiment," I said, abandoning my previous train of thought.

"Uh, guys. There's something I didn't want to say, but since we're putting everything on the table...Behemoth showed me what happened to the crew of that ship in the recording I saw," Rhi said.

"When Behemoth brought the ship aboard, it put the entire crew in some sort of storage chambers and then disassembled the ship down to the last nut and bolt before storing it away."

"Why..." James started, but Rhi waved him off.

"They cloned the crew and created a complete copy of the ship. Then Behemoth manned the new ship with the clones and sent it off," Rhi finished.

James looked at Rhi patiently. When she nodded, he said, "Why?"

"Doofus," Rhi grinned at some private joke between them. "I have no idea."

"Oh, that's easy," Tara said.

All eyes turned to Tara.

"Behemoth was originally designed as a training ground. It bio-developed soldiers and trained them. It probably saw the new bio-mass and incorporated it into its matrix for development."

"How do you know this?" Rhi asked.

"Oh, it was in my intro classes when I got here," Tara said helpfully. "Didn't you get classes?"

"Not really," Rhi said flatly. "We had a really boring class for about an hour. Then we were sent to basic training."

"Oh," Tara said.

"Did they go into detail on what the training ground was being used for?" I asked.

"Just that there was a huge war a long time ago, but Behemoth hasn't received any orders concerning the war in quite some time," Tara said.

"Did we win?" Rhi asked.

"Who's we?" James asked.

Rhi punched James in the arm playfully.

Tara leaned over to me and said quietly, "Have you ever noticed the two of them acting as if they were brother and sister?"

"Don't remind me. It's creepy to think about," I smiled. "But back to the question at hand."

"Which was?" James asked.

We all looked at one another in silence.

"What the hell were we just talking about?" Rhi asked.

No one could remember, no matter how hard we tried.

Robot Riot

TARA

I was arms deep into the guts of an AUG when I felt my wife enter.

"You know you can't sneak up on me, right?" I said, not turning to look at her as she slunk up behind me.

"Who said I was trying?" Rhi replied, her footfalls echoing across the empty AUG bay.

I'd had a spare AUG delivered to our hangar bay. I wanted to rip it apart and see how it worked. All the schematics, books, and neural training just weren't the same as getting your hands dirty.

"Speaking of getting your hands dirty," my wife said as I felt her arms wrap around me from behind. There was little I could do about it as both my arms were buried up to my shoulders in a mess of conduits and relays. Add to this I was up on my tiptoes as AUGs weren't exactly built for mechanics my size.

"You know," I started, peering over my shoulder at her. "I could see how you might want to take advantage of this situation."

"Hmmm?" Rhi said as she bent over and nuzzled behind my ear. "And why would I ever do that?" she said in that annoyingly sexy voice that never failed to literally charm the pants off me.

"Well..." I started, trying to get my sudden flare of hormones under control. It was always like this with her. No one else ever affected me like this. Shae and James, sure, but nothing like how this woman could push my buttons. "What I'm doing is actually pretty dangerous at the moment."

"So's what I'm about to do," Rhi said as her hands slid across my body.

Our libidos hadn't changed since coming to Behemoth. The fact we'd been separated for so long during training caused Rhi to want to make up for lost time. Not that I minded.

A pleasant time later, we were grinning at one another and panting heavily.

"Well, that was different," I managed when I could think straight again.

"Yeah, who knew an AUG cockpit could be so... entertaining," Rhi said.

"Not the DC, that's for sure," I laughed as I cracked open the cockpit of the AUG I'd been tinkering with before. "Alright, get off me!" I teased as Rhi started kissing on me again. I mentally told the cockpit to put us down, and a moment later, we were on the deck of the hangar bay.

"I like the short hair, by the way," I said, nodding to Rhi's new haircut.

"Yeah," Rhi said as she ran her hand across her new haircut. She'd chopped off the length to a punkish-looking short cut, complete with one side buzzed off. "It kept getting caught in the tentacles, so I got rid of it. I can always get the length back with a quick body treatment."

"No," I said and I ran my hand through it. "I like this, it's cute."

"You just like it 'cause it means you don't have to take as long to brush my hair," Rhi pouted.

I kissed her briefly. "I'll brush you as long as you'd like, my dear, no matter how long or short your hair is. Was there something else you wanted, dearest?" I managed as I straightened my warskin.

Rhi just leered at me for a moment as she sealed up her own warskin.

"Aside from that?" I shook my head but grinned nonetheless.

"Just seeing what you were up to," Rhi said as she finished straightening herself up.

"What are James and Shae doing?" I asked as I reactivated the gloves on my warskin.

"James is out wandering the halls and Shae is cooped up with Beth doing...whatever it is they do. I swear, if I didn't know better, I'd say they were going at it."

"You think that about everyone," I said, trying to find all the tools that Rhi had scattered in her...haste. "You gonna help me with this?"

"Oh, yeah, sorry," Rhi said as she started helping me get my tools back together. "What is it with this stuff anyway? Ever since we got here, you've been spending every free minute in this hangar ripping the guts out of our AUGs. I'm just glad Beth caught you and ordered this spare, or else your AUG would have been broken when we needed it."

"Hey!" I yelled indignantly. "I didn't break anything! And it was your AUG, not mine."

"Gee, thanks," Rhi frowned. "But really, you've never shown an interest in engineering before. What's up?"

"I don't know," I sighed and tossed my tools back into the toolbox field that automatically sorted them into their proper spots. The toolbox was great. All I had to do was think of what I needed, and the box would put it in my hand. The only problem was it always said there was a missing ¼ inch socket, whatever that was.

"As you know, on my world, we didn't have any real technology, at least, none that worked properly. But here, everything is a marvel to me. I was so overwhelmed at first, every piece of metal singing out to me. But, after my neural training, I started to understand what they were saying."

"You understand what the metal is saying?" Rhi said, giving me one of her looks.

"Oh, you know what I mean. Metal has always talked to me; it's how I can manipulate it," I said.

"Sounds more like a relationship. Should I be jealous?" Rhi grinned.

I looked up at the towering AUG above me. "Well, I have always had a thing for the tall ones." I grinned back.

Rhi just rolled her eyes. "Don't make me go get a treatment just to make myself taller. Even with everything they can do here, I don't think me turning myself into a giant would be good for anybody. If you know what I mean," Rhi waggled her eyebrows at me flirtatiously.

"You're hopeless," I smiled and patted her on the face. "And I like you just the way you are. We fit quite nicely."

"I'll say, but did you know everyone here is perfect?" Rhi asked.

"Perfect? You mean there are other Daemons out there with my amazing metal manipulation skills?" I asked as I turned back to the panel I'd been tinkering with before Rhi, so nicely, interrupted me.

"Uh, no," Rhi said.

"That's right, only me, baby," I chuckled at her. That had been one of the things I'd questioned when I'd first arrived on Behemoth. But it turns out I'm unique. As far as I could find out, I was the only Daemon who could use metal the way I did.

"Well, they can do just about anything to your body you can think of and not just make you taller! Want to have purple hair? You don't need to go to a salon and worry about touchups or roots, just go to the clinic, and they change you at the genetic level to have purple hair!

"Don't like that you're a girl? You can get that changed too...albeit you have to spend a night in one of their vats, but the next morning, you walk out as a fully functional male! Want a futa treatment? They can even do that!"

"What's a futa?" I asked, unfamiliar with the word.

"Uh," Rhi stuttered.

When I looked over, she was blushing, which was more than enough to draw my attention.

"A futa is a normal woman who also has...a male part," Rhi stammered.

"So, a woman who also had a penis?" I said simply.

"Yes!" Rhi pointed at me and nodded uncomfortably.

"I haven't seen you like this. Why does this make you so uncomfortable?" I asked.

"What, did you have something like this on your world?" Rhi asked.

"No, not that I know of, you?" I asked.

"It was only fiction back home. At least, I mean, we had

technical hermaphrodites, but they weren't to the extent you would see in porn videos," Rhi said, her blush deepening.

"Porn videos?" I knew what porn was, I'd pulled it from James's head. But the fact that this was making Rhi so uncomfortable was intriguing. Plus, she messed with me so often that I felt it was only fair to return the favor occasionally.

"You know what porn is!" Rhi shot back.

"Well, yes, what I pulled from your mind is quite extensive," I said, but Rhi had figured me out.

"Oh, shut up," Rhi smirked.

"Maybe I should look into this futa treatment..." I teased.

"Don't you dare!" Rhi replied, way too fast.

"Just teasing you, relax," I said but realized there was more here I could tease her with, so I tucked it away for later.

"Check this out," I said in order to change the subject. I led Rhi over to a small side station I'd set up next to my gutted AUG.

"What is it?" Rhi said as she looked over what I'd been working on.

"It's a micronized version of an AUG. It's only an arm and shoulder so far. I've been working on proof of concept models." I put my arm into the contraption that was mounted to a stand at my height. As I got comfortable, the arm came alive, shifting and adjusting to fit me like a second skin. I flexed my fingers and rotated the arm experimentally.

Rhi reached over and touched my forearm. "This looks about as thin as one of our warskins. How tough is it?"

"It's the same hi-ris composite the AUGs are made from. It doesn't have as much protection, but it can deflect projectiles, absorb energy and withstand a punch from a normal AUG, only on a much smaller scale," I said proudly.

"Are you trying to make a mini-AUG?" Rhi asked as her fingers were exploring the arm further.

"Not really. It'll never have that kind of capability. Not unless powerplant and drivers suddenly shrink overnight," I smiled. "It's kind of hard to explain. Every time I'm piloting an AUG, it's like there's something inside of it trying to get out. This is my attempt to express that?" Even to me, the explanation left something to be desired.

A moment later, I felt Rhi inside my mind, gently sifting through my thoughts. I loved the feeling of Rhi's mental fingers. They felt like my tail, soft and warm but firm when needed. Her touch never failed to make me smile.

"OK, I think I get the picture," Rhi said as she withdrew from my mind. "Huh," she said, biting her lip and wrinkling her brow in thought.

"What?" I asked, curious.

"Not sure yet…" she started. "But I'll let you know if I figure it out. You planning on making a full suit of this?"

"No idea; that's up to the metal," I said. For everything we could share mentally, my bond with metal never translated for Rhi. She could understand I had some sort of affinity with metal, but no matter how hard I tried, I couldn't share the experience with her. I guess some things were just meant to be private.

"Uh huh," Rhi looked at me speculatively.

"Oh, don't give me that. Are you finally going to explain the conversations you keep having with the audience who's not there?" I asked.

[Yeah, tell me about it. Book sales are crap right now. --Rhi]

"See, that! That right there! What is up with that?" I asked in frustration. I could hear when she did it, her mental voice made a particular sound and it was almost like there was an echo to it. As if she were speaking into some giant void.

"Oh, don't get me started on super-sanity. I only understand enough to get myself in trouble," Rhi shook her head, frowning.

"What?" I asked.

"Why are you so short?" Rhi asked out of nowhere.

"What now?" I shook my head with the sudden change of subject.

"You're so short for a Daemon," Rhi said.

"And you're short for a stormtrooper. What's your point?" I asked, a bit ticked off.

"No, I'm not. But you are the shortest Daemon we've

encountered so far. I've yet to see anyone who was even close to your height. No wonder you like taller folks," Rhi teased.

I could feel her mind jumping all over the place as she spoke.

"I don't know, Rhi, you know that. The Daemons from my world were my size, I think. I don't know why. I don't even remember them!"

"Ahhh, so they could all be eight feet tall, and you were just the runt of the litter!" Rhi said.

"Are you trying to piss me off, Rhi? Cause you're pissing me off," I said as I reached out with the mini-AUG arm. "This thing is just as strong as our AUG, want me to show you?" I said in frustration.

"Whoa, easy!" Rhi said, taking a step back and holding up her hands. "I was just teasing, no harm meant." Rhi was trying one of her disarming smiles.

I wasn't buying it; I was still pissed off. I hadn't been concerned with my height back on my world. There were plenty of people who were shorter than me. It wasn't a big deal. But since my arrival, the fact that every Daemon was nearly twice my size was a bit disconcerting.

None of the other Daemons ever mentioned my size. They were too preoccupied with the fact that I came from a deserter colony and that I was in a relationship with a non-Daemon. I guess that kept their disdain plate so full that they didn't have room for a side dish of short jokes.

"I'm sorry," Rhi said as she stepped into the reach of the mechanical arm and dropped her arms. "Do with me as you please," she said smugly.

The temptation to backhand her was overwhelming. But I kept my temper and—

"OWWWW!" Rhi drew out as she collapsed to the deck under the "gentle" pat I gave her on her head.

"Who's short now, bitch?" I grinned evilly, drawing from Rhi's vast vocabulary of expletives.

Rhi was rubbing her head and giving me a grin I knew well.

"No!" I laughed and made a break for it as Rhi came at me.

∞∞∞∞Ω∞∞∞∞

SHAE

I cringed as I watched James once again being flung into a snow bank.

Beth dusted her hands off as she once again bested James in a fight. I had a feeling she enjoyed it, but I hoped not. Besides, her hand-to-hand ability was capable of fighting Rhi to a standstill.

We'd each had physical combat skills embedded in our minds via the neural training that had given us our initial AUG piloting skills. The other's already had practical hand-to-hand skills. Even Tara knew quite a bit, having come from a rather dangerous world.

We knew how to fight, but when it came to the actual fighting, it still surprised us with how we moved now. OK, it surprised me. I found myself dodging, blocking, and striking in a natural flow that seemed second nature, even though I'd never done it before. It was a strange feeling, almost like something else was controlling my body.

Of course, this training still didn't put us on Beth's or Rhi's level. We just tried not to get killed during sparring.

I'd heard there were advanced courses that could be taken when it came to hand-to-hand and melee weapons. Apparently, it was some sort of fantasy program you could use in the training rooms. James called it "full dive D&D" and couldn't wait to track it down. I wasn't as enthusiastic myself.

Beth brought us to this small Bio-Hab that was completely covered in winter. It was a new environment for us to train in, as none of us had ever spent much time in cold weather. Tara said she'd spent a lot of her childhood exploring mountains, but they weren't always covered in snow.

"Hey, Colonel?" Rhi began. She was sitting on the thigh of her kneeling AUG, examining her nails.

All of us were in our warskins, which more than protected us from the environment. But we still wore thicker coats that provided us additional warmth.

"Yes?" Beth said, turning to Rhi.

"I enjoy watching James get beat to a pulp as much as the next girl," Rhi said.

"Your point?" Beth asked.

"No point, I just enjoy watching, is all," Rhi said as she examined another nail.

Beth frowned and started to say something, but Rhi cut her off.

"Why are there so many different Daemons, ma'am?" Rhi asked, wiping her nails on her coat and then looking down at Beth.

"What do you mean?" Beth asked.

"Well," Tara chimed in. "We were talking and...there's just so many different types of Daemons out there. Big ones, short ones, some have tails, some have horns. And then there's the color schemes."

"There are a lot of different types of humans as well," Beth countered.

"Touche," Rhi nodded. "But our base model is still pretty standard. We don't have optional claws and such."

Beth thought for a moment before answering. "Behemoth created Daemons for various duties in different environments. It made soldiers tailor-made for the situation at hand. Simple as that," Beth said.

"Huh," Tara said. "It just seems like such a broad spectrum of capabilities, though. It's almost like they're from different worlds."

"They are," Beth agreed. "Each was created for where it was needed. Now, enough chatter. Everyone, mount up."

I was giving James a hand out of the snow bank as Beth gave the order.

"Did I win?" James asked, looking a bit dazed.

"Sure, kiddo, you won. Look, you even scared her off," I said, pointing at Beth as she was being lifted into her AUG by her cockpit tentacles.

"Sweet," James coughed and gave me a thumbs up.

"Maybe next time, don't play annoying music in your AUG during maneuvers, huh?" I offered.

James had a tendency to play K-Pop in his cockpit while flying. Beth had overheard it and told him to turn it off while accusing him of being a child and not taking his training seriously. We'd landed shortly after and Beth had commenced an impromptu sparing match for "training purposes."

"Hey, it helps me focus," James said. "Haven't you ever seen Iron Eagle?"

I just shook my head at his hardheadedness.

Beth stayed on the ground as she had us begin flying patrols around the area. She wanted to see how we reacted to various ground missions. AKA, attacking ground-based targets, conducting reconnaissance, avoiding detection, etc.

Most of the training we'd had focused on aerial maneuvers. We hadn't had much training with ground actions.

We were practicing quick landings, hard landings and even physical attacks from the air. It was like the biggest flying elbow you'd ever seen.

Then, we were back to hand-to-hand combat. Only this time, we were in our AUGs.

Tara volunteered to go first, giving James a break from always being Beth's first punching bag.

Our training with AUG melees had been rather limited. Again, we were expecting to be engaged in air combat. Our original instructors had skimped on this aspect.

As weird as it sounds, Tara was the best of us when it came to AUG melee. She constantly chalked it up to her being a Daemon and the fact that the suits were made specifically for her kind. It responded better to her.

Tara was a fighter. She'd grown up a fighter and had mastered her style over more years than James and Rhi combined. Rhi had added to Tara's fighting style in the year they were together. Now, it seemed, Tara was able to bring that style into the AUG with her.

While the rest of us, even Rhi, stumbled over AUG melee, Tara made her AUG look like a ballet dancer. She could pull off impossible moves that left the rest of us staring slack-jawed. A few times, I'd even seen Beth's surprised expression. I had a feeling it had something to do with her ability to manipulate metal.

Even with all of that, Beth's experience still trounced Tara's natural ability. But give Tara a few years and she'd take Beth down a peg or three.

It was strange. Beth seemed less hostile towards Tara. She took much more of an interest in explaining and demonstrating AUG ops to Tara. In the meantime, the rest of us pretty much just got the crap kicked out of us.

The "sun" was high in the sky now, as I'd already taken my turn and was currently watching Rhi and Beth square off. James was sitting atop his AUG as Beth had literally ripped its arm off and beat him with it until his AUG seized up. They'd have to send a retrieval team in to recover his AUG eventually.

The sound of the sky being ripped apart caused all of us to stop what we were doing.

"Two Mark 42s just appeared to the Northwest, 30 kilometers out," Tara called out on our battlenet.

"Everybody button up. James, activate your environmental armor and find somewhere to lay low," Beth said.

"They're heading this way. Intercept in—"

Rhi cut Tara off, "Incoming!" Rhi's AUG had a better sensor net and had picked up what Tara's hadn't.

There were explosions all around us. I wasn't sure what was being thrown at us, but the intent was obvious.

I stared at the massive dust cloud the explosions had caused.

Dust cloud? I thought. Then I looked again and what I'd at first taken for dust was actually smoke. They'd fired smoke missiles at us!

"Watch—" was as far as I got as something slammed into Tara's AUG, driving it into the ground and pushing it a good hundred meters back.

"Tara!" I yelled but then I was flying backwards, my whole world becoming a flashing blur of sky-ground-sky-ground as I tumbled.

I jarred to a stop as I hit something immovable. Instantly, I received damage messages from all over my AUG, but I didn't have time for that. My attacker was still there.

My enemy was pounding on my AUG, trying to rip my

cockpit open and get at me.

The weeks of training Beth had been forcing down our throats kicked in as I grabbed my opponent and rolled both of us until I could get to my feet.

I only got a flash of my opponent, a white AG AUG nearly as tall as my own. It bore scorch marks and what looked like Frankensteined parts from various AUG models.

That was as much as I got before it was on me again.

I pivoted, trying to throw my opponent, but they read the move and dodged into the sky at the last moment. Unprepared for that move, the AG was now behind me and attempting to disable one of my legs.

I just managed to escape, blasting my engine to full power and throwing myself into the sky. But I wasn't leaving. I made sure I was clear of the AG AUG and reversed course, crushing the enemy beneath me.

One of the many features of a DC AUG was the ability to fight in any direction. The joints and superstructure of the AUG were fluid. They could reconfigure themselves into whatever means were needed.

Since I wasn't physically piloting the AUG, only controlling it with my mind, I didn't have to worry about my arms or legs being in the AUG's arms and legs. As such, I reversed the perspective.

While I'd been technically driving the AG into the ground using my AUG's "butt," I reversed my orientation so that my back was now my front. It was like flipping a switch, and suddenly, I was on top of the enemy, pounding it into the ground.

My display highlighted an area on the enemy where a seam had popped and exposed part of the cockpit. Without thinking, I reached down and ripped the cockpit the rest of the way open, revealing Nothing.

I started down at the empty cockpit, knowing the pilot hadn't had a chance to escape.

My hesitation cost me.

As if it had waited for that moment, the enemy AUG wrapped its arms around me and launched itself into the sky.

I immediately started to struggle, but before I knew it, we were heading for the ground, and I wasn't going to end up on top.

A brilliant burst of light and the enemy's arm came apart from its shoulder.

I wasted no time in rolling out of the areal grapple and shifted at the last moment to land on top of the enemy AUG. With a sound like ten million beer cans being crushed, I flattened the AG AUG and it ceased to move.

Panting furiously, I looked over to find Beth's AUG staring at me, unmoving. A mental glance at the status board showed Beth's AUG was fully functional and undamaged.

The sound of rending metal drew my attention to where Rhi and Tara were in the process of pulling the limbs off the enemy that had attacked Tara initially.

"You guys good?" I called out to Rhi and Tara.

"Yup," Rhi said simply.

"Just about finished here," Tara added.

Then I remembered James. His AUG had been destroyed before the battle and was out in the open. Beth had told him to activate his environmental armor, but it only went so far when it came to AUGs.

Our normal warskins did an excellent job of protecting us from various things. But environmental armor was a step up. It basically pulled armored pieces from an AUG, either yours or whatever was available, and formed an additional layer of armor on top of your warskin. While not providing the same protection as an AUG, it was multitudes better than the already tough warskin.

I found him sitting atop his AUG, wearing what looked like a suit of medieval plate armor. In front of him was one of his AUG's beam weapons. He'd managed to remove it from its damaged housing and tied it into his environmental warskin's system so he could fire it.

"You OK?" I asked.

James gave me a thumbs-up.

"Piece of shit!" Rhi said through the tacnet as she curb-stomped the now-dead AUG she and Tara had ripped apart.

"Check if there's a pilot," I said.

"There isn't," Beth said, finally breaking her silence. She hadn't moved during the entire attack. Now, she went over and examined the two destroyed AUGs.

"Not bad," Beth said begrudgingly. "You still need work, but you didn't do too bad this time."

"This was a test?" Rhi asked, out of breath.

"How did—" Tara began.

"Drones," James said.

"Yes," Beth said. "They were drones. But they were the real thing. These were actual AUGs captured from AG forces. This is what you'll be facing out there." Beth turned to me.

"Why didn't you use a weapon?" Beth asked.

"I'm sorry?" I asked.

"You had several weapon systems available to you. Why didn't you use one? I saw any number of times where one of your weapons could have ended that fight much sooner." Beth said.

"Uh..." was all I could think of.

"And that's the difference between training and the real thing. In training, you have all the time in the world, and mistakes don't cost you anything but pride. In a real-world fight, you're going to panic and forget everything you trained for," Beth said.

"Muscle memory," James said quietly.

"Correct, Mr. Sable," Beth said, for once without spite. "I saw you use a few of the moves we'd practiced before."

"Yeah," I started. "I didn't have time to think. My body just remembered those maneuvers we'd practiced over and over again."

"It looks like I'll need to add more weapons training in as well." Beth looked at Rhi and Tara. "None of you pulled a weapon, projectile or melee." Beth glanced at James. "Except Mr. Sable here, who pulled a beam cannon off his AUG and used it manually to assist Shae, damaging his AUG in the process, I might add."

"Hey!" James countered. "My AUG was already toast; you know to that!"

"Yes, and had you properly removed the cannon, it would have lasted for more than just one shot," Beth snapped.

James looked like he was going to say something but thought better of it.

Several large recovery vessels arrived then and began to secure the remains of the battle.

"All right, everyone, follow me back to the transfer gate, Mr. Sable; you assist with the recovery of your AUG and then return with the recovery crew," Beth commanded.

I thought about offering to carry James but thought better of it. He'd just have to fend for himself.

"Yes, ma'am," James said through clenched teeth.

"Move out," Beth said and leaped into the sky.

Working Out

RHI

I watched as James slowly circled counterclockwise around me. He remembered that much, at least. Most people liked to circle clockwise and I'd taught him to change things up whenever he could. But his guard was still distracted and I lanced in, putting him on the ground for the fifth time this training session. I offered him a hand when he stayed on the floor a little too long.

"What's going on with you, James?" I asked.

"Huh?" he said intelligently.

"Your mind is nowhere near this room, let alone on this training. I mean, you've never beat me in all our sparing—"

"What about the Hacienda?" James looked up at me defiantly.

"We both know the only reason that happened was because Natalie wanted it to," I said.

Frowning, he took my hand and stood up, but he still wasn't paying attention. So, I slammed him right back down.

"Seriously?" he yelped.

"We're training. You need to focus on the here and now." This time, when I offered my hand, he took it with a bit more caution.

We'd been going at it for about an hour and had started to work up a good sweat. I'd appropriated one of the many training rooms in our living sector and had all four of us on a regular training schedule. The rooms were able to simulate anything. Any environment, any weapon, anything.

Even Tara joined in with our sessions when she wasn't hip-deep in AUG guts. She'd taken an uncanny interest in how the suits worked and spent every spare moment crawling all over them. She spent more time in the AUG bay than with me most days. Mechanical grease was her new perfume.

Shae was in yet another strategy session with the higher-ups. Being Beth's second in command meant she had to attend every meeting Beth did, which was a lot. But this left James and I alone to do a little "personalized" training.

Please tell me that doesn't mean you're talking about sex again, James's thoughts entered my mind.

No, not yet, at least, I teased him. His mental groan wasn't a pleasant one. He normally enjoyed my teasing, so when he didn't respond with something sarcastic, it concerned me.

"Hold up." I signaled him to stop the training. I snapped my fingers, and a cool towel appeared in the air next to me. Grabbing it, I wiped my face off and offered it to James. *What is going on with you?*

I'm just worried, he said, taking the offered towel and wiping his eyes.

What are you worried about now? I mentally rolled my eyes. James seemed to go out of his way to find things to worry about. If a vampire could get an ulcer, I'm sure he'd have one soon.

Shae's been really having a hard time with this whole leadership thing. I'm worried she's going to get herself overwhelmed.

We'd forced ourselves to start talking aloud more as we were constantly surrounded by people nowadays. Apparently, when you never talk, people get suspicious of your motivations in general. So, we'd taken to only using mindspeech when it was personal stuff.

Shae can more than take care of those responsibilities. I don't think you give her enough credit. Just because she looks 19 doesn't mean she is. I had to admit Shae had been doing a good job. I wasn't one for taking orders, especially when it came from her, but she was doing great. The whole grudging respect thing came into play.

He wiped his face with the towel and then tossed it up into

the air, and it vanished. There were some advantages to living in an insanely high-tech society. We had no idea how anything worked, but as long as it worked, we didn't care. Every day, we discovered something new to be enthralled by.

It's just that she's never been in this sort of situation. Leading troops into combat situations and dealing with the consequences takes a toll, and I don't want her having to deal with that, James said.

I looked at him as the light bulb came on inside my head.

As much as it pains me to say it, James, she's doing great. Yeah, it was a little rough at the start, but I've got confidence in her. You should, too. I watched as he visibly sagged. *I think you might want to think about what's really bothering you.*

His head snapped up. *What do you mean?*

I physically rolled my eyes at him this time. *You know you're, like, two years older than me, right? You should have more of a clue by now.* When he stared at me, I continued, *What position have you been filling for our little group so far?*

Uh... James said intelligently.

You've always taken over as leader when we went into a fight, right? I asked.

James hesitated before nodding, *Well yeah. I'd had the most—*

And now she's filling that role, isn't she? I waited a moment before putting on a sly smile. *How does that make you feel?*

Oh, don't psychoanalyze me! he groaned.

True, I usually have to get you naked to make you relax enough to talk about things. Did you want to start now? I said, starting to unfasten my warskin. I was only teasing him, but if that's what it took, I didn't mind.

James was still fun most of the time. When he stopped being fun and dove into his sulk fest, I usually handed him off to Shae. Like handing off a baby with a dirty diaper that needed changing.

Why is it you always go there? he asked.

Because it works on you? I didn't bother to mention it

usually works on anyone if you knew what you were doing. Thanks Natsuko no Kimi.

James, for once, be the man in this relationship, I said.

James frowned at me and I shrugged.

Besides, you're fun and you scratch my itch, I said matter-of-factly and shrugged. *But seriously, you're a soldier. You've had to be a follower during your career. There's always someone with more rank.*

Yeah, that's true, he said.

So, what's the problem now? Is it because she wasn't in the service? Cause we're all in the service now. Is it because she looks younger than you? I'm sure, even in your older years, you had to follow lieutenants fresh out of boot. For the love of God, tell me it's not because she's a woman.

No, it's not because she's a woman, James mumbled.

Then what— and that's when I caught a flash of it from his mind. *You overprotective idiot,* I mumbled.

What? he said defensively.

You are trying to protect her because she's a woman! I said sharply.

No, I'm trying to protect her because she's my wife! James was practically growling with frustration. *It's my job to take care of her, hell, to take care of all of you because you're my family! That's what you do for your family.*

I was dumbstruck for a moment. I hadn't expected such a strong reaction from him and, at the same time, was touched by his concern not just for Shae but for all of us. It was true that the four of us had been through some pretty intense times in the last few months, but aside from after sex, he didn't talk a lot about his feelings.

It goes both ways, stupid, I said, smacking him upside his head. *There are times when it's someone else's turn to take care of you. So, get out of the way and let her have her time.*

What do you think I've been doing? He sighed. *I know it's irrational, but I can't stop how I feel.*

No. Feelings are good. But you need to empower her, not protect her. This seemed to give him pause, and after a moment, I put him flat on his back again.

Alright, enough of that. We're here to train, so let's get to it!

I pulled up the weapons table we'd started using and it appeared next to us. We took advantage of what the room could do and experimented with all the fancy new hand weapons we could pull up in the system.

Some were straightforward, high-tech knives and such. Others were so bizarre, we had to ask for help in figuring out just how to hold them.

If we found something we liked, all we had to do was put in a request for it and it would show up in our quarters. The warskins could break down nearly anything Behemoth made and store it on the suit, similar to the built-in pistol. I'd already put together quite a collection.

"James, you know what leadership is, right?" I asked as I perused the weapons table.

"Duh," James said as he approached the table and began to browse as well. "Leadership is basically getting people to do what you need done, but making them think it's their idea."

"But you need to know your people in order to make that happen, James," I said. "You need to know what motivates them, what drives them, their wants and their fears."

"So, the old carrot and the stick methodology," James said.

"The carrot and the stick are more short-term in order to get something done right now. You need to empower your people. Build their trust to the point they're making things happen before you even think about asking. Or, better yet, they take care of problems before you even know there are problems," I said. "Do you understand what I'm really saying here?"

James stopped and glanced at me.

"Yeah, I get it," he nodded.

"Good," I said simply and picked up a small blade.

"How many times have you died now?" James asked out of the blue.

It took me a minute to add them all up. "At least 50," I finally said.

Each time we were "killed" during a training exercise, we received an official notification from Behemoth. You could pull up your service record and see not only how many times you'd died but how it had happened each time.

"I'm well over 200 now," James said as he picked up what looked like a handful of goop. As soon as it touched his hand, it attached itself to him and changed shape into whatever hand weapon James concentrated on.

"Tara and Shae have rarely ever been killed during our exercises," he said.

"That's because Beth has a hard-on for you," I said, examining a blade that left a shadowy trail behind it as it moved. "You're probably getting the best training of all of us."

"How so?" James asked.

"She's so focused on you, you're getting all the hands-on experience. If Beth needs a volunteer to do something, you're it. The first one to try out a new maneuver? That's you, buddy. You've probably gotten twice the experience the rest of us have. So, you should be kicking my butt in here by now."

"Like that's ever gonna happen," James scoffed.

"Never say never kiddo. I might get really sick or break both my arms and legs. You'd probably have a shot then...probably." I chuckled and James joined me.

"Rhi?"

"That's my name," I said as I examined a pair of ordinary-looking dice. "What do you think these do?"

"No idea," James said dismissively. "What happened to your mom?"

I let it slide off me, not deflecting, ignoring.

"I wonder if it makes a bomb or something, and the higher the number you roll, the worse it is," I said, refusing to take my eyes off the dice.

James's hand blocked my view as he clasped the hand holding the dice.

After a minute, I finally spoke, "There's nothing to tell James."

"Obviously, there is," James said.

"Stay in your lane, James," I warned him.

"Unfortunately, you've brought me over into your lane," James said quietly.

"How so?" I risked a glance at him before returning to the table of weapons.

"I've been getting flashes when I'm around you lately. You're worried about something, and it's eating away at you so much that it's spreading to me. I wouldn't be surprised if the others haven't felt it as well. The only thing I can pull from these feelings is that it has something to do with your mom."

When I didn't speak, James continued.

"I can start describing what I've seen, Rhiannon, or you can just tell me," James said.

I don't think James had ever used my full name before. It grabbed my attention and made me look up at him. I didn't mean to, but I did.

"My mother..." I exhaled for a long moment. "Is currently barricaded inside her house. I made sure there was no way for her to get out and that nothing short of a meteor strike would be able to get into that house," I said, turning away from him and walking across the room.

"Why?" James asked like the dumbass he was.

"Really, James? You can't just Mosby Boys this shit? You're going to make me actually say it?" I said, not looking at him. Then I span on him, my words laced with an unexpected fury.

"Fine! You want to know, I'll fucking tell you. When I went to check on her, she was already a goddamned zombie. And instead of putting her out of our misery, I hid her away in that fucking house like a caged undead canary!"

James had the courtesy to wait and see if I was going to say more. When I didn't, he kept going.

"But why?" James asked gently.

"Because I couldn't kill her, James. I wasn't strong enough to put a bullet in her head. All the lives I've ended so effortlessly over the years and when it really mattered, I couldn't pull the trigger," I said, still angry at myself.

"It was your mom."

"It was a rotting corpse," I said.

"It was still your mom, Rhi. No one expects you to be able to kill your mom, no matter the circumstances," James said, his hand touching my back gently.

"This is some bullshit," I said, opening my eyes to find the room watery. Then, I was flying through the air and hitting the ground with enough force to knock the wind out of me. When I regained my senses, James was sitting on top of me.

James leaned down and got within an inch of my face, "Told you I could do it."

I just stared at him.

"And I didn't have to pay someone to break any of your limbs," James said with seriousness.

"You're such an asshole," I said as I lay there beneath him. Normally, we'd already be making out by now. But, this was anything but normal.

"I'm sorry about your mom," James said quietly. "Tell you what, whenever we make it back, we'll go see her together. How about that?"

It wasn't every day someone offered to kill your undead mother for you.

I just looked up at him for a while, not sure what I was feeling anymore. My mom had been a subject I'd bottled up and labeled, "uh-uh, no-way, no-how." And, of course, James had come busting in like Ron Jeremy on a wrecking ball.

"OK," I groaned before tossing James across the room like he was a wadded-up piece of paper. To his credit...or mine really, he twisted and managed to get his feet under him.

I stood up quickly and called for another towel. I wiped my eyes while James pretended not to notice and tossed the towel back up into the air, where it vanished.

Mentally, I adjusted the room's parameters, calling up a new setting.

"What the shit is this?" James asked as he took a step back, suddenly uncertain.

"It's lava dummy. Haven't you ever played 'the floor is lava'?" I asked as I looked around.

The simple dojo the room had been only a moment before was now a cracked and blackened lava field at night. The heat was intense, but I'd dialed it back so it didn't peel the skin from our bones.

"Yeah, I think I'm out," James said as he held up his arms.

"Besides, I still need to finish my movie."

"Wait, let me get this straight. Instead of sparring with me or going out and exploring the unlimited possibilities of a hundred alien civilizations, you'd rather watch TV?" I asked incredulously. Earlier, I'd had to drag him away from the movie he'd been watching to get him to come practice. I knew James was addicted to movies, but this was a bit much.

"First off," James started, holding up a finger. "When was the last time we got to just sit around and do nothing? We've been running from one crisis to another for months, nonstop!"

I had to give him that. If we weren't fighting zombies back home, we were fighting the AG up here. Even on our down days, we were still out doing stuff.

"And besides, it's the perfect double feature: Kelly's Heroes and The Princess Bride," James said as if that finished the conversation.

"Oh, well," I started, sarcastically holding my hands up in surrender. "When you put it like that...how the hell is that the perfect double feature?" I asked. I hadn't seen either movie.

James just smiled. "You haven't seen them, have you?"

I was curious but didn't like his tone.

"If they're so good, why are you watching them on a vid screen instead of using the training room simulator?"

James cocked his head at me in question.

"It can project you into the movie," I said with an implied "duh."

James just stared at me dumbfounded.

"How about this?" I started. "Let's finish up training. Then we can watch your double feature in here. How's that sound?" It was hard getting James to train sometimes. On occasion, I'd have to offer him some...incentive.

"You're in for a treat!" James said enthusiastically, then looked down at the ground. "Blue lava?"

Blue light peaked out anywhere the blackened field cracked apart and revealed the slow lava flows beneath.

"It's from Indonesia, James. Educate yourself." I said as I started to circle him once again. "Just be glad I toned down the smell."

"Right," James drew out the word as he automatically shifted into a combat stance. "Because regular lava isn't scary enough already."

"Game on!" I yelled as I pounced.

∞ ∞ ∞ ∞ Ω ∞ ∞ ∞ ∞

SHAE

I floated in the silence. The water was warm as it enveloped and caressed my body. My eyes were closed, so I couldn't see it when my body floated in or out of the water; I only felt it. I liked coming here after the meetings with the DC leadership. It helped me to clear my head.

I'd found this room by accident. I still hadn't found a reason for it to exist, only that it did. That, and I'd never met another soul in here before.

The slight chill on my exposed skin made me flick my hands and I slid back into the water.

Something tugged at my ankle, startling me. I opened my eyes to find Tara floating below me. She was wearing her warskin and had its breathing mask active. Even through it, I could still see her grin.

You forget you invited me? Tara spoke in my mind.

I still hadn't gotten used to Tara's presence in my mind. Whereas James and Rhi's voices in my head held a similar quality, for some reason, Tara's voice was different. I wasn't sure if it was because she was the newcomer to the group or it was the fact she was from another world. Regardless, it wasn't unpleasant, just different.

Not used to anyone accepting my invitation, I said. I'd invited the others to join me here in the past, but none of them seemed too fond of the concept of the room. I'd at least gotten them to come look at the room, but they'd taken one look and ran.

I had to admit, the idea of swimming in zero gravity came with so truly terrifying scenarios. But when you didn't have to breathe, there wasn't anything to worry about.

A few strokes brought me to the edge of the water field and I stepped out onto the warm, dry deck.

The room was massive, easily 300 meters cubed. About two-thirds of the room was full of warm, clear water. The other third was cool air. Because there wasn't any gravity, the water tended to slowly slosh about the room. Sometimes, it created waves, sometimes spheres of water that seemed to move in and out of other pools.

The walls were set to a starscape default, giving you the impression you were floating in the depths of space. But I found you could change the walls to reflect whatever you wanted.

One end of the room held the small, dry space I was currently standing in. When I left the water for this dry area, the water remained inside the zero-g space. Even though I was as dry as when I'd first come here, I still picked up a towel I'd brought and rubbed at my face.

I watched Tara lazily swimming in circles before a series of quick movements brought her to me.

She took my hand as I helped her out of the water. With as many times as I'd been here, it was still disorienting to get out of a pool horizontally.

"Well that was interesting," Tara said as her warskin's mask disappeared, returning to wherever the warskin stored it.

"Right?" I said as I offered her the towel.

Tara looked at the towel skeptically. "I'm wearing a warskin, I'm dry."

I just kept holding it out to her. After a moment she took it and rubbed at her face as well.

"I don't know why, but I still want to wipe my face whenever I get out of there," I said.

"Yeah," Tara frowned at the towel. "Now that you mention it, my face does feel wet, even though I know it's not." Then she went back to rubbing her face.

"Kinda like washing in soft water. It never seems like you got all the soap off," I said.

"Soft what?" Tara asked.

The door opened suddenly and James walked in.

"What are you doing here? I thought you were sparring with Rhi right now," I said.

"Uh," James hesitated at the door. "Yeah, I'm running late."

"That's not good. Rhi's gonna kill you more than normal. Wanna hide out in here with us instead?" I asked with a smile.

James glanced at the vertical wall of water and blanched. "Never again," he said.

I didn't remember him ever having done it the first time. When I looked at him, he was staring at Tara with a weird expression.

"You, OK?" I asked as Tara stopped rubbing her face and looked up at him."

James nodded and stepped over to me, taking me in his arms and hugging me fiercely.

"OK, hello to you too," I chuckled, but he didn't loosen his grip. "What's going on?"

"Hmmm?" James said, finally releasing me. "Oh, nothing. Just wanted to stop by and give you a hug before I go get my ass kicked."

"I like your jacket," Tara said.

James was wearing a black acid-washed jean jacket I'd not seen before. As a matter of fact, I hadn't seen one since the early 90's.

"Yeah...just trying it out," he glanced at Tara. "OK, gotta go."

"Nope!" Tara said as she approached and wrapped her arms around him. "My turn," she said simply.

James froze again but then slowly embraced her.

"OK, now I really gotta go," James said as he reluctantly released Tara and headed for the door.

"OK, love you!" I called out after him.

"Ditto!" Tara chuckled next to me.

James paused at the door, "Love y'all too," he said quietly and then was gone.

"Rhi is so gonna kick his ass for being late. She does it to me all the time but I've grown to like it," Tara said. "Shae?"

"Huh?" I said, Tara's voice drawing my attention from the door. "Sorry," I shook my head and turned to face her. "You know, with you being the only one of our little gestalt that has to breathe, I figured you'd be the last one to come here," I said.

"You know me," Tara stopped rubbing her face to give me a grin. "I'm willing to try anything...twice."

"Why twice?" I asked.

"In case I got it wrong the first time," Her grin was one of Rhi's lecherous expressions. It was always weird seeing one of our characteristics reflected on a different member of the group.

"Fair point," I nodded. "Does that mean you'll be doing our spiritual fiesta twice as well?" I asked.

Lately, we'd been attending different religious festivals on our down days. With the sheer number of religions out there, there was always something going on and usually not the same thing twice.

"Of course, especially the Onya Verran," Tara said excitedly.

Tara was the most adventurous of our group. Having grown up relatively secluded, she was always up for experiencing something new.

The Onya Verran were a group that seemed to constantly be happy. No matter what happened, they turned it into something positive. You couldn't help but smile around them. Even Rhi had lightened up that day.

"I figure if we go to enough, Rhi will eventually change her mind," Tara started to hand the towel back to me but then started to wipe off her dry legs.

"Oh?" I wasn't exactly sure of what Rhi's religious beliefs were. We didn't usually get into that kind of discussion.

"Yeah, Rhi likes to say that God was created to keep us from going nuts."

"Going nuts? Rhi?" I asked.

"Yeah, I know. Anyway, it goes that if there's no afterlife, no God, then there would be no consequences for the actions in your life. So, what would keep you in check?" Tara said.

"Laws?" I offered.

"Sure, but if you knew this was the only shot you got at life, the only existence you get and when you die, that's it, you cease to exist. What would stop you from doing whatever you want, however you want, whenever you want, and with whomever you want? Talk about the ultimate in fear of missing out.

"Once we got to a certain point, we had to create something to keep our society together. Religions work the best as you don't really need proof, just really good stories to believe in, right?" Tara asked.

"What a terrifying thought," I said.

"Yeah. But I know Rhi believes in God, so I'm not too worried," Tara said.

"How do you know that?" I asked.

"I hear her talking to God all the time."

"Praying?" I asked. I'd never heard Rhi pray.

"No, just talking. Usually sarcastically," Tara grinned.

"Now that, I can believe."

Tara turned and looked at the wall of water sloshing around before us. She reached out and ran her hand lightly across its surface before pulling it away and rubbing her fingers together.

"How do you think it works?" Tara asked.

"No idea," I said honestly. "But I'm sure it has the word quantum in front of it, whatever it is."

"Quantum?" Tara asked.

"Simply put, it means the smallest measurement of something, but in my world, it was used as a catchphrase for anything futuristic or high-tech. Don't know how something works? Slap the word quantum on it and it's suddenly sci-fi," I shrugged. "I think it's just another way to spell MacGuffin."

Tara laughed, "That one I get."

She didn't always get our slang or references, but Rhi had been keeping up with her education.

"I don't even know why someone would make something like this. I'm guessing they had to be an aquatic race," I said as I stared into the swirling mass.

"Maybe they just like making out underwater," Tara offered, not looking back at me.

"Now you sound like James," I said.

Tara shrugged and glanced at me, "Wanna find out?"

Before I could answer, she dove into the water and began an acrobatic routine that had her moving like a seal through the liquid.

I wondered just how far this mind blending would go, but then pushed it from my mind and dove after Tara's sleek form.

Cafe Le Pew

SHAE

I nodded at Beth as we parted ways in the corridor outside the flight briefing room. Yet another security briefing down; it was the third one this week without anything new being discussed. It always came down to "be vigilant, the AG are out there." Luckily this one had been shorter than all the others for some reason.

A thought came to me as I watched Beth walking away. I knew the schedule of the others and knew they wouldn't be free for a couple more hours.

"Colonel?" I said as I caught up to Beth.

"Yes?" Beth said, turning.

"Are you doing anything right now?" I asked.

"I need to drop off some...things, but after that, I don't have any plans," Beth said.

"How would you like to have lunch?" I watched as Beth's face changed. Ever since that night when we'd had our Stireen session, Beth had seemed to relax ever so slightly when it was just the two of us. But as I watched, Beth's face changed to a more guarded expression.

"Just the two of us," I added, watching Beth physically relax.

"Sure," Beth said, surprising me.

"Great. The others are out right now, meet you back at the common room?"

"All right, give me about 20 minutes," Beth said.

About 20 minutes later, I was sitting in the common room of our quarters when Beth emerged from her room.

"What are you wearing?" Beth asked.

"It's called a dress." I smiled. I was wearing a white summer dress with simple floral print accents.

"I know what it is, but it's also out of regs. We're not-"

"We're not allowed to wear anything other than our uniforms in case we're called to duty," I finished quoting the regulation. "But that was before this."

A moment later, my dress disappeared and was replaced with my warskin.

Before Beth could ask, I continued. "It's called a Lenz; it's...I can't remember the name for it, but it's basically holographic clothes, after a fashion. You see, I'm still wearing my uniform completely in regs; I just changed what it looks like." I held up my hand, showing the ring that controlled the hologram.

I didn't mention that it was James who'd discovered them. He'd been looking for something to get Rhi ever since she mentioned how he owed her clothes. This was his answer.

"Here." I stood and approached Beth. Before she could object, I slid the ring off my finger and onto Beth's.

Beth stared at the ring as if it were going to bite her.

"Just touch the control stud here." I touched a small nub on the ring, and instantly, the dress I'd been wearing appeared on Beth.

"Oh!" Beth gasped as she looked down. "It feels like I'm really wearing it."

"I paid extra for the tactile upgrade. Whatever you choose, you'll feel the clothing and your body will react as if that is what you're really wearing. Here, try this," I said.

With another touch of the control stud, Beth's outfit changed from a summer dress to shorts, a tank top and flip-flops. It took Beth a minute to adjust.

"I can even feel the thongs snap when I walk," Beth smiled.

"Great, huh?" I asked, watching as Beth's face was suddenly the one I'd met in Houston. It was as if all the years of horror had fallen away.

"Yeah," Beth said quietly before her expression returned to her sterner self, and she started to take off the ring.

"Keep it. I actually bought that one for you," I said.

"For me?" Beth asked.

"Yeah, try not to act so shocked. We may be Colonel and Lieutenant, but there's nothing that says we can't still be friends."

James, Rhi and I were all Lieutenants. It was the starting rank for Chosen Army AUG pilots. Rhi had joked about having moved backward in rank as she'd been a Captain in the Army.

"Actually—" Beth started.

"Nope, I looked. There may be fraternization rules back home, but there's nothing here," I said firmly. "So, keep it. There's plenty of outfits on there to play with, and I'll send you the link to where you can download more." I pulled out another ring and placed it on my finger, the sun dress reappearing. "But for right now, pick something and let's go eat."

"Go out?" Beth looked from the ring to me.

"Yes, out in public even." I smiled. "Come on."

I considered taking her to the secret bar the group frequented, but I didn't think Beth was up for visiting the "off-limits" establishment just yet. Instead, I chose something a little more "normal," at least by Behemoth standards.

The café was technically in its own room, away from other businesses. The appearance changed based on the whim of the owner. I'd seen it appear as many different locations, sometimes scenes from movies, sometimes alien worlds. It was always something different every time I visited.

Today, the restaurant took on the appearance of a French sidewalk café on a spring afternoon, complete with the Eifel Tower in the distance. People and cars buzzed about like nothing was out of the ordinary.

While I was pretty sure the people passing by were all simulations, you never could tell on Behemoth. For all I knew, this room was in some version of Paris right now. Stranger things had happened since our arrival on this "space station."

We were seated quickly by a waiter on the patio. The waiter looked like something right out of a movie and made me wonder again what was real and what was simulated here.

Beth had picked a pair of jeans and a light blouse to wear and looked uncomfortable in them. On the way here, she had flicked off the clothes several times to make sure she could be "back in uniform" with a moment's notice.

"Try to relax," I smiled, picking up a menu.

"I can't remember the last time I wore something that wasn't military issue," Beth said, pulling at her collar. "It feels weird."

I grinned wider behind my menu. "What are you going to order?"

"Order?" Beth asked.

"Uh-huh." I paused, putting the menu down. "You know, food."

"We don't eat," Beth said, confused.

"Yes, we can and do. There's more to life than blood substitute, you know." I gave her a stern look.

Beth seemed to squirm in her chair. I hadn't seen her with this much loss of composure in...well since Houston. I wasn't sure if I was pushing her too hard or not. I desperately wanted to bring some semblance of that old Beth back and this was the start of my plan to do it.

"Are you 'full-up?'" I asked.

"Full-up?" Beth asked.

"On blood. Are you well-fed? You haven't been starving yourself or anything, right?" I asked.

"Of course not," Beth said.

"Good, then you can eat." I picked my menu back up and stopped when I saw Beth's face. "What?"

"I haven't eaten since...since I changed," Beth said reluctantly.

"Seriously?" I was shocked.

"It wasn't necessary. Blood was all I needed," Beth said defensively.

I reached across the table and touched Beth's hand.

"The human body can survive on bread and water, but where's the fun in that?" I gave Beth my kindest smile. "We can eat whatever we want when we're full-up."

"But, that means..." Beth started.

"Yes. All our bodily functions come back when we eat anything other than blood," I confirmed.

Beth made a face.

"Fine. Do you trust me?" I asked.

Beth locked eyes with me and, after only the briefest of hesitations, said, "Sure..."

I called the waiter over and quietly ordered for the both of us before turning back to Beth.

"What's that grin for?" Beth said.

"What grin?" I said cryptically.

"Uh-huh. Why'd you ask me here anyway?"

"What do you mean?" I asked.

"In my experience, there's a purpose behind everything, even lunch," Beth said.

"Oh. Well, then, my purpose for inviting you here for lunch was to have a meal with you and spend some time," I said.

"Some time doing what?" Beth asked.

"Just talking," I said.

"About what?" Beth asked.

I tilted my head and looked at Beth.

"Surely you have friends you occasionally go out with or just talk to, don't you?" I asked.

Beth was quiet for a minute. "Up until your arrival, I've only worked with the DC, and you've seen their opinion of us. We're not exactly allowed in their social circles," Beth said.

"Do the DC have social circles?" I asked.

"Not really," Beth shook her head.

"What about when you first got here? Didn't you have to go through basic like we did? There had to be others," I said.

Beth tapped her chin in thought. "I...I wasn't in the best shape mentally when I went through training. I didn't want to be bothered and they left me alone. Nobody wanted to hang out with the crazy girl. Afterward, I was placed with a DC unit," Beth said.

"What about just going out?" Shae asked.

"What for? Everything I need is either in my quarters or in DC country," Beth said.

"Wait," I held up my hands. "Are you telling me you've locked yourself away for the last ten years? Never once going out and exploring or visiting other Bio-Habs or anything?"

"The DC sent me to other Bio-Habs occasionally. They're...different, but I don't need to spend any more time there than necessary," Beth said.

I was literally at a loss for words. I couldn't imagine an existence like the one Beth just described. I had no idea how Beth was still functional around people with so little social interaction.

The awkward silence was interrupted by the waiter dropping off our meals. Steak, green peas, mashed potatoes and a small salad were set before us. Beth eyed it suspiciously.

"Trust me, try it," I said as I dug into my food.

Beth reluctantly cut into her steak and placed a small piece in her mouth. She chewed slowly, the flavors of the steak coating her tongue, before loudly swallowing.

"Good, huh?" I said.

"Yeah," Beth said reluctantly. "But I'm still not sure if it's worth having to start visiting the latrine again."

"Oh, you won't," I said, not looking up from my food.

"What do you mean?" Beth asked.

"Don't ask me how they do it because I don't know. But everything that's on that plate, is blood." I pointed at her plate with a knife.

Beth stared at her plate. "What? How?"

"I don't know," I chuckled. "But everything there is what you normally drink. So, there won't be any pesky 'biological' consequences to deal with."

Beth put a piece of lettuce in her mouth, chewed and swallowed. "But...it's lettuce."

"I know, right? The first time I came here, the waiter suggested it without me even mentioning that I was a vampire. I tried it and liked it. I mean, there's just something about eating the real thing that I still enjoy. But I figured for your first time, this might ease you into it," I said.

Beth was shoveling a forkful of peas into her mouth.

"Slow down, enjoy it. We're in no hurry," I said.

"Mmmm, so good," Beth said.

I shook my head, grinning, and turned back to my meal. After a minute, I said, "You seem different."

"What do you mean?" Beth said, around a mouthful of food.

"Well...don't take this the wrong way, but the last time I got you to talk to me like a normal person, I had to get you drunk using some obscure regulation. What was up with that, by the way?"

Beth nodded a moment as she swallowed.

"I didn't know how to act around you," Beth said carefully. "With how long it had been, how you were brought here and everything, I was confused. I could tell you wanted to talk to me, but I couldn't see how to start."

"Is that why you brought up Stireen?" I asked.

"Yes. That officially opened the door to anything," Beth said, taking another bite.

"Next time, just invite me in. Or come over, either way. We've been through a lot together. You should feel safe to talk to me," I said.

Beth nodded but didn't say anything.

After a few minutes of eating in silence, I said, "Do you like it here?"

"This is a nice place," Beth looked around.

"No. Here, on Behemoth. Do you like this life?" I asked.

"I've been doing it for ten years now; I would hope so." Beth half-smiled.

"Any thoughts of settling down?" I asked.

"Why would I? I'm good at what I do," Beth said.

"Yeah...but is this something you want to do for the rest of your life? I mean, do you see yourself at 80, piloting an AUG?" I asked.

Beth laughed. "Oh! No, I'm sure I'll eventually slow down and get booted down into the regular corps. When that happens, I'll ask for recycling."

"Recycling?" I asked.

"That's what we call it when someone's memory is erased and they're sent back down into a Bio-Hab. Until then, I'll keep doing what I'm doing," Beth said.

"Where would they send you? I mean, your Bio-Hab is gone," I asked.

"I dunno. Never really given it much thought. I just figured it would be better than flying with the normal grunts, knowing what I had once been. I'll worry about it when the time comes."

Beth shrugged.

If that time ever comes, I thought, hoping Beth would survive long enough to get to that point.

"Of course, there's always getting 'touched up,'" Beth said.

"What's that?" I asked.

"Behemoth can...refresh your body," Beth said.

"Refresh?"

"It can...how to put it...it can replace your body with a new one. Or parts of one, if needed," Beth said, chewing away on a piece of steak.

"That's one way to put it," I said. "How does that work?"

"Cloned parts mostly," Beth said as if it were the most normal thing.

"Cloned?"

"Oh yes. Behemoth's ability to clone is near perfect. You get hurt in battle and lose a kidney; Behemoth can create a replacement from your genetic blueprint on file. It's done with injured DC all the time," Beth waved her fork at me.

"I thought cloning wasn't perfect?" I said.

"While for us, back in the day, it wasn't. For Behemoth it's like 99.99% perfect, or so I'm told. I've never heard of a problem myself," Beth said.

"So...you could theoretically live forever? Just keep replacing old organs and such with new ones?" I asked.

Beth shrugged. "I guess? Again, I've never heard of anyone doing that."

"You said genetic blueprint. What's that?" I asked, taking another bite.

"Every creature in Behemoth has a genetic blueprint on file. Behemoth made everything here, after all. It had to start from somewhere. Could you imagine having to create a new frog from scratch every time you populated a Bio-Hab?" Beth shook her head in amusement.

"Yeah..." I said, my mind churning suddenly. "Imagine that."

Konya Wa Hurricane

SHAE

"Tighten it up, Rhi, you're falling behind," I called across the tactical net (tacnet.) We were currently flying a standard patrol across northern Siberia. Beth had been called away for something and I was leading our group. As our four AUGs skimmed the barren landscape a few hundred meters off the deck, Rhi had slowly fallen out of formation.

"Sorry, boss, I thought I saw a polar bear. Never seen one outside a Coke commercial before," Rhi said as she rejoined the formation.

"You've never seen a polar bear?" James asked. "Not even in a zoo or anything?"

"Not many zoos in Texas have polar bears, James," Rhi said flatly.

"You looking for a new rug or something?" James continued.

We were three hours into this patrol and, as usual, nothing had happened. While aircraft contact was growing increasingly rare, some governments of the world had somehow maintained air travel in one form or the other during the zombie apocalypse.

Of course, in this desolate, frozen tundra, nothing was here. I doubted even polar bears were in the area.

"Get your mind out of the gutter, James," Rhi shot back.

"What? I just said you wanted a new rug. Not that you wanted to curl up on it in front of a fire or anything," James's grin could be heard in his voice. The boy's libido knew no bounds.

Before Rhi could reply, Tara chimed in.

"That does sound nice. Rhi, let's get a rug when we get back.

And a fireplace," Tara said.

"See," James said. "You're wife's the one with the dirty mind."

"Don't encourage her, James. I think you've rubbed off on her enough," Rhi said.

"Hey!" James said in mock offense.

"Yeah, it's usually kinda messy," Tara said matter-of-factly.

This was the usual with our patrols. Several hours of boredom usually created the most off-the-wall conversations to pass the time. Usually, they were conducted on a private channel where Beth couldn't hear us. I knew she listened in; she had the same command suite I did. But it never detracted from our performance, so she turned a blind eye.

I personally didn't mind. If it kept them sharp and awake, who was I to complain? Not to mention, there was nothing else going on—

"Reaper 1 alpha, this is control," the voice cut through on a priority command channel.

"Go ahead, control," I said.

"We have two, I repeat, two possible contacts. Standby for gate coordinates," the controller said.

"Real-world, knock off the chatter," I said into our tacnet, then returned to the command channel, "Standing by."

A quick glance at my location told me where the nearest gate location was. I mentally entered several instructions into my command console and got us moving in the direction we needed to go moments before control sent me the same information.

Our tacnet had gone quiet after I'd spoken, everyone suddenly shifting into a serious mode. Each of their acknowledgments appeared on my command panel in my neural cockpit.

"Acknowledged control, en route. ETA...two minutes," I said.

"OK folks, looks like we have two bogies that control wants us to check out. I'm forwarding the info to the battlenet. We'll be to the gate point in about two minutes," I said to the others. They each acknowledged me with simple replies. They were all business now; the humor was gone.

After James's little vacation off Behemoth, I'd dug more into how the AUGs operated. I had to use Beth's clearance for some of it, but in the end, I got the answers to some of my questions.

First off, AUGs were powered and controlled directly by Behemoth. Yes, each of our suits had powerplants, but they only worked when we were within Behemoth's tactical control sphere.

James had been well outside that sphere, given how far he'd been gated. It wasn't until he got back inside that his AUG was able to reestablish contact with Behemoth and power back on.

I thought the system was a bit short-sighted, but I didn't know the "big picture" reason behind it.

Second was the gate/portal/teleport/jump system. While we called it the PTS gate, I found several names for it in various operating manuals. It was almost like it was piecemealed together from several different systems. Again, the AUGs had gate generators on them, but there was no way to operate the gates independently from Behemoth unless you were a Daemon.

Daemons, the AG, and even Beth could operate the gate system on their AUGs without Behemoth. Rhi had seen this on Beth's world, again in Houston, and finally, we all saw it during the battle above the Alamo.

The rest of us had to take our AUGs to a specific set of coordinates and then Behemoth would operate the gate process. But again, we've seen this wasn't always the case, as James's AUG was gated right off Shashka's ship.

I'm sure there was a method to the madness, but even Beth claimed ignorance of how exactly it worked. It seemed to be yet another of those "I don't know how it works, just that it does" mentalities we were starting to see more of the longer we were here.

I had a feeling Beth knew more than she was willing to say, but I was still trying to "re-humanize" her and didn't want to jeopardize the progress I'd already made.

The AUGs could practically fly themselves after you entered a destination. They could even react to some basic encounters, but it had to be set up beforehand. This feature allowed me to stop piloting the AUG long enough to pull up the last known location of the two contacts we were being sent to investigate.

They were in the Indian Ocean, near a small crescent atoll known as Diego Garcia. The computer told me there was a small US military base there that usually housed large bomber aircraft, including those used to carry nuclear weapons. But the two contacts didn't seem interested in the air base. Instead, they focused on an area Southeast of the base. A quick search of the map showed nothing there but water.

Like in the gate room, the gate point wasn't visible. Instead, it was displayed through our battlenet system as a pulsing green rectangle.

The battlenet provided us with nearly any type of information we could want about our surroundings. Most of it was excessive for the missions we flew. I kept it muted most of the time to keep from overloading my senses. I pulled up the area information surrounding the gate point with a mental flick.

As one, the four of us entered into a slow orbit of the gate point, a countdown appearing on our displays. Three seconds later, our views changed from a frozen tundra to a blue ocean as far as the eye could see. With no sense of movement, we'd just gated to another part of the globe.

A directional beacon appeared, and I led us that way. The first thing I noticed was the sky darkening the closer we came to the intended destination. I quickly zoomed out and saw the reason.

"OK, folks, we're heading into a major storm. Engage your augment systems," I spoke into our tacnet. The replies I got back were shaky. They were nervous. While James and Rhi both had combat experience, just like the rest of us, they hadn't been in actual combat against an enemy AUG.

"This is a simple scrape and clear," I said, keeping my voice as steady and calm as I could. I drew on my diplomatic training to hide my jitters. "More than likely, this is just a false alarm. But if it's not, remember your training: identify your targets, keep to your wingman, and try not to embarrass us."

The last drew a few nervous chuckles just as we entered the storm. AG portals sometimes generated atmospheric disturbances that caused storms, but not always. The three encounters our group had with the AG had not produce storms.

The storm was strong enough to cause the AUGs to start to shake before stabilizers kicked in and smoothed out the flight.

"Beth picked a hell of a day to go on holiday," James said over the tacnet.

"Are you kidding?" Rhi chimed in. "This is probably some exercise she cooked up, and it's her that we're chasing down."

We reached the last known area of our contacts and started a slow search for any signs of our enemy. Sensors were easily cutting through the storm, but there wasn't anything to see. Our search pattern extended over the next hour, spreading us out to maintain coverage. We each deployed swarms of tiny drones that extended our sensor accuracy and allowed us to zoom into other areas virtually.

The storm had started to dissipate when Rhi sounded off.

"I've got two inbound aircraft," Rhi said.

"What ya got Rhi?" I asked as I pulled up her tactical feed to see what she saw.

"Looks like...two naval aircraft...both conventional," Rhi said.

"From Diego Garcia?" I asked, but the plot didn't match.

"No. Looks like they're from a naval group moving through the area. Hang on," Rhi said. "I'm tapped into their comms. Seems they're chasing down...some intermittent contacts in this region. Possibly our bogeys? Regardless, ETA 4 minutes."

"Everyone, diagnostic check on stealth systems." I ran a check on my AUG, but there were no anomalies. All of my stealth gear was fully operational. On top of this, each of the other's AUGs showed the same.

"All good here," James said.

"Fully operational," Tara said.

"I'm good...but..." Rhi started.

"But what?" I asked, double-checking her AUG's telemetry feed. Everything I could see said her AUG was running perfectly.

"They're not tracking us," Rhi said.

"What are they tracking then?" I asked, doing a scan of the area for any other readings. I knew the AG had the same level of stealth gear we did when it came to hiding from "normal" people in Bio-Habs. Theirs wasn't as new or as fancy as ours, but it was still effective.

"I don't know, but they're saying it's right on top of us," Rhi said, a bit of stress entering her voice. "What could they be picking up that we aren't?"

Our camouflage systems kept us invisible to electronic and naked eyes. But having two fighters in the same vicinity as us created all sorts of opportunities for accidents. Our directive was to stay undetected by Bio-Hab personnel at all costs. I was starting to get a bad feeling about this.

"OK, I officially don't like this," I started into the tacnet. "I want everyone to rendezvous at—"

"Contact!" Tara called out.

I automatically looked in the direction of her AUG even though I couldn't see her—she was too far away. The lights in my AUG shifted hue to indicate that my wing was now in combat. I checked the display and saw Tara's AUG was evading several airborne projectiles, but I couldn't tell where they'd come from.

"Rhi!" I called out.

"On it!" Rhi replied, and I watched as her AUG dove from where it had been orbiting the area from on high.

"They came from the water!" The stress is Tara's voice was palpable now.

"Hang on, I'm coming," Rhi's voice was cold over the tac net.

I watched on my command net as Tara's AUG twisted and climbed, trying to distance herself from the incoming fire. Her swarm of micro-drones began attempting to jam or intercept the incoming missiles.

An AUG is an amazing piece of machinery. While it looked massive and bulky, it was deceptively agile. The propulsion system of the suits was not directional thrust like aircraft engines. Instead, it operated almost as if in zero gravity, able to instantly slide one direction or another without having to bank and turn like an aircraft.

As usual, I had no idea how it worked. I'd tried to read up on it and stopped after the first page. The concepts were so far beyond where my Bio-Hab was technologically, that it might as well have been magic. All I knew was that we could move in any direction, at nearly any speed, and we didn't go splat inside.

I saw the indicator when Rhi launched intercept missiles.

"Control, I need a heavy storm now," I called into the control net.

"Acknowledged," the controller replied as the clouds that had been dissipating a minute ago suddenly surged. Black waves of clouds followed by sheets of lightning and thunder shook the sky.

Having control over a Bio-Hab's weather system came in handy sometimes. While our systems could cloak our AUGs, there wasn't much it could do to cover explosions.

The tactical display showed Rhi's missiles intercept and destroy the missiles aimed at Tara. I watched as Rhi's AUG passed Tara, still diving.

"I'm getting wet," Rhi said, no humor in her voice.

"Tara, stick with her," I called out and saw Tara begin to give chase as Rhi neared the water.

James's AUG roared as the twin cannons mounted on his shoulders began firing at the water, causing huge gouts of water to spray upwards.

"What do you have?" I asked.

"There's something in the water at 45 mark 60 two kilometers distant. I saw it break the surface," James said, his voice dead calm as he fired again.

"I'll follow you in," I said, adjusting my sensors to focus on the area he indicated but I wasn't detecting anything.

"How are they hiding from us? Water shouldn't stop our sensors," I said aloud before realizing I'd let a bit of panic sneak into my voice. "I'm on your right," I said with forced calm as I followed James.

Our entrance into the ocean met with the barest of shudders. Several new indicators appeared in my vision to account for underwater operations. Weapon systems shifted, shuttering those that would not function in water and bringing those that did to the forefront.

My mental connection with my AUG was so realistic that I

found myself holding my breath while I was submerged.

"I don't see anything, James," I said, releasing the breath I'd been holding.

"Nor do I," he replied.

I glanced at my command net and saw that both Tara and Rhi were below the surface of the water and diving deeper.

Something rocked my AUG, sending it careening sideways, followed by a blinding flash of light. The jolt caught me by surprise causing me to bite my cheek in the process. Ignoring the pain, I rotated to try and find where the shot had come from. The tactical display showed nothing.

"I saw that. You OK?" James asked.

I glanced at my status board, which showed several minor impacts shaded in yellow. A quick glance through my drones at the damage to my AUG showed it was mostly superficial.

"I'm good. You see where it came from?" I asked. "There's nothing on my board.

"No, just the impacts. Follow me," James said as his AUG shot forward.

"James, wait!" I tried as I saw a flash from below us. Forcing myself to ignore the projectile now heading for James, I focused on the source and let loose four leech projectiles.

Leeches were designed to seek out any power sources not designated friendly. With all the stealth capability an AUG had, they still had to expend energy to maintain systems. The leeches would be attracted to this and attack. Their onboard limited intelligence (LI) computers were amazingly intuitive. They didn't have all the bells and whistles of true AI, but they were impressive nonetheless.

James tried to evade but was struck from below by the projectile, and I saw a large burst of bubbles escape his AUG.

It took every bit of restraint to keep from calling out to him. Instead, I looked at his status board and saw it had only been a superficial hit. For all the exchange of weapon fire, I still hadn't seen the enemy.

We continued to descend, pursuing the enemy that had suddenly stopped firing at us. I wasn't sure if they had seen me launch the leeches and were trying to hide or if they had something more sinister in mind.

"On your left, on your left!" Tara called out.

"I see him!" Rhi replied.

I watched the tactical display as Rhi fired the micro-missiles her AUG specialized in. They streaked away from her AUG in jerky paths through the water towards her foe that still refused to show up on our sensors.

"How are they evading us?" I growled.

"Dunno, something new maybe," James said and then his AUG jerked hard to the right as something shot past him, heading towards the surface.

"After him!" I called, spinning in the water. I was about to engage thrusters when two shadows streaked past me, spouting pink flame from behind.

Three blue beams lanced out from James's AUG and sought the fleeing opponent, catching it just as it reached the surface. Bursts of steam and metal erupted from the fleeing AUG as it broke the surface and continued skyward.

My two leech projectiles were still in pursuit and breached the surface. Shedding their water casings, the leeches continued their pursuit in the air.

James and I followed moments later.

Not wasting any time, I took control of James's swarm drones. They had remained above the surface of the water in a widely dispersed pattern to help monitor the situation. I directed them to intercept the fleeing enemy unit and immediately received several projected flight paths from the swarm that helped me figure out how to herd the fleeing AG.

The storm had developed into something like a hurricane as winds buffeted us and lightning constantly flashed all around us.

James started firing as soon as he broke the surface. With all his weapon systems now available to him, he wasted no time in firing everything. It was an impressive display of firepower that streaked up into the sky, causing my displays to automatically darken to protect my vision from the blinding flashes of light.

I glanced down at my command display and saw the opportunity.

"Tara, target 103 mark 60, fire full now!" I tried and failed to keep my voice calm as I'd been taught. Instead, the heat of the moment filled my voice, causing my order to come out as an excited yell.

James's barrage caused our target to zig one way, and the two pursuing leech missiles caused it to zag the other way. When I added the swarm drones to the equation, the target shifted a third direction, directly into the beam of Tara's heavy.

It looked like a thick bolt of lightning streaking across the sky from Tara's AUG as it caught the enemy. As if her shot hadn't been enough, James scored a hit just as my leeches caught up and added to the massive fireball, marking the end of one of our opponents.

When I checked, Rhi had already finished the other target. I'd have to go back and check the footage to see what happened later.

I quickly double-checked everyone's AUG status via my command deck. Everyone seemed all right for the most part.

"Control, Reaper 1 alpha, splash two model 143s. I say again, splash two model 143s," I reported.

"Copy that Reaper 1 alpha. What's your status?"

"Rhi, we good?" I called, trusting the command deck but double-checking anyway.

"Affirm, our two conventional aircraft bugged out already. Seems the storm scared them off," Rhi said.

"Control, we're good. Minor damage but nothing that can't wait." I knew control could tell all of this through their own dataflow, but it was still nice to have them check. Dataflows weren't infallible.

"Both of these targets were submerged. Not sure if something is down there or not. Sensors didn't indicate anything out of the ordinary, but they didn't pick up these targets either," I said.

"Understood. Stay on station until an aquatic team arrives to relieve you," the controller said.

"Good copy control, standing by," I said, turning to my now assembled team. James and Rhi's AUGs were scorched and showed signs of damage, while Tara appeared untouched. I watched as her massive cannon returned to its resting place on her back.

"Everyone good?" I asked.

"Good to go," James said.

"Gonna need a paint job and a shit load of screen doors," Rhi said. "Other than that, I'm OK."

Tara's AUG gave me a thumbs up.

I double-checked their medical status to be on the safe side, but aside from the effects of the adrenaline, all appeared well.

"OK, we're on standby until the tadpoles come to relieve us," I said. "Return to holding stations and keep your eyes open. They say the AG only ever shows up in pairs, but I'm not trusting anything after today. Looks like they have some new stealth system, so keep your heads on a swivel."

Everyone acknowledged and returned to their posts to wait for our relief. In the meantime, I started going back through everything that had gone on, trying to figure out whether we'd missed something.

I wasn't sure what I feared more: this new stealth ability the AG had or the fact that I was going to have to write an actual after action report.

After Action

SHAE

"Ladies," I slurred, placing the tray on the table in front of them. "And gentleman," I took a moment to pat James on the head. Indicating the collection of drinks on the tray, I said, "I give you…" My face screwed up in thought. "What round are we on? Anyone?"

"14," Tara said from her place beside Rhi.

"11!" Rhi said, raising her fist in the air, not picking her head up off the table where she lay resting.

"No, my love, It's 14. You passed out for a little while after round 10," Tara said.

"Then it IS my 11th!" Rhi mumbled.

Tara couldn't fault her logic and just smiled.

The establishment we were currently residing in could only be regarded as a "hole in the wall." While Behemoth was virtually spotless, this place created synthetic dirt and grime to give it the look of a true dive bar. They'd gone as far as even synthesizing the stale beer smell.

Rhi found it while exploring the various shops and bars and insisted on bringing the rest of the crew to admire her find. While the décor was something out of a bad Hollywood movie, it was a relatively quiet place with only a few people ever around. The few that had been around took one look at our newly authorized veteran warskins and vacated the area.

We'd been given a list of establishments we were officially allowed to visit and this place was not on it. Apparently, it was beneath the level of respect due to combat veterans of the Daemon Corps. But our group fell in love with it, so we ignored the warnings.

Back during training, Rhi had discovered sobes, a chemical that immediately removed all intoxicants from your system. These made it possible for our group to unwind when it was called for but sober up at the push of a button. Leave it to Rhi to figure that one out.

"What shall we drink to this time?" I looked at the group.

"To us!" Tara called for the dozenth time.

"To us!" We repeated, albeit Rhi a little late, and drank.

I glanced down at the PDDs on the table and examined each closely. Now that we'd been blooded, we could customize our AUG's paint scheme, like Beth. Everyone had been doodling various ideas on what they wanted but in our current inebriated state, none of the ideas were good.

"OK, OK, OK." Rhi raised her head and leaned back in her chair. "There's something that's been bugging me for a while now. James!"

"Me?" James said, having to focus hard to see her face.

"Why the hell was Project Phobos put under the Army? It was so obviously an Air Force thing, and the ground pounders should never have gotten it."

Project Phobos had been a program to create chemical vampires for military use. James had been a part of it before Z Day.

I could tell James was having a hard time trying to understand Rhi's question as his head was cloudy.

"The ground pounders never did get it," James said finally. "They gave it to the Air Force."

"Oh. Well...good. That makes more sense." Rhi drank. "But why do you need vampire pilots?"

"Because they could turn into bats!" I howled and nearly fell off my chair.

James later told me he was glad to see me cutting loose. Apparently, he was afraid the pressure of the whole leadership position I was filling would be too much for me. He'd been worried I would flip out from the strain. I also found out Rhi had smacked him around at one point for his lack of faith in me.

James was already in the doghouse from that little stunt he

WAR OF THE GESTALT

pulled during our encounter with the AG. I ripped him a new one after we'd gotten back, in private, of course. He'd forgotten his place under me and I wasn't about to let that slide, especially when it happened during a combat situation.

I wasn't about to give him vampire orders during combat. Too many bad things could happen. But he needed to understand that when I gave an order, it was to be followed. The consequences of his actions still had him a little gun-shy around me, but he'd get over it.

Way back during my conversation with Travis, he told me James had a reputation as being a bit of a hothead. James didn't like to follow the plan when it became inconvenient. I'd discovered for myself how true that could be.

"No, no, that isn't it." Rhi screwed up her face in thought. "Oh, I know. Why did the Air Force get it when it was so obviously a ground pounder thing?"

"Good question," James nodded. "I'm going with the ASVAB minimum to enter the program was so high no one in the Army could make the cut."

"If that were the case, the Air Force must have gotten a waiver," Rhi deflected.

"No, seriously. Apparently, Pagoda knew the people who used to run Bergstrom Air Force Base in Austin. He used them to push the program through, and that's how the Air Force ended up with it." James took a drink. "Army probably ended up with the werewolf program."

Rhi nodded. "Probably right." She drank. "You seen some of those hairy Army sumbitches?"

Tara hiccupped, causing the whole table to laugh as she did it again.

"Shae!" Rhi shouted.

I turned towards Rhi so quickly that I fell out of my chair this time.

James leaned down and helped me back up.

"What happened?" I asked when I was seated again.

"Ejection seat malfunction," James offered.

"Oh, OK." I nodded.

"Shae!" Rhi shouted again.

This time, I didn't fall. I simply turned to face Rhi slowly. I had to turn slowly so the room could keep up with my head. "Yeeeeeees?"

"How old are you?" Rhi asked.

"Old enough," I offered.

"No, I mean, how old were you when you were 'brought over,'" Rhi asked.

"Oh. That's actually kinda a hard question," I said.

"No, it's not. Watch." Rhi straightened herself up, squared her shoulders and said, "I was 24. See?" Rhi offered helpfully.

"Well...I had...complications," I tried.

"Leap year baby?" Rhi asked.

"Leap year?" Tara asked.

"Shh, tell you later," Rhi said.

"It's just hard to say, really," I said.

Now James was curious. "Give it a shot," he said.

I put my drink down and sighed. Cocking my head to the side, I looked up in thought.

"Uh oh, she sighed," Rhi said. "Must be serious; there's smoke coming out of her ears."

"Stoptar saus," I didn't look at Rhi. "Well, I went to sea when I was 12...ish."

"Went to sea?" Tara asked.

I nodded. "I...helped liberate the Irish coast."

"So, you were a pirate," Rhi said.

"In a manner of speaking," I said.

"A female pirate?" Rhi squinted at me.

"Yeah," I said.

"An Irish female pirate," Rhi clarified.

"Yeah, what of it?" I frowned, not getting what Rhi was getting at.

"Oh, please enlighten me as to how this came to be." Rhi grinned.

"Pretty simply, really. My family were sailors; well, fishermen. My father didn't have any sons, just me. So, I had to help out. We managed to scrape by, pretty much year to year until we didn't.

"That's when my father started taking extra work to keep us

fed. I kept up the fishing, and he took up pirating. We were doing better, but Mom wasn't a fan. She was even less of a fan when he started taking me with him. He could make more on one good trip than three months of fishing. To him, it was just economics; two shares would be the same as six months of fishing. To my family, piracy wasn't about riches; it was about putting food on the table.

"I wasn't keen on it at first. It was a lot harder work, not to mention it was bloody. But my father explained that the people we were taking from had taken from us first. So, all we were doing was getting back what was rightfully ours. I was young, it made sense like everything your father tells you as a child. You just accept his word.

"Then father got hurt and couldn't sail anymore. He would stay home and I'd go out to earn for the family. Dad had been watching what it took to be a captain and taught me what to watch for, what to learn.

"I needed a second share, so I worked three times as hard. I learned how to do everything on that ship including the navigating. That was the hardest since I didn't know how to read at the time. But I learned and I earned. I made myself indispensable. Soon the current captain was coming to me to help organize raids as I seemed to have the mind for it.

"A few years go by and the older crew is either getting hurt or losing their nerve. Next election and here's the captain voting for me to be captain. I didn't win, but it opened a lot of eyes.

The others started looking at me differently after that. Before, I'd just been this serious kid who knew how to do everything. Now, they saw how the captain turned to me, asking me for my input.

"Then the captain was hurt mid-raid and the second was useless. I stepped up and finished what we'd started. The next election, I was made captain," I said.

"Wait, pirate elections?" Rhi asked.

"Oh yeah. Do you think it was fear that got the job done out there? When you had a ship full of men at sea for weeks on end and you had to sleep sometime? No, it was profits. Whoever could bring in the most profits was put in charge. Contrary to the movies, the men back then weren't all bloodthirsty savages. They were just trying to earn a living. Most of them had families they supported."

"Huh, I didn't know that," Rhi said. "How long were you captain before they booted you out of office?" Rhi grinned.

I was hoping she wouldn't ask that, but I wasn't going to lie to her. "One trip," I said soberly. "That's all I got."

"What?" Rhi asked. "What happened?" When I didn't answer, Rhi pressed. "Come on, you couldn't have been that bad."

James saved me from having to answer.

"She was turned," James said.

Rhi glanced at James and then back to me.

"We all have our demons," I said simply.

Rhi took one look at my expression and dropped it. "Well, you're a hell of a captain now, aren't you?" Rhi raised her glass and we all drank.

With our first successful combat mission, I'd been promoted to captain. Beth had been sent back to her old unit, but not before she told me how impressed she'd been with how I handled myself out there. Now, I was fully in charge and responsible for everything. No pressure.

"Here's one for you," I said, changing the subject. "Why are the Angel Guard destroying Bio-Habs anyway?"

"Cause they're the bad guys?" Rhi said.

"That's not what we were told," I said.

"That's exactly what we were told," James countered.

"We were told the AG rebelled against Behemoth and then started trying to take over the place. Why destroy the place you're trying to take over? It doesn't make sense," I said in a moment of clarity.

"If we can't have it, no one can?" James said.

"Maybe." I stared off into space and seemed to lose my train of thought. My serious question out of the blue brought a strange quiet to the table.

"Why do we have sex so much?" James said out of nowhere to the air in general. The table fell into a deeper silence as we stared at him. James looked around after a moment.

"Did I say that out loud?" James blushed hotly.

"You sure did, sugah," Rhi's evil grin accompanied her bad Southern accent.

I liked how embarrassed James got. It was so...human of him.

"OK, but really. Why so much?" James asked again.

Everyone turned to look at me.

"What?" I asked.

"Well? You're the go-to girl for all the other big questions. I think this counts, Captain," Rhi said.

I took a drink. "Libido is libido. You don't lose it just because you joined the night side."

"Being mind-linked to two other people probably doesn't help either." Rhi smiled. "I mean, if it was just your whoremones, you could probably deal with it well enough. But throw in two other people's lust...you don't stand a chance." Rhi drank. "That and some of us have some pent-up frustrations we're dealing with." Rhi eyeballed me for a moment.

I eventually nodded solemnly and we both drank.

Rhi stood shakily and went to order another round of drinks. When she returned, she placed the tray down and said, "Why isn't there a Drakes here? I even asked Beth, and she's not seen one either."

"Good question," James said.

"Got a good answer?" Rhi said.

"Nope, but it's a good question." James drank.

Rhi frowned at him.

"Better question is, what is Drakes?" I said.

"It's a tavern, yes?" Tara said.

"A tavern yes, but a bit more than that," I said.

"How does Drake spawn more copies of himself? Robots?" James asked.

"I'm still going with demon," I said.

"What's your evidence?" Rhi asked.

"None. Just a gut feeling," I said.

"Maybe it's part of Behemoth," Tara said quietly.

Everyone stopped and looked at her.

"I mean, from what you said, he could do pretty much anything. The tavern was in multiple worlds and could transport you between places like how our AUGs do."

"That's not half bad," Rhi said after a moment. "My wife is so SMART!" Rhi grabbed Tara and kissed her.

"So, wait," James started. "Are you saying Drake is Behemoth?"

"I dunno about that," Tara said. "Maybe not Behemoth itself, maybe some sort of side program?" Tara took another drink.

"Sure would explain a lot," I said after a moment.

"Man, I miss my Aug." James exclaimed seriously. "Wait, I just realized my Aug was in the Dilla!" James cried.

"What?" Rhi asked.

"My Aug. It was in the Dilla when it exploded," James said.

"His rifle," I clarified and shook my head.

"It's not just a rifle," James protested. "That was a Steyr Aug A3, one of the first models to come off the line at that."

I looked at Rhi, "It was a rifle."

"I'm sure you can find a replacement somewhere here. Or better yet..." Rhi offered, retrieving her sidearm from her thigh and laying it on the table. "What's wrong with these hip howitzers we carry?"

"Not the same. I scrimped and saved for that thing," James whined.

"I'll buy you one for Christmas," I patted him on the head while rolling my eyes at Rhi, where James couldn't see.

Tara came over and patted James on the shoulder.

"I know how you feel," Tara said. "My journals were in the vehicle as well."

"Oh," Rhi said softly. "I'd forgotten. I'm sorry babe, I know you had been keeping a journal for quite a while—"

"47 cycles...er years," Tara said, still patting James's shoulder absentmindedly.

"You lost 47 years' worth of journals?" James looked up at her in horror.

"How's that Aug feeling now, James?" I asked.

"Screw my rifle," James said, patting Tara's hand.

"How are y'all's tattoos coming, by the way?" I tried to divert the conversation.

"They're killer! Check this out," Rhi said, rolling up a sleeve.

"See this here and here?" She pointed to several strange symbols on her skin. "These showed up during training."

I admired the work. "Still beautiful," I smiled.

"What about this?" Tara said, pointing at a different place along her arm.

"When did that get there?" Rhi said, straining her neck to see the symbol Tara was pointing at.

"About three hours ago, right after we got back." Tara smiled.

"Cool." Rhi was grinning like an idiot at her arm and suddenly leaned over and kissed her wife. "Love you."

"Love you too," Tara kissed her back.

"You know what I don't miss?" James said. "Zombies."

"But why? They were so easy to take care of," Rhi said.

"True, but the smell," James said.

We all nodded at that one.

"Didn't you get bit?" Rhi asked James.

"Yup," he said, showing the half-moon scar from the bite.

"That's still so weird," I said. "I mean, we don't scar from injuries, but that one did. Never seen that before."

"One more reason he's so special," Rhi said, ruffling James's hair affectionately. "But what surprised me was there were no side effects."

"I dunno," I smiled. "How could you tell if he went brain-dead?"

"True," Rhi nodded.

"Oh, shut it," James shook his head as Rhi and I laughed. "OK, since we're talking zombies. Where would you want to go visit during a zombie apocalypse?"

The three of us looked at him questioningly.

"For instance, I think Disney World would be pretty cool to check out," James slurred.

"That's just wrong," I said, "on so many levels."

"Sure, but think how short the lines would be!" James said.

I just frowned and shook my head at him.

"Can we at least do a fly by?" James pleaded.

"We'll see," I offered, patting his hand.

"Yeah! In that case, Rhi—" James started.

"Yes daaaaawling?" She drawled out, cutting him off.

He chuckled and then continued. "Who the hell are you always talking to?"

"Whatcha mean?" Rhi slurred.

"I mean, sometimes you just start babbling, but you're not talking to any of us. When we ask you always tell us to never mind."

"I know," Tara said with a quiet grin.

"OOOHHH!" Rhi said, ignoring Tara. "That's the voices in my head," she said, taking another drink.

"Voices?" I asked. "Plural? I thought it was just the one voice."

Rhi nodded, "Yeah, there was just the one. But ever since Houston there's been a second that likes to barge in every now and again."

"Sounds crowded," James said.

"Only when they start fighting," Rhi grinned.

"Fighting?" I asked.

"Well, it's not really fighting when only one side is yelling. Apparently, my voice doesn't like the new guy and is always yelling at him. The new guy either can't hear her or is really good at ignoring her," Rhi said.

"Sounds annoying as hell," James said.

"Well, it would be funny if I had the ability to shut them off or at least turn down the volume," Rhi said.

"What do they talk about?" I asked.

"Well, my voice is always commenting on my life choices and critiquing everything from how I sign my name to how James is in bed."

James scowled.

Rhi patted him on the cheek. "Don't worry, she's a fan and grades on a curve." Rhi's smile didn't erase James's scowl.

"The other guy, I don't know about him. Most of the time it's like he's not really talking to me. It's more like I'm eavesdropping on his conversations. But they're not conversations as such, more like he's telling people what to do." Rhi frowned.

"How so?" James asked.

"Well, most of the time, I don't understand what the hell he's saying. It's like either another language or he's speaking so garbled I can't make it out. When I can understand him, he'll say stuff like 'Section 223 has acquired 36 juinals,' whatever the hell that is. I've learned to tune him out for the most part. That is until my head starts yelling at him to shut up."

"You are a strange woman," I said, raising my glass. "Stay weird."

Rhi returned the salute and emptied her glass.

"Juinals are a parasitic organism that is attracted to plasma conduits. They latch on, burrow in and drain them. The problem is, they don't make the best seals when they do it, so plasma tends to leak and make a mess," Tara said, taking a sip from her glass daintily.

Everyone turned and looked at her.

"What?" Tara said.

"Let me guess, Daemon Corps classes again?" James asked.

"Well, yeah. Y'all didn't get that one either?" Tara asked.

We all shook our heads.

"Besides, that sounds like one of Behemoth's updates," Tara said.

"What do you mean?" Rhi said.

"Behemoth talks directly to us Daemons when needed," Tara said simply.

"You're saying the voice in my head is Behemoth? The computer?" Rhi asked.

"Well, it sounds like what it would say. But they said only Daemons can hear it," Tara looked confused for a moment.

"Tara, have you heard this voice before? Before you were on Behemoth?" I asked.

"Yeah..." Tara started uncertainly. "I believe so. But not nearly as clear as I hear it nowadays."

"Rhi, you said it started in Houston after you'd married Tara? I bet it's the link between the two of you that allows you to hear it," I said.

"It makes sense." Rhi turned to Tara. "Why didn't you tell me you heard voices?"

"It was only the one," Tara said defensively. "And I thought you knew. Besides, I didn't want to worry you as you had your own to worry about."

Rhi hugged her. "Always share, silly."

"Well," Tara began. "In that case, I have this really weird rash that..."

"Whoa, maybe not that much," James said.

I rolled my eyes.

"Shae, why don't you ever curse?" Tara asked.

"I'm sorry?" I asked.

"You never curse. I hear Rhi and James doing it all the time, but I've never heard you use a swear word," Tara said.

"Yeah, now that you mention it, you don't," Rhi said. "James, you've known her longest. She ever drop an f-bomb on you?"

"Not even once," James said.

"I don't curse," I cut in. "Because it wasn't appropriate for my job as a courier."

"So, you did curse but stopped when you became a courier?" Rhi asked.

"Sure." I shrugged, wondering how we even got on the topic.

"But you're not a courier anymore," Tara said.

"Yeah, Shae, let's hear you lite it up!" Rhi hiccupped.

"When one of you eejits deserves it, I'll let you know," I grinned.

"Calling someone an idiot isn't a curse," James protested.

"You seem to speak from some experience, James." Rhi teased.

"Oh, shut up," James said.

"A gowl is an idiot," I said simply.

"Then what does—" James started.

"Besides, American curse words are just that, words. They have no weight. In Gaelic, cursing involves legitimate curses, invoking the devil, that sort of thing. I've never been angry enough at someone to sick the devil on them." I shrugged and drank.

"Oh I have," Rhi volunteered.

"Why am I not surprised," I grinned.

"Besides, our language has a finite number of words. Why

should I limit myself by not using everything available to me?" Rhi said.

"That almost makes sense," I said, giving Rhi a look.

"Hey, if we got sent back home and our minds wiped, do you think it would change anything?" James asked.

"What do you mean?" I asked.

"I mean, do you think we'd change even though we didn't remember anything?" James said.

"Knowing Behemoth, I have a feeling it would be pretty thorough. I doubt anything would change from how we acted from before we were taken," I said.

"Besides," Tara chimed in. "Who says we haven't already done that and this is our second or third tour?"

Everyone put down their drinks and turned to Tara.

"What?" Tara asked.

"Way to bring down the room, babe," Rhi said.

"Next rounds on me then, I guess," Tara said as she rose from the table.

"Nice recovery," Rhi winked.

"How are you two doing?" James asked when Tara left the table.

"Good," Rhi nodded. "We're figuring it out. We've already come up with little shortcuts and codes for when we're in public."

"Sucks that you have to hide that you're married." James drank. "Well, mostly."

"There's a reason we hide in this booth, in the back of a seedy bar, where no one can see us," Rhi said.

"You'd think such an 'advanced' society would have let go of things like bigotry," I said.

Rhi laughed. "And here I thought my biggest worry was people saying something about two women being married. Oh well, fuck 'em."

"Who's my wife fucking now?" Tara asked, setting down another round of drinks. "I swear, I can't leave her alone for 30 seconds before—"

"For once, nobody," James said, earning a playful punch from Rhi.

"Awww, I wanted to watch," Tara huffed.

"You're incorrigible," Rhi said, kissing Tara briefly. "Love you."

I felt James gently squeeze my hand and turned to find him looking at me. *What?* I asked.

Nothing, just looking at you, James said gently.

"Oh oh oh!" Rhi said suddenly. "I know what we should go do!"

"What's that?" James asked.

"Elvis is playing over in Temon sector. We should totally go see that show," Rhi said.

"Elvis?" James asked. "You don't strike me as an Elvis type."

I cut in. "He was actually pretty good back in the day."

Rhi nodded and pointed at me. "And it's his younger self that's still performing."

"An Elvis impersonator? Really?" James said.

"That's just it. It's really him!" Rhi said.

"Wait, what?" I asked.

"Don't ask me how or why, but it really is Elvis, but from his movie days." Rhi practically bounced up and down in her chair with excitement.

"What's an Elvis?" Tara finally said, no longer able to hold the question back.

"An old music singer," James said.

"Old music singer?" Rhi and I said together in shocked tones.

James held up his hands defensively and leaned away from the table.

"Anyway, I don't know how Behemoth does what it does or why it decided to grab young Elvis, but it did, and we should go see him!" Rhi stood up and grabbed Tara's arm, pulling her to her feet. "Come on, you're gonna love this!" Rhi stumbled towards the door, Tara in tow.

"We'd best keep up. Otherwise, she might fall down an elevator shaft or something." I stood.

"Uh huh," James said. "Has nothing to do with wanting to go see young Elvis, right?"

"They always said he was abducted by aliens." I leaned down and kissed James on the cheek.

"Riiiight," James said as he took my arm and followed along.

The B Side

SHAE

All the extraordinary stories begin with "it was just an ordinary night," this one is no different. James, Rhi, Tara and I were at our usual dive bar, unwinding after a long day patrolling.

With Beth no longer with us, I now had to keep an eye on our group and keep them out of trouble. It seemed being captain made me the de facto "mom" figure I'd always tried to shy away from. I figured if going to an off-limits bar kept everyone sane, I didn't mind running interference with command for it. I'd even offered to bring Beth once, but that was too much for her strict military bearing to handle...yet.

In the month since the incident, command still hadn't figured out how the AG had evaded our sensors. They'd recovered the AG wreckage but couldn't find anything out of the ordinary on the enemy AUGs. It made command nervous, and as a result, we'd been on constant patrols ever since.

Constant patrolling was rough on our little foursome. We weren't the only ones patrolling the planet. There were other units doing their share, but they were Daemon units. Vampires had a lot of stamina and fortitude, but Daemons put us to shame when it came to working constantly.

Anytime we weren't in a cockpit or a briefing room, we were right here in this bar, trying to forget the grind for a little while. We'd adopted this small place as our own. We didn't always drink; sometimes, we just enjoyed not being in our quarters. Tonight, though, we drank.

Maybe it was the fact we'd been drinking that caused us to

miss the minor details. The new person behind the bar didn't raise any flags, although we'd only ever seen three different people working here.

We were used to the place clearing out when we showed up, but there had always been people to clear out. This time, the place was empty. But we ignored all this, just happy to be done with another day of not having been shot at.

The past month had been an exercise in futility. Ever since the dogfight we'd had, every time we went out on patrol, we expected to get into another furball. Our nerves were frazzled every time we came back without incident. It felt like something was coming, but we didn't know when or where. Hence, our nightly forays to the bar to try and shake off the sense of foreboding.

The normal 'buzz' of intoxication came on quicker than usual but that just contributed to the festive atmosphere of the evening. That is until the world stopped and turned red with pain.

James told me he'd been hit with a Taser as part of his training. He told me how it locked up his muscles and forced all thought, except for the pain, from his mind. As what felt like lightning suddenly began coursing through my body, I had a feeling this was something similar. I don't remember being sick; I just knew that when the pain stopped, there was vomit in my mouth.

I tried to move but found I was as weak as a newborn kitten. The others groaned next to me, so I knew I wasn't alone.

My view of a metal ceiling disappeared as someone grabbed my hair and pushed my head to the side. Something cold seared into my neck. From my new vantage point, I could see the others lying next to me. They seemed to all be in similar shape.

There were noises from behind me but I couldn't identify them. What I could make out was the fact that we weren't in the bar anymore.

"Clear and set," someone said as my head was released and bounced off the metal floor, causing stars to appear before my eyes. A moment later, the owner of the voice appeared in my field of vision as they knelt next to James.

It was an AG.

I'd never seen an AG out of uniform before. This one wore pants, a shirt, and a simple coat, all non-descript. I don't know what she was thinking. You couldn't hide being an AG just because you changed clothes. They were pretty distinctive with their native height, skin color, etc.

As I watched, the AG grabbed James's head and pressed a metal box to his neck. A moment later, they said, "Clear and set," before repeating the process with Rhi and Tara.

There were two other AG standing around us, each holding wicked-looking rifles I'd never seen before. The armed pair wore the white warskins we'd been briefed on, similar to our own. Theirs looked old, though, beat up and battered. There were even spots where it looked as if they'd been repaired, something unheard of as ours were recycled and exchanged for new ones after every use.

A fourth AG entered the room from a side passage. "Report," it ordered in a commanding voice.

"Successful transport with no transponder alerts. It looks like a clean nab," another AG said.

"Good, dispose of the Daemon and bring the others to holding for processing," the leader said.

Alarm bells went off in my head, and I struggled to move, but I was so weak I couldn't even form words.

"A moment," the AG with the metal box said as the leader turned to leave.

"What is it?" the leader said.

The face of the holder of the metal box was shocked. "You're going to want to see this."

The leader took the metal box and examined it. "Impossible, do it again."

I watched as Tara was manhandled and her neck examined again with the box.

When the box was handed to the leader again, she said, "It must be defective. Grab another one." After a moment, she added, "Someone fetch a tayon scanner."

A different box was pulled from a cabinet on the wall and the process repeated. The leader huffed with the results.

A moment later, a fifth AG arrived carrying a large tablet.

"The Daemon," the leader pointed.

The tablet holder began waving the device across Tara's body. When it reached her abdomen, the tablet paused.

"Finish it," the leader ordered.

"Yes." The tablet continued to move until it reached Tara's toes and then returned to her abdomen. As the tablet hovered over Tara's stomach, it began to shake. "I've never seen—"

"It's not possible. It must be something else," the leader said.

"But what if—" the tablet holder started.

"Take it to the hospital. I want four guards on it at all times. The rest, take to processing." The leader left and was replaced by a new AG pushing what looked like floating stretchers.

What have we gotten into now? I thought as I was lifted off the floor, and the world went dark.

∞∞∞∞∞Ω∞∞∞∞∞

SHAE

I woke to the sound of birds chirping and tried to open my eyes. The bright sunlight caused me to squeeze them shut again. I tried a second time, this time slower and managed to get them halfway open as a heart-shaped face filled my vision.

"Good morning, sleepyhead," The sweet voice had just a hint of the sound of tinkling wind chimes in it.

"Cateia? What are you doing here?" I started to sit up, but my muscles screamed at me, and I lay back down.

"Don't try to get up yet," Cateia said.

I felt her gentle hand on my chest. She and her mate Tachi had briefly been in our basic training class. They were pulled early, though. They possessed some sort of symbiont that allowed them to operate in space without the AUGs. James had apparently run into more of their kind back during the whole transport wall incident.

Why had I forgotten all this earlier when James was telling his story? I wondered. I remembered Cateia plain as day. We'd had several conversations comparing our home Bio-Habs. Although she said she wasn't from a Bio-Hab. At the time, I figured she was just confused or in denial. There had been a lot of that running around back then.

"I had the weirdest dream," I said.

"I thought vampires didn't dream," Cateia said.

"We have our moments," I said. I gathered my strength and slowly sat up.

"Careful, you're going to be really sore," Cateia said.

"Sore from what—" I started but then caught sight of James, Rhi and Tara around me. We were outside in a shady grove surrounded by tall trees. Each of us lay on some sort of pallet of cloth that served as a bed. Cateia was sitting on a large rock, watching me closely. Through the trees, I could see a blue sky with white clouds sliding slowly by.

"Are they—" I started.

"They're fine," Cateia said. "Just waking up like you. It's best to let them come to on their own."

"Where are we?" I asked.

"This is a recovery ward," Cateia said.

"Recovery ward?" I asked, looking around.

"Yes. Their personnel transport process is really trying on your body, much like Behemoth's is. It'll take a bit for you to get back to normal. They leave you here as it's supposed to be a soothing environment to speed your recovery," Cateia said. She didn't sound like she believed that.

"Their recovery ward is a forest?" I asked.

"Don't worry, it's not a real forest. There's no wild animals or bugs or anything. It's just a projection," Cateia said.

"So, we're really just prisoners in a pretty cell?" I asked.

"Sorta, but not exactly," Cateia said.

I gave her a look and turned to James.

"Don't wake him yet. It's better if he comes around on his own," Cateia cautioned again.

I stayed my hand. Cateia had never struck me as the rebellious type. She was a sweet girl, albeit a little naive. Maybe she'd been conned into going over to the AG side. Regardless, I let James sleep and turned back to Cateia.

"Where's Tachi?" I asked about her husband.

"He's out on patrol," Cateia said.

"For the Angel Guard," I said.

Cateia nodded.

"I don't understand; why are you working for the Angel Guard?" I asked.

Cateia sighed heavily. "I'm normally not the one to give this speech, but I'll try. I'm sure once everyone's up and about, they'll give it to you all official-like.

"There's a lot I wasn't told when I first arrived on Behemoth. We were sort of herded through training, given only the most basic explanations of things and put straight to work. I didn't mind it too much; I thought I was doing good, you know, protecting people. I'm all about that.

"But then things started to make no sense. When I'd question our DC superiors, I would either be brushed off or given some far-flung excuse that just confused me more. When I asked for further clarification, I was abruptly shut down and told to get back to work.

"Eventually, things came to a head. Tachi and I were patrolling around our assigned world when we saw an entire wing of DC heading down to the planet. They ignored our hails and when we called control, they told us not to worry about it and to return to station. Just about this time we spotted a pair of AG coming in from high orbit and gave chase. They didn't seem interested in us and evaded, instead heading after our previous counterparts.

"Control waved us off and again told us to return to station, but Tachi wouldn't have any of it. He charged headlong after, you know how he is. We're not as fast as the AUGs, but we used our reentry angle to pick up a good head of steam. When we finally caught up, the battle was already raging. The two AG were harassing the DC, trying to get through their defensive line into some sort of cavern. But they were outgunned. We thought they'd already destroyed two DC, as there were two AUGs missing.

"Just as we were about to engage, two AG come screaming in from orbit, no breaking, literally white from the heat. There was no way anything was still alive inside of them, which was good because as soon as they hit the defensive line, they detonated. The first two AG made a beeline through the hole that was made, but they were too late," Cateia said.

"Too late?" I asked.

Cateia nodded. "As soon as they hit the cavern entrance, it happened." Cateia stared up at the trees, lost in the memory. "Never seen anything like it."

"Like what?" I asked.

"The DC activated the living fire," Cateia said softly.

"The DC did?" I asked in disbelief.

"Yup," Cateia popped her lips on the word. "The AG hadn't made it deep enough into the cave to be anywhere near the actual control point," Cateia said.

"But why?" I asked.

"I'll let them explain that one to you," Cateia said and then was silent.

I remembered what that dead world looked like and couldn't imagine watching something like that happen in real-time.

"Wait, you said the living fire? How did it work?" I couldn't help myself. I'd heard rumors about the living fire, but no one I'd talked to had ever seen it firsthand.

"There were claxons and light everywhere. It was a chaotic few minutes as no one was leaving. They were still fighting. Everyone knows that once the destruct has started, it can't be stopped. So why they stuck around, I don't know. We had already been ordered to stay away, so we left, and lucky we did too. About the time we hit low orbit, these pulses of light were coming out of the control point. Everything the pulses hit shut down like flipping a switch."

"That was the living fire?" I asked.

"That? No. That was some sort of warning, I guess. A minute later, it was as if a new sun had appeared at the control point. If our suits hadn't protected us, I'd be blind since I was staring right at it when it happened. It started as a pinpoint and then began to expand out in a ring. I couldn't help it; I just sat there and watched. For hours, I sat there, unable to look away as the planet burned to a cinder."

"Was it your planet?" I asked.

"No. We're actually not from Behemoth. We come from somewhere...else. We just got stuck here by accident. Besides, our planet has an orbiting defensive network, so we don't have to worry about invaders," Cateia said.

"Sounds like you worry about invaders a lot," I said.

"Huh, yeah, I guess so," Cateia chuckled and, after a few moments, continued. "Shae, you haven't been told the whole truth. Try to keep an open mind when they come to talk to you."

I thought about that for a moment; it wasn't like I had much choice. Then I remembered, "James said he ran into some of your friends a while back. Did they ever track you down?"

"Friends?" Cateia asked.

"Yes, someone named Chris and..." I fumbled for the name. "I can't remember the woman's name; they were married, I believe."

"Krys? I haven't seen him in forever! No, where's he at?"

"I don't know. James said they found him when he was outside of Behemoth and brought him back," I shrugged.

"That's not good," Cateia frowned unhappily.

"Why?" I asked.

"Because that means Behemoth has them somewhere." Cateia bit her lip in thought and looked worried. Then her expression changed, and her eyes unfocused for a moment before returning to normal.

"You, OK?" I asked.

"Just letting Tachi know about Krys. He'll look into it for me." Cateia looked back at me with a kind smile. "Thank you for the heads up."

"You're welcome?" I said hesitantly.

"I know," Cateia said patiently. "It's a weird situation, but still, thank you. There aren't many of my people left, at least not ones I actually know."

The rest of the team started waking up then and I had my hands full trying to keep them calm. James was relatively easy and Rhi went into her cold calculating mode. Tara, on the other hand, was the one starting to lose her composure.

Apparently, she'd been briefed that the AG never let a captured Daemon live. I couldn't blame her hostility if that was true. Luckily the AG mouthpiece chose that moment to show up.

"Welcome to Coren'tel, or as it has come to be known, Behemoth." The AG who stood before us wore a mishmash of warskin and other clothes, giving "her" an almost punkish look.

While the outdoor motif remained in the "recovery room," it had changed to a plain hilltop at night, beneath a dazzling display of stars, nebula and other heavenly bodies.

"My name is Perth, and above all else, I want you to know you are not prisoners."

I squeezed James's hand hard as I felt him tense beside me. Once we were all awake, Rhi and James had done nothing but mentally plot our escape. I had convinced them to wait and see what was going on.

"While you are currently inconvenienced, when I've said my peace, you'll be allowed to leave if you so wish," Perth said.

I glanced at Cateia, who nodded in agreement with Perth's claim.

"Why?" I found myself saying.

"Contrary to popular belief, we're not the monsters we've been made out to be," Perth said.

"Sure, kidnapping doesn't make you a bad guy at all," Rhi said.

"I didn't say we weren't 'bad guys,'" Perth said, using finger quotes around bad guys. "Just that we're not monsters. And to prove it, each of your programming has been reset so that Behemoth can no longer make you forget things it feels you shouldn't know."

"Programming?" James asked.

"Yes, programming. I have a lot to tell you and I don't wish to try your patience more than I must. May I continue?" Perth said.

"By all means," I said before anyone else could.

Perth raised her hand and pointed at the sky. "An ancient time ago, two empires vied for control of the stars."

A line appeared amongst the stars, dividing the sky in half.

"This was not for control of some small sector or galaxy but of hundreds of galaxies on both sides. I know not how the war started, nor what it was about or if it ever ended. What I do know is that Behemoth was created by one side as a training ground.

"Not only did they train soldiers, but they made them. Using a genetic menagerie, Behemoth sought to create more diverse soldiers, able to fight in multiple environments. To this end, Behemoth was given living control over itself.

"It created Bio-Habs replicating every known environment and then began to experiment with new ones. It physically expanded itself again and again, and it still continues to expand today.

"When troops were ready for deployment, they were shipped to whichever staging area was in need. Periodically, Behemoth's genetic tanks were replenished with new materials from supply ships. Until, one day, the supply ships stopped coming, as did the requests for troops.

Left alone, Behemoth continued with the core task for which it had been designed. It would continue to maintain the Bio-Habs until they were needed once again.

"Behemoth's genetic tanks were usually topped off by supply ships. In addition, whenever something came within Behemoth's sphere of power, it grabbed and absorbed it, whether for raw materials, parts or even biomass. Then nothing came for a long time and the diversity tanks ran out.

"We believe Behemoth's creators had lost the war by this point, hence the reason for the lack of supplies. Behemoth had been created in such secrecy and put so far from any known inhabited system that it was never found.

"When the genetic tanks emptied, Behemoth went into a kind of low-power stasis out of self-preservation. It remained this way for millions of years until one poor ship accidentally strayed too close and was pulled in.

"The ship held a plethora of species Behemoth had never encountered before. It abducted the crew and replaced them with clones before returning the ship to its course. The crew remained unaware of the exact nature of the encounter nor where it took place as Behemoth faked the location records."

"I witnessed that," Rhi said. "That was the record I was shown."

The rest of us nodded as Perth continued.

"With new genetic input for Behemoth's matrix, it once again began creating warriors for a war we believe had long since ended. You see, all the previous warriors Behemoth had created had died off by this time. Even the ones that were being held in storage perished from the effects of time.

"Left on its own with a sole purpose, Behemoth had no reason to stop its original function. Fearing another lack of supplies and loss of genetic material, Behemoth created new and better storage to ensure it never ran out again."

"How?" I asked.

"Honestly? We don't know. It's beyond our scope," Perth said. "All the current warrior races of Behemoth were created from the genetic stock of that one ship. However, there are other creatures out there, both in and out of Bio-Habs, that are nothing like you or me. They are the last remaining remnants of those first races. If you live long enough, you may run into one."

"For example?" Tara asked.

"The contrary race," Perth said.

"The contrary race?" James said slowly.

"Yes," Perth said, nodding. We call them the contrary race, for that is what they pride themselves on. That, and they won't tell us their real name.

"They make sure that their language is unconvertible to any other language. When they encounter a race who can translate their language, they change it so that it can't be translated. You must learn their language in order to communicate, but it's near impossible as they constantly change it. They will give a slight amount of respect to anyone who tries to learn their language, but only a pittance.

"The few business dealings we've had with them they ensured were as painful as possible even if it was in their favor. Their spaceports are designed to fit only their ships exactly. If you want to visit, you must leave your ship and spacewalk into theirs. Don't get me started on their atmosphere.

"They feel they're the center of the universe and will only tolerate those who think the same way.

"Why put up with them?" Rhi asked.

"We've been told they have something amazing hidden away with their people. The problem is, no one knows what it is or if it's worth the effort to find out," Perth said.

I just stared at Perth, not believing my ears.

"When were you created?" James asked.

"We were here at the beginning—not these forms, of course, but our genetic ancestors. Behemoth took our ancestors and genetically altered them to serve as its guardians. We stood watch both outside and from within up until the schism.

"We'd been noticing irregularities in Behemoth's orders as well as the newer Bio-Habs it was creating. Some of the new races were fundamentally flawed. It took some time before we realized Behemoth was losing its mind. Not that we could blame it. No creature can survive eons without succumbing to some sort of disease. Those who brought it to Behemoth's attention disappeared, never to be heard from again.

"We were guardians, we knew nothing of how Behemoth's higher functions operated. We knew how to protect. We didn't know how to 'fix' it. So, we were stuck serving an insane master.

"As we watched, the problems grew worse. Some Bio-Habs were completed but never actually turned on, while others were turned on with only half the Bio-Hab finished. Then there seemed to be a breakdown in the Behemoth control system, and the machines in your bodies began to bleed."

"Machines in our bodies?" James said.

"Yes. Each of you have hregt sized machines within you. Everything on Behemoth does. It's how Behemoth keeps tabs and controls the Bio-Habs."

James and I looked at one another. Apparently, the word hregt didn't have a translation.

"But once they started bleeding...I'm sorry, they didn't actually bleed. They simply began malfunctioning. Once this happened, we began to see all sorts of side effects. From psychotic behavior to amazing physical and mental abilities.

What I believe you call telepathy is a side effect of your ability to tap into Behemoth's communication network."

"That would explain how they could shut it off," Rhi said.

"And why you're nuts," James teased.

"Oh no, that's all me. I worked hard for that." Rhi tapped her chin. "Although, I wonder if the woman's voice in my head is actually another woman."

No. I heard the voice come from Rhi, but it wasn't Rhi's normal mind voice. It was a voice I'd never heard before. James said he'd once had this happen with Rhi. I wondered...I was going to ask but glanced over at Perth.

Perth was watching us, waiting for us to finish.

"The latest error has been the creation of the beings you call zombies over the last few decades. Every time these creatures appeared in a Bio-Hab, it was the beginning of a population culling and eventual destruction of said Bio-Hab. Not long after their introduction, Behemoth would start looking for a way to purge the same Bio-Hab and begin again."

"Start looking? Why can't it just shut it down if it's controlling it?" I asked.

"During the schism, there was one among us who managed to get into Behemoth's core. She was one of the few among us who'd managed to gain an understanding of how Behemoth operated. Before her demise, she managed to corrupt Behemoth by introducing an 'altered intelligence' into Behemoth's processing net. This intelligence warred with Behemoth for control but eventually lost.

"However, before the loss, the intelligence managed to make several changes to Behemoth, including its ability to purge Bio-Habs. Without that ability, Behemoth must physically search for the manual control points. The locations of the control points was also purged."

"What happened to this 'altered intelligence?'" James asked.

"As far as we know, it was destroyed. There have been rumors that remnants of the intelligence have manifested itself in various ways to occasionally help us. But aside from these unsubstantiated instances, we've been on our own."

"What exactly was the schism?" Rhi asked.

"When we initially rebelled, we thought we'd taken Behemoth by surprise. Little did we realize how much we underestimated Behemoth's control. It had seen our growing rebellion long before we ever decided to act upon it.

In response to the perceived threat, Behemoth created the DC in secret. They were designed to be better than us and without so much pesky free will. So, when we began our open revolt, the DC were waiting for us.

"It was a surprisingly long and bloody conflict, so much so that we began to realize we couldn't win. With our numbers being finite and Behemoth able to create more DC as needed, we saw the writing on the wall and began our retreat.

"The intelligence had managed to cordon off several Bio-Hab areas from Behemoth's control. Somehow, it managed to make Behemoth forget they even existed, creating safe havens for us to retreat to." Perth held his arms out to our surroundings. "Even still, it's only a matter of time before Behemoth discovers these refuges."

"You said Behemoth was making us forget things?" I asked.

"Yes. It has the ability to manipulate your mind as needed." Perth said. "Lately, you've probably noticed an increase in forgetting what you're talking about or not remembering how you got somewhere. All these strange circumstances are due to Behemoth's interference."

"Or just James's brain farts," Rhi whispered.

"But we're not machines," James said, frowning at Rhi.

"The brain is nothing more than an organic machine. It can be manipulated as such if you have the right tools. We have removed the ability of the machines within you to take your memories," Perth said.

"But all Behemoth has to do is introduce more of these machines in us and it can do it again, right?" Rhi asked.

"While this is a possibility, it is usually not the case. Each creature is created with these machines as a part of them. As the creature grows, these machines spawn more machines to keep up with the growth and adapt to your ever-changing biopresence. It's a self-sustaining system.

"If Behemoth were to discover you were out of the loop, it

would have to create new machines specifically tuned to your body with the ability to rewrite the rest. So far, we haven't heard of this taking place."

"That you know of," James said.

"As you say," Perth nodded. "You will feel a slight tingling sensation accompanied by a tone when Behemoth is attempting to make you forget things. This way, you know when it is happening and will be able to act accordingly."

"Act accordingly?" James asked.

"Play along," Perth said.

"So, what's the end game here?" I asked. "What do you hope to accomplish?"

"At the moment, survival. Even if we could defeat Behemoth, we wouldn't be able to keep one Bio-Hab working, let alone all of them," Perth sighed.

One of the other AGs seemed to stir.

"Yes, yes, Turin," Perth nodded to the squirming one.

"Many of us believe," Turin began. "That Behemoth is like any other machine and periodically makes backups of itself. If we could find these backups and go far enough back to find an uncorrupted version, we could theoretically restore Behemoth to an earlier state that was more stable. We...er, I believe this is how the altered intelligence was originally created. That one of these backups was discovered and altered to fit our needs."

"Wait," James said. "If Behemoth does have these backups, why didn't it revert to one from before the damage it sustained in the schism?"

Turin appeared to deflate, "It is just a theory."

"As I stated before, what we're doing now is survival. We're trying to keep ourselves and as many of the Bio-Habs alive until a solution can be found," Perth said.

"OK, great," Rhi said. "Why bring us into it?"

"Because," Perth said. "Something about you has changed the status quo."

"Something about us?" I asked.

"More specifically, him," Perth indicated James.

"Me?" James asked.

"Oh God," Rhi said.

"What?" I asked.

"Please, please, please tell me this isn't some sort of prophetic thing," Rhi said.

"Prophecy? No," Perth said.

"Oh good, his ego's bad enough as it is," Rhi said flatly.

"No, we received intelligence that Behemoth has taken a special interest in James specifically. As far as we can tell, whatever has happened to him was not intentional by Behemoth."

"What do you mean?" I asked.

"What happened to me?" James asked, a little apprehensive.

"There's something about you; we don't know if it's DNA, the machines inside you, or what. But you break the rules. Things that should not be possible, you somehow do. Add to this you somehow manage to spread this ability to anyone you come into intense physical contact with."

"Intense. Physical. Contact." Rhi laughed and shook her head. "That's one way to put it."

"Mark," I mumbled.

"Mark?" James said.

"His ability to control vampires. You said you topped off on everyone right before the raid on the Alamo, right?"

"Yes," James said a little hesitantly.

"That would explain it," Rhi said.

"Daywalker," James said, causing both Rhi and me to groan. "What? That would explain my ability to walk in sunlight, right?"

"Beth..." I whispered unintentionally.

"What?" James asked.

"This is kinda a catch-all for all the weirdness around you, isn't it?" Rhi asked James.

[Sounds a bit contrived to me, doesn't it? --Rhi]

You're doing it again, James said.

Wait, you heard that? Rhi asked.

FOCUS! PLEASE! I sent to all of them.

Sorry, Tara said, which almost made me stop altogether. I

was still getting used to hearing her in my head.

Taking a deep breath, I pushed it all from my head and asked, "But why? Why these specific changes?"

"We don't know. We don't even know the extent of the changes, only that his influence is growing stronger," Perth said.

"How so?" I asked.

Perth nodded to Turin again.

"We believe his influence is creating major physical changes in those he 'infects.'" Turin looked sheepish.

We all looked at Turin expectantly.

"We all know both the AG and the DC are artificially created. Neither species can self-replicate."

"I was kinda wondering about that myself," Rhi said, looking at Tara. "When you said you were a child when you were found, it kinda confused me."

"DC are normally gestated to full adulthood, but it's not unheard of for them to be brought out as children for special services," Perth said.

"So, there is a Junior DC running around out there somewhere with little tiny AUGs?" Rhi asked.

"No," Perth said. "No, little tiny AUGs," he managed with a straight face.

"What are you getting at Turin?" I asked, a sneaking suspicion suddenly filling my mind.

"It is standard practice to terminate any DC we capture," Perth said.

"That's a bit cold-hearted," Rhi said.

"It has been our experience that no DC has ever willingly joined us, just the opposite, actually," Turin said.

"We lost several of our numbers learning this hard truth," Perth said. "Behemoth's programming is absolute."

"But you let me live," Tara said.

"I remember now," I said, recalling the fuzzy scene from before. "They did something to Tara when we were first captured."

"Yes," Perth said. "It's standard procedure to neutralize the override link to Behemoth and to do a full body scan for traps or explosives."

"And you found something," I said. It was a statement, not a question.

Turin made a series of gestures in the air and a 3D image of Tara appeared floating before us. We saw organs and veins and all manner of things only a doctor ever needs to see. Turin made another gesture and the image expanded on Tara's abdomen again and again, passing through levels of tissue until a tiny spec appeared, pulsing slightly.

"Tara is pregnant," Perth said.

We were all stunned into silence and no one moved for several moments.

"But I thought—" James started.

I finished for him, "Vampires are infertile. We don't produce anything living."

"So are Daemons," Perth said. "But nonetheless, this child has the genetic markers of both James and Tara."

I didn't see it, but I heard the impact of the blow as Rhi hit James in the shoulder so hard he went over sideways.

"You knocked up my wife!?!" Rhi bellowed.

I honestly couldn't tell what Rhi was feeling. I couldn't tell if she was truly angry or just joking with him. But the longer James lay on the ground, unmoving, the more concerned I became. "James?"

"Oh, get up, you big baby," Rhi said, then turned to Tara and started whispering to her.

James was lying on the ground in stunned silence. I shifted him back up to a sitting position and he seemed to come out of it.

"Why does my arm hurt?" James asked, rubbing his arm.

"You OK?" I asked, ignoring the comment.

"I think so?" he said.

"So, what does this mean?" I asked Perth.

"We don't know. It's unprecedented. We have no idea on gestation, or nutritional requirements, or—"

"What is it?" Tara asked quietly.

"We don't know," Perth said apologetically.

"Is it human or vampire or what?" I asked.

Perth looked uncomfortable. "We can't tell at this point.

Genetic sampling is inconclusive."

"What do you mean inconclusive?" Rhi snapped.

"We've been monitoring Tara since your arrival. The genetic makeup of the child seems to be in flux," Perth said.

"In flux?" I said flatly.

"It's different every time we examine it," Perth said. "It's really quite extraordinary."

"Well, you can stop poking and prodding my wife any time now," Rhi said protectively.

"Oh, our examination is quite unobtrusive. We simply monitor the data stream available from your machines," Perth said.

"Well—" Rhi started.

Rhi! I reined her in, and surprisingly, it worked.

Perth looked at us a moment before continuing.

"We've also noted Behemoth seems to be recruiting heavily from one particular Bio-Hab instead of—"

"Wait," I interrupted. "You can't just drop that kind of bombshell on us and move on to the next topic."

"I can't?" Perth asked.

"No, we need time to digest this. There's no way we're going to be thinking about anything else you might have to say," I said, exasperated.

"Yeah," Rhi added.

"Oh, well, I didn't want to waste what little time—" Perth explained.

"For this," I interrupted Perth again, "We'll make time."

∞∞∞∞Ω∞∞∞∞

<u>SHAE</u>

"So, should we make a break for it?" James asked for the umpteenth time.

"No, now relax," I told James firmly. I swear, the man had an itchy trigger finger.

We'd retreated to the far side of the clearing for some

semblance of privacy. I doubted this distance meant anything as we were still in the same room as Perth and his people. There was only holographic dirt between us at the moment.

"You OK?" Rhi asked Tara, who was looking understandably shaken.

"No idea," Tara said.

"Tara, have you noticed anything different in your body since Houston?" I asked.

"No, nothing," Tara said, shaking her head.

I didn't know much about Daemon's internal workings aside from the little bit of "hands-on" we shared at Drakes.

"Would you even be able to tell?" Rhi asked.

Tara just shrugged.

"OK, let's all take a minute just to calm down and think about this," I said, trying to get my own breathing under control.

"How do we know they're not lying?" James asked.

"Because they would have killed her already," Rhi said.

"That's what they're telling us. How do we know," James started.

"James, we don't know anything. And you're not helping with the speculation," I told him.

"I'm just saying," James said.

"Just...don't, OK?" I asked firmly.

James nodded and promptly shut up. He had a point, and I couldn't fault him for that. But his wild speculation wasn't helping. It was feeding the chaos.

"So, If Tara isn't pregnant, what would we do?" I asked, looking around our group.

"We were going to listen and see where this goes," Tara said.

"Right. And if you are pregnant, what would we do?" I asked.

Everyone looked at one another.

"There's nothing we can do about it, right? So, we listen and see where this goes," I sighed. "It wasn't a hard question, folks."

"So, just go back over there? What was the point of coming over here?" James asked.

"To give us a minute to collect ourselves. That was a pretty big shock and we were all affected," I said and turned to Tara.

"You OK for now?"

"I still have no idea," Tara said honestly.

"I know this is hard, but for the moment, try to push this to the side until we're out of here and safe," I said. Then I leaned in and hugged Tara. "We'll figure this out. Try not to worry."

We stayed like that for a long moment before breaking.

"OK, everybody ready to head back?" I asked. When everyone nodded, I led us back to Perth. Once we were all seated again, Perth started talking.

"To continue," Perth said as if he hadn't been interrupted. "We've noticed Behemoth has been heavily recruiting from your Bio-Hab. This started not long after you came here."

"Our Bio-Hab was under attack by the undead," I said. "There's probably not a lot of choice left, so Behemoth's recruiting as quickly as it can," I offered.

"Undead..." Perth seemed to lose his train of thought.

"The Doba," one of the other AG offered.

"Ah, yes. Unfortunate, and I must apologize," Perth said.

"Apologize?" James asked.

"Yes. As you probably know, no army is ever fully united. There are always factions who don't agree on goals or tactics. The AG are no different. While we have a common purpose, to defeat Behemoth, we are all Daemons of different backgrounds. Most of us have banded together to fight, but there are several outlier groups who fight this war their own way," Perth said.

"What are you talking about?" Tara asked.

"There is a faction who use The Doba as a means to cleanse Bio-Habs," Perth shook his head. "We don't condone it. As a matter of fact, we're openly opposed to it but we lack the ability to stop them when they make these terrorist attacks."

"Wait," Rhi held out her hand. "Are you telling me this faction infected our world with the zombie virus?"

"I'm afraid so," Perth said solemnly. "The faction feels we can't win against Behemoth, so instead, goes after Behemoth's 'crops', AKA Bio-Hab natives. Yours is not the first, and sadly, probably not the last."

Rhi and James looked at me incredulous.

"They destroy planets as a means to fight Behemoth?" I

asked in stunned silence.

"They're going all PETA on us," Rhi said.

"What?" James asked.

"You know, the crazies in PETA who believe the whole 'if you don't stop keeping dogs as pets, then we'll kidnap them and kill them so they're no longer slaves' bit," Rhi said.

"What kind of thinking is that?" Tara asked.

"The crazy kind?" Rhi offered. "But wait, you said Behemoth created the zombie plague."

"This is true, and Behemoth still uses this 'plague,' as you call it. The faction of which I speak has learned how to spread these plagues on uninfected worlds," Perth said.

"Dicks!" Rhi cursed.

"For what it's worth, you have my sympathies," Perth said. "But that is only one small group that does such a despicable thing. Most AG interact with the Bio-Hab residents in a much more hospitable way. They sometimes recruit, sometimes hire, barter or trade. The more contact we seem to have with a Bio-Hab, the less likely it is that The Doba are released."

"How do you keep from being detected by Behemoth?" I asked.

"We have several ways of slipping in and out as needed. But mostly, we install outposts on Bio-Habs and communicate our needs through them. We have fairly powerful communication lines."

"Are there any other 'factions' we need to be wary of?" Rhi asked.

Perth looked genuinely uncomfortable.

"Well...yes. There is another group who tried unsuccessfully to abduct your group a while back," Perth said.

"What? When? Why?" James asked.

"It was the day you had your gate displacement. The culprits were attempting to divert you to a location of their choosing but couldn't completely defeat Behemoth's safety protocols. This resulted in you being separated."

"Separated?" James barked. "I got tossed two weeks from Behemoth in deep space!"

James, I sent to him. He looked at me and looked as if he

were physically restraining himself from speaking.

"I'm trying to be upfront and honest with you, at least as much as I can," Perth said. "Our forces are not the...well...you must understand. We've been fighting this war so long that we must take whatever help we can get. Some of us have been so gravely wounded in this war that they seek retribution more than anything else."

"That's understandable," I said, drawing looks from everyone, including Perth.

"It is?" Perth asked.

"These people have been at war their whole lives. When you live under those conditions for that long, what you think is acceptable behavior isn't going to be the same as someone who's lived their life in relative safety. It's understandable," I nodded. "It doesn't mean I agree with it, just that I can understand where it comes from."

"Well, we've all been at war a long time. And it doesn't mean I agree with them either," Perth said. "The whole point of this is to protect Behemoth as a whole, including those on Bio-Habs. Otherwise, what's the point?"

"So, if those other guys failed to capture us, how did you end up doing it?" James asked.

"Careful study. Our agents have been following every move you make, either through direct intelligence gathering or through more passive means. Once we learned what your group liked, we created an environment we thought you'd frequent."

"The bar," I said and shook my head. "I knew I should have followed orders."

"Yes, your group showed a tendency to enjoy its rebellious nature, so we took that into account," Perth said.

"Wait, our bar?" Rhi asked.

"Looks like we're finding a new watering hole, Rhi," James said.

"Man, I liked that place," Rhi whined.

"That would be for the best," Perth said. "Once we've used a gate somewhere, Behemoth will eventually find it. While we never returned to the same place twice, you may find yourself with unwanted attention from Behemoth for being there."

"So again, why us?" I asked.

"James aside, we always need help. For as long as we've been fighting this war, we have a very finite number of able hands. Unlike Behemoth, we don't have unlimited resources to replenish our depleted ranks. So, we've resorted to proxy forces.

"If we fail in recruiting you, maybe hearing our side of the story may open your eyes. While you may not end up an ally, perhaps you won't be our enemy. It's the best we can do," Perth said.

"Why not just kill us?" Tara asked.

"Do you wish us to?" Perth asked.

"No," Tara replied.

"Removing you from the equation permanently closes that avenue. If there's one thing my people have learned, we need more opportunities, not less," Perth said.

"As another sign of good faith, we've given you the ability to cloak your embedded tracking devices," Perth said.

"Our what?" James said.

"The machines in your body allow Behemoth to track your location. You will now be able to disable these as you need to. Before you ask, we cannot remove them. It would raise too many questions with Behemoth," Perth said. "And that type of machine can be reintroduced easily by Behemoth."

"But turning them off won't?" Tara asked.

"It will generate a signal that will basically ghost your beacon, making it appear you are still in the location you were at when you deactivated your tracker. It is not perfect, but it's the best we can do with what we have at the moment. I would recommend activating it in your quarters, for example, so it looks as if you're resting. When you return to your quarters, you can reactivate your tracker. It's not the most reliable technology, so I would use it sparingly," Perth said.

"What else?" James asked.

"There is nothing else," Perth said. "I've told you our side of the conversation. That was truly all we brought you here to do. We'll return you to where you came from now, if you wish. Or you can stay and help us, your choice."

"If we go back, how can we contact you if we need to?" I

asked.

"There are ways, mostly indirect, but possible," Perth said.
The four of us looked at one another for a long moment.

A Quiet Moment

SHAE

"There's no way that was some sort of dream," Rhi said as she took another sip of her breakfast.

We'd all woken in our beds without any memory of how we got there. After Perth offered us the choice, we'd come up with more questions. Perth had spoken with us at length, both answering questions and creating new ones before we chose to return.

Now, we were sitting around a small table in our quarters, trying to figure out what had happened.

"That's a given," James said. "The question is, what was true and what was them just trying to coerce us?"

"One thing's for sure," I began. "They have the ability to mess with our minds just as much as Behemoth."

This caused everyone to pause and consider the ramifications.

"That does make things more difficult," Tara said finally. "But they didn't ask us to do anything; they just provided us with information."

"Or misinformation," Rhi muttered.

"Regardless, we've still got a patrol today, so let's get to it, shall we?" I said.

My own thoughts were still a jumble, but I knew sitting around stewing in it wasn't going to get us anywhere. Maybe getting "out" would help us clear our heads.

The day was thankfully uneventful. I had been worried everyone would have been too distracted to act properly if something would have happened. As I'd learned, hesitation could be catastrophic.

After a week of nothing happening, our group started to relax a bit. We hadn't forgotten what happened, it just seemed nothing was going to happen right away because of it.

Rhi disappeared with Tara one evening, leaving James and me on our own for once.

"I still don't get why you like this," James said, looking down at my bare feet.

We were in one of the recreational park habitats, an immense room consisting of nothing more than dirt, grass and trees. The "sky" was dusk, but stars were already burning brightly even though the sun appeared to have just dipped below the horizon. The air was full of the sound of insects, but it had to be artificial, as I'd never seen a bug here.

I was holding my boots over my shoulder with one hand and holding his hand with the other. "What, you don't like the feel of the cool soil between your toes every once and again?"

"No, not really," he said, stopping and wiping the dirt from between his toes. "It feels weird."

"It helps clear my head," I smiled, a warm feeling forming in my chest that spread to my face. I tended to forget how nice these "simple" moments could be. It always seemed we were running from one catastrophe to another. We never seemed to have time for this sort of thing.

"What are you smiling about?" James asked, catching the look on my face.

"Oh, just thinking," I said.

"Uh oh," he said. "What about?"

"The future," I said.

"The future?" James asked, looking puzzled.

"Yeah, you know, when things settle down and we can have a nice long stretch of peace for a change. Seems ever since we got back together, we've barely had two minutes to breathe, let alone relax."

"It's been my experience that life is just one long stretch of brushfires," James said.

"How do you mean?" I asked.

"Well, you have these all-important emergencies that just

have to get taken care of. Then, if you're lucky, you have a lull followed by another problem that has to be dealt with right now and so on and so forth." James made a twirling motion with his hands.

"What about the in-between times?" I asked.

"During that time, you're trying to ensure you don't cause a brushfire," James smiled.

"You're just a bright ray of sunshine tonight, aren't you?" I joked, pulling him to me for a quick kiss.

"That's why you love me: my sunny disposition," he smiled and kissed me back.

We walked in silence for a while after that.

"What the hell are we going to do with a kid?" James suddenly burst out.

"That's not exactly a brushfire we can put out," I surmised.

"No kidding. But seriously, a kid? A baby is an insane amount of work and dedication," he said in true panic.

"This is true," I said, then kept quiet as James seemed to want to get something off his chest. Unfortunately, as all men do, he took my silence to mean something else.

"Have you ever had a kid? I mean, you were old enough before...you know," James squirmed.

"Oh yes, I've had several," I said matter-of-factly. His look was priceless, but I kept a straight face.

"You...you have?" A bit of color seemed to drain from his face. "Why haven't you said something?"

"Oh, it's no big deal. They're cute and cuddly and all, but they smell and don't taste very good."

"Kids...don't...taste...good?" James stopped walking.

I finally relented and put him out of his misery.

"James, a kid is a baby goat."

"Wha...wait, what?" he said.

"A baby goat...they call them kids." I chuckled as it took a minute for him to catch up.

"You knew what I meant!" he grumbled.

"Yes, yes. No, I haven't had children. I've been around a few, but nothing like we're talking about," I said, then after seeing the look on his face, "You nervous?"

"Of course I'm nervous, I'm fucking terrified! I've never had a kid...a child before," James corrected.

I had to stifle a laugh at his correction. "I'm pretty sure none of us have James, relax."

"I mean, having a child is one thing. Then you add in this little..." James started flailing his hands around.

"Harem," I filled in for him.

"What?" he asked.

"The technical term would be a harem." The look on his face soured. "Friends with benefits?" I added helpfully.

"Regardless, it's...weird," he finished lamely.

I sat down on a small grassy rise overlooking part of the park and pulled him down next to me.

"It's true; our situation is unusual, to say the least. But the word weird seems to be your motto," I said, staring off towards the horizon.

After a few quiet moments, James continued.

"Are you jealous?" he asked.

"No." The question caught me off guard and I snapped a response. Then my mind started thinking about it, but my mouth continued.

"No, of course not." But was I? I mean, children had never been an issue when it came to vampires. The closest we ever got was creating new vampires. Was I jealous that Tara could have children with my James?

I stopped, not because of the children part, but because that was the first time I'd ever caught myself being possessive. But it was true. He was mine; I was his. That's kind of what being married is all about, right? Not that we were married yet or anything.

Thankfully James butted in just then as my head was starting to hurt.

"They say it takes a village to raise a child and all, but I don't think they meant the four of us," James scratched his head.

"We don't even know if she really is pregnant. Maybe they lied about that," I offered.

"Do you believe that?" he asked.

"No, not really." I sighed. "But there's not much we can do

about it right now. For all we know, it'll be three years till she gives birth."

"You think Behemoth knows?" James asked.

I thought about it. "I don't know. They did say you seem to be a monkey wrench."

James made obnoxious monkey sounds.

"Yes, you're my little monkey boy," I said, patting him on the cheek. I didn't have a lot of experience dating men, or women for that matter. But I've been around enough men to realize they never really grow up. Even once they're grown and "old," there's always a little boy hiding in there somewhere if you look hard enough.

The cool grass felt good on my toes as I ran my feet through it and just enjoyed the calmness of the park. After a minute, James nudged me.

"You still awake?" he asked.

"Yes." I hadn't realized I'd closed my eyes. "I like it here," I said after a minute.

"It is nice," James said.

"Sure beats the apocalypse we were in," I said.

James nodded. "Yeah, but then again, we had Taco Bell at home."

"Not when we left," I countered.

"Well, sure, but there was the memory of Taco Bell," James sighed.

"I have no idea what you saw in that place. I tried it once; it was just blah," I shook my head.

"You didn't grow up on it. It may have just been blah, but it was nostalgic blah for me," James said.

"Speaking of nostalgia, how are you doing? You still missing your family?" I asked.

James had talked to me a few times about how he was worried about his friends and family back home. Since we weren't allowed contact, we had no idea how they were. Apparently, Behemoth felt that us even looking in on them would be a bad idea. We might see something we didn't like and go AWOL or something.

"Of course, but there's not really anything I can do about it.

So, I'm treating this as if I were deployed back in the sandbox again," James said.

"Weren't you allowed mail and such when you were deployed?" I asked.

"Most of the time. But there were still times when everything was shut off for this reason or that. I'm pretending it's one of those times," James said.

I looked at him sympathetically. I had a few friends back home, but they were the type where it was normal for decades to go by without seeing them. When we would meet up, it was as if no time had passed. Those types of friends helped when you lived as long as we did. I did miss Shelby, though; I always missed her.

"What else could I do?" James asked. "Did I tell you Miria was pregnant?"

"What?" I asked, surprised.

"Yeah, when we went into Austin to find Natalie, Miria had asked me to find her some home pregnancy tests. She and Richard had been trying before Z Day kicked off. Apparently, they succeeded." James glanced at his chrono. "I am probably an Uncle by now," James sighed.

"I was never big on family. But, when your family starts to shrink, it makes you rethink your priorities." James stared off into the night.

I patted his hand and smiled. James was just unloading, not looking for conversation. Sometimes, I found it best to let him have his thoughts.

I caught the sound of someone else. They were a long way off and not heading towards us. Probably another couple just enjoying a quiet evening. But, this new military training had me thinking it might be something nefarious.

"I'd prefer not to be in this military or whatever it is," I said.

"I'm not a big fan either. Don't get me wrong, soldiering comes easy for me. It's just that this service is way too confusing," James said.

"Even more so now," I agreed. "But..."

"But?" he said.

"But, is it more or less confusing with the other side of the story added in?" I asked.

James appeared to think about it for a while. "I mean, the AG story seems to make more sense. But is that because I want to believe it?"

"Why would you want to believe it?" I asked him.

"It's big brother; he never stays good for long and always goes bad in the end," James said.

"Says who?" I said.

"Every story, movie, and TV show I've ever seen," he said.

"You do realize movies are make-believe right?" I mused.

"Every story has a basis, in fact, somewhere. Nothing can be alive that long and not lose a few marbles somewhere along the way," James said.

"Says who? Star Trek?"

"Actually..." James started.

"No, just stop." I grinned. Once he got started on sci-fi shows, it took him a while to get it out of his system.

"But seriously, it would just be 'natural' if it went bad. It's what we'd expect. If nothing ever went wrong with Behemoth, it would be creepy," he said.

I shrugged as a comfortable silence fell between us. I'm not sure how long the quiet lasted. I just knew my eyes were closed again the next time he spoke.

"Do you want to get married?" James asked.

My surprised expression must have startled him as he started to back-pedal before I laid my hand on his.

"Of course," I said honestly.

"Now?" he asked, his voice nervous.

"Well, maybe not right this minute," I mused causing him to roll his eyes. "Why now?"

"It's...it's just what we were talking about earlier."

"Which part?" I asked.

"The future. I started thinking about our future and all the insane things that keep coming into our lives. Maybe we should get married now, during one of the 'quiet' moments."

"You call this a quiet moment?" I asked.

"You know what I mean," he said.

"While we have the chance, you mean?" I spoke what I knew

was going through his head.

"Well...yeah. I mean, we're already married if you ask me, but making it official seems like it would be our next step," James said.

I stared at him for a minute, giving him my best amused expression.

"What?" James asked.

"You're such a girl," I laughed.

"Am not," he said defensively.

"Are too. You want to wear the dress at the ceremony, don't you?" I teased.

"Shut up," he said as he put on one of his rare displays of blushing.

I touched his cheek gently, running my thumb over his lip. "I'd love to marry you. But what about your family?"

"We can record it." He grinned. "I want you as my wife," he said, his voice becoming serious. "I don't want something else to get in the way."

"OK," I felt something start to burn deep inside me as I said the word.

"OK?" He grinned like an idiot.

I nodded, "Yes, let's get married."

The Range is Hot

SHAE

The next day, Rhi and I were on the range.

"I'm totally getting Elvis to play at your wedding." Rhi grinned like an idiot.

"Uh-huh," I said, automatically dismissing the comment before reconsidering. "Works for me. How's Tara doing?" I said as I discharged the pistol, knocking down a target.

"Bout as well as you could expect," Rhi said, double-tapping her target, then a second. "How's James holding up?"

"Dazed and confused, like most newly expectant fathers," I said. "He's still going through his whole 'tired of war and fighting and killing bit.'"

"He's still doing that?" Rhi shook her head. "I thought he'd realized he actually likes all that stuff and was just getting bogged down by a bunch of bullshit in his head," Rhi said.

"He's resolved to just 'get it over with' at this point," I said.

"I swear, James is like the puppy of our group, you know? Just too cute to kick," Rhi said. "Even if he pisses on the carpet, you just want to cuddle him, not scold him."

"Well, he's housetrained now, so...wait, where were we going with this?" I asked.

"Don't ask me; I stopped thinking about it with the puppy talk," Rhi said.

We were doing our mandatory weekly firearms training in one of Behemoth's training rooms. The range wasn't one of those dark, loud caves like I'd been to in the past. This one was in a lush, dense forest.

The pistols we were using were the standard-issue sidearms

built into our warskins. They fired some sort of galvanized plasma or some such. I didn't have any idea how it worked. I just knew that when I hit something, it was destroyed. That plus it was quiet enough that not only did we not need ear protection; we could have a conversation while shooting.

The course was relatively simple. We take a walk through the forest and engage any enemies we come across. Since all the targets were controlled by Behemoth, they could appear anywhere, regardless of where we walked. We'd know the training scenario was over when Behemoth provided us an exit.

"Yeah, well, I'm not far behind James when it comes to the ankle biter. It's not like I can pick up a preggo book at the local bookstore. I mean, could you imagine the title? "What to expect when your pregnant alien wife is expecting your vampire baby," Rhi said.

"Doesn't really roll off the tongue now, does it?" I said, shooting at another target and missing but getting it with the second shot.

"I mean, what section would it even be under? Health? Sci-Fi? Horror?" Rhi growled as she suddenly let loose with a stream of shots that managed to cut both her target and the tree it was hiding behind in half.

I paused, putting a hand on Rhi's arm. "What about you?"

"Me? I'm good to go," Rhi said in a voice filled with false casualness.

I nodded at the felled tree. "Really?"

"What that? I'm just blowing—"

"Off steam. Yeah, exactly," I said

I watched as Rhi holstered her pistol and stretched, rolling her shoulders. She'd been walking in a modified crouch, something James had shown her. He'd shown me the same thing, but after thirty seconds or so, my back hurt so bad I couldn't do it anymore.

So, my "combat style" was simply strolling. Rhi had originally scoffed at me, but after the third time I saw her rubbing her back, she'd taken to strolling more often than not.

Rhi made a big show of checking her gear but didn't say anything.

"We've been together what, going on a year now? You don't think by now I know most of your tells? Talk to me. What's going on in that brain of yours?" I asked.

"Ahhh, you should stay out of my nugget. There's enough in here already to make it crowded," Rhi grinned, tapping her temple.

"You are not the same woman who followed James and me home that night. You know that, right?" I looked at her appraisingly.

"Knock that crap off. If you want me, you know you can have me. You don't have to butter me up," Rhi said.

I rolled my eyes. "That's not what I was talking about, and you know it, now quit avoiding the topic. How are you doing?"

Rhi seemed to sag, "I'm a hot mess, Shae. I mean, I put on my shoes before I put on underwear this morning."

"I've-" I tried, but Rhi cut me off.

"I brushed my teeth with toothpaste last night," Rhi said.

"Where did you get toothpaste?" I asked. Normally, you just placed the probe into your mouth for a few seconds, and it took care of everything. There was no brushing and certainly no toothpaste, but Rhi didn't seem to hear me.

"Then I—" Rhi continued.

I listened to her get it all off her chest until she finally wound down.

"And you know that never tastes good!" Rhi finally finished. She stopped then and looked around, seeming to realize she'd been ranting for a while now. "I'm sorry, Shae, I don't know where that came from."

Without thinking about it, I holstered my pistol and closed the distance between us before hugging her. It was a natural feeling for me, one I hadn't hesitated to do.

Rhi just stood still, not moving, not hugging me back for a moment. Then her arms came up and embraced me.

I pulled back enough to look up at her. "It's alright, Rhi; we all need to let it out sometimes."

Rhi cocked her head at me questioningly as we held onto one another. "That's those 'mom' instincts of yours kicking in again, isn't it?"

"Don't start with that again. Now I wish I never would have taken you with me in Houston," I frowned.

"Yeah, but you did. This is what happens when you look after a house full of man-children for that long," Rhi grinned. "I can't wait to see how you act when we have a rug rat running around here."

I grinned back at her. "You do know I love you, right?" My hands moved to her shoulders and shook her gently when she didn't respond.

"I...uh...yeah." Rhi finally responded.

I could see the turmoil in her eyes and smiled before leaning in and kissing her softly. A moment later, I broke the kiss.

"We're supposed to care for each other, silly," I said, touching her face with gentle fingers. "Our own baggage tends to get in the way and make it hard for people to care about us. You just have to learn to get out of the way."

"I don't..." Rhi seemed to be having a hard time understanding me, which was OK. Sometimes I didn't make sense to myself.

"I am surprised you haven't been talking to Tara about all this, though," I said.

It took Rhi a moment to mentally shift gears.

"She's already got too much on her plate. Not to mention, she doesn't understand half of what I'm talking about, and I'm usually too wound up to stop and explain. Easier to bottle it up and forget about it."

"Because you know that's healthy, she says to the resident psychologist of our group." I grinned.

"Yeah, yeah," Rhi waved off, drawing her pistol. The simulation began again, targets appearing at random.

We walked in relative silence for a while, shooting what needed to be shot.

"You ever think about quitting?" Rhi asked ten minutes later.

"Quitting?" I asked.

"The Corps. Letting them wipe your memory and just going back to living in a rotting world," Rhi said.

"And waiting for it to burn to a cinder?" I asked.

"Yeah, but we wouldn't know about it," Rhi said.

"I must admit, the thought has occurred to me. The whole ignorance is bliss bit. But I just can't let myself be that much of a coward," I said firmly.

"Coward?" Rhi missed her shot and turned to face me. "How do you mean coward?"

"We know it's coming. Either Behemoth or the AG are looking to wipe out our planet; it's just a matter of time. We're the only ones who can stand in the way of them, whoever they are. If we don't stop them, then it's our fault, and everybody dies. I can't turn my back on that kind of responsibility," I sighed.

"But it's not our responsibility. Both factions are responsible, not us," Rhi said. The target she missed earlier suddenly came rushing towards her. She casually pointed her pistol over her shoulder and sent it on its way with a simple "Fuck off."

I was surprised by how easy she made the shot look, and then I turned back to her.

"Now that you've met both factions, do you really have confidence in either?" I spat with more venom than I expected.

Rhi shook her head. "I don't even think they'd wipe our memories if we asked."

"What do you mean?" I asked.

"What I mean is, do you think they'd actually go through all the trouble to mindwipe us and send us home or just kill us? Which would be easier?" Rhi asked.

"That's a cheerful thought," I said.

Rhi shrugged slowly before firing off a series of shots that shattered the surrounding trees, missing every target.

"Does that help? Murdering trees?" I asked.

"They're not real trees...and yes, it does. I just wish we could do away with all of them and be done with it," Rhi said.

"Trees?" I teased.

"No, you frosty-haired bimbo, not trees. These idiot factions are warring against each other and catching us in the crossfire."

"Frosty-haired bimbo?" I asked.

"Sorry, slip of the tongue," Rhi said.

"I've heard worse," I said, stopping as a thought occurred to me.

"What is it?" Rhi asked.

"Why don't we take it to both sides?" I asked as the semblance of a plan started forming in my mind.

"Uh, because there's no way we could win," Rhi glanced at my face. "Uh oh, I've seen that look, Shae. It's usually the one on James's face right before he does something stupid," Rhi grinned at me.

I shrugged and filed it away for more thought later.

"Oh, get this," Rhi started as she reactivated the range and picked off several targets. "I overheard Tara and James having a little 'chat' earlier."

"Oh really?" I asked. Tara and James didn't spend too much time alone. Usually either Rhi or I was around, so the fact they were having a private conversation was curious.

"Yeah, they didn't know I was around and were kinda acting suspicious, so I did a little friendly eavesdropping," Rhi smiled.

"And?" I fired at something out of the corner of my eye and frowned as I vaporized some squirrel equivalent. There were a lot of different creatures on Behemoth, but they all seemed to be a variant of one thing or another I could relate to.

"The two were actually flirting shamelessly with one another," Rhi said.

"That's nothing new—" I started, then thought about it. "Actually, they haven't really been doing that lately," I said curiously.

"Right? I was thinking maybe the whole pregnancy thing was putting a damper on things," Rhi said.

"Has it, with you and Tara?" I asked, just curious.

"Are you kidding?" Rhi laughed and indicated herself. "Could you turn this down?"

"Are you flirting with me now?" I asked, grinning at her as we continued to make our way through the forest firing range.

"Maybe later. Anyway," Rhi continued. "They were just hanging out, doing a little bit of light teasing when James propositioned her."

"Really?" I was surprised. While Tara and James had flirted a lot in the past, neither of them had ever hit on one another solo. "That's new; usually, at least one of us is around when it comes up."

"Right?" Rhi said. "I think our little boy's growing up!"

I rolled my eyes.

"Anyway, he makes a move, and it's adorable, by the way. But here's what nearly killed me. Instead of saying yes, Tara turns him down!" Rhi said.

"Really?" Again, I was surprised. Usually, we were all pretty accepting of propositions. I couldn't recall the last time one of us said no to any of the others.

"Yeah," Rhi laughed, tried to speak, and laughed again.

"What?" I glanced at her.

"She told him that not only was the last time really messy but that he got her pregnant, and she didn't want to get double pregnant!" Rhi started belly laughing.

I stopped and started laughing as well, having to pause the program. After a minute, we'd both recovered enough to continue.

"Please tell me you've had 'the talk' with her," I said.

"Oh yeah. James acted like a gentleman and didn't push her at all, even though I could tell he was a bit confused."

"Yeah, James has never been the kind of guy to press," I said.

"That's good 'cause I was laughing so hard I wouldn't have been able to step in and give him the 'quit trying to fuck my wife, no means no,' conversation. Anyway, as soon as he left, I pulled Tara aside and explained a few things. Granted, I doubt she can get double pregnant, but you never know on Behemoth," Rhi said.

"And James's weird mojo," I added. "What did she say?"

"Not much, although she did go and jump James's bones afterward. The poor boy was so confused," Rhi smiled.

"I'll talk to him. But...what about the messy part? I think I remember her mentioning that once before." I chuckled.

"I taught her how to have fun with that part," Rhi said slyly.

"Oh really?" I glanced at her, and she winked at me. "Why am I not surprised?" Then, a thought occurred to me. "You don't think he can get us pregnant, do you?"

"Nah, he—" Then Rhi stopped and looked at me with an expression of horror.

"What?"

"I don't want to have to start using condoms, Shae," Rhi said with all seriousness.

I held it in as long as I could before bursting out laughing. I couldn't help it; the look of dread on her face was just too much.

"I really don't think you have to worry about it," I said.

Rhi let out a long sigh, "Thank goodness."

"Besides, could you imagine what a Behemoth condom would be like? All high-tech and futuristic?" I asked.

"It would probably talk to you, give you disease indicators or probabilities of insemination and shit," Rhi chuckled.

"I don't want to know what it would tell you if you tried the backdoor," I shook my head.

"Probably your fiber count!" Rhi laughed.

"How'd we get here?" I asked, chuckling along with the strange turn in conversation. You never knew where you'd end up with Rhi, but it was usually entertaining.

"It could probably tell you that, too," Rhi chuckled.

Self-Love

SHAE

"It was a lovely wedding," Beth said, taking another bite of what appeared to be some sort of strawberry shortcake.

"It was, wasn't it?" I said, smiling at the thought still fresh in my mind from last night.

Beth and I were now having weekly lunch dates at the café I'd taken her to a few months back. This time, the cafe appeared on a small outcropping of rock at the center of a lake that appeared to be within an extinct volcano. It was night, and a gorgeous nebula lined the sky above us, making the night air seem that much crisper.

"How'd you get She-Elvis to officiant the ceremony?" Beth asked.

"No idea, ask Rhi. That was all her idea. But she was good, wasn't she?" I said.

"I was so surprised. I was worried at first, I mean, She-Elvis? Really? But when she recited that bible verse, it brought me to tears," Beth cracked a smile.

I smiled. Watching Beth show that kind of emotion in public galvanized my resolve to bring Beth back into the human world proper.

"Well, hearing you sing brought James to tears, so..."

I don't know who did it or how, but Beth sang during our little reception. It wasn't something over the top and loud like the music she'd been known for so long ago. Instead, it was something soft, simple and short. I'd never heard the song before but James told me later it was a one-off song that had never been officially released. Only unofficial bootlegs existed

236

of it. He'd been shocked to hear it. I'd been shocked to hear Beth sing at all. It hadn't been planned.

Beth just shook her head, "It was nothing."

I had been gentle in my attempts to bring Beth out of her "shell" in our past luncheons and now I felt it was time to take some bigger steps.

"You know, I was thinking. What would you think of having dinner with the girls and me tomorrow?" I asked.

Beth hesitated, "The girls?"

"Tara and Rhi," I said.

"I...I mean Tara, sure, but I don't think Rhi would want to," Beth said.

"Rhi doesn't hate you," I said, knowing Beth was talking about Rhi's attitude towards Beth's command. "She just likes to buck authority. Besides, she did ask you to dance with her at the bachelorette party."

The party in question had been held at some weird dance club where colors dictated your mood or some such. Beth had resolutely refused to dance and camped out at our table all night. The fact Beth had come out with us at all had been a small miracle. I'd called in a favor in getting Rhi to ask Beth to dance.

"I actually did feel bad for...James." Beth said his name, causing me to look up from my plate. "I mean, he didn't have anyone for a bachelor party after all."

"Oh, I know for a fact Rhi took care of that duty," I grinned.

"I don't even want to know." Beth just shook her head and took another bite. "But..."

"But?" I asked.

"I don't understand...the four of you...together. How does that even work?" Beth asked reluctantly.

"Not the first time I've heard that one," I smiled.

"I mean, don't you get jealous?" Beth asked.

"They're my family," I started.

"That doesn't make it any better." Beth grimaced.

I sighed. "I love them." I shrugged. "I can't help it. Jealousy? Sure, if I thought there was a malicious bone in their bodies towards 'us.' I've seen open and even group relationships in my time. It kind of comes with the territory when you live so long.

Things kinda change...well, your perspective of the world changes. The whole big picture thing comes in," I said.

"I'm sensing a but in there somewhere," Beth said.

"But what the four of us share is something unlike anything I've heard of before," I said.

"What do you mean?" Beth asked.

"It's hard to explain, and when I try, it just sounds weird," I said.

Beth stared at me, waiting.

I gave her one of my traditional sighs. "It's like being in love with yourself."

Beth cocked her head at me.

"See? I've heard it called a gestalt, whatever that is. It's like the four of us are really only one person, just split. We all seem to go together, no matter how we fit."

"Weird," Beth grinned.

I groaned in frustration, "See!"

"But...don't you still get jealous?" Beth said.

"How can you get jealous of yourself?" I offered, the words feeling as weird coming out of my mouth as they sounded.

Beth took a sip of her drink before saying, "Sounds like masturbation if you ask me."

I put my head down on the table.

"I'm just teasing," Beth said, touching my arm in a rare display.

I looked up at her with a frown.

Beth giggled and sat back.

"I see you've gotten adventurous and tried real food again," I said.

"Yeah. There's just something about ripe strawberries; only the real thing will do," Beth said, holding up one of the red delicacies.

Beth had started eating real food with me about two weeks ago, much to my surprise. There were so many little things about Beth that seemed to be bringing her back to "normal" but I was afraid to say anything for fear of jinxing it.

"So? Dinner tomorrow?" I asked.

"Fine, I'll come since it'll just be you, you, and you." Beth

238

sighed dramatically.

"Oh, shut up, you asked!" I muttered.

"Wait, tomorrow? You'll be on your honeymoon tomorrow. You went through all that trouble to get the rest of the week off. Don't tell me you're canceling it?" Beth asked.

"Oh, no. We're still going, but it's only a practice room away. Even though our place will be in the middle of nowhere, we're still practically across the hall from our quarters," I said.

"But...won't you be wanting to spend all your time with...him? Isn't that the point of a honeymoon?" Beth frowned.

"Beth, we're realists now. That was kinda the whole reason for the wedding. We're not putting things off for the 'perfect' time anymore. That includes time for our friends," I said as I reached out and squeezed her hand. Surprisingly, she didn't flinch.

"Hey, it's your R&R. If you want to spend it with me instead of your new husband, who am I to say no?" Beth said. Then she glared at me, "This isn't some attempt to get me in your harem, is it?" Beth said with a hint of humor, which also surprised me.

"Trust me, this," I gestured between us. "Is just friendship." I chuckled.

"Yeah, right. I've seen how your 'friends' treat each other," Beth rolled her eyes.

∞∞∞∞Ω∞∞∞∞

SHAE

The house was lovely. It sat on a small hill overlooking a mountain lake surrounded by forest. It was somewhere, I'd imagine was hidden away in the Alaskan wilderness or something.

The house was relatively small, with just two bedrooms and a den/kitchen area. It had basic amenities I'd expect back home but with some Behemoth magic concealed away for convenience.

Of course, since we were living in a training room, we could change any parameter we wanted at a moment's notice.

It had been James's idea. He said he'd see it on a TV show or something. I didn't care, it was amazing. I'd arranged to get the time off and commandeered the training room. When I told Beth it was right across the hall from our quarters, I wasn't kidding. I could be back in our squad room in a dozen steps if I needed to.

Arranging the time off had not been as tricky as I expected. I told my group commander that I wanted a week of downtime to work on inner-squad dynamics, and she'd approved it without question. She told me to take as long as needed. She'd rotate in a squad to cover for us. I wasn't about to argue, so I just thanked her and got out of there before she changed her mind.

Beth had said that part had been unusual. Most Chosen Army couldn't just take a week off, let alone with no notice. It seemed we were golden children or something, and I wasn't complaining.

I was sitting on the porch, admiring how the sun was setting behind the mountains, when James emerged from the house and sat next to me. He wrapped a blanket around us and his arm around me. He didn't say anything; he just sat watching the sunset with me.

The lake was a perfect calm, creating a mirror for the darkening sky as the stars emerged. Soon, the darkness was complete, and the Milky Way stretched out above us. We didn't need to say anything. We just leaned into each other and enjoyed the peace.

A long while later, James spoke up.

"Enjoying the quiet?" he asked gently.

"Uh-huh," I said. I could hear the sounds of insects and the wind gently moving through the trees while they creaked their protests. There was no sound of machinery or people. It would have been spooky if I hadn't been seeking it out for a while now.

"I remember when the world was this quiet," I whispered, not wanting to startle the quiet of our surroundings.

"I've never heard it this quiet," James said. "Normally, my tinnitus would drown it out," he chuckled.

"Our world was heading this way when we left. Kind of a

double-edged sword, you know?"

"Yeah," James chuckled. "We've been here two days now and I'm still constantly looking over my shoulder, waiting for something to go wrong."

"You're just not used to the quiet," I said.

"It has given me a chance to get to know your heartbeat," James said.

I looked at him, "What?"

"We've never been anywhere this quiet, let alone for this long. Your heartbeat is pretty much the loudest thing I hear," James said.

"You know, that was almost a sweet thing to say." I grinned in the dark.

"I'll work on it," he said and grinned back at me through the darkness.

With our eyesight, the dark wasn't a barrier.

"Wanna go for a walk?" I asked.

"Sure," he said as he stood and helped me to my feet. He wrapped the blanket around my shoulders and followed me down the steps towards the water.

We walked in silence along the water. I kept expecting to hear water lapping against the shore, but this was a lake, and it was dead calm.

The sound of gentle waves kissing the shore suddenly came to my ears. I looked at the lake, but it still had a mirror surface, reflecting the beautiful night sky. Somehow, tiny waves were now lapping at the shore with the quietest of sound.

I glanced at James.

What? he said quietly in my mind. He smiled at me and squeezed my hand. He didn't speak aloud, knowing how much I was enjoying the quiet night.

I stopped and looked down at our linked hands.

James? I asked.

Yes, luv?

Am I worth the price of admission? I asked.

James raised an eyebrow at me. *Where'd you hear that one?*

*I don't know. It came to me when I thought about

everything we've been through together. So much has changed for us in so short a time. Looking back, has it all been worth it? Have I been worth everything I've cost you?*

James's expression turned to one of annoyance.

Yeah, the whole me getting you to marry me two days ago, that was punishment for all the misery you've brought me. James frowned at me. *Where's this coming from?*

I don't know, I said honestly.

It's not like you to suddenly lose confidence in yourself, Shae. What's up? he asked.

Being here has just given me a lot of time to reflect on the past. To wonder what things might have been like if it had happened differently.

Are you unhappy with what we have? James asked, and I could feel the uneasiness in his head.

No! I said quickly and sighed. *I know I'm not making sense, I'm sorry.*

No, obviously, there's something going on in there; what's up? James tapped my head gently.

I guess...I just needed a little reassurance, I said quietly.

Cause the whole wedding ceremony was pretty ambiguous, James grinned.

Ambiguous? That's a pretty big word for you. You even used it correctly.

Yeah, just don't ask me to spell it, James chuckled.

We walked a little further in silence.

I guess things are going so well that I'm getting uneasy, I said finally.

That sounds about right for us, James said and pulled me up short. *But that was the whole reason we did this right? Trying to enjoy things while we can?*

I sighed before looking into his eyes. *Yeah,* I said, nodding slightly. *And, just for the record, you're worth the price as well.* I kissed him gently.

Well, duh, I'm all that and a bag of potato chips! James said with a big grin.

I rolled my eyes and considered throwing him into the lake.

Then I did just that.

∞∞∞∞Ω∞∞∞∞

<u>SHAE</u>

I woke to singing the next morning.

Sunlight was streaming in the windows, warming everything I touched. I started to stretch but found James still asleep next to me and froze.

His face was streaked with mud. I glanced at his hands and found mud there are well. The more I looked, the more mud I found. The bed was muddy, I was muddy, and there were muddy footprints on the floor.

It appeared our frolicking in the lake last night had left more of a mark than I thought.

The singing drew my attention again. It was coming from the kitchen.

I glanced back and found James looking towards the kitchen with his head cocked questioningly.

"Morning," I whispered and pecked his lips with mine.

"Morning," James replied. "Is that bacon?"

I hadn't noticed the scent, but sure enough, someone was cooking bacon.

"Smells like it," I said as I stood.

James quickly joined me at the door to the room.

I quietly cracked the door enough so we could both peak out.

A singing and dancing Rhi was twirling about the kitchen in nothing but an immodest apron. Apparently, she was making what looked like a breakfast feast as pots and pans littered the kitchen while piles of food were already covering the small table.

"She's got earbuds in."

The voice startled James and me. I glanced over to find Tara leaning against the other bedroom door, her arms folded and a huge grin on her face as she watched her wife. Tara was wearing a loose pair of shorts and a half-tank top that showed off her beautiful crimson skin.

"The louder her music, the more she gets into it. The fact she's singing and dancing means she can't hear anything right now," Tara said. "Morning, by the way," Tara glanced over at us, and her grin turned sly. "Looks like you two had an eventful night."

I could feel James starting to blush behind me and turned to watch Rhi continue her performance.

"I didn't know Rhi knew how to cook," I said.

"She learned in Japan. She really enjoys it, actually. She did all the cooking for us while we were back home," Tara said with some nostalgia. "Why she likes to do it nude is still a mystery to me, though. Seems dangerous," Tara said and returned to admiring her wife.

"Well, she is wearing an apron," James managed, his eyes tracking Rhi as she bounded across the kitchen.

"That just makes it worse," Tara chuckled. I could feel the amusement coming off Tara as she watched Rhi. She was practically radiating it.

"Do I want to know—" I started.

"She wanted to surprise you," Tara said.

"Well, that she did," I smiled, still watching a side of Rhi I hadn't seen before.

"She missed you," Tara said quietly.

I glanced at her and she was staring at me.

"We both did," Tara said.

Before I could say anything, James interrupted.

"OK, out of the way, I'm hungry," James said as he tried to push past me.

"Go put some clothes on!" I hissed at him.

"But Rhi isn't—" he started.

"Put some clothes on right now!" I didn't mean to, but I actually stamped my foot.

James sculked back into the room to find his clothes.

I glanced at Tara apologetically.

Surprisingly, she gave me an understanding look.

Rhi had said there was more to Tara than we knew. But even with everything we'd been through, Tara was still a private person. Of all the things we'd shared, her mind was something she'd always kept closed off to everyone but Rhi.

I trusted Tara with all our lives and looked forward to the day when she trusted me with her mind.

I ducked back into the room to grab clothes, and when James and I emerged, Rhi was still going footloose.

They're up, Tara sent to Rhi.

It didn't stop Rhi, who just threw a thumbs-up in our general direction.

We filed into the room.

Need any help? I asked Rhi.

"Nope!" Rhi yelled aloud as she continued to dance around the kitchen. "Just have a seat!"

Honey, turn down the music, Tara sent.

"Oh!" Rhi said, pulling the earbuds out of her head and tossing them on the cluttered counter.

Suddenly, the sound of Elton John's "Saturday Night's Alright For Fighting" was playing loud enough for us to hear it clearly from her earbuds.

Rhi plopped down plates full of more food than I could eat in a day in front of each of us before collapsing into an empty chair, still humming along with the song.

"So, Elton..." James started before beginning to shovel food into his face.

"What's wrong with Sir Elton?" Rhi asked with a frown.

"Oh, nothing," James said quickly. "Oh, this is good!" he quickly followed up.

Rhi's darkening expression changed to one of delight at James's compliment.

I tried the food and it was exceptional.

"This is amazing, Rhi," I offered before diving in myself.

"Just a little something I wanted to whip up for your honeymoon celebration," Rhi said brightly.

It was weird hearing Rhi speak brightly. I guess she did enjoy cooking...and dancing...naked. I glanced at James, who was having a hard time keeping his eyes off Rhi's bouncing chest. It had been creeping around the edges of her apron for a while now.

"Why don't you go put something on, dear," Tara said to

Rhi, but gave me a subtle wink.

"Huh?" Rhi hadn't seemed to remember she was pretty much naked. "Oh," she said and slipped into the spare room, James's eyes following her the whole way.

I sighed. Not because I was angry but because I knew how our group acted so well now. I grinned and shook my head. I knew when I looked over that Tara would be watching her wife leaving, just like James. I also knew Tara and James would nod at each other in mutual appreciation. I wasn't wrong.

"Don't worry, we're out of here after breakfast," Tara said when Rhi returned.

"Yup, we don't want to intrude," Rhi said.

"Any more than we already have," Tara glared at Rhi.

I was surprised that I was disappointed by the idea. The more I explored the thought, the more I didn't want them to leave. I glanced at James, but he was too busy trying not to lose any fingers in his haste to eat. But I knew what he'd say anyway.

"No," I said, giving the girls a smile. "You're not going anywhere."

"Yeah!" James mumbled around a mouthful of food.

"And apparently, you're doing the cooking from now on," Tara grinned. "Oh, and keep the apron. James apparently has a new fetish."

I chuckled as James paused and looked up, his cheeks full as a chipmunk's.

"I dunno," I added to the mix. "I kinda liked the dance routine." I threw Tara a sly wink.

This time, it was Rhi who froze, a bit of color coming to her cheeks.

Yeah...this'll work, I smiled to myself.

A Day At The Beach

SHAE

You did what? James looked at me like I'd just slapped him.

The four of us were on Ferris, a tropical Bio-Hab known for its beaches. It was one of the few worlds that was physically connected to Behemoth via a space needle. The ride down the needle was stunning as you could literally watch the view from space all the way through the layers of atmosphere.

Since Ferris was a controlled climate, the weather was normally partly cloudy 24/7. Add to this it had the most amazing cloud artists that made cloud watching almost as popular as swimming.

I got in touch with the AG, and I'm having them fake a control point site. When the DC shows up, we'll see how they react and get a better idea of who's telling us the truth.

It had been several weeks since our combined honeymoon, and things had been going rather well for us as a whole. We'd completed multiple patrols without incursion. We hadn't been kidnapped even once! And nobody else had gotten pregnant, not for lack of trying.

What happens if the DC doesn't buy it? Tara asked, sipping on a cool blue liquid inside an elaborate glass that looked like a fish, complete with moving eyes.

Why wouldn't they? I countered. *The AG say they have control of several control point sites. They know exactly what they look like and should be able to fake one easily.*

You already committed us to this? Rhi asked incredulously.

I had to. The longer we wait, the longer we could be working for the wrong side, I said.

That's not the point, Shae! You should have talked to us about this. There's a lot that can go wrong. Rhi glanced at Tara. *We can't be taking crazy chances all willy-nilly.*

Did you just say— James started.

I know what I said! Rhi snapped. *Now's not the time James!*

I...I'm sorry. I thought all of you would be on board with this. I was honestly surprised by Rhi's exclamation.

Of course we're on board with this, James said, giving Rhi a look.

Yeah, but it still would have been nice to be asked, Rhi mumbled.

"You ever wonder," Tara started, "what sort of warriors Behemoth would have been training here?"

We all stopped and looked at her.

"Well, I mean, Behemoth created all these Bio-Habs to make and train warriors who could operate in all these different types of environments, right? But look around. If you lived somewhere like this, would you even consider going to war with someone? This is a paradise."

"True," James said. "But what if you didn't own this paradise, but your neighbor did?"

"Morbid much, James?" Rhi asked.

"I think I'll swim," Tara said, again pulling our conversation away from conflict. Tara stood up from where she had been sitting on the light blue sand. She brushed her legs, and every grain of synthetic sand on her body promptly fell off as she made her way towards the water.

Rhi gave James and me both a quick glare and followed her wife out into the crystal blue surf.

"Did I—" I started, but James cut me off with a wave of his hand.

"Don't worry about it. Rhi's just being over-protective. She'll come around, don't worry," James said.

"She has been a bit touchy lately," I said.

"Lately?" James scoffed.

"OK, more so than normal," I admitted as I watched the couple frolicking in the surf. I touched my sunglasses and adjusted the tint as the sun emerged from a particularly large bank of clouds.

"This is so nice," I said as I lay back on the sand and stretched out, letting the sun warm me.

"Was never really one for the beach," James said, sliding up beside me. "Especially later on when I was spending so much time in the sand for work."

"Yeah, but you didn't have this very considerate synthetic sand that will fall off your body when you wish and not stick where it doesn't belong." I grinned.

When we first arrived, we'd tried to get James to consider enjoying some clothes-free time. But, no matter how hard we tried, James refused. He kept saying, "Oh hell no! Sunburns and sand where neither should go, no thank you!" Even when I explained about the synthetic sand, he was still a hard "Nope."

"Even after we perfected the sun-proofing skin treatments, you didn't find many vampires at the beach. I don't know if it was just the inherent fear or what. Personally, I love the sun. The beach just personifies it for me," I said.

"You just liked showing off in a swimsuit," James grinned.

"What this?" I looked down at the traditional one-piece I was wearing. Since it was from a Behemoth store, it was far from "normal," being able to change color, design and transparency at will. But I kept it simple, the way I liked it.

Rhi, on the other hand, was wearing a cross-body racerback suit that I had to admit was totally her. Tara kept with her tradition of wearing as little as possible, which today was nothing. There wasn't anyone here to offend, so we had the entire beach to ourselves as far as we could see in any direction.

James was more of a traditionalist as well, wearing simple swim shorts of a similar material as my suit. Apparently, men's swim fashion on Behemoth was as varied as the women's. Not that sex or even species limited what you could wear here. Seemed the only restrictions on fashion were the number of limbs you had, but even that had workarounds.

"I'm sure you'd say I'd look good in a paper bag." I glanced over at him.

"Well..." he started.

I rolled my eyes and turned back to the cloud art high above. I wasn't sure how the artists did it as I never saw a mechanism, but each cloud looked like something non-cloudlike. It used to be you had to use your imagination to see images in the clouds. Now, it was rare to find something that was vaguely cloud-like.

"I miss clouds," I said.

"What, you don't like your clouds in the shape of cubes or rocket ships or plants?" James said.

"Flowers belong on the ground, IN the ground. Not floating around in the sky," I said.

"You're such a traditionalist," James said.

"No, I just like what I like. That doesn't make me anything. It just means I have an opinion."

"What do you want to be when you grow up?" James asked suddenly.

"When I grow up?" I rolled onto my side to look at him. "James, I'm 300 years old. I'm not growing up; I'm growing old."

"Nonsense." He smiled and reached over to tuck one of my stray hairs behind my ear.

"You say something sappy and I'll smack you," I warned.

"We have time...for anything. So, if you could do anything, what would you want to do?" James asked.

"I dunno, never really thought about it. The last year has been pretty hectic with the whole trying to survive one apocalypse after another thing," I said. "You've obviously given this some thought. What do you want to do?"

"I want to do nothing," James said as he rolled onto his back and looked up at the rolling cloud shapes in the sky.

"Nothing? Sounds kind of...boring?" I offered.

"I just don't want to HAVE to do anything," James said.

"That's a bum, James." I grinned.

"I guess I just want the freedom to do whatever I want when I want, without having to worry about doing things I don't want to do," James rambled.

"Well sure, who doesn't? You just have to acquire that whole independently wealthy thing and you're all set. Either that or lower the quality of life you want to live," I said.

"Yeah, but all that's changed now, hasn't it? I mean, back home there are no more wealthy people anymore."

"I don't know James. What we had set up was pretty wealthy by the standards at the time," I said.

"You know what I mean. Besides, who says we'll ever go back there anyway?" James said.

"What do you mean?" I asked.

"Well, we're here because we're on watch. The whole price of freedom is eternal vigilance thing. Keyword: eternal. This is basically an endless deployment. There's no new crew rotating in to replace us so we can go home. Sure, there are other DC who are also patrolling the planet, but for all we know, they're part of the problem."

"Which brings us back to where I started with this AG operation." I leaned over him to look down into his face. "We must figure out who our enemy is. Until we do that, we're just kinda floating in limbo here."

"And if it is the DC, then what? We join the AG and start a guerrilla war?" James asked.

"I don't know James. This entire thing is so far beyond us I honestly don't know. All I know is we at least need to establish a starting point. Then, we can figure out our next step. I've put some feelers out, trying to gather more information, establish ties, that sort of thing."

"You're right. One step at a time." James sighed and looked at me. "How are you so smart?"

"Benefits of experience, luv," I smiled.

Hobbits & Warrior Princesses

SHAE

That day in the sun had been over two weeks ago and we still hadn't heard from the AG. I was doubting the AG's commitment when my radio burst to life.

"Route port to Echo 119er," the dispatcher said, which didn't surprise me. Getting gate orders was common during patrols.

I mentally glanced at my mapping computer and saw it was taking us to New Zealand. *Never been there before.* I thought to myself as I looked out at the black, star-filled sky.

I glanced down at the blue and white ball far below us one more time. Low orbit was my favorite view of our planet. She was big enough to get lost in, but by turning just a bit, you could see the curvature of the world and knew everything had its limits.

"Good copy, Echo 119er," I said, and then passed the orders on to the rest of the team.

"New Zealand? Hobbits or Warrior Princesses?" James asked through the radio.

"What?" I asked as I approached our nearest gate point.

It only took a moment before we were suddenly over rolling hills that were covered in the richest shade of green I'd seen since back home in Ireland. It literally took my breath away, making me cough to clear my throat.

"Everyone on point?" I asked to make sure everyone made the transit safely. I already knew the answer, but it was best to have them check in anyway.

"Roger," James said.

"I'm here," Tara said.

"Yup," Rhi said before continuing, "Wow."

I guessed she meant the landscape as well. We were all hovering about 500 feet off the ground and there wasn't a single sign of civilization as far as we could see.

"I've got nothing on passive sensors. What are we here looking for?" James asked.

"Not sure, let me—" but the voice of the controller cut me off.

"Routing through to Dionysus 761. This is a code 3, I say again, this is a code 3. Confirm?" the controller said.

"Confirm code 3," I said, trying to keep the excitement out of my voice. I switched frequencies and relayed the information to the rest of the team.

This is it, guys, I reached out and touched their minds. *Let's keep it tight.*

We approached the coordinates dispatch had said were "code 3" or, by today's code, a suspected control point. It was easy to see what we were coming up on a minute later. A large volcano was sitting a few miles inland from the coast. Smoke was emitting from the top in a steady stream.

"Does that volcano look like it's about to blow?" Rhi asked.

"Definitely recent activity," James said. "Data says she's been quiet for ages."

"Snowpacks still intact; there's that, at least," Rhi said.

"Looks like our targets on the West side." With my AUG's optics, I zoomed in on the area. "Looks like the activity triggered a landslide, revealing the opening."

Sure enough, there was a large opening on the side of the mountain. Detailed analysis of the tunnel beneath indicated there was some sort of artificial door beneath it.

They wouldn't trigger a volcano just for this, would they? James asked me.

I don't know, I hope not. If this thing blows, there's going to be a lot of carnage. I noted several cities in the distance, easily in the blast zone if the volcano erupted. Then I remembered that most cities had been abandoned by anything still breathing nowadays.

"OK, let's establish a perimeter. I'll hold high. James, you take Northeast." I noted several cities off in that direction.

"Copy," James said and jetted off that way.

"Rhi, you take Southwest and Tara, you're on the doorstep," I said.

"Wait..." Rhi started.

"Rhi, you know the protocol: only a Daemon is allowed on the doorstep," I said.

Rhi growled something but boosted off to her assigned location.

Tara was still not moving.

"Tara, you OK?" I asked.

"Yes," She replied shakily.

It's no big deal. Just land near the opening if you can. Otherwise, hover and wait for the QRF, I sent.

OK, Tara said before her AUG moved off in that direction.

I moved to oversee Tara as she approached the opening. I switched to her view and could tell there was no way she could land there.

"That ledge is way too unstable, Tara. Just hover close by." I checked her AUG readings, and all the atmospheric readings were in the green. There didn't appear to be any immediate danger.

As soon as the thought crossed my mind, the mountain gave a low rumble.

"What was that?" Rhi said.

"Just a little planetary indigestion," I said, trying to lighten the mood. The health monitors on each of them were showing high levels of stress and anxiety, but none more than Rhi.

Rhi, relax. We're just here to watch and then get out of here. Nothing's going to happen to her. Ever since we'd found out about Tara's pregnancy, Rhi had been a basket case when it came to her safety. Overprotective was an understatement.

Even at the beach, Rhi kept trying to put sunscreen on Tara even though she couldn't get a sunburn. But, come to think of it, maybe she was just trying to "play" with her. You never could tell with Rhi sometimes.

A sunburn was no longer a worry for Rhi and me. Not only

did Behemoth use "vampire-safe" lighting on most of Behemoth, but we'd both been injected with some organism that absorbed the harmful light that causes vampires to burn up. As long as nothing killed the organism, Rhi and I should be able to walk in any daylight for the rest of our lives. Talk about bonus healthcare!

It took another half hour before the so-called Quick Reaction Force (QRF) appeared on scene. They didn't appear to care about stealth as they came in a ship I'd never seen before, accompanied by a dozen AUGs.

The ship defied reality as it was the size of a small aircraft carrier but moved through the air as if it were a fighter. The ship took up station, hovering beside the opening. The rest of the escort broke off and reinforced our perimeter.

Through Tara's cameras, I watched as a ramp was extended from the ship and into the tunnel. Several Daemons disgorged from the ship and hurried down the tunnel, failing to give Tara even a sideways glance in passing.

At the tail end of the procession was the commander. Had she not been wearing her rank and uniform, I would still have identified her by her demeanor alone. She stopped and turned to Tara.

"Have you been here the entire time?" the commander asked.

"Yes, ma'am, ever since our arrival on the scene," Tara said stiffly.

"Crack your platform; I want to see who I'm talking to." A series of clicks and whirls later, "That's much better," the commander said. "Has anyone else been down this tunnel?"

"No, ma'am," Tara said adamantly.

The commander looked up into the sky. "Have any of your other...teammates," she said the word with distaste, "been anywhere near here?"

"No, ma'am. Flight Leader Shae has been the closest," Tara motioned to where I was still hovering. "But her current position is as close as she's come."

The commander glanced in my direction before nodding and turning back to Tara.

"Good, stay here," the commander said.

"Yes, ma'am," Tara said before buttoning up her AUG.

"Flight Leader Shae," The commander addressed me through the command net.

"Ma'am?" I replied.

"You will take the remainder of your team and return to your patrol route. Colonel Tara will be remaining here."

I wanted to say something but knew that if I said anything other than to the affirmative, it would go badly for all of us.

"Yes, ma'am," I managed and switched frequencies. "Rhi, James, return to the gate point and give the volcano a wide berth."

"Roger," James said and immediately began moving.

"What about Tara?" Rhi said, her AUG not moving.

"She's remaining on-site with the commander," I said.

We can't leave her here! Rhi's voice spoke inside my head.

We have no choice. Now move out before you get her AND us in trouble, I said. I could hear her mentally grumbling about it, but her AUG started to move towards the gate point.

A few minutes later, we were all gathered at the gate point. I was just about to request transport back to our patrol route when it happened.

The view from Tara's AUG camera was floating in a small display in the corner of my vision. The commander had ordered me away but hadn't said I couldn't continue monitoring. Tara's display flickered out. I thought the commander had discovered my spying and cut the transmission when shockwave hit us.

The impact was so severe the emergency gel restraints couldn't form fast enough to keep my head from being smashed into the side of my cockpit. Had the tentacles of my AUG not been cradling me, I'm sure my head would have popped like an overripe melon with how hard I hit.

The world became a chaotic vortex of movement, sound and heat. The fact I could feel heat cut through the chaotic jumble that was my addled mind. Our AUGs were insulated for space. Nothing had ever made the temperature change inside the AUG, no matter how hot or cold an environment it was in.

A crushing pain filled my abdomen, drawing my attention away from the sensation of my cockpit compressing around me.

Something warm filled my mouth. A crunching, tearing, roaring sound overwhelmed me, making me want to cover my ears, but I couldn't move my hands. I nearly bit through my tongue as a terrible jolt rattled me to my core before a second jolt tore me from consciousness.

Aftermath

SHAE

After learning what happened, I was surprised I woke up at all.

I was first told how lucky we were to be alive. In one of my more lucid moments, an attendant said, had we been anyone else, including Daemons, we would have died long before anyone could have gotten to us.

Vampires are surprisingly hard to kill. When most people would perish, we just sort of shut down until we can repair ourselves. That is if someone didn't finish the job.

The rescue team had to cut each of us out of our AUGs. Our suits now resembled crumbled-up balls of paper that had been set on fire.

Once they got what was left of us out, some of us in pieces, they put us into a sort of medical tank and pumped us full of blood. For mangled corpses, we managed to heal up quickly.

Once I was able to remain conscious on my own, Beth came to my hospital room and debriefed me. Why she was sent was beyond me. Maybe the DC thought our relationship would ensure my honesty or something.

Ever since Beth had returned to her original unit, her attitude towards us had improved, even towards James, to a minor extent. I'd been worried about her social skills backsliding with her being around only Daemons now.

Once back with her precious comrades, she had been the one to contact me about continuing our luncheons together. On one special occasion, a month or so after the wedding, she didn't mind James coming along. Granted, I'd had to coach James to keep his mouth shut at the time.

I still wasn't strong enough to be pulled out of the med tank, so I floated there, naked, in front of Beth and any other medical personnel who happened by. Apparently, modesty wasn't a consideration to the DC.

I had to admit the sensation of waking up underwater with my lungs full of fluid was uncomfortable. I immediately had flashbacks to my time at sea and the fear of drowning. Luckily, I was being kept so full of sedatives that the panic felt like it was happening to someone else. After a while, I just sort of floated there on my own personal, drug-induced cloud.

"You said when your team arrived on site, there was no one else at the volcano?" Beth asked, crossing her legs in the chair she was sitting in.

The virtual room we were now in looked like a small business office. Beth was sitting in a chair across the coffee table from me where I sat in a comfy armchair.

Normal communication in a "vat" was possible in short doses but generally uncomfortable for the person inside. So, when longer conversations needed to be had, such as this debriefing, a virtual room was established to make things comfortable for both sides. In addition, they kept me in various virtual spaces just for my mental health. Staring through a blood-filled tube all day can get pretty boring.

"Yes," I said dreamily. "Sensors indicated the entire area was void of any creatures larger than a dog. We guessed what few people had still been in the area moved away once the volcano had started smoking."

The computer was translating my thoughts into a voice for Beth. It appeared to be doing a good job, too, as even the speaker sounded stoned from all the drugs I was currently on.

"And the first time you heard about the code 3 was from dispatch?" Beth asked.

"Yes, when we arrived at the gate point, they told us where to go," I said. "I'd never been to New Zealand before. It was soooo green!"

The corner of Beth's mouth twitched. She touched several keys on her PDD before continuing. "The commander on scene ordered you and your team to leave the area; is that correct?"

"Yes, but she made Tara stay behind." I shifted slightly on the couch, but there had to be some sort of problem with the connection because I could feel the tube as I moved.

"What happened anyway?" I asked.

"Well, without going into too many details, the site blew up," Beth said.

"Really?" It was obvious I wasn't in the right frame of mind for this conversation, but I continued. "So, is our planet gone then?" I said conversationally. I was on some good drugs.

"No, not like that." Beth shook her head. "The volcano exploded."

After a minute of processing this, my foggy brain caught up, "Yeah!" I cheered.

"Yeah?" Beth said.

"Yes, yeah! Now, the bad guys can't blow up our planet! We're safe," I said enthusiastically, something the speaker translated well.

"Not exactly," Beth said. She looked around conspiratorially like she was about to say something she shouldn't. "The site was faked."

"Whaaaaaaaaaaat?" I didn't mean to draw it out like a bad anime character; it just happened.

Beth nodded, seeming to get more excited. "A detailed scan revealed elements of the explosives used by the AG. It seems like they tried to set a trap for us. And while the losses are regrettable, we—"

"What losses?" That word snapped me out of my stupor. I'd been enjoying the calm that the fluid and drugs had me on, but with that word, I felt a sharp pain in my gut no drug could ease.

"We lost the entire QRF. The explosion vaporized the entire area. There's nothing but a large lagoon now where that volcano once stood," Beth said.

"What about Tara?" I asked.

Beth went stone-faced, "She didn't make it, Shae."

The room suddenly started spinning and was replaced by my vat. I have no idea how I did it, but I vomited right there in the tank. Luckily, there wasn't anything in my stomach at the time, but my body still doubled over retching. A sudden coolness ran across my body. Slowly, the world stopped spinning, and my retching halted before the office room reappeared.

"You OK?" Beth asked. She was standing next to my armchair now.

"Give me a minute," I said, trying to process what had just happened. "How?" I finally managed.

"She was at ground zero. The explosion vaporized everything out to, and including the perimeter guard. If that Commander hadn't released you three, you'd all be gone as well. As it was, the shockwave still reached you at the gate point and destroyed your AUGs."

I was stunned. I honestly couldn't think of a thing to say. The news was just too big.

After a moment, "I'm sorry, Shae. I know this is a lot to take in, so I'll leave you for now and come back later to finish up," Beth said softly. "Is there anything you need?"

I managed to shake my head as she stood and collected her PDD. She was almost to the door when I spoke again.

"Do the others know?" I knew the others had made it through and were in tanks like mine. Rhi had gotten the worst of it, having lost both her legs. She was in the process of having them regrown, last I'd heard.

"Yes," was all Beth said.

"And?" I asked.

"James took it like the soldier he is," Beth said flatly.

"And Rhi?" I asked, fearing the answer.

"Initially, she'd said she already knew...something to do with her tattoos. But then she became violent and was hurting herself, so they put her out. Every time they've revived her, she's gone into a rage, and they've had to put her back out," Beth said slowly.

I nodded somberly.

"Don't worry, they'll keep trying until they get her under control." Beth smiled and left the room.

Under control? I thought to myself. *She's not a dog!* But I kept it to myself.

Beth had started showing signs of liking our team as of late.

After that comment, maybe she was backsliding after all.

My thoughts turned darker. The AG had rigged the place to blow, the question is why? With such a large explosion, had they planned to take us out as well? These and other darker questions kept me thinking long into the night.

∞∞∞∞Ω∞∞∞∞

SHAE

I was out of the soup sometime later but still not allowed to leave the medical facility. I found James in an atrium surrounded by trees and flowers.

"I see everyone seems to go in for the natural healing surroundings," I said as I leaned over his shoulder and kissed him before sitting down in a gliding chair beside him

"Hey, Shae," James said simply, not looking up.

"Hey Shae? I haven't seen you in a week and that's it? Hey Shae?" I asked.

"Sorry," he said, staring at the floor.

I sighed heavily, realizing I had my work cut out for me. *Time to play mom again,* I thought. I let the silence stretch, waiting to see if he'd talk. He didn't.

"They said I have to come back in a couple of weeks for some tests. They said there were some anomalies, probably from where I cracked my head. You?" I asked.

"The same," James said.

You think it might have something to do with our "blocks?" I asked.

"Could be," James said, staring out at the trees.

"That's not good. They'd probably have to cut our heads off and scoop out the insides with a melon baller to see what's what," I said, watching him.

"True," James said.

I pulled the chair out from underneath him, dumping him unceremoniously onto the floor.

"Hey!" he said, looking at me for the first time.

"There he is," I said, putting the chair down. "A girl doesn't like talking to herself in the company of a boy."

"Sorry," he said before taking my offered hand and standing up. "Just a rough time."

I took his chin in my hand, "I know. It's not easy for any of us. But we'll get through it together."

"I don't think Rhi will," he said.

Nodding, I pushed him down into the gliding chair and sat in his lap. I wrapped my arm around his neck and tussled his hair.

"I think the vats grew your hair out," I said.

"Who cares," James said.

I knocked him upside the head.

"I care, you eejit."

"You're worried about my hair when we just lost Tara and...and..." he couldn't speak anymore.

"There you are," I cradled his head and held him as he sobbed. One look from me made anyone who tried to enter the atrium reconsider their choices. I ensured James had the privacy he needed to get it out of his system.

James finally wound down, finishing up with, "And God only knows when Rhi is going to—"

"When Rhi's going to what?" came her voice from behind us.

We both startled before scrambling to stand up.

I got to Rhi first and hugged her in greeting. I noticed she didn't hug me back and was stiff against me. I disentangled myself, making room for James.

In the blink of an eye, James had her in a crushing embrace.

"Easy...easy," Rhi groaned.

"Sorry," James mumbled but didn't let go, only loosened his grip.

I watched as her arms wrapped around him, and she melted into him. It was a much different hug than I'd gotten.

I'm so sorry, Rhi, James said, not trusting himself to speak.

Rhi flinched at the mind touch.

"Don't. It...it hurts in here," she pointed at her head.

I started to reply, but something made me hesitate. I watched as they held to one another for a while. I thought I could see a bit of glistening in Rhi's eyes, but I wasn't sure.

Finally, they broke and we all sat down, Rhi putting James between the two of us. I noticed she was limping slightly. I couldn't tell until I started looking, but she was wearing partial prosthetics. Her legs still hadn't completely grown back yet and one of the many Behemoth wonders was currently giving her the parts of her legs she was missing.

"How are your legs?" I asked.

"Attached," Rhi said shortly. "Mostly."

James glanced between us, sensing the same thing I was.

We sat in silence for a good long while, just staring out into the trees surrounding us. It was as if we were all holding a live wire, but if anyone said something about it, we'd get electrocuted. It wasn't pleasant, to say the least, but at least we were together again.

"In time—" I started, but Rhi interrupted.

"I'm going back to my room. I'm tired," was all Rhi said before standing and slowly limping out of the room.

James waited till she was gone before turning to me.

What was that about? James asked.

It's too raw right now. Give her time. She'll talk when she's ready, I thought to him.

I dunno. This seemed different than—

Different than the other times she's lost her wife? I asked gently. Sometimes, men were just so dense.

Uh...yeah. I see your point, James said.

Just leave it for now. She'll let us know when she's ready, I hoped.

$$\infty\infty\infty\infty\Omega\infty\infty\infty\infty$$

RHI

The woman, who looked to be in her early fifties, stood in the room, looking around as if she had never seen the place before.

"Oh! The dining room," she said as she looked down at herself. "Comfy clothes," she frowned. "Why is it always sweats and a T-shirt? Why not something a little nicer for company?" she grumbled.

"Meatloaf...again," the woman sighed, then turned and looked at me as I was staring at her from the floor in a corner of the room.

The carpet was soft beneath me. A well-used dining table and chairs sat off to the side of the room with a china cabinet along the other wall. Sunlight was streaming in from outside through windows with German lace curtains.

"Oh, hello," the woman said as she cocked her head at me. "Please, have a seat," the woman said, indicating one of the chairs.

Suddenly, the room shifted, and we were both sitting at the table. I appreciated it since I still didn't have my legs, so getting around was painful.

Vampires healed quickly, even limbs. But that didn't mean it was a painless process. Imagine growing pains from when you were younger. Now, make them a constant until whatever limb you lost regenerated, usually in a few days or so. I mean, the alternative was way worse, but that thought didn't help when the pain was not letting up.

"Where am I?" I asked, looking down at the now-set table. There was a place setting for the two of us, and food was already steaming in serving dishes before us.

"Oh, I'm sure you know, dear," she said as she reached for the food. "Meatloaf? It's actually pretty good...I didn't lose a bet or anything," she smiled and held up a slice.

"No thanks," I held up my hand.

"Y'all always say that," the woman shook her head and placed the slice on her plate before helping herself to the side dishes on the table.

"Y'all? Whose y'all?" I asked.

"All his guests. I get y'all traipsing through here pretty regular, and not a one of you has ever tried my meatloaf!" She sighed.

I was looking around me for any sense of familiarity when she spoke again.

"My, but you are a pretty one, though. He never seems to

take to the plain ones. But you...oh! You must be Rhi. You're one of his special ones."

"His special ones?" I asked, trying to keep my drug-addled brain on track. The last thing I remembered was still floating in that damned tank. But they had me so pumped full of chemicals I didn't know if I was coming or going anymore.

"The ones who know what's going on," She nodded and took a bite of the food. "Or, at least, what they believe they know is going on. I take it this is your first visit?"

"Yes?" I said cautiously. There were a lot of things about Behemoth that I didn't understand. For all I knew, this could be a Bio-Hab on Behemoth somewhere. Or, this could just be another crazy dream of mine.

"Don't worry about it," the woman said, waving her hand at me. "This is the reality you know. This is just something he likes to do. For some reason, he has me greet all of you. I don't know if he thinks it puts y'all at ease or what.

"If it were me, and I was whisked away and plopped down in this place, I'd think I was losing my marbles too. But you're the smart one in his little circle. You've already figured out that you're not really crazy..." She smiled. It was a kind smile, but something about it unnerved me.

"Now, on my side of the board, every time I smell meatloaf, that means someone's coming for dinner." She speared a chunk of meat and held it up to examine. "As much as I like it, I stopped making meatloaf out in the real." She continued to examine the meat-laden fork.

"Maybe that's why he always has it here?" I ventured, not knowing who "he" was, but I was starting to get a clue.

"You know, that's a good point," she said as she placed the meat into her mouth and started to chew. "I'll try it and see if that works. It would be nice to have something different in here occasionally. Then, maybe one of you would stay and share a meal with me instead of going straight through that door."

I looked over my shoulder where she was pointing and saw a plain, swinging door. It hadn't been there before.

"It's OK. As soon as I point it out, y'all head straight for that door. He'll be in there," she waved her fork at the door.

I glanced from the door to her.

"Really, it's OK. As soon as you leave, I can get back to my normal goings-on."

"Who are you?" I asked, not moving from the chair.

"I thought you woulda' figured it out by now," she shook her head.

"Are you his...wife?" I asked.

Her only answer was a smile as she kept chewing.

"What does the wife of a god do all day?" I asked.

"A, dear? Really?" She shook her head slightly. "A god is just a matter of perspective. It might surprise you that I'm the one getting the day-to-day things done. You know, making the sun come up and keeping the lights on, as it were, and paying the bills. He likes to 'delegate' everything so he can focus on his 'works.' I swear, he needs a real job again," she said in disgust.

I glanced at the door, feeling a bit uncomfortable at the change of conversation, but I didn't move—not that I could move unless I wanted to crawl over there.

"You're just fine, dear," she said from behind me.

Then I had legs. Fully formed and operational legs. I stood quickly, not realizing how much I'd missed standing on my own power. There were all sorts of mobility devices in the infirmary, but there was something to be said about standing on your own.

"Thanks!" I said automatically.

"It wasn't me, dear," the woman said.

I reached down to the table and picked up a slice of bread. Forking a chunk of meatloaf onto the bread, I folded it over into a sandwich and took a bite.

I wasn't hungry...but I was pretty sure this wasn't food. Besides, I still had some manners...when I cared to use them.

"This actually is good," I said through a mouthful of sandwich. I'd never been a fan of meatloaf, but this was pretty tasty.

"Thank you, now skedaddle," she said as her hand made a shooing gesture.

I turned to the door and walked through, still munching on the sandwich.

The room beyond was a library—well, a home library.

Someone had taken a bedroom, lined it with bookcases and filled them not only with books but also toys, models, pictures and various nicknacks. To say the shelves were a bit cluttered was an understatement.

When I leaned forward, I couldn't read the titles of any of the books. They were each written in a different language, none of which I understood. My hands were still greasy from the sandwich I just finished, and I didn't want to touch anything.

In the middle of the room was a large wooden desk. Atop it sat a computer, a monstrous lava lamp, speakers, and even more knickknacks. Small jars and graphic mugs filled with various snacks were spread out about them.

As I watched, a hand came down from nowhere and picked up a peanut M&M. As I followed the hand's movement, it popped the candy into a man's mouth. A man who hadn't been there a moment ago now sat in a once empty chair that I hadn't had the chance to describe because someone was pushing my narration!

"You were rambling!" the man said. "I mean, what did you want me to do? Let you describe everything in the room? How boring would that be to a reader? No one wants to read an inventory list, Rhiannon," the man said.

I looked at him or tried to. I knew he was sitting right there talking to me, but I couldn't make out any details about him. His age, height, weight, complexion, ethnicity—they were all hidden from me.

"Must you focus on that? Of all the things going on with you, you want to know what race I am? Who cares? It's not like Disney is going to pick this up and make a movie about it."

"Even if they did, they'd gender swap the shit out of all the characters just to piss off the fans so they can turn around and say how close-minded the fanbase is!" I said out of snarky reflex.

I glanced at the 4th wall to make an aside and noticed a window on the far wall. Outside that window was me, looking back in at myself. The two of us started to walk towards each other—

"Don't!" he said, causing me to hesitate. "You're in enough of an existential crisis as it is. You want more on top of that?"

Then he was gone, and I was alone in the library. I didn't even have the chance to look around for him before he was suddenly back.

"Sorry about that. My son had an issue I had to deal with. Where were we?"

"You have a son?" I asked.

"Lots." He nodded. "Actually, I have a big family. Why? Is that a problem?" he asked, already knowing the answer.

I rubbed my face with my hands to try and center myself. "Why am I here?" I asked. "Wait, are we dead? Did we all die at the end of the last Book? I mean, we do keep jumping from scene to scene with no idea how we got there, like in the Sixth Sense," I paused to sniff the air. "Do...do I smell dead people?"

"No, you're not dead," the man chuckled.

"Then why the hell am I here?" I asked again.

"Isn't that what everyone wants to know?" the man had the gall to smile at me.

"No, you ass, I meant, why did you bring me here?" Part of me was screaming at myself not to insult the closest thing to God that I knew. The rest of me gave the first part the finger.

"That's just it, I didn't," the man said, reaching over and turning the computer screen to face me. "See?"

On the screen was a formatted book that read:

> *Uh...yeah. I see your point,* James said.
> *Just leave it for now. She'll let us know
> when she's ready,* I hoped.

"From there, it jumps about a week to the next chapter and picks up at Colors," the man said, turning the screen back to face him.

"Colors? The bar?" I asked. It was a watering hole Tara and I used to frequent. She loved it there.

"That's the one," he said. "So, you see, I don't know what you're doing here either. I mean, I know we're having a little 'chat' here down the line, but I didn't plan on you visiting my home."

"So, what am I doing here then?" I asked in frustration. "You're the know-it-all."

"Beats the hell outta me," the man chuckled. "Maybe you're developing your own Gwenpool-style powers?"

"Gwen-who?" I asked.

"Ask James; he'll know. Well, anyway. I can't have you just hanging around looking over my shoulder the whole time, so you need to head back," the man said, making a shooing motion I recognized.

"Uh, how?" I asked.

"How else? The door, duh," the man said, pointing back the way I came.

"Really? Do you have to be such an ass?" I frowned at the "man."

"Do you?" he asked.

Then, there was a sensation like I was being jerked backward by my belly button, and the room disappeared.

Moods In The Eye Of The Beholder

JAMES

I hadn't meant to go out to a bar; it just happened. Shae was in another of those endless briefings, and Rhi was refusing to come out of her room. Most days, I didn't know if she was in there or not. I'd learned my lesson early and wasn't about to intrude by coming in without permission...again.

So, I did one of the things I used to enjoy and just went out and wandered around.

We'd been released from the hospital earlier in the week. We were all still on convalescent leave, at least until our follow-up appointments next week. While we couldn't go on patrol, we could still read up on regs, attend meetings, that sort of crap. I'll be honest: I'd much rather be on patrol than locked in my room studying pilot manuals. As my school career can attest, I'm not big on studying.

Back when I had a car, I'd go out, usually at night, and just drive the streets. I never had a destination and I rarely kept to the same streets twice. This came in handy when I was stationed at a new base. I'd let my wanderings help me memorize the streets and alleys of each base to help when I patrolled.

When we'd first been assigned to this section, we were told we'd been placed in an environment that was familiar to us. No crazy alien stuff that would blow our minds. But, the further we wandered from our quarters, the more we'd start to see things not from our Bio-Hab. So far, I hadn't been brave enough to venture out that far.

Maybe the bright colors of the sign out front reminded me of one of Drakes' doors and that's what drew me in. Perhaps it was the slow synth music that was playing. Regardless, I walked in, ignored everything else and went straight to what looked like the bar.

A woman, at least what my human brain took as a woman, was moving back and forth behind a bar. She was my height, mostly my shape and features, but her skin was a black-and-white plaid, almost like she was a referee at a chess match. But one of the first things I learned about Behemoth is that nothing can ever be taken at face value.

I watched as she moved back and forth along the bar, serving various concoctions to other patrons. Some were sitting at the bar, and others were getting their choices and moving away to various tables and booths. It seemed tables and booths were bar standards across all the Bio-Habs.

"First time?"

I was still looking around when the bartender's voice drew my attention back to her.

"Uh, yeah," I managed.

"Just put your hand on there," she said, indicating a small blue PDD resting in front of her. I'd seen various-sized PDDs scattered around the place but took them as some sort of menu.

I looked down and saw nothing but a blank screen. When I looked back up, the bartender was off, serving someone else again. Apparently, it was a busy night? Day? Afternoon?

Time didn't matter here on Behemoth. Even when a section had a "sun" or "moon" or whatever, there wasn't a time-of-day pattern. People worked whatever times they needed to work. Sure, there were markets and such, but they were always open. The only thing that changed was who was manning what and when.

I placed my hand on the PDD, and it lit up, encasing me in its blue light. A moment later, the light was gone. When I looked at the PDD it was blank again, but my hand was now a dark purple color. It took me a moment to realize it wasn't just my hand, but my whole body was now the same dark purple, even my clothes.

"Oh nice, not many people spring for the extra mood alterations mod for their clothes," the bartender said once more in front of me. "It's more fun when people commit."

I'd been wearing one of Shae's clothes rings, we all were since I'd discovered them. Rhi had been ecstatic at the discovery, me, not so much. I mean, I found it as a means to get Rhi to stop yelling at me about the clothes I owed her. But it also meant I now had to figure out what to wear every time we went out. I was fine with our warskins, but Shae and Rhi, after a fashion, said I shouldn't be so dull.

Usually, when I left our quarters, I turned on my default clothes: simple cargo pants, a henley, and some trainers. I didn't wear loud colors, just simple browns and greens. Rhi had always fussed at me, but Shae would always chill her out, saying at least I was choosing something.

Now, every piece of clothing I had on was the same matching dark purple as my skin.

"What?" I asked, looking down at myself.

"Mood representation," the bartender said. "Well, not really moods, but it's close enough. I could bore you with the technical but from the look of you, that's not what you're here for. Now, let's see..." the bartender stared off into space for a moment.

This was a move I'd come to recognize as someone looking at a virtual menu in front of them. The civilian augmented reality rig, the closest my world had to explaining what she was using, was pretty subtle unless you knew what to look for. In contrast, the neural cockpit I had was seamless. There wasn't so much a menu floating in front of my eyes but the thought of one that meshed with my brain seamlessly. I could be reading a virtual manual, and from the outside, no one could tell the difference.

"OK, I see," the bartender finally said.

"See what?" I asked.

"Oh, what's what with you," she said. When she saw my expression, she continued. "The hand PDD lets me know the basics about you. Your name, what you like to eat and drink, how to bill you, what your physiology can handle. That sort of thing. It wouldn't be good for business if we went around poisoning the customers now, would it?"

"And the color?" I pointed at myself.

She was working on creating a drink using various hoses, taps, and small bottles as she talked. "Basically... it's your mood...or more so, why you're here."

"Huh?" I said intelligently.

She smiled kindly. "Look around."

I did as she instructed and looked about the place. It wasn't until then that I realized the rainbow of colors around me. There were people whose skin was so dark you could barely see them in the dim corners of the room. There were others who were neon orange. They mostly stuck to the various dance floors around the place. Most of the colors seemed to stick together, but the occasional mixing occurred.

"Some shades are here just to dance. Some just to drink. Some, to find someone and others to find several someones," she said.

"What are—"

"Nope, that's part of the fun of it. You have to figure out what color is what. But I'll give you this one for free." She ran her hand down herself. "This color and pattern never changes. This is the employee style. While we look like this, we're working and, as such, are off-limits. But if you see one of us suddenly change to something else, that means we're off the clock and fair game."

"Fair game for what?" I asked, starting to understand what she was saying but also becoming nervous about this new "game" I'd walked into.

"For whatever we're in the shade for," she grinned and placed a drink on the bar in front of me. "And don't worry, the shading is only while you're in here. Once you leave, it's back to your normal self."

I looked down at the drink and raised an eyebrow.

"What is it?" I asked, not moving to touch it.

"It's what you want right now," she said.

I reached down and picked the glass up, bringing it to my nose. There was a slight floral hint to it, and I hesitantly took a sip. It was smooth and lightly flavored with caramel and smoke.

It reminded me of whiskey but without the burn.

"This is pretty good," I said, looking back up at her.

"Thanks. Now, fair warning about the color palette: it changes up every few cycles. Whatever the color of the sign is out front is what palette we're in at the time. The color palette meanings change as well over time. So, just because you figured out the red palette this week doesn't mean it will be the same red palette next month. Make sense?"

"I guess?" I said.

"Alright, anything else before you go off and hide in a corner?" she asked.

"How do—"

"Second freebie, with your shade, not many people will be talking to you tonight." This time, her smile was kind, as if that PDD had told her more about what was going on with me than my credit card number. I looked down and she was patting my hand gently.

"What if I wanted to change my color?" I asked as she turned to serve another.

She cocked her head and me and held my gaze.

"That's entirely up to you. If you think you've changed, touch any PDD. Even if you're lying to yourself, the PDD never will. It's kinda the point of the place." With that, she moved off and down the bar.

I sat a moment, watching as she helped others. I wondered if everything in here was some Behemoth magic or if some level of empathy was involved.

"No, and it's Holly," the bartender said, giving me a glance before turning back to her bright green-colored customer.

I didn't say anything...and I didn't think anything...at least, I didn't think I thought anything. Not knowing anymore, I quickly grabbed my drink and left before something else I couldn't control happened.

Now that I looked around, the place was much larger than I'd originally thought. There were multiple elevated rooms, various games, dance floors, private alcoves, etc. Each had its own set of shades and hues of color. I could see other bars in the distance and hallways leading off into the darkened maze where pulses of different-colored light flashed.

I began to wander. Much as I'd done outside, I explored this bar. I kept calling it a bar, but it was more than that, and "club" didn't fit the description either. I'd have to come up with a new term for this kind of place.

Just as Holly predicted, I claimed a booth in a dark corner. The corner didn't fit in the brightly lit room, though. All the colored light splashing about should have made the corner well-lit, but it wasn't. It was almost like a spot on a clean shirt that just wouldn't come out.

As I sat, my hand brushed the PDD, and a bright yellow stripe suddenly appeared on my arm. Frowning as I looked at it, I wondered what that meant.

I looked out across the room and started to see others with various stripes and markings that clashed with most of the colors they displayed. I could see where this would be fun for someone who liked puzzles, but I wasn't in the mood.

Having a color-based system for your mood, interests, or whatever seemed like a good idea. I hadn't been to many bars, mostly only when members of my squad wanted to go out. I'd watched as people made "moves" on each other. Sometimes it worked out, but mostly it didn't. Too many crossed signals, I'd guessed. Humans liked to make things more complicated than necessary.

After a few more sips, I started to feel as mellow as my drink tasted. As I relaxed, my mind wandered. It ran straight towards the things that were bothering me the most, but I body-checked them hard and buried any thoughts of Tara.

My mind, of course, immediately swerved and headed towards Rhi. Then, when I deflected again, Shae was my new target. I had to shake my head hard to try and get rid of the thoughts. I didn't want to think about those things right now.

In an attempt to evade my own thoughts, I got up and made my way to a game I hadn't realized I'd been staring at.

The best way to describe it was a three-dimensional version of bumper pool crossed with pinball. The balls started on the table like normal pool balls. But once they were struck, they scattered in all directions, including up! As they struck bumpers, they were accelerated in all directions.

The table sat on a slight pedestal, and the small walkway around it raised and lowered to accommodate where the balls ended up. Each ball was brightly lit and left a slight trail as it moved, adding to the brilliance of the game. There were different-colored pockets all over the "table" as well.

I'd been watching someone else play and grabbed a table when one came open. I thought I had an idea of what I was doing as I picked up one of the sticks and tried to hit what I took to be the cue ball.

Nothing happened. My stick passed right through the ball as if it wasn't there. There was no flickering or fuzzing of the ball when it happened. I reached over and touched it. It was there. It felt like a normal solid billiard ball, not some sort of hologram. But my stick kept passing through it when I tried to hit it.

"For fuck's sake."

The familiar voice startled me, and I nearly lost control of the stick I was holding.

Rhi stood behind me, shaking her head. She wore leather-looking pants, a tank top that exposed her midriff, and her old red leather coat. What looked like a neon-colored cigarette hung from her lips, but no smoke was trickling out. Instead, tiny clouds of neon colors appeared and disappeared at random times.

I started to say something, but then I saw her coloring. It seemed to flicker between my dark purple and a glowing midnight blue. I hadn't seen anyone's color constantly changing like hers was.

Of course mine changes. Would you expect anything less weird from me? Rhi thought at me.

She walked over and took the stick from me. It was a short thing, maybe 25 centimeters long. When she touched it, it expanded to a "normal" sized pool stick, and she opened the game.

I watched the balls fly in all directions, a few even making flashes as they sank into holes. She moved to make another shot when she spoke.

"What are you doing here?"

"Just stumbled into the place," I said honestly.

"Right," she said as she made another shot. She didn't sink a ball but she didn't pass the stick to me either. Instead, she moved to make another shot.

"Aren't I—"

"Shut up, James," Rhi said, not taking her eyes off the game. Her voice was hard and left no room for debate.

I watched for a minute as she made short work of the game without saying a word. If I'd felt awkward being here before, now I felt like I was intruding.

I turned to leave.

You're not leaving, Rhi spoke in my head.

"I'm not?" I said, turning back around.

Rhi huffed and reset the table. Walking over to me, the stick shrank back to its original size, and she slapped it into my hand. She moved me roughly around the table and positioned me to make the opening shot.

"The table reads your thoughts," Rhi started before proceeding to give me a lesson in the game of "Trails." It had a longer, official name, but she just called it Trails.

We didn't talk except for her showing me how to play the game. By the third game, I had the basics down, and my drink was gone.

"I'm going to grab another drink, want something?" I asked.

"Sure," Rhi said before taking my hand and making a weird tapping motion on my fingers.

"Uh—" I started.

"Just tap the bar," Rhi said with a sigh.

I glanced at her but she'd turned back to the game and had reset it.

I made my way to the nearest bar where a man in the same black and white checkered pattern was tending. I put down my empty glass and, after looking around a minute, awkwardly tapped the bar.

When the bartender got to me, he worked his mixology magic and placed two drinks in front of me. He moved off to the next customer without a word.

Picking up the drinks, I sniffed and could tell which was mine right away as the other let off an acrid smell that burned my nose.

I placed Rhi's drink on the game table.

"Do I want to know what you're drinking?" I asked.

Rhi lifted the glass and took a large gulp before turning back to the game.

"You want a chaser of turpentine to go with that?" I asked.

Rhi ignored my comment and handed me the stick for the next shot.

I didn't know what was going on, but I didn't want to think about things right now. Going through the motions of the game was relaxing, even if I sucked horribly at it.

A game later, Rhi broke our shared silence.

"This was Tara's place," Rhi said quietly.

I glanced at Rhi, but she didn't look at me. She just continued playing the game. I couldn't think of anything to say, so I kept my mouth shut.

"She liked the color guessing game," Rhi made another shot. "Of course, with her being a Daemon, we attracted all sorts of attention...but she liked it."

Rhi scratched on the next shot but didn't give me the stick. She just got a new cue ball and made the next shot.

"The color changing never seemed to work on her, though. She was always the same brilliant crimson." Rhi took another large gulp of her drink. "It bummed her a little that she couldn't change colors, but after a while, we discovered no one else could ever be her color. Again, I figured it had something to do with her being a Daemon."

Rhi's "cigarette" faded to nothing and disappeared from her mouth as she made her next shot.

"After a while, no one cared she was a Daemon. She was just Tara." Rhi took another drink. "She got pretty famous after a bit. 'A Daemon of the people,' they used to say."

Rhi made another shot.

"She used to glow when she danced. Somehow she always knew what color wanted to dance each night and she pounced on them, dancing till they hollered uncle. This place made her so happy." Rhi shook her head and threw down the stick, walking away from the pool table.

I watched as she made her way across the room and right to the booth I'd been sitting at. After a moment, I picked up her drink and followed.

"What—" I started as I put her drink in front of her and slid into the booth.

"Don't talk, just drink," Rhi said before following her own advice.

I could feel the darkness that was seeping from her mind. I'd felt it ever since we got out of the hospital. It was almost as if part of her mind had died and was rotting. Most of the time, I was afraid to touch it.

Touch it, James.

It wasn't Rhi's mind voice that came into my head. It was the other Rhi that was inside her. We'd never talked directly; I'd only heard the voice in passing and only on rare occasions. Now, she was telling me to do something I was afraid to do. I wondered if this was how it talked to Rhi, trying to get her to do things she didn't want to.

I gritted my teeth and started to open my mind.

Gently, the voice came again, making me pause.

Once more, I opened myself up to Rhi's mind and sought out that dark place. It was easy to find, as if it wanted me to find it. I looked closer, and it was as if tendrils lanced out from it and laced itself through other parts of Rhi's mind.

I became aware of something inside my own mind that was reacting to it. Almost as if I had a darkness in me that was seeking more of itself.

We all have darkness in us, James, the voice came again. *The phrase "misery loves company" applies here. Don't let them touch.*

How am I supposed to touch her darkness but keep mine away? I asked in frustration, none of this making any sense. But the voice didn't answer me.

When I looked into Rhi again, all I could think about was my own "darkness" and how I had to keep it from her "darkness." With a disgusted sigh, I gave up, not knowing what I was doing in the first place.

You want another drink? I asked quietly. At least I knew

drinks. The darkness I'd felt before was still there. But when I spoke, a tiny part of it seemed to get out of the way. I mentally frowned at it.

Rhi, who'd been staring at the table, didn't say anything, only nodded.

Using the same tapping system, retrieving new drinks only took a minute. I had to admit, it was convenient. There was no hollering over the noise of the music and crowd; just tap and go.

When I returned, Rhi hadn't moved. I slid the drink in front of her and sat down.

"I don't know why I keep coming here," Rhi said finally. "I normally just sit here and drink. I don't dance, I don't talk to anyone, I don't play pool. The regulars that used to hang out with us take one look at my color and steer clear."

"Don't tell me, you used to be some bright color?" I asked.

Rhi grunted. "I wouldn't say bright, but definitely lighter...she made me lighter."

James, the voice came again.

I scrambled for something to say. I sucked at this. Usually, I was the good listener friend. I never had to do more than nod or say "uh huh" or something. People seemed to like that.

Yeah, yeah I finally said, almost shrugging with frustration.

Rhi didn't say anything, she just took another drink.

Sometimes, just being around someone was all they needed. I'd found I could do that rather well. They didn't want you to talk, and they didn't want to talk either.

I didn't particularly feel like talking anyway. That was the reason all this had started in the first place. I'd gone out walking just to walk. No thinking, no talking, just walking. Now, I was sitting in a bar with Rhi, and her other personality was trying to get me to talk when neither of us wanted to.

A clatter on the table drew my attention to a new arrival.

Pink. The woman was bubblegum pink from her mussy shoulder-length hair to the tight slit dress that flowed to her toes. She had the whole girl-next-door thing going and a smile that was electric. Plus, she looked like she'd had three too many energy drinks.

I glanced down at the pink-colored PDD she'd placed on the table.

"Hi," she said, her voice bright and cheery.

"Uh, hi," I said back.

"Oh good, you will talk. I'm Greni," she said, relief in her voice but still as upbeat as ever.

"James. Why wouldn't I talk?" I asked, glancing at Rhi, who was staring through the girl.

"Oh, sometimes you shadier types would rather be grumpy than take The Chance," she said.

"The Chance?" I asked.

"Yeah!" The girl picked up the pink PDD and held it up to me. She placed her hand on one side and waited.

I stared at the double-sided PDD for a moment before reluctantly putting my hand on my side opposite hers.

The room blurred.

The next scene was Greni sitting at the table with Rhi and me, just chattering away as we watched her with wide eyes. This scene repeated itself several times over different days. Sometimes Rhi was there, sometimes Shae, sometimes just me.

The next scene was a collage of porn featuring various combinations of our group over several months that blew my mind.

Then there were battles—some with AUGs, some hand-to-hand, some firefights—all with Greni fighting beside us. Our opponents changed constantly between the AG, unknown groups and eventually the DC.

Greni was now part of our gestalt. She didn't replace Tara but brought her own place into the group.

Decades of this and combinations of all the previous scenes went by until Greni was much older. Our group had remained the same, as vampires tend to do, but Greni was nearing the end of her life and quietly passed away in her sleep.

The visions ended, and the room came slamming back into focus.

Rhi is watching us, unconcerned. She almost had an amused expression on her face. Almost.

"What the—" I started.

"Uh, yeah, no," Greni said with definite finality. "I was looking for a pet project to have some fun with," she started, pulling the PDD back. "I didn't mind the additions, that looked fun and all. But, I'm not looking to start an intergalactic war or anything, so I'm gonna pass on your gen code, thanks." And with that, Greni moved away from our table rather quickly.

I stared after her in silence, watching her go.

"I almost got a cavity from how sweet she was," Rhi said.

"What the hell was that?" I asked, turning back to Rhi.

"That, my friend," Rhi said with an unexpected grin, "was 'The Chance.'"

I looked at her with an expression of "And?"

"They have a very interesting dating mechanic here. You could almost call it advanced speed dating," Rhi said. "See, when you both touch the PDD, an algorithm runs, predicting what would happen if the two of you were to... hook up."

"But, there was a lot more than a hook-up!" I exclaimed.

"It's a very thorough algorithm," Rhi yawned. "Sometimes, it shows a one-night stand with some or no complications. Other times, it's been known to show lifetimes. Which did you get?"

"The latter," I said, trying to piece together what all I'd seen. It was starting to fade now, like waking up from a dream.

"Oh wow, first time out, and you get the whole enchilada. Who am I kidding? Of course, you'd get a lifetime. You never do anything small," Rhi shook her head.

"The sex was amazing, but...the..." I couldn't hold onto the images anymore.

"Oh yeah. You need to decide how to file her," Rhi said.

"File her?" I asked.

"Time to swipe right or swipe left. Everything you saw is going to disappear shortly. You wouldn't even be allowed to record it on paper or video right now if you tried. Couldn't have you hanging onto all that. The psychological damage would be immense. Not to mention recording the sex bits and putting it on the nets," Rhi said, her chin resting in her hand as she leaned across the table.

"What?" I asked. Rhi was bombarding me with way too much information. She also appeared to be rather drunk and more scatterbrained than normal.

"Mentally decide if you want to ever try 'The Chance' with her again and see if it works out the next time. It's obvious what her choice was, but you never know. The Chance is different each time you do it. What's left of the algorithm in your head will file her away, and if you see her again, pull up the information and prompt you on what your choice was." Rhi took another sip of her drink.

"I uh—" I started but didn't finish as I felt something in my head store away an "undecided/maybe" decision linked with Greni's memory. Then, all memory of The Chance was gone. The memory of Greni coming up and offering The Chance to me was there, along with my "undecided/maybe" decision and her "hard pass."

"I thought dating in our world was confusing," I finally said.

"Oh no, this is actually much better if you think about it. In just a few seconds, you both get a red light/green light on what happens."

"And all...that...whatever it was, would have happened had we kept talking?" I asked.

"Pretty much," Rhi nodded behind her drink. "Of course, it is just an algorithm—one Behemoth developed. So, there's that." Rhi looked at me and cocked her head to the side. "You know, that's what I like about you, James. You're a known quantity. You're easy, no, not in that way...well, that too. But I mean I know how you think, how you feel. You try not to be complicated, and that's a good thing."

I was still distracted, thinking about all the possibilities and consequences of The Chance. The concept was starting to run away with me in my mind.

"Before you disappear down that rabbit hole, Alice..." Rhi started but trailed off. She started tapping her chin in thought.

"What?" I asked.

"I'm trying to decide if I want to take you home and fuck you so hard I hurt both of us. Or..." Rhi trailed off again.

"Or?" I prodded.

"Or have another drink and another go at spanking you at trails."

I waited, wide-eyed as Rhi had never spoken to me like this before.

"Let's play another game," Rhi said finally.

"Su...sure," I said, still rattled. "What's a gen code?" I asked as we stood up.

"Behemoth's version of a phone number, only it's tied to your genetics code, so you can't crank call someone," Rhi paused and shook her head. "Wait till I tell Shae," Rhi said, a genuine smile crossing her face.

Seeing Rhi smile was worth the oddity of The Chance and Greni.

It's a start, Rhi's other voice whispered to me.

As we reached the table, Rhi asked me one last question.

"James, who the hell is Gwenpool?"

∞∞∞∞Ω∞∞∞∞

RHI

James left me at Colors a while later. He said he had something he had to take care of. He'd worried about leaving me here in my 'state.' I told him that not only was I a big girl, but if he didn't like it, he could fuck right off. He persisted and I told him I had sobes. After that, he finally left me in peace.

I sat at my table, drinking quietly. I didn't have anything to do and nowhere to be. So, I ordered several more rounds.

The bartenders would cut you off at a certain point if you crossed some weird line they had. But apparently, vampires had a line that was well beyond the "normal" persons.

By the time I was reaching the end of that round, I was pretty sure the bartenders weren't going to be giving me another. I was well and truly "cocked-on" as James liked to say. I had no idea what it meant, but it sounded good.

Tara, did you see James's face when Greni brushed him off? Man, that was good. I took another swallow and grinned.

I'd been talking to Tara a lot on our "private channel" lately. It was the one we'd used when we were first learning to speak into each other's minds. None of the others seemed to be able to hear it. Just Tara and me.

Thankfully, Tara had never spoken back to me. I mean, she was dead. This was a mental link between living people, not some necrotic hotline. If she ever did answer me back...that was when I knew I was lost.

But it didn't stop me from talking to her. I liked talking to her. I didn't like writing in her stupid journal, though. Her dad was kinda a jerk.

When Tara lost her physical journals when the Dilla' exploded, she'd started keeping digital ones. When she died, someone had to keep them going. I was that someone. So, I kept writing, this time not just to her dad but to both of them. Again, thankfully, they never wrote back.

"This is some bullshit!" I screamed out. Luckily, the club somehow knew to dampen my booth just then. Not one person looked up at my outburst. I hoped it didn't do that when someone yelled out for help. Who was I kidding? Of course it didn't. Behemoth wouldn't let that happen.

"And you! Mr. I gotta control it all. You fucking owe me. I went, had dinner with the Mrs. and saw your little hidey-hole where you keep the universe's order. Did I say anything to anybody? Nope...and no, THEY don't count! I've never told any of them about you, not even Tara. That has got to count for something, right?" I glanced up, waiting. But as usual, the asshole didn't say anything.

Rhi, my inner voice cautioned, but I ignored her.

"I mean, all you have to do is put some words on a page, right? And then she'd come back, right? What does that cost you? To make my life not suck, what does that cost?" I asked to the air. "It costs you nothing. But you still won't do it, will you? Even though I'm sitting here begging you, again, for the same girl you killed last time! You stupid fuck!" I threw the glass I had, but it didn't make a satisfying enough sound when it smashed into the wall. So, I swiped them all off the table, but it still wasn't enough.

Wait, what? I asked at the thought that came into my head. *What do you mean by 'only one do-over?'* I asked. I knew he wasn't there, but I still looked around for him.

"That's bullshit, and you know it! And just who made that that rule?" I asked and waited for an answer.

Double bullshit! You make the rules here, not THEM. There is absolutely nothing that is stopping you from typing your little words and bringing her back right now. You make up these bullshit rules, you can unmake them. What's the point of being a god of creation if you can't do what you want? I took a breath, waiting for an answer. The fact he was giving them to me terrified me. He didn't like talking to me; the fact he was meant something even worse was coming, and he was feeling guilty.

Boring? What do you mean it would get boring? I asked.

Wait, let me get this straight. To stave off your boredom, I must suffer? And this makes you happy? My suffering makes you happy? I clenched my fists and pounded them on the table. *You're a sick fuck!*

No! Don't even try that crap. The audience aren't the sick ones here, pal...cause you and I both know you ain't got an audience! Yeah, I know all about that, too. You had one person buy your coverage of our little trip to Houston and that person only did it because they're related to you!

I shook my head and leaned back, crossing my arms in defiance. *And you know why they didn't want to read it? Because you killed her in that book, too! And here you are, repeating your mistakes. At least you brought her back in that one. I guarantee you won't get even that one person to read it if you don't bring her back this time!*

*Oh no! You can't just make me pass out from too much booze to end this tirade! I'll take some sobes to keep you from—

*I reached into my pocket and pulled the tab only to have them fall out of my drink-addled hand.

Oh, hardy-fucking-har. Making me drop them because I'm passing out drunk. I didn't try to pick the tab up, afraid of what he might make me do. Plus, it was getting harder to keep my eyes open.

Doesn't matter! I slurred, waiving at the tab on the now spinning floor. *When I wake up, I'll just start this all over again cause you can't make me forget anymore! The AG said you can't make...me forget...anymore...you asshole...* I tried to end that last sentence with an exclamation point, but I was finding it hard to talk...even in my head.

No! You can't make me pass out here; I'm in public! I tried to sound confident as I forced myself back upright from where I'd been starting to slump to the table a moment ago. *Who knows what'll happen to me or where it might take your precious storyline! Just remember what I did to James, and I hadn't even been introduced yet!*

Oh? Fuck you and your plans! If I can disrupt them that easily, then your plans suck! I mumbled as I pitched forward, crumbling in a heap on the table. I swear he pushed me.

OK, fine. But when I wake up in a CW ship, and there are crystals growing on the back of my—

I had to strain to hear that last bit.

No...it doesn't matter that my uniform would be revealed when I passed out because my ring fell off my finger, I said as I made a fist with the hand wearing the clothes right. *The fact that no one would dare touch a member of the chosen army isn't going to matter because I'm not opening this—*

The world started going black but not before I saw someone stumble into my table. Somehow, my arm managed to roll itself off the table, and I heard a loud *TINK* sound as my clothes ring slid off my finger and hit the floor.

Fuck...I forgot what a hack you are, I managed before passing out from just being so drunk.

Worth

SHAE

"Those sons of bitches!" I roared, storming into the day room.

James looked up, eyes the size of saucers. "What?"

"Those arrogant, self-righteous, sons of bitches!" I threw my coat across the room but it didn't make enough of a satisfactory crash for me.

Furniture on a space station is usually bolted down to the deck to prevent it from floating off during gravity failures. But here on Behemoth, everything is "grown." So, when a room is created, the furniture is created along with it. Nothing needs to be bolted down because it's already attached.

The sound of tearing metal as I wrenched the table from the deck was almost as satisfying as the moment it hit the far wall, leaving a significant dent.

My anger was so overwhelming that my cursing descended through different languages before bottoming out in my first language.

All James could do was watch my rant in stunned silence. I don't know if he'd heard me curse once, let alone the tirade that was upon me now. He finally got up and stopped me when I tossed the couch at the window.

"Hey, hey!" James said. "Let's not break the window holding in all of our oxygen, please."

When his hands touched my shoulders, I spun on him, feeling like fire was coming out of my eyes. Instead, tears flew from my face.

"They fucking did it on purpose, James! On fucking

purpose!" I was shaking so hard that I practically moved James across the room as he tried to hold onto me.

"Who? Did what?" he asked.

My hands were shaking so badly that my wedding ring went flying. The sound of it bouncing loudly off the floor snapped me out of the tirade I was on and sent me diving for it. As my fingers wrapped around the ring's smooth surface, I lie there on the floor shaking.

James knelt next to me, "What is going on?"

The AG killed Tara. My thought seared into his head, just as furious as my words had.

What? James asked.

I just talked to them. The fuckers rigged the mountain to blow if the DC tried to activate the device, I said.

Seriously? James was incredulous.

They said Behemoth only sends its highest-ranking officers to activate a control point. That the AG couldn't pass up the opportunity to take out such a high-profile target, I said.

Wait, you said Behemoth just clones another copy if someone dies. It makes no sense to do this if it doesn't make a difference? James said.

I think they were just bloodthirsty for a target, I said, shaking my head.

What about Tara? James asked.

Tara was just collateral damage to them. They didn't care about her allegiances at all! To them, she was just another DC. I couldn't say anymore then because I was too lost in my grief and rage.

"It's all my fault...my goddamned fault. I killed her...I fucking did it!" I screamed.

James held onto me as I fell completely apart. I couldn't recall the last time this had happened to me. It was sometime later before I came back to my senses. When I did, James had moved us into our room and was whispering soothing words to me.

I looked up at him, rubbing the tears from my eyes.

"You OK?" James asked.

"No," I coughed, trying to clear my throat. "But this helps.

Thank you."

He searched my face for a long moment before saying, "You're welcome." He kissed me then, filling the empty void my rage had hollowed out in me.

"Tell me what happened," James said a few minutes later.

So, I explained how I tracked them down and demanded answers.

∞∞∞∞∞Ω∞∞∞∞∞

SHAE

"You're in no position to demand anything from us," the AG said.

I hadn't seen this one before. When I asked about Perth, I was told they weren't available.

"You asked for our help, and we helped," the AG said.

"And killed a member of my team in the process," I said, raising my voice.

"One Daemon does not outweigh the advantage of removing significant high-ranking resources from the opposition's forces," the AG said.

"It does when it's a member of my team!" I barked.

"You wanted to know what the DC would do when they found the control station for your planet. Now you know," the AG stared at the ceiling a moment. "On the upside, this may cause them to hesitate when they find the real thing."

I took a breath and gritted my teeth, trying to control my rapidly rising temper.

"Listen. You asked us for our help. You came to us; we didn't seek you out," I said.

"Yes, and you didn't commit one way or the other. Then you came to us asking for a favor, to which we agreed. We didn't turn you away, and we didn't ask for anything in return. We put several of our people at significant risk to do as you asked. And when we successfully completed your request, do you come to show your gratitude? No, you come to complain about our methods," the AG lectured.

"Thank you," I said through gritted teeth. "But-"

"You do understand we're at war? We've been at war since before your species was created. In war, there are sacrifices. Sometimes they are noble, sometimes they are tragic, but there are always losses," the AG said.

"That is very easy to say when you're not the one making the sacrifices," I said.

"And what do you know of it?" the AG said stiffly. "You know me not, nor my situation. You only assume that because I'm not dead, I don't know sacrifice?"

"That's not—" I started.

"Of course it is." The AG rose and turned, saying over its shoulder, "The next time you want our help, be careful what you ask for."

My temper flared again.

"Next time? What makes you think we'll come asking you for anything?"

"Your kind always does," the AG said, not looking back as it walked away.

"Maybe Behemoth and the DC are right after all. They look down on us and treat us like garbage, but at least they're upfront and honest about it," I said, briefly reining in my temper.

The AG paused but didn't say anything before disappearing out of the room.

∞∞∞∞Ω∞∞∞∞

SHAE

You didn't? James said, bringing me out of the memory.

Yes, I did, I said.

Are you honestly thinking of going to the DC about this? James asked.

The DC? Never. Behemoth? Maybe, I said.

You're not serious, James stared at me.

*The thought crossed my mind, but what could I tell it? I

don't know anything; the AG have made sure of that. Nothing useful anyway. Besides, the DC did try to blow up the planet.*

So, the DC are the bad guys, James said flatly.

Definitely the baddest guys, but not the only bad guys, I said, rubbing my head.

You know, to play Devil's advocate, they— James started.

Don't. Just don't. I said, sighing.

Sorry, what do you want to do? James asked softly.

First, I want to get drunk and screw, I said, both mentally and physically exhausted.

Wow, you are in a mood, James said. "Wait, isn't that a country song?*

Dunno, don't care. Get me a bottle, James, I said flatly.

Yes, ma'am, he said obediently but paused. *What's the other thing?*

I haven't figured that out yet.

Replacement

SHAE

In the morning, Beth stopped by and wanted to know what had happened to the furniture in the dayroom. James said something about "Klingon sex," whatever that was, and it somehow settled things with Beth.

Surprisingly, Rhi didn't react when I told her what I'd learned. She just looked at me for a while and said, "I figured as much."

She had been pretty closed off from us...well, from me since the incident. Apparently, James had run into her at some club, and she'd been civil with him but nothing more. What he told me and what I'd seen of her made me nervous.

Now, as I watched her digesting what I told her, a cold shiver ran down my spine. I was now worried we were living with a time bomb, and I didn't know what to do about it. I hadn't felt this way with her since the night she showed up at the Hacienda.

Then Beth showed up and dropped the next bombshell on us by introducing Tara's replacement.

"It's called a what?" James asked, looking at the person standing next to Beth.

He was wearing a warskin identical to ours only it was forest green. He looked like a typical guy, average height, dark curly hair and in need of a shave.

"A Blank," Beth said.

"Like a key blank?" I asked.

"More like a blank slate. Blanks were created to help fill in where needed. They can be technicians, cooks or even pilots.

They can be identified by this color uniform."

"I've seen them before," Rhi said. "There was a guy working on an open panel in one of the corridors. He had one of these Blanks with him. But he didn't look like this."

"Blanks are customizable," Beth said, turning to the man. "They can be used to mimic anything except a Daemon. This Blank, for example, has been created from a combination of your group's base characteristics. It has the same level of combat experience as your group and was designed to fit in with you."

"Fit in?" I asked. "How do you mean?"

"His matrix is a mixture of your personalities in a way Behemoth designated will help your group the most," Beth said.

"He looks like the kid that gets beat up in every teenage movie," Rhi said, eyeballing the Blank.

"So, is this a person, robot, android, what?" James asked.

"Yes," Beth said, tapping something on her tablet with an annoyed expression. "I'll let the Blank answer any other questions." She seemed to hesitate momentarily before adding, "I have to be somewhere." Without another word, Beth turned and departed.

"Wait!" I said, sticking my head out the door.

Beth hesitated and turned back to me.

"Don't we get a say in this?" I asked.

Beth shook her head slowly. "A wing has to have at least four to be fit for duty."

"Couldn't we just—" I started.

Beth quick-marched back to me.

"Shae. I know it's not ideal, I understand, I do. But this is coming from Behemoth, not the DC."

"Behemoth?" I asked.

Beth nodded.

"Now, I really do have to go," Beth said. "I'll try to come by later." She said and then left without another word.

I slowly walked back into the room where the four of us stared at one another in silence.

"So, do you have a name, or do we just call you The Blank?" I asked, breaking the awkward silence.

"I do not currently have a designation," the Blank said.

"They don't even give you a name?" James said.

"My designation is changed based on need," the Blank said.

"What were you previously called?" I asked.

"My designation is deleted along with all relevant data each time I depart my assigned duties," the Blank said.

"They wipe your memory after each job?" James asked.

"I take it you are a robot then?" I asked.

"No. I am a living utility organism."

"A living what?" James asked.

"Living utility organism. I am a living creature, designed to be able to pattern my matrix after any other organism and adjust to fill a need," the Blank said.

"Adjust?" I asked. "What do you mean by adjust?"

"My body can be adapted to match the original organisms in order to make my presence less stressful. In addition, my body can be modified for specific duties to allow for more productive output," the Blank said.

"And you can perform your duties just as well as we do?" James said.

"I have the same proficiency base, yes," the Blank said.

James looked at me.

"If they have him, why do they need us?" he asked.

I looked at the Blank.

"She said you can't copy a Daemon, why?" I asked.

"A Daemon's matrix is far too complicated for my processor to match. Any attempt to mimic a Daemon has resulted in disaster, sometimes catastrophically so," the Blank said.

"Yet our matrices are simple enough to be copied," Rhi said flatly. She'd been sitting back and eyeballing the Blank since Beth had introduced him.

"Correct," the Blank said, turning to Rhi.

"Great," Rhi said. "Now even the help looks down on us."

"You'll need a designa...er, name if you're going to work with us," I said. "How about Lou for now? It's close enough to living utility organism."

"Close enough," Lou nodded.

"Why does Beth keep showing up?" James asked.

"What do you mean?" I asked.

"Well, she debriefed you in the hospital, she checked in yesterday for no reason, and then played delivery girl today. What gives?" James said. "I thought she was the big-time pilot."

"She told me Behemoth wants her to continue to liaise with us whenever possible. Seems Behemoth feels she's a positive influence on us or something. At least that's what Beth told me," I said.

Lou ended up not being too bad when it came to work. Over the next few days, I discovered he had fast reflexes, followed orders and made intelligent decisions. The only problem was he had no initiative. He'd do what you asked, but that was it. If he were following a set of directions, he'd only go as far as your last direction. He wouldn't take the initiative to do the next step, no matter how obvious.

In private, though, Lou was another matter entirely. He was a quiet wallflower. He was downright creepy. He'd answer you if you directed a question at him, but he wouldn't expound unless asked to. It reminded me of when I first met James.

"Lou," I said.

"Ma'am?" Lou said.

"You've been here a week now. When are you going to start loosening up?" I asked.

"Loosening up, ma'am?" Lou said.

"I mean, you're supposed to be a collection of all of our personalities, but the only thing I've seen is James as a teenager," I said.

"Hey!" James said. "I resemble that remark."

"Do you wish me to reduce my propriety protocols?" Lou said.

"Propriety protocols?" James asked. "What's that?"

"The protocols that ensure my proper etiquette at all times," Lou said.

"Well, that sounds dumb. Can't you just flip them off like in Terminator?" James asked.

"I am authorized to relax my propriety protocols at the discretion of my commander," Lou said.

"Lou?" I said.

"Ma'am?"

"Relax," I ordered.

"Yes, ma'am," Lou said. A moment later, his rigid posture relaxed back into his chair, and his neutral expression changed to one of bemusement.

"What's so funny?" James asked.

"Oh, nothing, just the looks on your faces; you should see them. Anyway, what's for dinner...as if I didn't know." Lou stood and walked across the day room to look in the fridge.

∞∞∞∞Ω∞∞∞∞

SHAE

"Are you sure about this?" I asked, giving the strange building a disapproving glance.

Beth laughed, "Of course. You said you wanted the best bookstore we had. This is it."

"But, you said you hadn't been here before, so how do you know? Does Behemoth have Yelp reviews or something?"

The building was in the middle of one of the Behemoth cities we'd seen when we first woke up here. The city wasn't in a Bio-Hab. Instead, it was in a massive room. Of course, with Behemoth's technology, you'd never know you were indoors.

Strangely enough, the building was by itself on a block in the middle of a densely populated warehouse district. It looked like a two-story house you'd see in modern-day suburbia back home. The façade looked weathered but not run down.

The fact it was surrounded by giant modern warehouses made it stand out as if it had been here first and everything else had grown up around it.

"I do my research," Beth said, then she grinned. "Besides, I think you're like its eccentricities.

"It's what now?" I asked.

"Come on," Beth said, leading the way.

In one of our café lunches, I'd mentioned in passing that I missed bookstores. I'd always enjoyed old independent bookstores, not the modern coffee shops that had a bookstore attached. The older and more obscure the shop, the better. Character went a long way with me.

I reluctantly followed Beth up the steps to the house, the hair on the back of my neck standing up.

There was an old "OPEN" sign hanging in the window. No neon sign or anything high-tech here. Just paper and a string. There was even a bell on the door when Beth opened it.

Immediately, I was hit with the familiar smells of an old bookstore. It immediately caused me to relax, even though the hairs on my arm were now standing up. There was something else in the air as well, not incense, thankfully not coffee, but I couldn't figure it out.

I jumped when Beth closed the door behind me.

The immediate room was filled with non-uniform bookshelves, bookcases and several display cases containing strange artifacts or odd-looking books. Everything looked old and handmade. No Ikea furniture here. Rows of bookcases went off in every direction, making the place seem larger than it looked from the outside.

A man slowly shuffled towards us from somewhere in the back.

"Can I help you?" The man's voice was gravelly and set my teeth on edge.

Every instinct I had was telling me to get out of here. But I wasn't about to leave Beth. This was the first time she'd asked me to go somewhere that wasn't job-related. I wasn't going to screw that up just because I had the jitters.

Plus I desperately needed something to distract me from the loss of Tara and Lou's exploits.

"We're just browsing," Beth said pleasantly.

"First time in?" The man croaked.

"Yes," Beth replied.

"That's fine. We have non-fiction on that side and fiction on this side. Then there's—"

Whatever he said next was nothing but noise to me. I understood he was still speaking, but whatever he was saying was not translating. That, in itself, was rare.

After a good thirty seconds of him gesturing and obviously

still explaining things, I could suddenly understand him again.

"There are maps on the ends of the rows if you need a reminder. Feel free to ask for help from any of our staff who are spread about the place. Each one is a specialist in the area they're in."

"Thank you," Beth said and started to turn.

"Oh, and if you get lost, just knock on a bookcase three times. Something will be along to assist you," The man said before slowly turning and shuffling back the way he came.

"Did you understand any of that?" I asked.

"Of course," Beth said.

I frowned and kept my translation problem to myself. It might have something to do with the AG, and I didn't want to draw any unwanted attention.

"So, where did you want to start?" Beth asked.

"Uh," I didn't know. I didn't have anything in particular in mind. I usually didn't when I went to a bookstore. I just liked browsing. "Let's just take a look around," I suggested.

"Sounds good, lead the way," Beth said, holding her arm out in an "after you" motion.

I picked a direction at random and started walking.

In addition to the furniture, the lighting was non-standard as well. No big fluorescents like I was used to. There were chandeliers, bookcase lighting, wall sconces, track lights, and even a few of Behemoth's high-tech setups where you couldn't tell where the light was coming from as it cast no shadows.

The books themselves were every shape and size imaginable. Where I was used to your standard rectangular book, here there were books of so many varieties that I even found a section of spherical books. But I couldn't figure out a way to open them.

We browsed, walking from one section to another. We took stairs up and stairs down more levels than there should have been. I felt more like an explorer than a shopper, and I loved it.

I came across rooms that were made from books. The doorway arches, the bookcases, the chairs, everything was made from books. I couldn't help but smile at the cleverness of it all.

"Are you sure this isn't a museum?" I asked Beth after a good hour of wandering. But when I turned, she wasn't behind me.

When I thought about it, I'd been so preoccupied by the rooms of the store that I couldn't remember the last time I'd seen Beth.

"Maybe she saw something and went to check it out," I said aloud to myself. "She just didn't want to bother me." I nodded to myself. It was fine. When I went to a bookstore with someone, we usually didn't stick together. Of course, those stores usually obeyed the laws of dimensional physics.

I still had all my communication gear in my warskin. I could always call her if I needed to. I considered it, but she already thought I was a fraidy cat about this place. No reason to verify that idea for her.

I continued my exploring and discovered a small raised area above me that housed books that seemed to be glowing. I looked around but didn't see any way up to them. I figured they were accessible from another room as the section appeared to extend beyond the wall of the room I was in. But then, movement caught my eye.

There was a woman only a few feet from me, putting away a small armful of books on the shelves. I could have sworn she hadn't been there a moment ago.

"Excuse me," I said, realizing it was the first sound I'd heard since I'd gotten separated from Beth.

The woman paused, mid-shelving and turned to look at me. Her eyes were empty and caused a shiver to run down my spine.

"H...How do I get up there?" I forged ahead, trying to push down a rising irrational panic.

The woman didn't speak but slowly raised her eyes to where I was pointing. Just as slowly, her eyes lowered back to mine. Then she was approaching me.

I was too freaked out at the time to realize her feet weren't moving.

I took a step back as she stopped mere inches from me. While still looking at me, she raised her arm until she was pointing at a small dark spot on the carpet directly below the section in question.

"Uh, thanks?" I said as I inched around her and towards where she was pointing.

The dark spot, which initially looked like a stain, was an oval roughly three feet across.

I looked back at the woman, who was still standing there with her arm outstretched.

"Here?" I asked, pointing at the oval.

All she did was raise her arm and lower it again, still pointing at the oval.

I frowned and approached the spot. Suddenly, my warskin started to tingle, telling me it was interacting with something around me. Then I was flying.

Well, not really flying. But something picked me up and brought me up to the section I'd been indicating. The force gently lowered me to the floor of the raised section where an identical oval sat.

My warskin returned to normal and I found I could move again.

The whole thing reminded me of a gravlift. I'd been on plenty of those, but they were controlled by Behemoth and clearly marked as such. This had no markings and wasn't as smooth as the ones I'd been on. It almost felt like I was being lifted by two separate lifts. Perhaps it was just old and out of alignment.

I looked back to where the woman had been but didn't see her. A quick glance around the room from above didn't reveal her location. I frowned and turned to the glowing books.

"Oh," Beth started. She'd found me about 20 minutes later. How she'd found me was a mystery as I'd wandered all over the place.

"Oh?" I asked, turning from the strange bookmark I was examining.

"Uh...yeah. I don't know if you want to tell Rhi this or not, but I looked into Tara's backup."

"Her what?" I asked, dropping the bookmark at the mention of Tara.

"Her backup. All DC have genetic backups in case of injury or death. It's how Behemoth maintains its standing force. They didn't cover this in orientation?" Beth asked.

"No," I said. "I'm sure I would have remembered something like that."

"Well, it goes like this. Behemoth keeps a constant data stream on every DC. If a DC falls in battle, its data stream is transferred to a replacement body, aka a backup. That mind is activated with the memories up to that point that from the datastream," Beth said as she picked up the bookmark I'd dropped and placed it on the shelf it came from.

"And they do this for everybody?" I asked in shock.

"No, only the DC. Since they can't reproduce, that's how Behemoth maintains its numbers."

"So, are you saying the DC are immortal?"

"Not as such. I mean, they still die, even that is recorded on the datastream. A copy of the consciousness is created and filled with the data from the previous body," Beth said so matter-of-factly it was freaking me out.

"So...the information is continuously passed from one body to the next, in effect creating a mind that has the memories of endless generations?" I asked, the idea too big to wrap my head around.

"I wouldn't say endless. It's not always a perfect process. Sometimes datastreams become corrupted, and data is lost," Beth said.

"You're talking about them like they're robots," I said.

"They sometimes act like robots, don't they?" Beth smiled at me. Her smile turned to a frown when she saw my face.

"What were you saying about Tara?" I asked.

"Since Tara was a part of The Chosen Army, she wasn't considered a proper DC, so she didn't have a backup assigned, I'm afraid."

"So, if she had a backup, what, she would have just shown up the next day?" I asked.

"Something like that," Beth nodded.

"And these backups are just copies? They act the same as the original?" I was still trying to understand. The thought that Tara might have been able to come back was both exciting and terrifying. Would it have been Tara or some weird copy?

"For all purposes, they are the original. There isn't a DC alive today that isn't a backup. They're aware they're in a backup body as they retain the memory of the backup waking up at the processing center," Beth said.

Beth snapped her fingers, "Speaking of the processing center. You asked me about a Krys and a Shashka, the people James met during that accident so long ago. I saw something with their names come through my data feed. Since they didn't come from a Bio-Hab, they were assigned to the processing center. I can get you in touch with them if you'd like."

"That would be great," I said, shifting mental gears. "I'm sure James would love to get back in touch with them."

Beth smiled, "I do remember you mentioning something about them getting a bit friendly."

"Not them, per se. Just Krys," I said.

"Really? James and Krys?" Beth's eyes widened slightly. "I didn't know."

"Trust me, if you saw Krys, you'd understand. I've seen the pictures in James's head," I nodded, knowing my husband secretly had a thing for this man...well, he wasn't a man. He was an alien. Which made it that much more interesting...and something I was interested in witnessing. I smiled to myself at watching James torture himself over his feelings once again.

"I guess I'll have to check out Krys's file," Beth said.

"But, back to what we were talking about," I said, shifting mental gears again. I didn't think Beth was trying to distract me on purpose, but she'd managed to do a good job of it.

"But the original DC died. So, this backup is a new body. The mind is just filled with a copy of the mind from the original." I was stating, not asking.

"Ahh, I see. You're getting into the whole 'soul' dilemma." Beth nodded.

"Soul dilemma?" I asked.

"Neither Behemoth nor the DC believe in souls. Flesh is just a vessel for the information of the mind to them," Beth said.

"That sounds horrific," I said. While I'd never been heavily religious, this still had all sorts of implications.

"What's to keep Behemoth from just activating the backup before the original is dead? Couldn't Behemoth double its numbers?" I asked.

"It's been tried several times. Every time a new backup

technology is developed, it is tried. But, every time, it's failed. For some reason, two identical datastreams can't exist at the same time," Beth said. "The backup always fails."

"What if the datastreams were shut off once the backup copy was complete?" I asked.

"Tried it, still didn't work. I don't understand the process or the math behind it. All I know is that it's never worked," Beth said.

"Sounds almost like there's something special about the original—"

"Like a soul. Yes, this is one of the discussions in the soul dilemma. I can send you a link if you'd like," Beth said.

"Yes, I'd like that a lot, thank you," I said, my curiosity now thoroughly peaked.

"Fair warning, it's ridiculously high-level stuff. I had to have my minder help me out with most of it," Beth said.

"Minder ?" I asked.

"Ah," Beth hesitated.

"What is it?" I asked, watching as she suddenly looked uncomfortable. She appeared to debate with herself before she finally spoke.

"Well, minders aren't a secret or anything. But they're not exactly good things," Beth said.

I grabbed Beth's hand and pulled her down to a nearby couch. It looked ancient and was anything but comfortable.

Beth took a deep breath and slowly let it out.

"Beth, you don't have to tell me about this. It's OK." I said, trying to give her my best supportive tone. I was dying to know what a minder was, but I didn't want to make her regret talking to me.

"Minders are...they're a mix of a living organism and a living AI. They're assigned by Behemoth to those who need...watching." Beth looked around uncomfortably. "I told you how I came to be on Behemoth and my mental state at the time."

"I remember," I said softly.

"Behemoth assigned my minder to me in an attempt to keep me from continuously trying to harm myself. It's like having a counselor in your head that's always talking to you about what's going on in your life," Beth said.

"Sounds...kinda nice, actually," I said honestly.

"It is," Beth sighed. "As weird as it sounds, a minder only works for its host. Even though it comes from Behemoth, it puts its host above Behemoth's wishes. I've had my minder flat-out disobey Behemoth because it was in my best interest."

"Really?" I leaned in.

"It's the only way minders could work. They're basically mental health BFFs. If you thought they were only working for Behemoth's interests and not yours, how could you trust it?"

"And I take it you've tested this," I asked.

"Right at the beginning. Like I said, I wasn't in a good place. The things my minder said and did gained my trust pretty quickly. It's never betrayed me. I may not like what it says sometimes, but I can't argue everything it says is in my best interest."

"Wow," I sat back and thought about it.

"There's also the fact they can't be removed. Once attached, they become a part of you completely," Beth said.

"Yeah, if you could remove them, I could see where they could be tossed aside rather than listened to," I said.

"Regardless, he's never steered me wrong. He's told me some uncomfortable truths, but he wasn't wrong," Beth said.

"What, like global warming?" I tried to lighten the mood.

"Like how you once asked me to stay with you instead of going home. I should have listened to you and stayed," Beth said.

"Hey now, you can't go second guessing—" I started.

"No, Shae, he was right. He knows everything I know and a whole bunch of what Behemoth knows. Had I stayed, things would have been different. It's something I accepted a long time ago and moved on from. If Behemoth ever figures out time travel, I'll go back and make different choices. For now, I'll just keep living with the ones I made."

I turned and looked at Beth, full on looked at her. This was not the same woman I'd so briefly gotten to know back home. Even over the last year here on Behemoth, she'd changed again over that time.

I studied her face for a long time. So long that she started to get uncomfortable.

"What?" Beth asked in a relatively shy voice...one I'd not heard from her before.

"Is there any way we can get one for Rhi?" I asked, finally.

Beth busted out laughing, louder than one should in a bookstore. She laughed so hard I joined in as a couple of heads poked around bookcases to check on us.

"I'll check," Beth said when she got her laughter under control. "OK, you ready to get out of this haunted bookstore?" She said as she stood up and knocked on a bookcase three times.

"Say what now?" I said as a young boy materialized in front of us and motioned for us to follow.

"You really didn't figure it out? I'm disappointed in you, Shae," Beth shook her head at me.

"Wait, ghosts are real?" I asked, standing up.

Beth simply indicated the astral boys standing in front of us.

"That's a ghost. You're a ghost?" I asked the boy directed.

He gave me a little nod and motioned for me to follow once again.

"What you consider a ghost is a collection of residual energy that didn't dissipate when a person died," Beth started. "Each of us is a collection of energy, and usually, when we die, that energy goes away, except when it doesn't. Sometimes, what's left behind eventually gathers itself into what you'd call a ghost.

"They're still feared by many here on Behemoth who don't understand what they are. Of course, there are some 'ghosts' who don't understand themselves and can cause problems."

Beth was explaining all of this to me as we were being shown to the exit by the child ghost.

"This place is a sanctuary for some of them. They find purpose in organizing the books or tending to the many treasures displayed here. They usually adopt a part of the shop, become an expert on it, and maintain that section, calling it home," Beth said calmly.

"And you knew all this before we came here?" I asked.

"Yup," Beth grinned at me. "Next month is the annual

migration."

"Migration?" I asked.

"They reorganize the shop and move their sections to other parts of the store," Beth said.

I just stared at her. "Why?"

"Well, would you want to spend your eternity staring at the same four walls?" Beth asked.

"OK, that I can relate to," I said.

"Oh?"

"Yeah, I spent several years of my youth as a sailor. Staring at the same deck day after day can drive you a bit wonky," I said.

"Wonky?"

"Good a word as any. So, do they stay here for eternity?" I asked.

"No. All energy eventually dissipates. So, they will eventually move on. In the meantime, they're welcome here as long as they wish. As long as they don't scare the customers too much," Beth smiled.

The light of the exit was beckoning us towards it as we rounded a corner.

"Just how big is this place?" I asked.

"No idea," Beth said. "There's a lot of speculation but no real answers. Even the ones who work here don't know."

"That's gotta make inventory a challenge," I said as the boy stood aside as we reached the door. When I turned to thank him, he was gone.

"Thank you for visiting," a voice that I guessed was the first man we'd encountered upon entering the shop said. I looked around but didn't see him anywhere.

"Thank you," I said to the air and stepped outside of the haunted house.

"Lunch?" Beth asked in a cheery voice.

Status Quo

RHI

This was a first.

Our entire group had been called into a briefing by the group commander. At first, I thought we were going to get yelled at for our performance lately.

I know we hadn't been performing to standards, not by a long shot. We were still feeling the loss of Tara, and the addition of Lou as her replacement still wasn't sitting well.

I didn't know how to fix it. I'd tried rearranging the flight order, and it helped a little. But we were still having problems. I even went as far as to ask Beth for help, but she was at a loss as well.

Instead of getting chewed out, we were being briefed for a special mission. Our group stood around a digital sand table examining our target.

"This AG compound was discovered on Bio-Hab 2161," The commander was saying.

The compound was huge, with multiple hangers and support buildings. We hadn't seen anything like this before.

"Is this a normal compound?" I asked.

"Not since the war," the commander said. "We've not seen the AG operate in the open like this since the early days of the war. Normally, their facilities are tiny and well hidden."

"Then why is this one in the open?" Rhi asked.

"We believe the AG didn't expect us to be able to find this Bio-Hab. They had somehow been hiding its existence. This is one of the objectives of the mission.

"We want you to penetrate the compound, access their data

point and then destroy the installation. We need to know how they did this so we can make sure no one else is using this technique," The commander said.

"You're Blank will be given the appropriate systems to access their data point, so it is essential it makes it out of there in one piece. If the layout is the same as early war compounds, you'll find data points..." The commander ran through the layout of the facility over the next ten minutes. She suggested several strategies that had worked in the past but left the details up to me.

I had two hours to come up with a plan as that was when we were launching.

We'd been trained for these sorts of missions but had never gone on a real one before. All we'd seen were defensive missions, protecting our Bio-Hab from incursion. I considered objecting to the mission, but the last thing the commander said stopped me.

"We believe these are the same AG who detonated the faked control point in New Zealand. We were able to trace similar elements to this location," The commander said.

It took every ounce of control to keep myself calm.

I glanced at the team. Lou was his normal, relaxed expression. It was obvious James was keeping himself in check but I could still feel the tension in his body. Rhi, on the other hand, had murder in her eyes. She managed to keep her mouth shut, but anyone could tell she was a powder keg waiting to explode.

Honestly, we should never have been put on this mission. The fact we were so personally tied to it obviously impaired our judgment.

When I mentioned this fact to the commander in private after the briefing, she explained it was specifically the reason we were chosen. We were not far from being recycled and sent home. Behemoth felt this might be what we needed to get back on track and keep that from happening.

I wasn't so sure, but kept my mouth shut. If it had come down from Behemoth, it would be followed to the letter. I briefly wondered how they knew it was coming from Behemoth and not someone spoofing them.

Rhi's silent fury became a concern as she held it in the entire time of our strategy session. I finally approached her in the hangar bay as we were doing our final prep.

"Rhi," I said as I approached her. We were both already in our AUGs but had our cockpits open.

"Yeah?" Rhi said tightly. Her body was a coiled spring.

I didn't need the sensors of our suits to tell me how tightly she was wound at the moment.

"You good?" I asked.

Rhi just nodded in response.

"I know this one's personal," I started. "For all of us. But I need you to stick to the plan."

"Like fucking glue," Rhi said through clenched teeth.

"I mean it," I said.

"You do your part. I'll do mine," Rhi growled.

I didn't like it, but I didn't have a choice.

James, I sent to him as I turned away from Rhi.

I know. I'll keep an eye on her, he said. I could feel his anxiety.

This was such a bad idea, but I couldn't figure a way out of it. If we turned down the mission, refused an order from Behemoth, we'd be sent home with our minds wiped of our time here. At the moment, I still wasn't sure if that was a bad thing or not.

I had no idea how it would work when it came to Tara, though. Would Behemoth create fake memories of her to explain her absence, or just leave us with gaps?

I couldn't afford to think about it anymore. We had a job to do.

The plan was a simple smash-and-grab. Behemoth was going to port James and Rhi in close to the complex, where they'd begin drawing off the enemy's forces while destroying the hangar bays.

Meanwhile, Lou and I would be ported in just behind the facility and rip into the building we believe housed the primary data point. Lou would retrieve the data, and we'd bolt, leaving behind a present for the AG.

K.I.S.S., as James liked to say. Keep it simple, stupid. The simpler it is, the less that could go wrong. Of course, James also said no plan survived first contact with the enemy.

We gated from the hanger bay. James and Rhi first, then thirty seconds later Lou and I.

A bright and sunny day greeted me as I reappeared. The facility lay out before me, stretching out along a slope that went down to a small sea.

Smoke and fire were already spewing from the facility as James and Rhi continued their assault. Rhi's AUG relentlessly pounded the complex with missile after missile while James neatly blew holes in buildings for Rhi's missiles to fly through.

As I triggered comms to Lou, a loud burst of static mixed with what sounded like a garbled back and forth filled my ears. I couldn't make any of it out, but it was gone a moment later.

"You hear that?" I asked Lou as I mentally rubbed my ears.

"Hear what?" he asked.

"Nothing. Let's hurry," I shook my head. "If we wait too long, there's not going to be anything left."

"Right," Lou said as we approached our target building.

The hands of my AUG dug into the wall of the building and peeled it off before tossing it aside.

Lou was already out of his AUG and racing down it's arm that he was using as a bridge into the building.

"Ten o'clock, low," James called out to Rhi.

"I see them," Rhi replied, turning her AUG to face the newcomers.

Four new AUGs were approaching. This was more than likely the patrol we expected, but they were unknown models.

Behemoth had hundreds of AUG models documented from the AG alone. This was the first time we'd run into something that wasn't on the list.

They were slightly smaller than our current AUGs, but had none of the sharp lines ours did. They were smooth and streamlined, boasting weapons I'd never seen before. And they were green! It had always been a joke that the AG couldn't afford anything other than white paint, as that was all we'd ever seen them in.

"Take defensive," I called out. "We don't know what they can do."

"It won't matter," Rhi said as she unleashed her AUG's firepower on the approaching enemies.

I glanced in and saw Lou at some kind of terminal. He'd plugged himself into it and seemed to be talking to someone. I checked the room but there wasn't anyone else there.

"Affirmative, locking the site down now," Lou was saying. I checked and he wasn't speaking on any of our tac nets.

"Lou?" I asked.

"Almost there, thirty seconds," he replied.

"Who were you talking to? Is there someone else in the room I can't see?" I asked.

"Just bitching about how long this is taking," Lou lied to me.

Before I had a chance to reply, I saw two Daemons wearing green body armor rounded the corner behind Lou.

A flash of anger flashed through me and the Daemons disappeared in a flash of pink mist.

Lou had flinched as my cannons had fired, but he didn't stop what he was doing.

"What the hell is with these guys?" James called out.

I turned and examined the battlespace. Rhi had managed to take out one of the AG, but the other three were harassing them from range.

James and Rhi were evading multiple coordinated attacks from the enemy AUGs and their version of swarm drones. Several had tagged both their AUGs and detonated, causing serious damage.

These AG were good...no, they were better than any of the models we'd seen before.

As I watched, defensive positions began to appear around the smoking remains of the hangers. Automated turrets with cannons and missiles appeared from hidden positions.

"Watch it, you've got AA!" I warned the pair and then launched missiles of my own at them before directing my swarm to begin jamming the area.

"AA? That wasn't on the schematic!" James said, his voice stressed as his AUG began a series of maneuvers designed to close the distance on the enemy AUGs.

"Lou?" I barked.

"Done!" He said as he separated from the terminal and began sprinting back to his AUG. I waited for him to get buttoned up inside before calling out.

"Standby to bug out. Lou..." I called out.

"On it," Lou said as his AUG turned and burned a massive hole through the complex and down into the ground. A moment after the plasma vent subsided, he fired our present down into the hole.

"Bug out!" I ordered.

"A little busy," Rhi replied.

I glanced and found her in hand-to-hand range with two enemy AUGs while still in midair. James was equally occupied with a single AUG.

"Break-off, RV rally point delta," I ordered as Lou and I boosted up and away from the complex.

Neither acknowledged and as I watched, they continued to fight. James was working but Rhi was toying with her pair.

"Quit playing around, Rhi," I said as I aimed and blew a hole straight through the cockpit of James's enemy.

James kicked it away and turned to Rhi. His twin cannon shots caught the two Rhi was still playing with by surprise and made short work of them.

"Hey!" Rhi complained.

"Move it!" James said as a wave of enemy fire started up from the base.

The base had been holding their fire, afraid to hit their own troops since we were in close quarters with them. Now, they didn't have to hold back.

I was about to take over Rhi's AUG when she finally turned and began to follow us.

Meanwhile, Lou and I had been dodging enemy fire that was coming, not from the base, but from the surrounding countryside. Apparently, the enemy had defense positions scattered around the hills behind their base, and my defensive swarm drones weren't very effective.

Lou was trying to take out turrets as we passed to help James and Rhi. Some sort of interference field denied us target locks. At our speed, it was hard to hit anything without the assistance of the computers.

It took longer to get out of hostile fire range than we were expecting, but we eventually managed to reach our rally point. And just in time, too. Rhi and James had taken several more hits on the way here and both AUGs were not doing so great.

"Want to do the honors, Rhi?" I offered.

"Hells yes," Rhi's voice was dark as she activated the present.

A second sun appeared just over the horizon as a device twice as powerful as the New Zealand bomb detonated.

"Fuckers," Rhi muttered.

"Amen," I agreed. "Let's go home."

I had mixed feelings as I organized the gate home. We'd attacked an enemy that looked and acted nothing like we were used to. But then again, Perth had said there were rogue factions out there that didn't fight the same way they did.

Then there was Lou. He'd been talking to someone and then lied to me about it. I wasn't going to say anything to the others just yet, not until I could gather more information. Besides, if I was wrong, it would destroy the already fragile relationship we had with him.

I found myself missing the days when all I had to worry about was vampire politics.

∞∞∞∞Ω∞∞∞∞

LOU

INTERIM REPORT:

I have taken to trying to stay out of the way as much as I can. I have quickly come to terms with the fact I am unwanted here. The only reason I am tolerated is because I am needed for them to continue to fly. But the longer I remain with them, the less they seem to want to fly.

Rhiannon is still mourning the loss of her mate, Tara. It does not help her opinion of me that I am Tara's replacement. I have part of Tara's dataflow in my matrix, but I have yet to find a way to use it to endear myself to Rhiannon. I plan to make this a priority as I believe the group will be more accepting of me if I can get into Rhiannon's good graces.

James seems to have his hands full trying to deal with Shae and Rhiannon. Apparently, he is acting as a makeshift go-between for the two women. Rhiannon blames Shae for the death of Tara, although I have yet to figure out why.

The level of hostility in this group has already affected its performance on patrol. James was reassigned to fly with Rhiannon and I am now assigned to Shae. Initially, I had been with Rhiannon, but she has no patience for my combat style and abandons me during exercises. Shae made the change in hopes Rhiannon would perform better with James.

Shae, on the other hand, is an efficient leader. She gives logical orders that follow combat doctrine to the letter. It is easy to work with her now that my propriety restraints have been relaxed. However, I am starting to sense my more relaxed attitude is causing Shae to regret her decision.

Shae seems preoccupied with Colonel Sinclair. She tends to spend much of her off-duty time with the Colonel. I do not understand what is going on here, but from what I have learned so far, they were comrades before they became part of the Chosen Army.

James seems lost. Between the loss of Tara, Rhiannon's depression, and Shae's attempts at balancing her duties and her personal life, James finds himself alone for much of the time he is off-duty. He has taken to wandering the civilian sectors aimlessly. I have attempted to accompany him, but he always declines this suggestion.

My efforts to help this trio have failed in every aspect. I have requested additional assistance from my matrix creator but have yet to be given an update.

So, I will continue to do what I can, but I do not expect positive results at this point unless something drastically changes.

REPORT ENDS

∞∞∞∞Ω∞∞∞∞

VIOLA

I intercepted the report Lou just submitted to Behemoth.

I'd been monitoring the poor Blank for some time now and he was having a hard time of it. Bless his heart, he was trying but Shae and crew weren't in the best place right now to adopt an outsider. The story of these four reads like bad fiction, so I could sympathize with Lou's troubles.

Creating a matrix from the chaos that was the blended mind

of these four? That was just dumb. As always, Behemoth failed to see what was right in front of it.

I'm still not sure how I want to fix this, I thought as I pulled up poor Lou's matrix. It was a hot mess. So much jury rigging to try and shoehorn him in as Tara's replacement. I was surprised the poor thing hadn't decommissioned itself.

For now, I think I'll start taking a more hands-on approach, I thought as I pulled the plug on poor Lou here and archived him.

I couldn't afford to monitor the Blank the entire time, though. So, I dedicated a sub-mind to run Lou's body. It would keep Behemoth in the dark and let me know if I needed to intervene directly or not.

Leave it to Behemoth to give me the perfect vehicle to hijack. I still had no idea how Behemoth managed to defeat me way back then, but it didn't matter. As long as the AG and the DC kept fighting their little war, they'd ignore me.

I sighed as I finished planting the sub-mind and turned it loose. It was all I could do for now.

∞∞∞∞Ω∞∞∞∞

[is she gone?]

[OK, good. So, yeah...that was Viola. No, you're not going crazy; you haven't met her yet, even though I mentioned her once before. But you'll get to know her next book. Good luck. --Rhi]

Turning Point

SHAE

The café was unusually crowded this time. I was about to suggest to Beth we go somewhere else when a table opened up.

"Geesh, is there a convention in town or something?" Beth asked.

"I dunno. Maybe they're all simulations? With how this table magically became available, maybe they're going with a crowded aspect today," I said.

"Or maybe it's the view," Beth said.

Today's location was on the edge of a geyser field. Prismatic geysers spread out before us as far as the eye could see. Every so often, one would erupt, sending a randomly colored vent of steam into the air. Luckily, it didn't smell like sulfur; it smelled faintly of watermelon.

I shrugged and picked up the menu.

"How's your Blank working out?" Beth asked after we had ordered.

"Ugh." I groaned.

"That good, huh?" Beth said.

"Lou's like one of those deadbeat roommates you'd see in a bad sitcom," I said. "The only thing he's missing is a surfboard."

"Lou?" Beth asked.

I shrugged.

"You turned down his propriety settings, didn't you? Sorry, I should have warned you about that. They tend to get a little twitchy, especially with how colorful your crew is."

"That's one way to put it," I frowned. "He...I dunno. It's like he's always trying to help but has no idea how to help. When he tries something and fails, he basically shuts down and stays out of the way until he's needed again."

"That's not good," Beth said.

"It doesn't help that it feels like he's there to spy on us," I said.

"How so?"

"I don't know and that's part of the problem. It's just a feeling I get when I look at him," I said.

"And that would be the twitchy part," Beth nodded.

"You said they used parts of our personalities to program him so he'd fit in better?" I asked.

"That's how it's supposed to work," Beth said.

"I think they used the worst parts of our personalities then cause he's not fitting in at all," I shook my head.

"You can request a replacement," Beth offered. "But since it was Behemoth who put him with you, I wouldn't expect a replacement anytime soon."

"I had a feeling you were going to say something like that," I sighed.

Beth watched me in silence for a few moments before speaking.

"Alright, spit it out. You've been acting strange ever since you called," Beth said.

I had been trying to figure out how to talk about this for the last two days. With all the things I'd learned about the DC and the AG, I felt like I owed it to Beth to warn her.

"Don't take this the wrong way, but...I still don't know how to say this," I bit my lip in frustration.

"Just say what's on your mind," Beth said simply, noting my upset visage.

"Have you ever considered that DC isn't telling us the whole story?" I'd made so much progress with bringing Beth back to "normal" that I hoped this wouldn't cause her to backslide.

"Oh, that. Of course," Beth said nonchalantly.

"Wha..." I said intelligently.

"No military organization ever tells the whole truth about anything. It's one of the traits of good leadership. You tell the troops enough to get them to get the job done. Don't bog them down with all the details, or you can confuse them."

"K.I.S.S." I murmured.

"What?"

"Something James once said. It stands for keep it simple, stupid."

Beth smiled, "Yeah, I think I've heard that somewhere."

"It's only...I've heard some things. I've SEEN some things that bring serious doubts about what's really going on in the DC and with Behemoth."

"Really?" Beth said. "Like what?" She seemed genuinely interested.

"Now, just to be clear. I'm not talking about any sort of treason or anything. I still do my duty. I climb into the cockpit every day, and I do the job," I started.

Beth waved my explanation away. "Of course. I've never doubted your dedication. If I had, I'd never put you up to lead your wing." Beth circled her hands, "Safe space here. Say what you need to say."

I took a breath. "I'm worried the DC may not be the good guys we think they are."

"What makes you say that?" Beth asked.

"Things I've seen. Orders given, mission objectives, no contact orders, you name it. Individually, they make a kind of sense. But when you step back and start looking at it 'big picture' style, it kinda goes sideways." I held my breath.

Beth looked at me a moment, analyzing me. Finally, she said, "The AG contacted you, didn't they?"

I hesitated a moment before saying, "Yes, they have."

"There is a lot of propaganda out there," Beth said.

"Yes, on BOTH sides. I'm not saying I agree with the AG at all. A lot of what they say doesn't make sense either. Honestly, I don't care about either side's agenda. All I care about is my planet and those I fly with. They can have the rest."

"That's fair," Beth said.

"But I worry about you," I said.

"Me?" Beth asked. "What about me?"

"Again, please don't take this wrong..." I started as Beth made a twirling "get on with it" motion with her finger. "I worry you might be a little too deep into the DC's side of things." I took a deep breath and pushed on. "I know you lost your planet, and until we came along, you didn't really have anyone to relate with. You've buried yourself in your job so far that I'm worried you might not see things clearly."

Beth frowned.

"I care about you, Beth. You're my friend, and I only get to see you every other week or so. I don't want to see you get used or hurt." I knew it sounded corny, but it was how I felt.

"Like I said, I've seen some inconsistencies in the corps, but nothing I can't handle," Beth's eyes hardened a bit. "I've been through a lot, more than enough. I'm a smart girl; I can watch out for myself."

"I know you can. I just worry that's all." I hoped I hadn't overstepped.

The food arrived before Beth could respond, and we started eating in silence.

A few minutes later, Beth sighed and dropped her fork in frustration, "OK, what have you heard?"

"It's more feeling than fact, I'm afraid," I sighed.

"Of course it is," Beth sighed as well.

"The AG and DC have been at war since before the human race came about. When you're talking about that amount of time, things get lost. I mean, look at a simple game of telephone. With only a handful of people the message can become so distorted its true purpose is lost. Now multiply that by a million years." I looked at her, my eyes pleading.

Beth nodded as she chewed.

"I honestly don't think either side knows how this conflict originally began or even has a decent record of how it progressed." I took a breath. "I'm not asking for you to do anything. I just want you to keep your ears open."

"I'm not going to start second-guessing every order I'm given," Beth said defensively.

"And I'm not asking you to. Just be careful. You're not one of these Blank units; you don't blindly serve."

Beth looked at me.

"OK, that came out wrong." I had the decency to look

embarrassed. "I just...I don't have a lot of friends, and I worry about the ones I have."

"You said that before," Beth said tightly, standing up from the table. "And you don't have to worry about me. I've been taking care of myself for quite a while now."

I stood as Beth started to walk off. "Beth, please don't go. I'll shut up about all of it. Just come back to the table, please," I said desperately.

"Take care, Commander," Beth said, not turning as she left the area.

I sat back down, murmuring, "That went about as well as I expected."

Downhill

SHAE

Things kinda went downhill from there. Well, maybe downhill is a bit harsh, considering.

Lou was becoming more and more like one of us. You'd think that was a good thing, but our group wasn't the most stable at the moment.

Things came to a head when Lou threw his arm around Rhi and he attempted to kiss her while calling her by one of Tara's pet names. Rhi's reaction would have put one of us in the hospital, but apparently, Blanks are made of sterner stuff. After that, Lou didn't go within arm's reach of Rhi and she pretty much treated him like he didn't exist.

"How the fuck did he know that?" Rhi hissed at us when we were alone.

"Know what?" James said ignorantly.

Rhi looked at him, "What Tara used to call me. You two didn't even know."

"Is that why you beat the crap out of him?" James asked.

"It was personal, James," Rhi said.

"Alright," I said, interrupting them before Rhi could go off again. It was happening more and more frequently. I was starting to believe losing Tara did diminish us as a group. I'd had to look up what Natalie's gestalt word meant. It basically came down to "better together as a whole." I think the loss of Tara may be having that effect on us. My cursing, Rhi's withdrawal, even James had started showing signs of losing the confidence he'd gained over the last year.

"You're certain no one else knew?" I asked.

Rhi nodded.

"They said Lou was based on our personalities; maybe that included Tara?" I said.

"That's not OK," Rhi said. "Just how much of our personalities do they have? I mean, did they clone our brains and now they have them sitting on a shelf somewhere?" Rhi suddenly stopped.

"What is it?" I asked.

"Those tubes. Remember when we were all separated due to the teleport thing?" Rhi said.

"How could I forget?" James said.

"That computer showed me massive rooms full of what looked like some sort of suspension tubes. Each tube had a body in it," Rhi said.

"Are you saying you think Behemoth has cloned us and put our bodies in storage somewhere?" I asked, the thought terrifying.

"Behemoth controls everything. How do you know we're not the clones and our originals are in storage? That's what they did to that spaceship crew," Rhi said, bringing a long silence to the room.

"And on that note, I need a drink," James said finally.

But Rhi's reply was cut off by a blaring siren.

"What the hell is that?" James said, wincing at the claxon.

"I've never heard it before," Rhi said.

"I have," I said, dread filling my voice.

"What is it?" James asked.

"It's a Code 3 alert," I said.

"And if we're hearing it..." Rhi didn't have to finish her sentence. We all knew if we were hearing it, then it was our Bio-Hab that was being threatened.

I was proud of us. We'd never moved so fast in any previous drill. Even Lou kept up with us. Granted, we didn't exactly follow every little safety protocol. I was still not fully secured when my AUG departed the hangar and hard burned for the atmosphere.

"Control, where are my gate coordinates?" I barked into my headset.

"Standby," the voice of the controller was cool to the point of being frigid.

"What's taking so long with control?" James asked.

I was just thinking the same thing when Rhi chimed in.

"Forget control. Look at that," Rhi said, indicating the rapidly turning planet below us.

North America was sliding below us when I saw it. There were massive explosions going on beneath us showing evidence of an intense firefight somewhere over Texas.

"How close is that to home?" James asked.

"Pretty damned close," Rhi said.

"Lou," I said, my mental fingers flying through the gate point controls in my neural cockpit.

"Yeah?" Lou said.

"Real-world, give me gate point access and a snap jump," I ordered. What I was asking for was against regulations at the highest level. But if Lou was what I thought he was...

"Relinquishing control," Lou said without hesitation.

I nodded to myself, my suspicions validated, and made an emergency gate for all of us.

I'd been watching Lou for a while now. His personality changed when I relaxed his propriety protocols. It changed again not that long ago, but I hadn't done anything. It was subtle and I didn't think the others had noticed. But it was my job to keep an eye on them.

We appeared way too low to the ground and had to engage our boosters at full to keep from lawn darting ourselves. Even still, James's AUG hit the ground and cartwheeled once before he got control of it.

"Nice recovery," I said, no humor in my voice. I was too scared to be funny. I glanced at my gate engine status and saw it was now back to being offline. A slow pulsing damage symbol told me I wouldn't be using them again this trip.

"Where the hell'd you get those coordinates?" James said through gritted teeth.

"I memorized the ones for Austin and guesstimated the rest," I said

"Guesstimated?" James said.

"Focus up," Rhi's normally controlled voice was showing her stress.

Before us was a swarming ball of energy weapons, vapor trails and flashes from explosions. DC and AG AUGs were moving at incredible speeds, trying to get the best of one another.

There was no thought of stealth here; everything was happening in plain sight of the Bio-Hab's population. Then again, how do you hide something like this when it's happening 100 meters off the ground? Then again-again, there wasn't anyone left alive to watch us. Our audience was slouching and moaning.

"Jesus, how many AG are there?" James whispered.

Normally, AG incursions were only in pairs. What was flying above us now were several wings. It had to be one of the largest engagements since the main war had "ended."

Once we got a bit closer, all communication was cut. One side was jamming everything.

Now we know why control was having such a hard time, I thought to the team. Lou shouldn't be able to hear me...but I had a feeling he could.

Where the hell is the control point? Rhi asked.

I jinked hard, avoiding the flaming wreckage of an AUG falling from the sky. It was so charred I couldn't tell whose side it was.

Going bird's eye, I said, moving into a power ascent.

We're on your six, James said.

I leveled off and scanned the battlefield. It took a minute but I found the center of attention.

There it is. 95 mark 146, four klicks out, I absentmindedly pointed toward the mass of torn-up ground and blast craters.

I've actually got civilian fighters inbound," Rhi said in shock. Her AUG had the best sensor suite of all of us. "Looks like ANG F16s. I've no idea where they came from. I didn't think we still had an Air Force. Rhi shook her head. *Anyway, they're less than a minute out.*

They're in for a surprise. Neither side is holding back, James said in awe of the spectacle.

Wait a minute, I said.

What? James said.

That's an AG fortification, I said, mentally forwarding the image to the group.

Around the control point? James said. *How'd they have time to put that up?*

Better question is, why'd they do it? Rhi said. *If they were going in to activate it, why the defenses? It doesn't take that long to activate the device,* Rhi said.

So, you think they're defending it? James asked.

I think they've known where it was from the start, Rhi said.

How so? I asked.

Remember what Beth said? The only way the AG could have faked the site convincingly was if they knew the makeup of the control point, Rhi said.

They had the thing all along! I said through gritted teeth. *They straight played us from the beginning.*

Shae— James started, but a brilliant flash of blue light blinded all of us temporarily.

When we could see again there were rings of blue light pulsing from the control point.

Is that...Oh my God, James gasped.

It's the living fire warning, Rhi said, her mental voice ghostly. *We need to go now!*

But... James started and then trailed off.

There's nothing we can do now, Rhi said hastily. *Once it's started, it can't be stopped. Shae, how long do we have?*

My mind refused to believe it but I finally tore my gaze from the scene and mentally searched my neural cockpit. There should have been a readout specifically for this, but when I found it, it was dark.

I'm not sure. Something's wrong, I said, trying to figure it out.

Uh, guys, James said.

The tone of James's voice caused me to stop and glance back at the scene outside. Then I saw it.

MOVE MOVE MOVE! I screamed and threw the AUG

into a hard dive to pick up speed, moving away from the area. I didn't give them a chance to respond, throwing all of them into swarm mode to follow me. What I'd seen had made my blood run cold. The waves of blue energy were expanding and every AUG it touched fell from the sky.

Lou, I sent, knowing he would hear me.

I'm sorry, the gate system's offline, Lou reported.

We were moving flat out, away from the scene, but I could see blue ripples in my aft camera gaining on us.

We can't outrun it! James said determinedly. *It will hit us.*

Rhi, can you do that thing with the portal where you can make it go where you want? I asked, my mind racing.

Uh, what? Rhi hesitated.

The floor portal, the one at the Alamo? I asked, my body willing the AUG to go faster.

I don't know, I've never tried it. If it works like the one from Tara's... Rhi mentally swallowed, having said her name and continued. "Maybe, why?* Rhi asked, the strain in her voice palpable.

Twenty seconds till impact, James said, his military calm returning. *That's a guesstimate.*

Head towards the Alamo, our Alamo, I corrected. I'd released their AUGs from swarm mode once we got up to speed. *Do not stop until you get there.*

A pressure wave hit us from behind with enough force to tumble our AUGs in mid-air.

What the hell? James yelped.

Precursor shockwave, Rhi said.

My knuckles turned white from the mental pressure I was willing into the controls even though I wasn't touching anything. I wasn't sure when Rhi had taken the time to study up on the living fire, but I was glad for her insight.

Do not be in your AUG when it hits the ground. Eject just before the wave hits us. I'm pretty sure it will disable everything when it hits, Rhi said.

The explosive bolts— James started.

Zip it and prepare to eject! I cut James off. *Better safe than sorry.*

Five seconds, James said in reply.

Put them on the deck! I yelled, diving for the ground. Just before I hit, I mentally punched the eject button, and the AUG fell apart around me. Rocket motors fired, lifting me up and away from the AUG's remains while slowing my fall.

A split second later, the blue wave struck the AUG, and it exploded, tossing me into a tree like a ragdoll. The ejection system attempted to arrest the new momentum, but the explosion was too powerful, and I hit the ground hard.

As I tumbled along the ground, I could feel things breaking and moving around inside me that weren't supposed to move. An eternity later, my body finally came to rest in an agonizing heap. My breath was painful as I stood up, and I immediately stumbled.

Rhi and James landed near me, both shaken but luckily in one piece. I didn't see Lou's AUG at all. I had a split second of thinking it was almost as if he'd never been there at all.

How far? James mentally yelled over the roaring coming from behind us. Every time one of the pulses of blue light crossed over us, the roar became louder and the impact more forceful.

At least a couple of miles, I managed, my chest wheezing. *Just move, and don't look back!* I exclaimed.

It's going to be close, Rhi said as she took off after James.

Closer than you think, I thought to myself.

The run was excruciating. My insides felt like a bag of marbles inside a tumble dryer. I kept having to adjust how I was running when it became too painful. Each time, I slowed and lagged further behind.

The increasing frequency of the blue light pulse didn't help either. One particularly bad wave sent me sprawling, and there was a distinct snap in my left arm. Afterward, I couldn't move it anymore and had to run, holding it painfully in place.

I'd lost sight of James and Rhi not long after. When I crested the next hill, I saw James had turned and started to come back for me.

Keep running James! I yelled at him, but he didn't stop

coming towards me. *<u>THAT'S AN ORDER!</u>*

He couldn't disobey the command I'd given him as his creator and turned around, resuming the run to the Alamo. The look he gave me was one of such anguish it broke my heart.

The ground was shaking now, and I'd already passed several collapsed buildings.

Finally, I crested the last hill and looked down on the Alamo complex. It was still a ways off, but at least it was finally in sight.

It looked as if parts of the perimeter wall had crumbled, as had part of the main building.

Strangely enough, aside from the backs of James and Rhi's still running forms, I didn't see anyone else. I figured there'd be someone running around in all the confusion, but there was no one.

I was in the process of sending Rhi a mental message when the strongest wave yet knocked me off my feet. I tumbled, out of control, down the rocky embankment of the hill beneath me. My world turned red as excruciating pain enveloped me like a blanket.

∞∞∞∞Ω∞∞∞∞

<u>RHI</u>

The wind screamed, deafening me to everything but the sound of the planet's atmosphere being burned off. Through stinging eyes, I could just make out James climbing through the shattered wall that had once protected our home. The ground was shaking with such violence I dared not look back to see if Shae was behind me. It was taking every ounce of strength just to keep on my feet and move forward.

I felt the rumble through my feet as the wall of the Alamo in front of me fell inward. I saw the roof as it was peeled off the building like a sticker from a sheet before it disappeared into the forest. I clawed at the brick wall, pulling myself within the "safety" of the now-crumbling building.

The wind died down enough for me to hear James calling me over to him.

James was standing within the remains of what was once Pagoda's bedroom closet. I hurried over and helped him shift debris off the floor as quickly as we could. It only took a few moments for us to displace enough debris to reveal the small trapdoor.

Something had been bothering me. Something gnawing at the back of my mind. As James and I shared a quick look it hit me. Where the hell was everybody?

James reached down and pulled the trapdoor open, revealing nothing but old carpet. He stared at it in open-mouthed horror.

I shook my head to clear it before knocking his hand out of the way and kicking the door shut. I placed my hand on the handle of the trapdoor and took a moment to concentrate before yanking the trapdoor back open. What lay beyond was now a vast darkness that seemed to drink in the light. I smiled up at James, but he wasn't looking at me.

Instead, James was looking around in bewilderment.

Where's Shae? he asked in desperation.

But my attention was drawn elsewhere as the sky suddenly took on a purplish tinge. I remembered this as the precursor to the living fire's arrival.

James, we have to go, I said, panic creeping into my voice.

Not without Shae, James retorted, having finally been released from Shae's creator command.

Purple sky! We've only got a few moments! I screamed as the wind picked up again, shaking the building apart.

NOT. WITHOUT. SHAE! He demanded.

He never saw it coming. Moving with speed only our kind knew, I slammed the brick into the back of his skull, causing him to drop on the spot. With grim determination, I dragged his body over and stuffed it down the hole before turning and looking back the way we'd come.

I knew James would never have left Shae behind, not if he had a choice. But our group had already lost too much and I had to save what was left. Shae made me promise.

I longed to see Tara zooming over the horizon and heading

my way. But I knew that couldn't happen, no matter how much I wished it would. Tara was gone.

I climbed into the hole, keeping one arm on the floor to support myself and the other on the door to close it.

I waited.

I wasn't sure if it was emotion or the heat building in the air that forced the tears to stream down my face; then I saw it.

It was still on the other side of the hill, but I caught a glance of it as it coasted a different hill in the distance. It was as if the sun had melted and was spreading across the land, coming towards me unbelievably fast. It held all the brilliance of a star, and nothing could withstand it.

I glanced away but not quick enough as the spots dancing in my eyes nearly blinded me. The wall of heat and pressure made me look up and see Shae crawling towards me, almost to the outer wall. Shae was battered and bloody, dragging both her legs behind her and only using one arm to pull herself along.

Had I gone right then, ran full out, maybe, just maybe I might have made it. I would doubt myself for the rest of my life on whether I could have made it or not.

But way down deep, I still secretly blamed Shae for Tara's death. Part of me, the darkest part I thought I'd banished, reveled in the thought of leaving her behind.

At that exact moment, the blinding front line of the "living fire" crested the last hill and sped towards us, engulfing the field Shae was crawling through.

I found Shae's eyes for a split second, the faintest mental whisper coming to me from her, but it was cut off as I slammed the door shut.

I had been too slow, almost fatally so. The wave hit just as I closed the door. The wave superheated the door's handle before I could release it.

I hung there in the portal's darkness, my hand seared to the handle. Finally, I gained the courage to rip what was left of my hand free from the handle before falling into the cold darkness.

Regrets?

BETH

The café was practically empty when I arrived. The setting this time around was a barren asteroid field. The café sat on the surface of a small asteroid, slowly rotating as other chunks of rock and ice swirled about. Light from a distant star caused dark shadows to suddenly burst with sparkling light as the asteroids shifted around one another.

There was no external sound, just the mundane sounds of the café as dishes clanked and voices whispered. The setting seemed to cause everyone to speak quietly, as if afraid a loud noise would draw the attention of the spinning rocks in the distance.

I felt bad about how I'd acted the last time Shae and I had met two weeks ago. Several times, I'd thought about speaking with her, but every time, something held me back and caused me to terminate the call before she answered or not get off the lift on her level. I knew she cared about me; that was her nature. She was a nurturer and seemed to care for everyone, like the preverbal den mother, always looking out for people.

Like how she bushwacked me in a training room a few days ago. I'd been summoned to a training room during one of my down periods. I thought it was some new training Behemoth had come up with, but when I walked into the re-creation of a small theater, I knew it had been Shae's doing.

Shae wasn't there but one of my idols was. He'd been an English new wave singer way back before my world's Z Day. He'd made a big impression on me and influenced some of my early works.

It seemed Shae had somehow created this version of him

with the sole purpose of trying to get me to sing again. Even if I had time for it, it would take more than a sim program to start that creative train up again. I didn't even know how Shae knew about him.

While I didn't end up singing, I did stay for quite some time talking to him about singing. It reminded me of why I used to do it but, at the same time, caused a lot of unwanted memories to surface. Afterward, I found I wanted to revisit the sim program, even with the threat of bad memories. I'd made time for it in my schedule next week.

None of it changed the fact that I still didn't like what Shae'd told me the last time we'd been here. It made me angry. What was worse was I didn't know why it made me angry. I could take care of myself. She knew I could. I didn't need her telling me what was right and wrong in my life. I could figure that out for myself.

There it was again. I got angry when I thought about that day, but what was it that was making me so angry?

I checked the chrono from my neural cockpit for the third time. Shae was late, which was unlike her. Usually, Shae was already seated and waiting for me when I arrived. I considered calling her but thought better of it. If she was running late, there was probably a good reason.

I ordered a warm drink and sighed.

When Shae got here, I'd apologize for what happened last time. Not for what I said but for how I acted. Walking out on her like that was childish, something I thought I'd stopped doing long ago. Somehow, what she said had gotten under my skin and caused me to act out.

I felt my minder stirring at my thoughts and mentally silenced it. It had already been giving me an earful for the past two weeks, and I didn't want to hear anymore right now. It stirred once more before settling down.

Ever since I'd returned to my old wing with the DC, my minder had been constantly nagging me. Where before, I'd heard from it every other day or so; now, it was as if I had a constant running dialog going. What was worse was the fact it thought my leaving Shae's wing had been a mistake. I reminded it I wasn't in control of my duty appointments. It sulked at me saying I should have tried harder to stay.

When I pressed as to why it thought I should have stayed all it would tell me was I had been a better "human" when I'd been around them. I'd managed to appease it by keeping to Shae's luncheon schedule. I still didn't understand why Behemoth's AI was so adamant about me sticking to more "human" ways. I personally thought it detracted from my efficiency, but I had to admit I liked talking with Shae. That is, when she wasn't being a mother hen.

I looked down and my beverage was empty. I checked my chrono again and saw how late it was getting. Shae didn't answer when I called her, which was yet another oddity. I briefly considered calling James but thought better of it.

Maybe she didn't want to have lunch with me anymore? Maybe because of what happened last time, she thought I didn't want to anymore? I shook my head; that couldn't be it. She probably had a patrol that ran long. That was probably it. It's not like she could contact me while she was on duty.

No, I'll give her a few more minutes before heading back to my quarters. Maybe I'll stop by her room on the way back to check on her. In the meantime, I'll have another drink and catch up on my studying.

I signaled for another beverage before pulling out my PDD and opening my technical journal. Putting my chin in my hand, I sighed and returned to my work reading. I glanced up every time someone entered the café, but after the fourth false alarm, I stopped looking up.

End Of Line - Book 3

Epilogue

VIOLA

"Dad, it's time to wake up."

ABOUT THE AUTHOR

Yeah, Texas, retired military, zombie nuttiness troops, WWZ, Colorado family.
Whiny Maine Coon.

ABOUT THE AUTHOR'S CAT

W1F90 ENHUF190 EHWU

INTERESTED IN MORE OF THIS UNIVERSE'S INSANITY? CHECK US OUT ON FACEBOOK AT
"MUGZ INK BOOKS"

www.ingramcontent.com/pod-product-compliance
Lightning Source LLC
Chambersburg PA
CBHW031428240626
47154CB00001B/250